Empire of Flame and Thorns

BOOKS BY MARION BLACKWOOD

The Oncoming Storm

A Storm of Silver and Ash
A Storm of Shadows and Pearls
A Storm of Smoke and Flame
A Storm of Glass and Stars
A Storm of Mist and Thunder
A Storm of Blood and Swords
A Storm of Light and Darkness

***

Court of Elves

The Traitor Spy
The Wicked Betrayal
The Beautiful Liar
The Fire Soul
The Lethal Deception
The Desperate Gamble
The Last Stand

***

Ruthless Villains

Ruthless Villains
Wicked Villains
Heartless Villains
Vicious Villains
Merciless Villains

***

Ruthless Enemy

Ruthless Enemy
Wicked Enemy
Heartless Enemy

***

Flame and Thorns

Empire of Flame and Thorns

EMPIRE OF FLAME AND THORNS

FLAME AND THORNS
BOOK ONE

MARION BLACKWOOD

ISBN 978-91-989042-6-0 (ebook)
ISBN 978-91-989042-7-7 (paperback)
ISBN 978-91-989042-8-4 (hardcover)
ISBN 978-91-989042-9-1 (special edition)

www.marionblackwood.com

CONTENT WARNINGS

If you have specific triggers, you can find the full list of content warnings at: www.marionblackwood.com/content-warnings

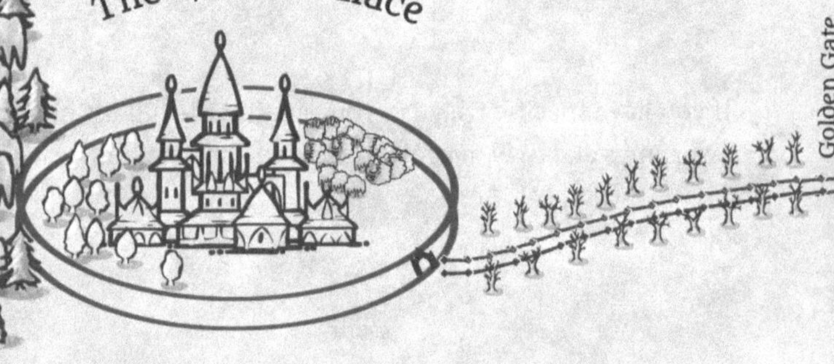
Seelie Court
The Golden Palace
Golden Gate
Dragon Field

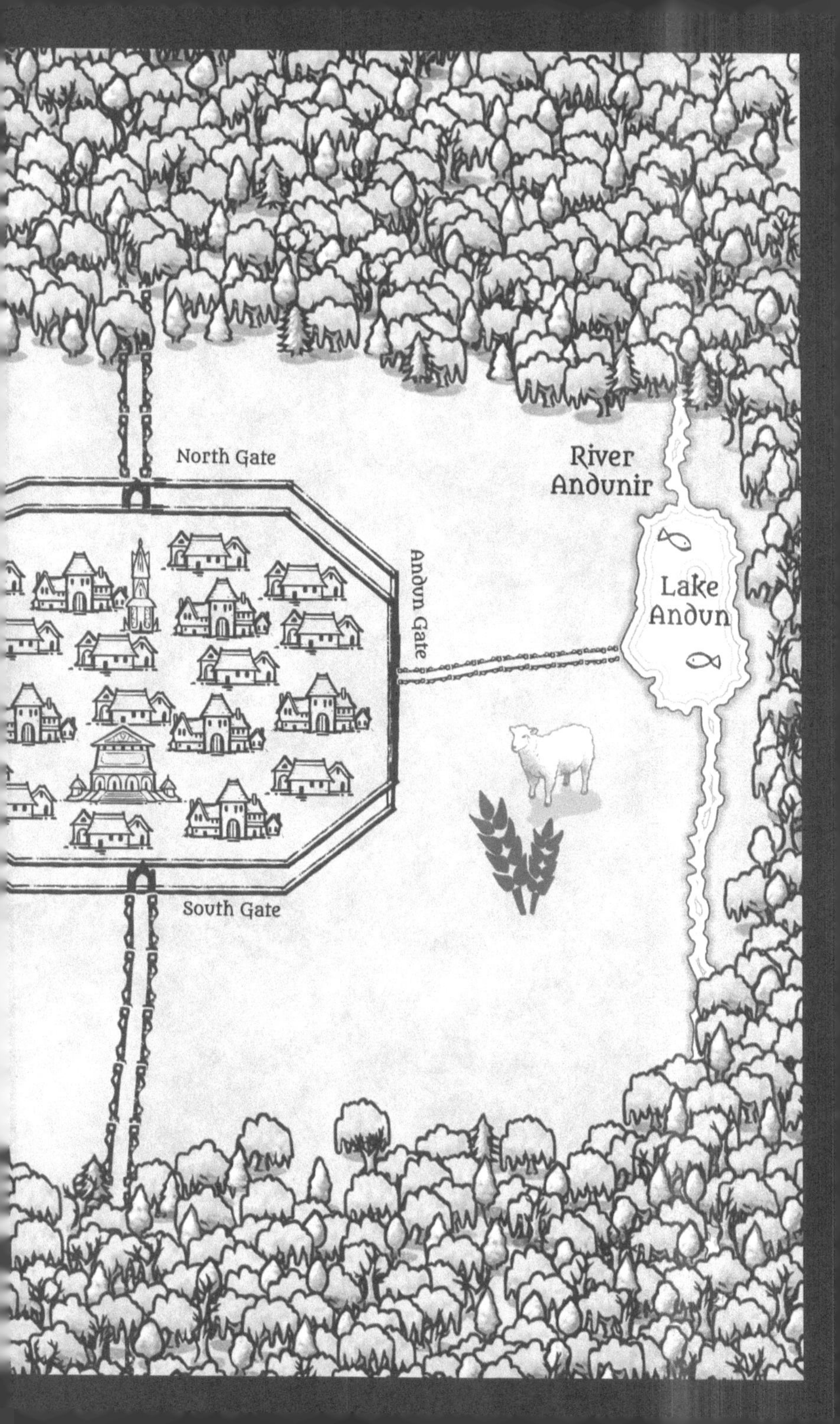
North Gate
River Andunir
Andun Gate
Lake Andun
South Gate

For everyone who dreams of being
swept away on a grand adventure.

Especially if that adventure involves
an enemies to lovers romance with
a smoking hot guy with wings.

And dark hair.

And very questionable morals.

CHAPTER ONE

You'd think that being a part of a badass secret resistance movement would involve something a lot more glamourous than sitting on a cold stool, wrist-deep in fish guts. But apparently not.

Shifting my weight on the wooden stool, I discreetly scan the street around me for dragon shifter patrols while I continue to gut the mountain of fish waiting for me in the buckets below my stall. Only other fae like me occupy the street at the moment. Or maybe not exactly like me. As far as I know, the young brown-haired guy a little farther to my left is the only other member of our resistance group out here. Everyone else on this particular street is a civilian. Mostly because the real action, the actual important work that the resistance is doing, is taking place *inside* the building behind me.

A chilly fall wind whirls down the street, tugging at my clothes and my long silver hair. I resist the urge to raise my hand and push a stray strand out of my face since it would only smear fish guts across my cheek. Instead, I flex my cold fingers around the knife handle in an attempt to get some warmth back into my hands.

Gutting fish might not be the most desirable job ever, but after the dragon shifters slaughtered all the dragon riders and conquered the Seelie Court, we lost the ability to decide our own lives, so I can't really choose anything else. It has been millennia since then, and generations have come and gone for both our races, but they still rule over us with the same brutal iron fist.

But not for long. Or at least, not if we can finally organize a strong enough resistance to overthrow them.

I cast a discreet but very longing glance up at the windows high above me. The leaders of the resistance are meeting somewhere in there. Plotting. Scheming. Discussing crucial plans and making important decisions. I so desperately want to be in there. But instead, I'm out here. Gutting fish.

A faint clanking sound comes from the left.

My heart leaps into my throat, and I snap my gaze towards it.

Jeiman, the young brown-haired guy who is also watching the street, frantically tries to straighten the stack of copper pots that he almost knocked over.

I shoot him a look before returning my gaze to the street.

Mabona's tits, how did I get stuck with him for this job? I've been working for the resistance for years, and yet I'm still assigned as a lookout together with this damn rookie who started last month. I should have moved up the ranks by now. I should be inside, helping them plot and scheme. Not sit out here as if I'm some fresh recruit that needs to prove herself. I have proven my loyalty. And yet, they still don't trust me.

Stabbing my knife into the wooden board before me, I blow out a bitter sigh before reaching down to switch from the now empty bucket to one filled with dead fish. Another cold wind rushes between the buildings. The few fae civilians who are walking down the street flip their collars up against the chill. One particularly miserable-looking guy stops right in the middle of the road and heaves an endless sigh.

Behind me, warmth and the soft murmur of voices spill out from the door to the tavern.

The miserable-looking fae man turns towards it. Then he abandons whatever it was that he was doing and instead marches straight through the door and into the tavern's alluring warmth.

I can't really blame him. It's an overcast and chilly afternoon, and the winds that keep rushing between the rows of wooden buildings aren't exactly helping either. I once more flex my hands to get some warmth back into my fingers while wishing that I was indoors, doing something important at the meeting upstairs.

Though I suppose I can't be too bitter about the fact that the higher-ups still don't trust me. They barely trust each other. They always wear masks at their meetings so that no one knows who they really are. It's to keep the resistance safe in case one of them is captured. If they don't even know who their co-conspirators are, they can't have that information tortured out of them by the Shadow of Death.

A ripple pulses through the air.

My breath catches.

There is no sound. No movement. Nothing in sight.

But something is wrong. I can feel it.

The fae on the street tense up. Then quickly hurry down the road.

One second later, a dragon shifter patrol rounds the corner and marches onto the street.

My heart jerks.

Shit.

While twisting as if reaching for another fish to gut, I discreetly smear some of the slimy stickiness that coats my fingers on the window behind me. Another lookout, who will be mixed in with the civilians inside the tavern, will see that mark and sprint upstairs to inform the leaders of the resistance that it's time to get the hell out.

I keep an impassive expression on my face as I pick up the fish that I pretended to reach for while keeping one eye on the dragon shifters.

They look like humans. Or at least what I think humans look like, since I have never seen one in real life. Only fae live in the Seelie Court. Well, fae and some shifters from the Red Dragon Clan who are here to make sure that we remain exactly where they want us. Which is on our knees and underneath their heel.

Gray light from the overcast sky falls on their red leather armor as they continue in my direction. Thankfully, they don't appear to be in a hurry. If they continue at that pace, our resistance leaders will be able to leave the building by the back door before they can make it inside the tavern.

I place the fish I picked up on the wooden board of my stall. Now, I just need to—

A loud clattering noise explodes across the street.

I whip my head around.

To my left, Jeiman has leaped to his feet, knocking over the pile of copper pots in his haste. Panic is written all over his face. His gaze darts down to the metal pots, which are still bouncing and rolling across the cobblestones. Then he casts a panicked glance at the patrol that has turned to stare at him from farther up the street.

Don't, I beg silently in my mind while trying to catch Jeiman's eye. *Please, don't—*

He bolts into the tavern.

Fuck.

The dragon shifters lurch into motion as well. With one hand on their swords, they pick up the pace and stalk after him. Suspicion swirls in their eyes.

I have to suppress the urge to growl in frustration. Jeiman might as well have put up a bloody sign that says: *suspicious shit is happening in here*. Why did they have to assign such a rookie as my lookout partner?

Quickly wiping off my knife, I hide it in my clothes and then dunk my hands into the bucket of water to clean off any traces of fish guts. Then I slip away from my place on the stool and disappear in through the side door while the soldiers aren't looking. I need to find a way to stall them inside the tavern so that our leaders can get out unseen.

Warm air hits me like a vibrating wall as I sneak into the packed tavern. After the long hours gutting fish in the crisp air outside, the warmth is almost suffocating.

I flick a quick glance around the room. As always, most people are already deep in their cups despite it only being afternoon. A fire burns in the hearth by the opposite wall, bathing the room both with golden light and warmth. At the bar, the tavern keeper is pouring drinks as if nothing is wrong.

My stomach flips when I notice that there is a small gap in the door that leads to the stairwell and the secret back door. Through it, I spot someone in a cloak and mask shoving Jeiman up against the wall in what is no doubt rage and panic. Behind them, the other leaders of the resistance are still sprinting down the steps, trying to escape before the patrol barges in. I need to—

The front door of the tavern is yanked open.

Dread pulses through my chest as the soldiers in their blood red leather armor stalk into the room.

Dead silence spreads like a wet blanket across the whole tavern. The fae who were drinking close to the door shrink back and lower their gazes, trying not to draw attention even though they're just normal civilians. By Mabona, if they only knew that they are not the ones who need to hide right now.

A man with blond hair, who appears to be the captain and leader of the patrol, sweeps his hard gray eyes over the room. "What's going on here?"

No one even dares to breathe.

From this angle, I can still see our leaders quietly running down the stairs and out the back door. It's not visible from where the patrol is, because the door is thankfully blocking the view from that angle. But if they move a little closer, they will see it. And then, we will be well and truly fucked.

I need to do something.

The captain takes a step forward.

Snatching up a glass of liquor, I adopt a drunk expression and walk straight towards the soldiers.

Since everyone else is sitting still and quiet, my movements draw their attention immediately. I make sure to keep my steps a little wobbly and my hips swaying a lot more than necessary. The captain narrows his eyes at me.

"Wow," I say, coming to a halt in front of him. I make my voice breathless as I tilt my head back to look up into his stern face. "You're hot."

Shock pulses across his features, and he jerks back a little. Whatever he had been expecting me to say, that had apparently not been it. Clearing his throat, he draws his eyebrows back down in a scowl.

"I said," he begins, his voice once more filled with menace. "What's going on in here? And where's the guy who rushed in here?"

I make a disappointed noise. "Oh, you're into guys? That's such a shame."

One of the soldiers chokes on his breath.

The captain's cheeks flush bright red, and he splutters out, "No, that's not what I—"

"Because you have such a handsome face," I continue, interrupting him.

"Well, I…" He seems to be unsure of how to react because he simply trails off and stares at me as if I've grown a second head.

To be fair, this must be a first for him. No fae would ever be stupid or suicidal enough to willingly go near a dragon shifter, let alone flirt with one.

"Though I still don't understand how you can only have one eye color," I say, keeping my voice slightly slurred and my words the epitome of drunken ramblings. "Such limited combinations."

He scowls now, almost looking a little offended. Which was exactly my goal. Anything to keep him distracted and entirely focused on me while the resistance leaders escape out the back door.

"Better than having two colors like some kind of freak," he bites out.

Dragon shifters, and humans too presumably, all have only one eye color. Like brown or gold or violet or something equally mundane. We fae seem to be the only ones who have normal eyes with two colors. Not one in each eye. Instead, both colors are mixed like swirls of paint in both eyes, offering lots of combinations. My own eyes, which are turquoise and lavender-colored, are not unique by any means. But I much prefer them to the odd one-colored eyes of the shifters and the humans.

"Hmm," I murmur in response to the captain's insult while taking a sip of the drink I swiped earlier and swaying a little, as if I'm severely drunk already.

The captain looks like he's about to stalk past me and continue searching the room, so I reach up with my free hand to trace my fingers over his cheek.

His hand shoots up.

Fingers wrap around my wrist like steel bands, stopping my hand.

"Do not touch me with your filthy fucking hand, you worthless fae bitch," the captain growls at me.

Rage burns through me at his words, but I keep the expression firmly off my face and instead just lower my hand again. "I just—"

"Is there a problem?" a voice dripping with command cuts through the room.

Clothes rustle as the whole tavern whips towards the source of the voice.

My heart stutters as my gaze lands on the man who has just walked in through the side door.

He is wearing black dragon scale armor, and his black hair has been swept back from his face as if he has carelessly run his hand through it. Unflinching power radiates from his muscular body, and there is a calculating and highly ruthless glint in his golden eyes.

As opposed to the other dragon shifters in the room, his wings are also out. The vast majority of dragon shifters can only maintain two forms: fully human or fully dragon. Only the most powerful ones can do what is called a *half-shift,* which is to shift into a human form but with wings.

I stare at those imposing black wings that are clearly visible behind him even though he hasn't even spread them out fully. Then my gaze drifts to his tall and powerful body. Then back to his lethally handsome face.

He is, by far, the hottest man I have ever seen.

And yet, all I want is to never have to lay eyes on him ever again.

Because this is Draven Ryat. The Shadow of Death. Leader of the Black Dragon Clan. Commander of the Dread Legion and second only to the Empress and Emperor of the Iceheart Dynasty themselves.

He is one of the most powerful and dangerous dragon shifters in the world. And the most ruthless. According to rumors, he sold out his own clan to the Icehearts in exchange for power. He has slaughtered thousands. Burned cities to the ground. Conquered and destroyed. He and his Black Dragon Clan are crucial in keeping all the other dragon clans firmly underneath the rule of the Icehearts.

If anyone can break the entire fae resistance before it has even had a chance to fully grow, it's him.

The tavern is dead silent as Draven prowls towards me and the captain from the Red Dragon Clan. The captain might be from a different clan, but Draven is still his ultimate commander. So when he approaches, the captain takes a step back and lowers his chin in deference.

"Just some fae who—" the captain begins, but Draven cuts him off.

"I wasn't talking to you." His golden eyes slide to me, fixing me in place with a penetrating stare. And when he speaks again, threats lace his tone like sharp blades. "I said, is there a problem?"

My head spins with different plans and choices and decisions. What is he even doing here? The Red Dragon Clan is responsible for maintaining order in our city. So what is Draven Ryat doing here? And what am I supposed to say in response to his question? Yes, there is a problem? No, there is no problem? I don't know which answer will keep him from searching through the whole tavern. I don't even know if all resistance members have already made it out. Maybe they have. It has been long enough that they must have. But from this angle, I can't tell.

All I know is that I need to do something to keep the Shadow of Death from breaking our resistance before we've even had a chance to fight back.

So I do the only thing I can think of.

I throw my drink in his face.

CHAPTER TWO

The collective gasp that rips through the tavern could probably be heard halfway to the Unseelie Court. All the fae patrons, and all the shifters from the Red Dragon patrol too, stare wide-eyed at the scene before them.

Clear liquid slides down along Draven's sharp cheekbones and over his chiseled jaw before dripping down on the front of his black armor. Firelight from the hearth makes the drops that cling to his dark eyebrows glint before they slip down to curve around his eyes on their way down his face. His mouth was slightly open when I threw the drink, so a few drops rest along the top of his bottom lip as well.

For what feels like an eternity, no one says anything. No one moves. No one even dares to breathe.

My head spins, dizzy with disbelief. Mabona's tits, I just threw a drink in Draven Ryat's face.

I stare at the drops sliding down his skin. Well, at least it was a glass of *firechaser*, which is a strong and clear liquor, and not a sticky and foul-smelling ale or something. If anything, the concentrated alcohol should help clean the dirt off his armor.

Which I realize now is absolutely spotless, so there is no dirt to clean off. But that—

Draven's tongue darts out, running lightly along the seam of his bottom lip to lick the alcohol off. The sight of it snaps me out of my spinning thoughts.

His golden eyes sear through my very soul as he stares me down.

Only mere seconds have passed since I threw the drink.

The whole tavern is holding its breath.

Draven cocks his head.

I bolt.

Clamor and raised voices echo behind me as the soldiers snap out of their stupor and lurch into motion to stop the lunatic who just threw a drink in their commander's face, but I'm already out the door.

I use the tavern's front door so that, in case there are still some resistance leaders escaping through the back door, the soldiers won't see them since they're chasing me in the opposite direction.

My heart slams against my ribs as I skid out onto the cobblestones and sprint towards the nearest side street. I need to make the soldiers lose sight of me. If I can do that, I will be able to disappear into the crowd. The dragon shifters might patrol these streets, but they don't know them like we do. Like *I* do. This is my home. I know every nook and cranny like the back of my hand.

Boots pound against stone behind me as the soldiers give chase. I throw myself around the next corner. But shouts split the air, informing me that they saw me. I push myself harder.

Wooden buildings flash past on either side of me as I hurtle down the next street while praying to Mabona, the fae goddess, that I will have luck on my side today. Because there is one gigantic flaw in my plan to disappear into the crowd. The soldiers might have to chase me on foot, or shift into dragons and try to find me from above in their huge hulking forms, but Draven is capable of a half-shift. He could simply fly after me through the streets. And if he does, I'm doomed.

So I pray to Mabona that he is too prideful to chase after me himself and that he will instead leave that to the grunts who serve underneath him.

I leap over a broken crate of half-rotted turnips and swerve around a barrel of potatoes. The people who were trying to sort through the root vegetables to find which ones can still be saved scramble back so quickly that they knock over their stools. Wooden clattering echoes between the crooked buildings around me as the stools hit the street while I continue sprinting down the road.

A narrow alley is coming up on my left, but the soldiers are still too close. They will see me if I dart into it. So instead, I take an abrupt right and leap straight in through an open window.

Shocked cries ring out as I roll right over someone's kitchen table. But I can't stop to see what they're doing, because I need to make it to the door on the other side before the shifters can spot me.

Shoving a chair out of the way, I barrel through the kitchen and out towards where I assume the back door to be.

"Where is she?" the captain demands from outside the open window.

"B-back door," the terrified owner of this house replies from the kitchen right as I yank open the back door and slip out.

A frustrated snarl rips from the captain's throat. It's cut off when I throw the back door shut behind me and sprint out onto the empty road behind the building. The dragon shifters must either pass through the house too or go around the entire length of buildings. Either way, it buys me enough time.

I take a quick left and then a right before running along another deserted street. The sound of pounding footsteps from behind is no longer audible. And there are no black wings of death following me either. I breathe a small sigh of relief but still continue to weave in random patterns through the city to make sure that they have truly lost me.

Eventually, I end up at the Golden Gate, the gate on the west side of the city which leads to the Golden Palace.

In the shadows of the gate, I stop and lean my back against the rough stones of the city wall. My chest heaves after my lengthy run. Tilting my head back, I rest it against the cold stones.

Gray afternoon light from the overcast sky paints the grasslands outside in bleak hues, making the dead trees that line the walk to the palace look even more miserable.

Aching sadness fills my chest.

It didn't used to look like this. In the old paintings, saved and kept secret and passed down from generation to generation, this path was magnificent. Grand trees with vibrant leaves and colorful flowers lined the walk from the city to the palace, making it look like the trees were forever living in a glorious season of spring. Now, only burnt trunks remain.

I raise my gaze to the palace itself that is visible across the grasslands. Made of shimmering pale stone, it shines like it's filled with golden light when the sun reflects against it. It used to be the seat of power in our court. A jewel in the beautiful landscape and a testament to the marvelous power of the Seelie Court.

Now, it's a deserted relic. A reminder of everything we can never have.

Rage burns through my heart, fierce as wildfire, as I shift my gaze to the iron wall that now circles our beautiful castle. Cold iron. A metal that drains our energy and blocks our connection to our magic. And those sadistic fucking dragon shifters built an entire wall of it around our most precious building.

Another burst of fury pulses through me, and I squeeze my hand into a fist. Isn't it ever enough? I get that what our ancestors did to the dragon shifters was wrong, but by Mabona, it has been thousands of years since then! Haven't they already gotten their revenge?

Closing my eyes, I heave a tired sigh. Even after all these years, I can still hear the voice of the dragon shifter teacher at school who taught me and the other kids before we became old enough to work. Can still hear his nasally voice as he tells us about how awful our ancestors were. How we deserve everything we got. Because it will never be enough. No amount of penance will ever be enough to absolve us of our cruel acts.

He used to tell us that thousands of years ago, fae and dragon shifters were allies. That we lived in peace and harmony. But then the fae discovered a new metal deep within the roots of a long dead volcano. A metal they called *dragon steel*. Though it's not actually real steel. It's harder and, more importantly, it can bend a dragon's will.

My old teacher used to say that just as we are weak against iron, the dragon shifters' weakness was dragon steel. And our ancestors used that to their advantage. Apparently, they forged bracelets and collars from the steel and forced them onto the dragon shifters. And then when the fae of old channeled their magic through the dragon steel, the shifters had no choice but to obey them. So the fae turned the shifters into slaves and became dragon riders, treating them as if they were no better than horses.

Eventually, the shifters rose up and killed all the dragon riders. My old teacher was always very vague about the details of exactly how that happened, for obvious reasons. But apparently, the dragons slaughtered everyone who had enslaved them, and all the other adult fae too. They spared the children but trapped them inside the Seelie Court so that they would be isolated and vulnerable.

My gaze drifts to the thick forest of gnarly trees and sharp thorns that completely surrounds our court. The old roads to the rest of the continent are still there, running right into the dense woods, but they're useless now. It's possible to walk a limited distance into the forest, but then the thorns become so thick that it's impossible to get through.

Since this unnatural vegetation apparently continues for miles upon miles around our court, it has made us entirely isolated from everyone else. We have no idea what happened to the Unseelie Court, but I can only assume that they suffered a similar fate. I don't even know how the dragon shifters managed to raise this strange forest of thorns all those millennia ago, but it has kept us prisoner ever since.

I still remember the vicious smugness in my teacher's voice as he told us that this is what we deserve. That it is our turn to live in poverty. To live as slaves. Our turn to suffer so that we might pay for our ancestors' crimes.

Heaving a bitter sigh, I shake my head. It's time to fight back. To take back our home. Reclaim our freedom. That's the whole reason why I joined the resistance. If only they would actually let me *help*. It has been years, and still all they ever let me do is be a lookout. I want to do something meaningful. Something important. Something that will actually aid our cause.

With another angry shake of my head, I push off from the wall and straighten again while I squeeze my hand into a fist. Determination pulses through me as I start back towards the city. I need to do something to prove myself to the leaders. Something that will finally make them trust me. Something—

My gaze snags on a poster that has been nailed to the wooden news board.

Stopping in my tracks, I blink at it.

That's it. That's what I need to do in order to actually make a difference for our resistance movement.

After quickly checking the address at the bottom, I hurry towards the correct building. It should be open for another half hour before the administrator closes up and goes home for the day. Picking up the pace, I sprint towards the building.

Once again out of breath, I arrive at a well-kept wooden building with about ten minutes to spare.

All around me, people have started heading home for the evening. A tired-looking fae man with silver hair limps past, supported by another guy who carries an axe in his other hand. Given their clothes and equipment, they must be from the Lumber Guild. Across the street, a member of the Painter's Guild continues trying to give the rundown building before him a much-needed facelift. Green paint is splattered across the sleeves of his white shirt.

I draw in a deep breath to refill my lungs and then push my hair back behind my pointed ears in an effort to make myself look more presentable and less like I have just spent the past hour trying to escape from a patrol that was hunting me.

Once I'm reasonably sure that I look as composed as I'll ever be, I open the door and stride across the threshold.

A small brass bell tinkles above me when I open the door. At the sound of it, a male dragon shifter looks up from a document that he was reading. He is sitting behind a large desk on the other side of the room, facing the door. Apart from that, and the chair he is sitting on, the small room contains only bookshelves filled with leather tomes and documents. There is a door to my right, leading farther into the building, but I'm pretty sure that everything I need is right in this room.

"What?" the shifter behind the desk snaps, his voice laced with impatience.

His blue eyes lock on mine as he raises his eyebrows expectantly. Since dragon shifters have very long lifespans, just like we fae have, it's difficult to tell how old he is. Their physical age stops around the same time as ours do, so everyone looks like they're somewhere between twenty-five and thirty. This man in front of me might be twenty-five or five hundred years old, and there is no way to know just by looking at him.

"I'm here to register for the trial," I reply as I walk a little closer to his desk.

He heaves an annoyed sigh as if this is something that takes great effort on his part when it's in fact his literal job. Setting down the document he was reading, he twists in his chair and reaches towards a stack of papers on the shelf behind him. The paper rustles in the air as he yanks one out and then turns back to me. After slamming it down on the desk, he picks up a pen and then levels yet another impatient look at me.

"Name," he demands.

"Selena Hale," I reply.

Faint scraping sounds drift through the room as he writes down my name. Without looking up, he asks, "Age?"

"One hundred and sixty-seven."

"Guild?"

He could technically look that up on his own since the dragon shifters are the ones who assigned everyone to their guilds, but I answer anyway. "Fishing Guild. I'm a fish cutter."

With his eyes still on the paper, he wrinkles his nose as if he can smell the stench of it. I have to suppress a sudden flash of anger. It's not my fault that I'm still working a low-level job in the guild. Just like everyone else in this city, the other people in the Fishing Guild don't trust me, so they never move me up to better jobs.

"Magic type?" the shifter asks.

"Emotion magic."

At that, he looks up from his paper for the first time since starting the interview. Suspicion pulses across his whole face as he looks at me. I just remain standing there, keeping my chin raised.

"Emotion magic?" he asks at last.

I nod. "Yes."

Almost subconsciously, he moves a little farther back in his chair while he looks at me with suspicion in his eyes. They always do. Whenever people find out that I possess emotion magic, they always look at me like that. As if I'm going to use my magic on them and start manipulating their emotions without them knowing. As if I'm going to make them do things that they don't want to do.

Don't get me wrong, I can do that. Well, part of that anyway. It's a bit more complicated than people think. But what I can't do is hide it. As soon as I mention my magic, it's as if everyone forgets that no fae who was born with magic can use it without people seeing it. Because our eyes glow when we channel magic. So if someone is looking me in the eye, they will know whether I'm using my magic to manipulate their emotions or not. But because emotion magic immediately makes people nervous, they seem to forget that.

The dragon shifter behind the desk seems to finally remember that my eyes will glow if I use magic, because instead of looking down at his paper again, he now keeps his eyes locked on mine while he continues the interview.

A dull ache buries deep into my heart. Even though I haven't done anything to earn their mistrust, no one ever feels truly comfortable around me because of my magic type. It's why I can't move up in the guild and why I can't move up in the resistance either.

But this… this is going to change all that.

"Alright," the administrator says as he takes the finished paper and slams it down on top of another pile. "That's it. You're registered for this century's Atonement Trials. They will begin sometime in the next two to four weeks. Be ready at any time." He jerks his chin. "Now, get the hell out of my office."

I swallow down an angry remark at his rudeness and instead just give him a nod in acknowledgement before I turn around and walk back out the door.

Cold winds rip at my clothes as I step back out onto the cobblestone street, but there is a fiery sense of anticipation burning in my chest now. I grin as I flip my collar up and start down the street.

The Atonement Trials. Every one hundred and fifty years, the Emperor and Empress of the Iceheart Dynasty hold a tournament in the Seelie Court. The Atonement Trials is supposed to be the one scrap of mercy that they will bestow upon us. It's a series of competitions that pits fae magic users against each other to prove who is the strongest and most worthy. The three people who win the tournament are deemed to have atoned for the sins of their ancestors, and they are awarded with a highly sought-after prize. They are allowed to leave the Seelie Court and are given funds to set up a new life in the world outside.

Last time the Atonement Trials were held, I was too young to compete. I was only seventeen back then, which means that I had barely started practicing with my magic. The other contestants would have mopped the floor with me.

But now, I'm much stronger. Now, I have a chance to win.

This is how I prove my worth to the leaders of the resistance. If I win, I will get to leave the city and have access to the rest of the world. I can find out what happened to the Unseelie Court. I can be a spy. A real asset. I can help the rebellion more than anyone in this entire city.

All I need to do is to win the Atonement Trials.

CHAPTER THREE

Nausea rolls through my stomach as I stand in front of a plain wooden door on the north side of the city. It doesn't matter how many times I try to convince myself that I'm a badass resistance fighter and a skilled magic user who will help free our people, every time I stand in front of this door, I'm reminded of who I really am. Of what I really am.

I might act all tough in the face of dragon shifter patrols, but as soon as I'm with other fae, with my own people, my bravado crumbles and I revert back into this. And I hate it. But I don't know how to stop it.

Drawing in a bracing breath, I raise my hand to knock on the door.

After about half a minute, the door is opened and a fae man with blond hair becomes visible on the other side of the threshold. His turquoise and silver eyes are soft and friendly for all of two seconds. Then they fix on my face, and disappointment briefly flickers in them instead before he manages to hide it.

He presses his mouth into a thin line.

"Hi, Dad," I say.

"Selena," he replies, but he doesn't move from his place in the doorway.

"Can I come in?" I ask when he still doesn't step aside.

The fact that I even have to knock on the door and then ask if I can come inside, into my own childhood home, makes a tiny fragile part of my heart crack. But it has always been like this. Ever since I moved out when I was eighteen. Or rather, ever since I was asked to leave the day I turned eighteen, I have always had to act as if I'm just an uninvited guest every time I want to come back and visit my parents.

After an extended moment, my father finally steps aside with a sigh.

I carefully walk inside. Fabric rustles from the kitchen. I move towards the sound and find my mother sitting at the kitchen table, mending a pair of pants.

She looks up when I walk into the room, and uneasiness flits across her face for a second before she too covers it up. But I've seen it so many times now that it's impossible to miss it. Another piece of my heart still cracks at the sight of it.

"Selena," she says.

"Hi, Mom," I reply.

Footsteps come from behind me. I quickly move farther into the kitchen so that I'm not blocking the doorway. Dad arrives a few seconds later and takes up position in front of one of the wooden counters. I hover awkwardly by one of the sturdy kitchen chairs, wondering whether I should sit down or not.

Dad crosses his arms and remains standing, leaning back against the counter, while Mom is sitting down. Indecision flashes through me as I try to decide if they would feel better if I sat down or if that would just make them think that I was planning on staying long, which would just make them more uncomfortable.

In the end, I gently pull out a chair at the other end of the table and sit down. But I sit on the very edge of the seat, so that they will know that I'm just sitting down for a few minutes and will be leaving soon.

A small clock on the shelf behind me ticks loudly into the oppressive silence. My parents simply continue looking at me. Mom's silver hair has been pulled back in a braid, and there is an impatient look in her lavender and yellow eyes.

I clear my throat. "I, uhm… I just wanted to tell you that… uhm… Yesterday, I did something exciting. Important, I mean."

Dad furrows his pale brows. Mom just looks like she wants me to get to the point.

Dropping my gaze, I start wringing my hands before I remember myself. With a soft breath, I force my hands flat against my thighs and then look up to meet my parents' eyes.

"I registered as a contestant for the Atonement Trials," I blurt out before I can change my mind.

All of last night, and most of today while I was gutting fish, I was debating whether or not to tell my parents that I signed up. We have a complicated relationship, and I didn't want to burden them with any upsetting news. But a small part of me, the desperate child still inside my heart, wanted them to be excited for me, or worried about my safety, or wish me luck, or all of the above. And that part of me won.

"Why?" is the first thing my dad says. He sounds angry.

Swallowing, I suppress the urge to wring my hands in my lap again. "Well, I just… If I win, I will be able to leave the city. Then I could go anywhere and do… things. I could make a change. Help make your lives better and—"

"Do not say things like that in my house," Dad cuts me off, his eyes flashing with both anger and panic. He flicks a quick glance towards the windows, as if to make sure that they are truly closed. "That kind of talk is dangerously close to treason."

They don't know that I'm actually an active member of the

resistance, and I intend to keep it that way. Because I knew that this is how they would react.

"It's not *your* house," my mother snaps before I can reply. Irritation pulses across her beautiful features as she locks eyes with her husband. "It's *our* house."

"You know what I mean," he huffs. Then he throws his hands up and blows out a forceful sigh. "By Mabona, you always do this. You always twist my words into something else."

"Twist your words? Those *were* your exact words!"

"Please," I interject, trying to mediate. "You have every right to feel upset, but I'm sure he didn't mean it like that. Right, Dad?"

"Don't," both of my parents growl, whipping around to lock hard eyes on me.

"Don't meddle," Dad warns.

Mom blows out an angry breath. "You've done far too much of that already."

Pain pulses through my heart, and I shrink back on the chair. Not because of the harsh words, but because they're right.

I know that my parents resent me. I can feel it every time they look at me. And the worst part of it all is that they have every right to.

When I first manifested my powers, my parents were excited. Neither of them was born with magical abilities, so to have a child with magic was supposed to bring them great benefits. Instead, I only brought them pain.

As a child, I couldn't control my powers. Which is normal. It takes years for any magic user to gain full control of their powers. But because of the nature of my magic, it caused more destruction than usual.

My powers would randomly activate without me even realizing it, making me manipulate my parents' emotions. I tried to control it. I tried to master my magic faster than any fae had ever done before, but it simply wasn't possible. It takes time. And training. So my parents continued to be influenced by my magic for years. It made them question what was real and what wasn't, and it led to problems in their marriage that still remain to this day.

They didn't want me near them. They didn't trust me not to mess with their emotions. And they started resenting each other too because of all the fights that their magically increased emotions led to.

So their dream of a happy family was destroyed by me. Not only because of the problems in their marriage that I unwittingly caused, but also because they couldn't simply try again. Since we fae have such long lifespans, we can only give birth to one child. So my parents wasted their one shot at having a perfect family by having me. The daughter who ruined it all.

So I sit there on the chair and quietly wait for my parents to finish arguing.

Once it has died down, I look up from my lap and meet their frustrated eyes again.

"I… I just wanted to tell you that I registered, so in a few weeks, I will be in the trials," I say before trailing off.

Mom puts the pants and the needle and thread down on the scratched wooden table in front of her while Dad shifts his weight by the counter.

"Thank you for informing us," she manages to press out, but the words come out sounding stilted and unnatural.

I just nod in reply.

"If you win, don't contact us," Dad says, turning eyes full of warning on me. "We don't want the dragon shifters to think that you're some kind of rebel. That *we* are some kind of rebels."

"She's not going to win," Mom interjects with an impatient sigh and an annoyed look at Dad. "She's a fish cutter with emotion magic."

"You know damn well the damage she can cause."

"To a relationship! Not to an opponent in battle."

"Who says it's going to be a battle?"

"What do—"

Their arguing is interrupted by the grating of wood against wood as I quickly stand up and then push my chair back in underneath the table. My heart aches and I need to leave before I drown underneath the weight of it.

"I just wanted to tell you that," I repeat uselessly before clearing my throat. "I need to go and eat now before all the food places close for the night."

"Right," Dad says, still sounding flustered. "Yes."

Mom nods.

I wait for them to wish me luck. To tell me to be careful.

They don't.

So I lick my lips, swallow, and then walk back towards the front door. Only silence follows me.

Once I open the door and take one step across the threshold, I can hear their argument start back up inside the kitchen again. I close the door behind me and try to keep my heart from fracturing as I walk away from my childhood home and the family that I ruined.

I had planned to go to my usual tavern, but I only make it a few streets before I can't take it anymore. I can't take one more second of simply walking alone with my thoughts, so I duck into the nearest tavern.

Just like most of our city, it's in desperate need of repair. But at least it's warm and brightly lit by a hearth and several faelights along the walls. The faelights are white gemstones that glow and produce light without giving off any heat.

I scan the dark wooden tables as I step across the threshold. The room is packed with people. Some of them sit alone, but most are crammed together around the tables in pairs or groups as they eat and drink. I note an empty table by the wall while I head straight for the bar.

Reaching into my pocket, I pull out the meal ticket that I

received at the end of my workday. I stare at that piece of paper while I wait for the tavern keeper to finish up with the customer before me.

The dragon shifters control everything. Even our ability to eat. We're not allowed to own or produce money, so we can't simply buy the food we need with our wages. Instead, we receive one meal ticket at the end of each workday. One ticket that can be exchanged for one meal at any tavern in the city. Even the people who work in those taverns only receive one ticket. Though I'm sure they've figured out some kind of system to stealthily eat some more while they work.

But the rest of us have to make do with one meal a day. The hunger is meant to keep us weak and to keep us so distracted by our empty stomachs that we can't find the energy to resist.

"What can I get you?" the tavern keeper asks from behind the counter.

I look up from my meal ticket and open my mouth to respond.

"The fish stew," replies the woman who has suddenly appeared next to me.

My gaze flits from her to the tavern keeper. It was my turn to order. Not hers. For a second, I consider saying something. But in the end, I just let her order first. No point in being difficult.

Once she has received her meal, I finally meet the tavern keeper's eyes.

"What can I get you?" he asks.

"The mutton stew, please," I reply.

Since I work with fish every day, I'm usually sick of the smell and taste of it, so I always order the beef or the mutton stew.

He nods distractedly, one eye on the long line that has started to form behind me, before he heads over to the massive pots that contain the different stews. I roll the corner of the meal ticket while I wait for him to come back. My stomach grumbles, but I'm so used to it that I barely notice it anymore.

"Alright, here we are," the tavern keeper says. A thud sounds as he sets down the bowl on the dark wooden counter before me. "One fish stew."

I reach for it before his words register. Pausing with my hand halfway to the bowl, I meet his tired gaze and open my mouth to speak.

Indecision flashes through me. Should I tell him that he got my order wrong? I really don't want the fish stew. But I also don't want to cause any trouble.

My hand hovers in the air. The tavern keeper raises his eyebrows in question before his distracted gaze once more flits to the long line of people waiting impatiently behind me.

Anxiousness slithers through my stomach.

"Thank you," I press out, and take the offered bowl while handing over my meal ticket.

Deep inside, frustration rips through me. I should have said something. I *wanted* to say something. Because I didn't want the fish. I wanted the mutton stew. But I just... I didn't want to annoy him. People already keep me at arm's length, and I don't want to give them any more reasons to dislike me.

Blowing out an exhausted sigh, I take my bowl of fish stew and head straight for the table I spotted earlier. It's a table for two, so I slide into the rickety chair and immediately pick up the spoon from the bowl.

The fish tastes like... fish. But I eat it anyway.

While I eat, one of the waitresses comes by and places a mug of ale in front of me. I watch her flowing brown hair sway across her back as she walks up to the next table and does the same. At the third table, she swaps out the empty mugs for full ones.

I shake my head. We only get one meal ticket per day, but all alcohol is free. Another cruel but effective tactic to keep us all on our knees. Drinking alcohol eases the hunger and numbs the pain and depression that most people feel. It also makes people addicted and keeps them too drunk to fight back.

With another sigh, I shake my head once more. We need to change this. *I* need to change this. And once I win the Atonement Trials, that is exactly what I will do.

CHAPTER FOUR

Steel rings faintly through the chilly midday air as I use a whetstone to sharpen my knife. One of my fellow guild members rolls a wooden barrel along the street. It produces a wooden rattling sound as it turns over and over. I keep my eyes on my blade.

"Here's the next barrel," he says when he reaches me.

With a grunt, he grabs the side of the barrel and tips it back up so that it's in an upright position. I raise my gaze from the whetstone right as he uses a crowbar to pop the lid of the barrel.

The smell of fish wafts towards me.

I stare at the mountain of fish waiting for me in the barrel. It's the same thing every day. Transporters bring me barrels or buckets of fish, and I clean it, gut it, and cut it. It's boring, monotonous, and smelly. But at least it has helped me develop great skills with a knife.

"Thanks," I say to the transporter who is dusting off his hands after straightening the barrel.

He nods and then heads back down towards Lake Andun, where the actual fishermen work to catch the fish that I and other low-level guild members get to clean.

My gaze flits down to my hands. After I finished the previous barrel, I had a few minutes to spare, so I was able to wash and scrub my hands. And since I want to enjoy the sensation of clean and soap-scented hands a little longer, I keep pretending to sharpen my knife even though I'm already done.

Hopefully, it won't be too long now before—

"DRAGONS!"

I snap my head up right as the massive bells atop the watchtower start to ring.

"DRAGONS!" the watchmaster bellows across the city again, his voice amplified by magic. "THE DRAGONS ARE COMING!"

I leap up from my stool so fast that I knock over the empty buckets next to me. The wooden clattering joins the loud metallic clanging of the bells and the shouts that rise from people up and down the streets.

My heart flips in my chest. But not out of fear. No. My heart lurches with excitement.

It has been two and a half weeks since I signed up for the Atonement Trials.

If the dragon shifters are coming in force now, it can only mean one thing.

The tournament is about to start.

Anticipation burns through me as I ram my knife into the holster on my thigh. Then I leave the barrel of fish behind and take off down the street.

All around me, people are doing the same.

The shifters from the Red Dragon Clan fly in and out of the Seelie Court all the time since it's their responsibility to manage us. But sometimes, other clans, or even the emperor and empress themselves, come to visit for one reason or another. And when they do, they expect us to greet them properly.

One time, about forty years ago, the farseer atop the watchtower, the fae man or woman with magically enhanced eyesight who is responsible for watching the skies for approaching dragons, didn't spot the Brown Dragon Clan until they were almost at the city. We didn't make it out to the Dragon Field in time to greet them. It… did not end well.

So the moment the announcement comes, we all rush out to the grasslands on the west side of the city, which have been named the Dragon Field since that's always where they land.

My heart pounds in my chest as I race through the streets and out through South Gate.

Brisk winds whirl across the grasslands, making my hair flutter behind me. But the midday sun shines down from a clear blue sky and warms my cheeks.

I draw in deep breaths as I slow to a walk and then come to a halt on the grass. Anxious murmuring fills the air as we arrange ourselves into neat rows, but I feel only excitement. The time has finally come. At last, I will get to show everyone just how much of an asset I can really be to our cause.

Sunlight shines down over the palace to my left, making the pale stones glitter like gold. I cast a glance at it while both pain and longing tug at my heart. The dragon shifters will be living inside the palace for the duration of the trials. As will the contestants. I don't want those damn dragons in there, desecrating our sacred halls. But soon, it will be all ours again.

The woman next to me sucks in a sharp breath.

I whip my gaze back to the grasslands in front of me.

My stomach dips.

There.

On the horizon, high over the massive forest of thorns, dragons become visible as they swoop across the grand mountains to the north called the Peaks of Prosperity.

I draw in an involuntary breath at the sight. I might hate them all with every fiber of my being for how they treat us, but by Mabona, I can't deny that it's a magnificent sight.

Two massive silver dragons fly at the front of the procession.

Light glints against their scales, making it look like glittering starlight.

To their right and a little behind them flies another gigantic dragon. This one is black like a moonless night.

There is a larger space behind that dragon, after which an entire row of dragons can be seen. One red, one green, one orange, one white, one blue, one brown, and one purple.

An entire host of dragons, in all colors, fills the sky after that.

I let out a long exhale. We can do this. *I* can do this.

The booming of wings fills the air as the mass of dragons draws closer. Trees shake as the winds that their wings produce slam down over the forest. The red dragon at the edge of the row lets out a deafening roar.

Gasps and whimpers rip from our ranks, and several people around me shrink back.

I stand my ground even as the two silver dragons and the black dragon swoop down towards us at breakneck speed. Others around me scramble back. The dragons get closer.

Booms cut through the air as the first three dragons hit the ground in a cloud of smoke.

Everyone holds their breath.

And out of the dissipating smoke stride the Wings of Freedom, the Forger of Worlds, and the Shadow of Death.

As one, we all drop down on one knee and bow our heads.

Side by side, the Empress and Emperor of the Iceheart Dynasty stride towards us. Draven Ryat walks on their right, two steps behind them.

Briefly closing my eyes, I send a quick prayer to Mabona that Draven won't recognize me. After all, there is nothing about me that stands out. Silver hair is rather common in our court, and all fae have elegant facial features, so it's not as if I'm unusually beautiful or anything like that. Nothing special. Nothing remarkable. Which means that Draven won't recognize me. Probably. Hopefully.

I open my eyes again as several more booms echo across the grasslands. While still keeping my chin lowered, I study the scene before me.

The second row of dragons has landed and shifted. When they shift, it produces smoke, so it temporarily blocks the view of the forest behind them.

Once the smoke clears, the leaders of the other seven dragon clans are standing there on the trampled grass.

Gremar Fireclaw, the leader of the Red Dragon Clan, sweeps a glare dripping with threats over all of us, as if to warn us to be on our best behavior. Since he is responsible for managing our city, any wrongdoing on our part would reflect badly on him. But he doesn't need to warn us to behave. None of us would be stupid enough to try something when the leader of every dragon clan as well as the empress and emperor themselves are here.

I keep my chin lowered but watch discreetly as Draven and the Icehearts come to a halt a short distance in front of us.

Empress Jessina Iceheart, nicknamed the Wings of Freedom, stands with her back straight and her chin raised. Her pale gray eyes shift casually over the sea of kneeling fae before her. A strong wind makes her long white hair ripple over the regal silver dress that she is wearing. It matches the elegant silver wings visible behind her shoulders.

Beside her, Emperor Bane Iceheart, also known as the Forger of Worlds, watches us all with a smug tilt of his lips while he flares his silver wings slightly. His long black hair has been swept back, barely a strand out of place as it cascades down his back, and a cruel glint shines in his black eyes.

In terms of physical appearance, they couldn't be more different. And yet, they are mates. Both of them are equal leaders of the rare Silver Dragon Clan. An incredibly powerful species of dragon that, as opposed to all other dragons, breathes ice flames instead of fire. It was those dangerous ice flames that made it possible for the Silver Dragon Clan to conquer all the other clans and bring them to heel underneath their rule.

"Well," Jessina Iceheart says, sounding incredibly bored. "Is this it?"

Tense silence hangs over the Dragon Field like a suffocating cloak. No one dares to respond since we don't know who she was addressing.

Behind them, Gremar Fireclaw flicks a quick glance between us and his monarchs while a hint of panic pulses across his face. He opens his mouth to speak, but Bane beats him to it.

"Just wait until the tournament starts." A wicked smile curves the emperor's lips. "Then we'll have some fun."

"Yes," Jessina agrees. Then she sweeps her gaze over us again while a sharp smile spreads across her mouth as well. "We traveled a long way for these trials. Make it interesting."

Before anyone can figure out how to respond to that, the Icehearts turn as one and start towards the Golden Palace. The leaders of the other dragon clans follow. In the sky above, the rest of the dragons are circling as if to keep their leaders safe from threats.

I stare at Gremar's broad back as he reaches the path lined with dead trees that leads to the palace. He tilts his head up and scowls at something. Following his gaze, I find one tiny little leaf that has sprouted on one of the dead branches.

Hope fills my heart.

Gremar raises an arm, making his red dragon scale armor shift with the motion.

And then he uses his lava magic to incinerate the leaf.

A collective sigh of misery washes through our ranks, but no one says anything. I shake my head at his back as he continues towards the palace with the others.

"Everyone who has not registered as a contestant for the Atonement Trials, get back to the city," a commanding voice suddenly calls.

Clothes rustle as the vast majority jump to their feet and hurry back to the city. I remain on one knee since I haven't been told that I'm allowed to rise.

Glancing over my shoulder, I find other people still on one knee as well. My competitors. I'll have to study them more carefully later, so that I can make a plan for how to beat them.

I turn my head back so that I'm facing forwards again once all the non-contestants have left. The blue-eyed dragon shifter who interviewed me and filled out my registration form two weeks ago is standing on the grass before us.

And so is someone else.

Dread flits through my chest as I notice a pair of legs wearing familiar black armor.

Crap.

Why hasn't he left with the other clan leaders?

I keep my head bowed while I silently try to force Draven to leave by simply the power of my mind. I even consider using my magic to manipulate his emotions so that he will feel impatient and restless enough to leave. But I decide against it. I can't risk the administrator seeing it. If he does, he might disqualify me before the trials have even started.

Clothes rustle as the final non-contestants hurry away to my right.

I barely dare to breathe as I keep my eyes on Draven's black boots.

He takes a step forward.

Shit.

Dry grass crunches underneath his boots as he strides towards me.

Shit, shit, shit.

I discreetly slide the knife from my holster and hide it behind my back instead.

Draven continues advancing on me.

My heart slams against my ribs.

His boots stop right in front of me.

The distinct ringing of steel fills the air as he draws his sword.

I tighten my grip on the knife behind my back. If he tries to execute me right here, I will have to fight him. I know that I won't win. But I'll have to try.

Sunlight glints against metal as Draven moves his sword towards my neck.

My fingers tighten on the hilt of my knife.

Cold steel kisses my skin as Draven places the tip of the sword underneath my chin. With a firm push, he tilts my chin up so that I'm forced to meet his gaze.

His golden eyes lock on mine with such intensity that I forget how to breathe.

"You," he says. "I remember you."

"No, you don't," I blurt out before I even know what I'm saying.

Mabona's tits. I want to slap myself. What the hell was that? I sounded like a delusional five-year-old who tries to deny that she was found during a game of hide-and-seek.

Something almost like a breath of amusement escapes Draven's lips. But the smile that follows is all threats. "Yours is a face I'm not likely to forget."

"Understandable." I flex my fingers on the knife behind my back. "And now, you've... what? Come to take an eye for an eye?"

That lethal smile on his mouth widens, and his eyes glint. With a firm push of his blade, he forces me to tilt my head farther back, exposing my throat completely to him.

"An eye for an eye sounds too fair." He flashes me a wicked smile. "I'll be taking the whole head."

My heart skips a beat. I squeeze the hilt of my knife hard, getting ready to yank it forward and slam it into his leg.

But right before I can begin my desperate and doomed fight, he abruptly removes the sword from my throat, flashes me a threatening smile, and walks away.

I stare after him, dumbfounded. My head spins, and I'm not sure if I should be relieved or even more worried.

"Right," the administrator says, a tad awkwardly, as if he's not sure what to make of that either. His blue eyes flick to me for a second, and a scowl creases his brows, but then he simply clears his throat and presses on. "My name is Imar, and I am the overseer for this century's Atonement Trials."

Everyone who was staring at Draven immediately snaps their gaze to the blond dragon shifter still standing on the grass before us. He raises his eyebrows expectantly. We all dip our chins in a quick bow of acknowledgement and respect.

"The trials will begin tomorrow," Imar says.

Relief washes through me. That's great. That means that I can go home and get a good night's sleep and pack everything that I need to bring before heading off to the Golden Palace.

A knowing smile blows across Imar's lips as he watches us in silence for a second. Then he adds, "But the registrations will finish tonight."

Some of the fae around me exchange glances since no one seems to understand what that's supposed to mean.

The smile on Imar's lips grows into a full-blown smirk as he spells it out. "You have until sundown to make it inside the iron walls. Anyone not inside the walls when the sun sets will not be allowed to compete in the Atonement Trials."

Deafening silence falls over the grasslands.

We all turn our heads to look at the palace and the iron wall that circles it. The Iceheart monarchs and all the other clan leaders have already made it inside. And so have the rest of the dragons who were guarding their leaders from the sky. I watch as Draven, in his half-shift form, flies the final stretch and disappears through the now open iron gate as well.

Clothes rustle faintly as we glance around at each other.

Because we all know what this means.

The trials haven't *technically* started yet, but they have started.

The people who make it to the gate first can hold it so that no one else can enter. That way there will be less competition once the trials actually start.

I cast another worried glance at the people around me. I won't be able to fight my way through the gate. Which means that I must make it there first.

Imar flashes us another broad grin filled with wicked glee. "Dismissed."

We all sprint towards the gate.

CHAPTER FIVE

My breath saws through my lungs as I hurtle across the grass. Boots pound against the ground as everyone tries to make it to the gate first. I push myself to the limits, running with everything I have. But it's with growing dread that I realize that I'm not fast enough.

The first two people reach the gate.

Both of them simply sprint through and disappear inside the palace grounds. The next four people do the same.

Hope swells in my chest as about half of the contestants simply run inside without trying to stop others from following. Maybe I can make it through anyway. If I can just—

A group of five reaches the gate, spins around, and then spreads out to block the way.

Goddess damn it. Why did I have to jinx it?

The people who were right behind them throw themselves to the sides as the fae man with curly blond hair in the middle of the gate shoots a torrent of fire straight out.

"Shit," I hiss under my breath, swerving to the side to escape the heat of the flames.

While slowing to a careful walk, I study the people now

blocking the gate. I recognize them all, but I only know the name of the guy in the middle with the curly blond hair and the green and orange eyes and the fire magic. His name is Alistair Geller, and he is an absolute bully.

I've only had a few run-ins with him myself, many years ago, but almost every time I see him around town, he is doing something to make other people feel small and helpless.

And now, he is blocking the damn gate.

Fantastic.

The other contestants around me watch them warily as well. Most of them have trailed to a halt, and some people cluster together in groups as if to strategize together.

Only three people keep running.

I watch with brows furrowed in confusion as a fae woman with black hair and eyes that are blue and silver runs straight for the iron wall farther down from the gate. Right before she can crash into it, a block of ice shoots up from the ground underneath her. It pushes her into the air, and she sails gracefully over the wall.

A few seconds later, a fae man a short distance from her does the same thing, except with a block of stone instead of ice.

The third person who kept running continues farther down along the wall. Her brown hair flutters in the wind as she moves. Right before she reaches the wall, a tree sprouts right out of the ground.

I jerk back in shock.

Tree magic? With wide eyes, I stare at the fae woman as she nimbly climbs the tree. I didn't even know that we had someone with that kind of magic in our city.

The people around me seem equally surprised, because they also stare at her while she jumps over the wall and into another tree that she must have grown from the ground. Both trees then sink back into the grass.

A scream shatters through the air.

I snap my gaze back to the gate to find that a guy is trying to fight his way past Alistair and his gang. The sound seems to jolt everyone else out of their stupor too, because they all lurch into motion as well.

Magic flashes through the air as several people try to force their way through.

Desperation rips at my chest. I know that I won't be able to fight my way through. My magic isn't suited for that kind of brute force attack.

My gaze slides to the guy on the far right, and an idea forms in my mind. Maybe I can sneak through while they're otherwise occupied.

Sneaking around the group of increasingly frantic contestants, I approach the edge of the gate.

The person who is supposed to guard that side is a muscular guy with brown hair. But his red and brown eyes are currently fixed on the three people trying to force their way past him from the front.

I stick to the shadows, creeping along the wall until I'm right next to the gate. My heart patters in my chest. I suck in a quick breath.

Then I dart forward, intending to quickly slip around the corner and in through the gate.

Pain pulses through me as a large hand wraps around my upper arm and yanks me back out before I have gotten more than one foot inside. I try to pull my arm free, but the grip is impossibly strong. It might as well have been a steel manacle.

"Nice try," a voice growls.

Looking up, I meet the red and brown eyes of the man I thought was too preoccupied to notice me. His eyes glow, indicating that he is using some kind of magic, though I don't know what kind.

Wicked satisfaction blows across his face. He moves his arm, and I can feel that he is about to use his grip on me to physically throw me away from the gate.

"I'm sorry," I blurt out.

That stuns him enough that he pauses for a moment.

I quickly bow my head and make my voice pleading. "I'm sorry. I just really want to compete in these trials. Please."

From his perspective, it looks like I'm begging. But what I'm really doing is hiding my eyes so that he won't see that I've begun channeling magic.

Reaching out with my magic, I push at an emotion that I hope will be there after my little show of pitiful pleading.

It's not there, so I keep speaking.

"I've been dreaming of competing in this tournament since I was a kid," I lie, keeping my voice soft and sad and pleading. "I just want to prove that I'm good enough. Please."

I push with my magic again.

Victory pulses through me when I find a small pink spark of sympathy inside him. I pour my magic towards it, making it grow.

His grip on my arm loosens a little.

I keep manipulating that pale pink spark inside him, increasing the sympathy he now feels towards me.

He relaxes his fingers even more.

I keep my magic flowing. Almost now. He will release me fully in three, two—

A strong hand wraps around my jaw and wrenches my head up.

My glowing eyes come face to face with Alistair Geller.

"Don't be fooled by her," he snarls at his friend, his fingers still digging into my jaw. "This is Selena Soulstealer."

Soulstealer. That's the name people call me behind my back because they think that I can manipulate people's emotions to such a degree that I can change them into an entirely different person. It's not true. But I haven't told people that. Because revealing secrets about how your magic works is not only stupid, it's dangerous as hell too.

The other guy snatches his hand off my arm as if I have a contagious disease.

But Alistair keeps his hand around my jaw. His eyes begin to glow as he summons his fire magic.

Alarm blares through my skull.

Yanking out the knife from my thigh holster, I slash it through the air towards his face.

He leaps back, shock pulsing in his eyes.

The moment he releases me, I whip around and sprint away along the wall.

Fire roars behind me.

Throwing myself to the side, I dive down right before a blast of flames shoots through the space I was just occupying. The heat of it singes a few strands of my hair that were still fluttering above me from the dive. Twisting around, I cast a frantic look back. But thankfully, Alistair and his gang are already engaged in another fight with the other contestants.

I push to my feet.

My heart slams against my ribs. I draw a deep breath.

Alright, so the gate is out.

Looking from side to side, I scan the iron wall as far as I can see.

There might be some other way in.

After making sure that my hair isn't on fire, I slide my knife back into its holster and then start down along the wall.

I check every side of it. Every inch. For an opening. A crack. Something. Anything.

The sun is slipping lower towards the horizon with every passing hour.

But after circling the entire palace grounds twice, I'm forced to conclude that there is no other way in.

I head back to the gate but stop along the wall a safe distance away.

Alistair and his gang are still blocking it. There are fewer people still outside, though, so some of them must have succeeded in getting inside. Regardless, it doesn't matter. Because *I* will never be able to get through them.

Tilting my head back, I stare up at the iron wall before me. Up above, the sky has started to turn pink and orange. Crows caw in the trees somewhere inside the forest of thorns.

I heave a deep sigh. I guess there is nothing else for it.

I'm going to have to climb the wall.

There are small spikes on it that I should be able to use as hand- and footholds. If only I can actually manage to hold on to them.

My mind balks at the very idea. But I'm out of options.

So I steel myself and close the final distance to the wall. Then I reach out and grip the first spike.

A hiss rips from my lungs, and I snatch my hand back.

"Fuck," I growl, shaking my hand to relieve the pain.

Then I grit my teeth and try again. This time, I don't give myself time to react. I grab a spike with both hands and start climbing.

My magic is immediately suffocated.

Pain sears through my palms as the iron meets my skin. It doesn't cause physical damage, but it burns cold, like gripping a frozen block of ice. And it completely blocks off my ability to channel magic.

I keep climbing, as fast as I can manage.

Burning pain spreads from my palms and shoots up through my arms.

A whimper slips from my lips.

My body is already weakening, and I haven't even made it halfway up the wall yet.

I climb faster.

My boot slips from the spike.

Throwing my hand up, I desperately grip one of the spikes hard to stop myself from falling. Freezing, burning pain spears through my arm and up to my collarbones.

I cry out in pain as I heave myself up until I can get my foot on another spike.

Energy is draining from my body like a rapid flood.

I need to make it over the wall. Right now. Or I won't make it at all.

Black spots dance before my eyes as I throw everything I have into a burst of speed.

Pain and exhaustion tear through my whole body, but my hand finally reaches the top of the wall. With a scream of pure desperation, I haul myself up and roll over the edge. Icy pain streaks through my back as my bare skin meets the iron. But I don't have enough energy left to reach up and yank my shirt back down to cover my skin. I don't even have enough energy left to sit up. Let alone climb back down the wall.

So I do the only thing I can.

I roll over the edge and simply plummet down to the ground.

My body hits the grass with a loud thud.

More pain pulses through my body, but I can barely feel it. The prolonged contact with iron from something as massive as a wall has left me completely drained. I know that the fall from the wall won't be enough to break any bones. And I can survive the bruises. So I just lie there on my side, staring at the soft grass before me. It smells of damp soil.

Everything hurts. I don't have even a smidgen of energy left inside my body right now. But I made it.

Without my magic, it would never have been possible.

The fae who don't have magic would never have been able to climb this wall, because the iron would go straight for their energy. And the strength of the iron is in direct proportion to its size. Something as small as a bracelet would steal much less energy than something as massive as this gigantic wall around the entire palace grounds. So climbing this without any magic would leave people catatonic.

But if you have magic, the iron feeds off that first. It blocks our ability to channel magic and it also leaves us weakened, but not nearly as much as those without magic.

Except if the iron happens to be this gigantic fucking wall. Then I would argue that I feel damn close to being catatonic too even though the wall fed on my magic first.

Rolling over on my back, I draw in a few shuddering breaths. It's going to be at least half an hour before I've recovered enough energy to stand up.

But it doesn't matter.

Because I made it.

I'm inside the palace walls. My registration is finished and I will be able to compete in the trials.

I smile up at the orange and pink streaks in the sky above. This is the beginning of the rest of my life.

Footsteps sound from somewhere on my left.

It's probably Imar, the administrator for the trials, who has come to register my presence. I know that I should probably try to sit up or do something to show a smidgen of respect, but I still can't make my muscles obey me. So I just lie there, my chest heaving and victory sparkling in my soul.

A shadow falls over me.

I shift my gaze to the person now standing right next to me.

The breath freezes in my lungs.

Draven Ryat stands there, looming over me like the Shadow of Death that he truly is.

Shadows from the wall fall across his face, painting it with harsh lines. He is no longer holding a sword, but the furious look in his eyes is just as damning.

"You really should have given up and stayed out of this when you had the chance," he declares, his voice dark and low.

I want to shoot to my feet. Or sit up. Or do literally anything other than simply lie on the ground before his feet. But I can't. I can barely even summon the energy required to speak.

"I made..." I begin, gasping out the words. But then I have to wait for air to return to my lungs again as my chest continues to heave. Sucking in another breath, I try again. "I made it inside the walls." I drag more air into my lungs before I manage to finish with, "So you can't exclude me from the tournament now."

A sly smirk tilts the corner of Draven's lips as he holds my gaze. "I could always just toss you back over the wall before anyone sees you."

Dread snakes around my spine.

I stare up at him. He stares back down at me. My chest continues heaving. And I know, without a doubt, that he could pick me up and throw me back over the wall if he wants to, and there is absolutely nothing that I can do to stop him.

The very air around us crackles with tension.

Draven opens his mouth.

But before any words can make it out, Imar comes jogging across the grass.

"Another lunatic desperate enough to climb the wall," he says, and snickers when he reaches us. His blue eyes scan my face. "Selena Hale, right?"

"Yes," I gasp out.

Draven draws his dark brows down in a scowl. Then, without another word, he turns and stalks away.

Imar looks up from his paper in surprise, but then just shrugs. Shifting his gaze back to his paper, he continues scribbling something for another few seconds. I focus on trying to get air into my lungs.

Then he looks up and meets my gaze again. Clicking his tongue, he slides his pen into the slot at the top of his writing board and gives me a curt nod.

"Welcome to the Atonement Trials."

CHAPTER SIX

Torchlight illuminates the large gathering hall inside the Golden Palace's south wing. I sweep my gaze over the burning torches that have been mounted on the pale stone walls. The swirling gold and glass lantern holders that used to contain faelights are still there on the walls too, but the faelight gems have been ripped out. So instead of the soft white light of our people illuminating our sacred palace, it's lit by fire, which is the dragon shifters' element. It's a petty yet effective reminder that this is no longer our castle.

I cast a glance out the window. The sun has set now, which means that only the people who are in here with me now will compete in the trials. I shift my gaze back to the crowd around me. Some of them are standing in groups, speaking in soft tones, but most are standing alone on the gleaming white floor. It looks as if roughly three quarters of our original group made it inside.

"Alright, listen up, because I'm only going to say this once," Imar declares as he suddenly strides in through one of the open doorways. "And if you're too stupid to remember these instructions after only hearing them once, you don't deserve to be here anyway."

A ripple goes through the crowd as we all turn slightly so that we're facing him. Most people simply ignore the insult in his words, but a little to my left, Alistair squeezes his hand into a tight fist before flexing his fingers again.

I'm so used to people treating me like the plague, both dragon shifter and fae, that I barely even consider Imar's words an insult.

"When you entered the palace, you were given a key with a number on it," Imar says. "That's the key to the room you will be staying in for the duration of the Atonement Trials. There will be no switching rooms. What you've been given is what you get."

I glance down at the golden key in my hand. The number forty-two is engraved on it. Despite what Imar just said, I fold my fingers around it and hold it tightly in case someone might try to steal it.

"There are shared bathing chambers at the end of each corridor," Imar continues. "Food will be served for you in the south wing dining room." A smug smile tilts his lips. "Both the cleaning and the food preparation is done by volunteers from your city. So whatever mess you make, they will have to clean up. Understood?"

The way he said *volunteers* made it clear that there was nothing voluntary about their decision. They were ordered to do it, and if we make trouble, they will pay the price.

Most people around me appear to have understood that too because several of them clench their jaw in anger. To my surprise, Alistair is one of them. I flick a confused glance at him. I didn't think he cared about anyone else.

"Which brings us to the most important rule of all," Imar says before pausing as if to make sure that everyone is paying attention. His blue eyes sharpen as he cuts a hard look across our group. "You are not allowed to harm each other outside of the trials. Anyone who causes physical harm to another contestant in the times between trials will be executed immediately."

Several people shift their weight uncomfortably.

A fae woman with long blond hair raises a tentative hand. "I'm sorry, did you say exiled? Or executed?"

"Executed."

"Oh." She swallows. "What if it's an accident?"

He just continues staring her down in silence, his expression unyielding.

She edges a step back and lowers her chin.

I blow out a soft breath. At least that means that I won't have to worry about someone breaking into my room and slitting my throat while I sleep.

Draven's words from earlier suddenly echo through my mind. *An eye for an eye sounds too fair. I will be taking the whole head.*

Uncertainty swirls through me, and I run a quick hand over my throat. Draven doesn't have access to our rooms, does he?

"That's all," Imar announces, yanking me out of my thoughts and back to the present. "The first test will begin tomorrow at midday." He flicks his wrist. "Dismissed."

The sound of shuffling feet fills the room as everyone starts towards the doorways in search of their rooms. I do the same.

Just like the gathering hall, the white stone corridors are lit with torches. But the rest of the Golden Palace looks to be mostly unspoiled. Soft red carpets line the hallways, and in this wing, the gilded paintings on the walls depict breathtaking nature scenes. I gaze longingly at one painting of a beautiful forest that must be located somewhere close to our court. Or maybe that forest has now been consumed by the thorn forest that the shifters raised.

When I at last reach a door with the number forty-two on it, a few stories up, I find myself in a wide corridor with lots of other doors along the walls and then a larger one at the very end. I've never been inside the Golden Palace before, for obvious reasons, but if I were to guess, the entire south wing is probably a guest wing.

Several other people walk past me and continue down the hall towards rooms farther down. I quickly unlock my door and slip inside my room.

My breath catches as I stare at the room that meets me on the other side of the threshold. It's elegant and spacious. Sparkling windows offer a view of the trees in vibrant fall colors that remain in the palace grounds outside. A white wooden closet stands next to them, and there is a gilded full-length mirror on the wall too. By the wall on my left is a massive double bed made of the same white wood as the closet.

Staggering forward, I run my hand over the fluffy covers and smooth sheets.

Something between a whimper and a sob escapes my lips.

It's the softest bed I have ever seen.

I sweep my gaze around the room and suck in a stunned breath when I realize that, in here, the faelights have been left untouched. No flickering firelight dances menacingly over the walls. Instead, soft white light fills the room, making the walls shimmer.

My heart both aches and feels like it's bursting with joy at the same time. This room is beautiful. And the most luxurious room I have ever stayed in.

I turn back to the bed.

A neatly folded pile of white fabric waits there atop the covers. Moving closer, I carefully pick it up. As I lift them, the garments unfold to reveal a white silk nightgown and a thigh-length robe made of sheer white lace.

For a few seconds, I just stare at those two pieces of clothing.

All I want to do is to put them on and jump into bed to see if it feels just as heavenly as it looks.

However, before I can do that, I catch sight of myself in the mirror on the other side of the room. Turning, I face it fully. A dusty and exhausted-looking fae rebel stares back at me from the mirror.

I drop the nightgown and robe in a flash, suddenly afraid that they're going to start smelling like fish guts if I hold on to them for too long. Shaking my head, I take a step back from the bed.

I'm covered in dust and sweat from the sprint across the grasslands and the hike around the iron wall, and blades of grass still cling to my hair from the half-hour I spent lying on the ground after I made it over the wall. Not to mention that I spent all morning with my hands wrist-deep in fish guts.

Backing towards the door, I shake my head at the beautiful room again.

No. I need to take a bath first. Then, and only then, can I climb into that wonderful bed without fear of ruining it.

The hallway outside is empty when I slip back out of my room. I take that as a good sign and hurry towards the large door at the end of the corridor. Imar said that there would be a bathing chamber there. Hopefully, everyone else is still trying to find their rooms so that I can wash off alone.

For once, luck is on my side and I find the bathing chamber empty. However, voices start echoing from the hallway before long, so I finish washing off quickly. Right after I've finished getting dressed, another person strides in through the door.

It's the woman with ice magic who jumped over the wall earlier. Her blue and silver eyes are sharp as she scans the bathing chamber. When her gaze lands on me, I give her a small smile. She doesn't return it, but she does give me a nod in acknowledgement.

Since I can tell that she's not in the mood for conversation, I leave it at that and instead walk back out into the corridor.

My heart jerks when I find Alistair and his gang standing clustered together close to my room.

"Shit," I mutter under my breath.

Even though we're not allowed to hurt each other in here, I don't want to show him which room is mine. Just in case. So instead of heading back to my room, I slip past them and continue out into the next hallway. I might as well scout out this wing so that I know where the dining room and everything else is located.

Firelight dances over the stone walls as I make my way through the palace.

There are lots of twisting hallways containing doors with numbers on them, which further strengthens my assumption that this wing is entirely dedicated to guests.

As I skulk down an empty corridor behind the dining room, I wonder where all the dragon shifters are living. When I walked through the main palace doors, I was immediately ushered towards the south wing. But I know that there are several other wings too. The Icehearts are probably staying in the royal chambers, but I wonder where Draven and—

I slam to a halt, yanked out of my thoughts, as I round the next corner and suddenly find myself face to face with the ruthless dragon commander that I was just thinking about.

Draven Ryat comes to an abrupt halt as well, looking equally surprised to have found me in this corridor at this hour.

I flick a glance out the nearest window, realizing that the night has grown later than I thought. Scouting through all the different corridors and levels and public rooms has taken more time than I had intended.

For a few moments, only the soft hissing of the torches breaks the tense silence.

Then Draven cocks his head, a sly smile spreading over his mouth. "Well, aren't you a little rebel?"

Panic cracks through my chest like a lightning strike. *Shit.* Does he know that I'm a member of the resistance? How could he possibly have found that out? How could—

"...sneaking around at night like this."

My brain malfunctions for a second as his words register.

Then my mind finally catches up.

Oh. He didn't mean *rebel* as in *member of the fae resistance.* He meant *rebel* as in *someone sneaking around the castle late at night while she should be in her room.*

Relief washes through me. Thank Mabona.

Draven takes a step closer and narrows his eyes at me, and I suddenly realize that I still haven't actually responded to his statement.

"You shouldn't be here," he declares as he advances on me.

Instinctively, I back away. But then I remember myself right before my back can hit the wall behind me. Raising my chin, I stop a stride away from the wall and meet his eyes instead.

"Roaming the halls isn't forbidden," I state. That burst of relief has filled me with pulsing confidence and makes me feel bold. Arching an eyebrow, I give Draven a look full of challenge. "No one ever said that we're not allowed to leave our rooms at night."

"No." He takes a step closer. "But that's not what I meant."

He moves until he is standing barely half a step in front of me. This close, I can almost feel the heat radiating from his skin. His intoxicating scent envelops me. Dark and mysterious, like night mist and embers. It makes my head spin.

While his intense eyes are locked firmly on mine, he flexes his right hand, as if he's barely restraining himself from drawing his sword. I inhale softly to steady myself, but that only makes me breathe him in more, causing my head to spin yet again.

Draven holds my gaze with hard eyes. "What I mean is, you shouldn't be in this tournament."

"Look, I'm sorry that I spilled my drink on you," I blurt out.

"Spilled?" A laugh rips from his lungs. With a wicked glint in his eyes, he advances on me again. "You threw it in my face."

Since he's both taller and more muscular than me, I'm forced to step back to avoid being mowed down by him. My back hits the stone wall behind me with a soft thud.

"It was a mistake," I reply.

He adjusts his wings, spreading them wider, as he closes the final distance between us. Even though he's not touching me, his powerful body and massive wings now block off any escape route and trap me completely against the wall.

"A mistake?" he echoes. "It looked very deliberate to me."

Since there is no point in trying to further deny that, I instead just hold his gaze and repeat, "I'm sorry."

Apologizing to a dragon shifter makes me want to vomit, but having Draven Ryat as an enemy is a really bad idea. If he decides to start interfering, my chances of winning the Atonement Trials are going to be very slim.

"It's too late for apologies." His eyes are as hard and unyielding as iron as he stares me down. "Do you know what I do to people who step out of line?"

A jolt shoots through me as he draws his fingers over my throat. The soft brush of his fingers against the sensitive skin on the side of my neck sends fire licking through my veins. The touch is gentle, but the implied threat is clear.

He braces his other hand on the wall next to my head and leans down until he's so close that I can feel his breath against my lips.

"This is your last chance," he warns. "Drop out of the Atonement Trials before the first test tomorrow."

My heart beats erratically in my chest as I hold his gaze. "Or what?"

"Or you're going to regret it."

An absolutely insane burst of laughter rips from my throat, but I can't stop it. Because I have just come to the crystal-clear conclusion that there is nothing that I can do or say to stop this man from hating me. I'm pretty sure that I could even get down on my knees and lick his boots and grovel for his forgiveness, and he would still never accept my apology. He hates me for humiliating him in front of everyone in that tavern, and he's going to do whatever it takes to ruin my life. And there is nothing I can do to change that.

And for the first time in my life, I don't even care. Because I despise him and everything he stands for too.

To my surprise, that realization is so liberating that I almost feel lightheaded. I don't have to make myself less in front of him. I don't have to be polite and self-sacrificing. Because he is going to hate me regardless of how I behave, and I don't care if a ruthless enemy commander, and the biggest threat to our resistance, likes me anyway.

Another chuckle slips from my lips. This one is a lot more mocking.

"Oh?" I taunt with a sly grin. "You'll make sure of that, huh?"

In a flash, his fingers go from lightly tracing my throat to gripping my jaw. The back of my head is now pressed against the wall, and with the firm hand right underneath my jaw, I can no longer open my mouth.

Draven leans down until his lips almost brush against mine. "Watch your mouth."

My heart flips and then pounds against my ribs. But it's not out of fear.

Tension crackles around us like lightning in the air.

"And do as I say." He slides his hand down to rest around my throat instead. Firelight from the torch next to us flickers in his eyes as he stares me down. "Or you're going to wish that I had killed you here in this corridor tonight."

Before I can unscramble my brain and form a reply, he abruptly takes his hand off my throat. His wings flare before he tucks them in tighter and turns around.

I remain there, slumped against the wall, and watch as he stalks back down the hall.

A deep sigh escapes my chest.

Well, that went splendidly.

CHAPTER SEVEN

There is a nervous tension in the air. A quiet murmur. It's so palpable that I can almost feel it vibrating against my skin, even without using my magic. I desperately want to, though. I want to reach out with my magic and calm the anxiousness in the room so that it's easier to breathe. For everyone. But I've learned from experience that people hate it when I use my magic on them without being asked. Even if I'm trying to help. So instead of decreasing the worry that I can see on people's faces, I just grab a plate of food and sit down alone to eat my breakfast.

Even though the dining room is large, at least compared to what I'm used to, it's filling up quickly because of the number of contestants. Yesterday, Imar said that the first trial wouldn't start until midday. But apparently, no one was keen on sleeping in. Instead, we're all up at sunrise. Ready to face whatever today might bring.

I look down at my plate as I settle into my seat.

There is bread and cheese, eggs and sausages, and even a pile of diced fruit. Joy pulses through me. It's the most luxurious breakfast I have ever had. In fact, it's the *first* breakfast I've ever had, since we usually only get one meal a day.

Picking up my knife and fork, I carefully cut into one of the eggs. The warm yolk runs out a little on the plate as I cut through it. I use a piece of bread to mop it up.

A soft moan escapes my throat as I eat.

Goddess above, this alone was worth the climb over the iron wall yesterday.

While I continue eating the delicious food, savoring each bite, I study the people around me. These men and women will be my competition for the three winning spots in the trials. I need to figure out what I'm up against.

My gaze lingers on a group sitting in the middle of the room, right underneath the golden chandelier. Alistair and his four friends. He is lounging in his chair as if it were a throne, and based on the way people around him behave, it might as well be. Everyone averts their eyes and gives his table a wide berth when they pass. It appears to be out of fear rather than respect, though. I don't blame them. After all, Alistair has fire magic. It's not only a rare magical ability among our people, it's also *their* element. The dragon shifters' element. That alone would make people wary of Alistair.

I pick up my slice of fluffy bread and take another bite while I shift my gaze to the table next to mine. The woman with ice powers sits there. Her long black hair lies neatly down her back, and her blue and silver eyes are focused on the food before her as she eats. She doesn't even look up when two guys, one with silver hair and one with blond hair, pull out the chairs opposite her and sit down.

"Hey," the silver-haired one says.

The woman looks up from her eggs. Her dark brows pull into a scowl at finding them there, but she gives them a curt nod in greeting before she goes back to eating.

"What? No hello?" he pushes.

She simply continues eating.

"Rude," he scoffs. Then he and his friend exchange a knowing look. "Though I can't say I'm surprised. We've heard that you're very unapproachable, Isera."

The woman, Isera, simply slices through a sausage and spears it with her fork.

"Want some advice?" the guy says. But he doesn't wait for a response. "How about actually replying when a man tries to make small talk?"

"Yeah," the blond one fills in. "And you should smile more."

At that, Isera finally looks up. Her face is an expressionless mask and her tone is flat as she replies with one single word. "Why?"

"Because it makes you look pretty."

"And why would that be my goal?"

Stunned silence falls over the table as the two guys stare at her, uncomprehending, while their mouths work up and down a few times.

Isera lets out a scoff and goes back to eating.

"No wonder you're still single," the silver-haired one huffs. "Fucking ice lady."

Utensils clink as he and his friend angrily gather up their things and stomp over to another table. Isera doesn't even watch them leave. She just picks up her slice of bread and arranges some cheese on it. Three other people quickly take the empty seats at Isera's table, but as opposed to those guys, they don't bother her with annoying comments.

A smile steals across my lips as I watch her. Goddess, that was epic. The next time someone tries to walk all over me, I'm going to do that as well. Just treat them like they're less than air. I'm going to—

"Sorry," a man's voice says from right next to me.

Setting down my fork, I look up to find two people standing next to my table.

"Are you finished?" the fae man asks.

I flick a glance down at the still half full plate on my table, which is a very obvious clue that I am in fact not finished. I once again look up at the man and the woman with him.

"Uhm..." I begin, not sure what to say.

"It's just, all the other tables are full," he continues, waving a hand to indicate the now packed dining room. "And you're taking up a table for two."

I shift uncomfortably in my seat. But I force myself to laugh so that they won't feel uncomfortable too. "Yeah, I suppose I am."

"So could we...?" He motions at the table.

My chest tightens, and I glance between them and my table. Then my gaze flicks to Isera for a second. I want to do what she did. Mere seconds ago, I told myself that I was going to do what she did. I want to tell them *no*. I want to tell them to find their own damn table. That I want to sit down and eat my food too.

But I don't. Because no matter how much I try to convince myself otherwise, I still desperately want people to like me. I want them to trust me. I want to be accepted.

So I force a smile and pick up my plate and say, "Sure."

Pain and frustration swirl like a restless storm behind my ribcage as I walk away with my plate. I hate that I am this way. I hate that I desperately want people's approval. I hate that I make myself less so that others won't feel uncomfortable around me.

I just want to scream. I want to say what I really feel sometime instead of just saying what I know that other people want to hear. I want to push back. I want to stand up for myself.

And I will.

After I win the Atonement Trials, everything will change. People will accept me and the leaders of the resistance will finally raise me to the top levels. I will make a difference. I will help free our people. And then everyone will finally trust me.

But first, I need to actually win the trials. Which means that I need an advantage.

With my plate still in hand, I scan the dining room again.

My gaze snags on a dark-haired fae man sitting alone by the

pale stone wall to my left. The man who sat opposite him has just taken his empty plate and left. But an empty seat is not why my heart jolted when I spotted him. It's because I recognize him.

His name is Kevlin, and he has entered the Atonement Trials the previous two times as well. Some people call him Kevlin the Double Loser behind his back because of it.

Before someone else can claim that seat, I hurry over to it and sit down.

"Hi, sorry, is it okay if I join you?" I say, my voice breathless.

He frowns a little but then shrugs. "Fine."

I give him a smile in thanks and then eat a piece of bread. He continues eating too.

After I deem an appropriate amount of time has passed, I make my voice soft as I ask, "So, you've been in these trials before, right?"

Annoyance flickers in his eyes, but he replies, "Yes."

"Are the trials the same every time?"

He narrows his eyes at me. "Why should I tell you?"

I curse silently in my mind. Of course he doesn't want to share anything that might give him an edge.

Indecision flashes through me. I don't want to use my powers on him, but I also really need this information.

Making a snap decision, I lower my gaze to my plate and make my voice small. While he can no longer see my eyes, I channel my magic and reply, "Because I really need help. I'm not a threat to anyone here, and I'm so scared that I will be eliminated in the first trial. It would be such an embarrassment for my family."

Just like I did with the guy at the gate, I reach out with my magic and push at his sympathy. To my relief, I find a small pink spark there that I can latch on to. I pour my magic into it, making it bigger.

Kevlin heaves a deep sigh. "Fine. But just because you asked nicely."

Or because I used my magic to manipulate your emotions. Potato, potahto.

"No, the trials are not the same every time," he says. "Or at least, they haven't been the last two times. But one thing that has remained the same is the very first one. It's not actually a trial at all. It's more of a test. One final hurdle before the real trials start. It's basically just a demonstration where everyone displays their skills individually."

Victory shimmers inside me. Fantastic. Then I can use the remaining hours to prepare.

"Oh, I see," I reply. "And how does—"

"Check it out!" a male voice booms across the room. "Soulstealer is manipulating Kevlin the Double Loser."

I immediately cut off my magic, but the damage is already done. Snapping my gaze up, I find the muscular guy who I tried to manipulate at the gate smirking at me and Kevlin from where he sits next to Alistair.

Kevlin, who also turned to look towards him when he spoke, shifts his gaze back to me. Embarrassment, indignation, and anger flash across his face. I open my mouth to apologize, but he cuts me off.

"You manipulated my emotions," he accuses.

"Uhm..." is all I manage to reply.

Wood scrapes against stone as he shoots out of his seat and lunges towards me. I barely manage to push my own chair back before he grabs me by the collar and yanks me up. His eyes, a mix of brown and lavender, are pulsing with fury as he tightens his grip on my collar.

"You slippery little snake," he growls in my face. "I hope you humiliate yourself at the test today." He raises his voice. "And I hope that no one here ever lets you get close to them. After all, no one wants a backstabber as an ally."

My stomach lurches as he uses his grip on my shirt to throw me away from his table. I stumble sideways, slamming into another table a few strides away. Utensils clank and a mug clatters as the force makes the table rattle, tipping over several items.

"Don't ever approach me again," he warns.

Nausea rolls through my stomach.

I can feel the eyes of everyone in the room watching me. The distrust radiating from them sears into my skin like iron pokers. I swallow back the lump in my throat as I straighten from the table I crashed into.

A pair of eyes that are a breathtaking mix of pink and purple meet me. They belong to a fae woman with an incredibly beautiful face, which is marred by a scar that cuts along her cheek and across her jaw.

I blink, recognizing the brown-haired woman from yesterday. She's the one who grew a tree out of the ground so that she could climb over the wall.

My gaze darts down to the toppled mug and the small pool of water that now covers part of the tabletop.

Clearing my throat, I tentatively reach out and straighten the mug. "I'm sorry."

For a few seconds, she just watches me in silence. Her eyes are completely blank. As is her expression.

Just when I think that she's going to ignore me, she cracks a smile. "No worries. Everything I have has already been spilled more than once anyway."

"I, uhm..." Blinking, I trail off, because I have no idea what that's supposed to mean. But she doesn't appear angry at least, so I simply clear my throat once more and repeat, "I'm sorry."

Giving her an apologetic look, I back away and start towards the door.

Oppressive silence fills the dining room.

Everyone is watching me. The look in their eyes varies from disgust to wariness to shrewd calculation.

I swallow and try to walk as naturally as I can through the sea of staring contestants. I feel like I'm going to be sick.

We're not even one day into the trials, and everyone already despises me.

My chest constricts, making it difficult to breathe. I shouldn't have used my powers like this. Now everyone hates me. But I needed that information.

I draw in a shuddering breath as I try to settle the war between my heart and my mind, torn between wanting people to like me and wanting to win. It doesn't work, so I decide to just block it all out instead.

The first test is today. And regardless of how I found out and the consequences that my actions had, I now know what it is. A demonstration. A simple display of our powers.

A small smile blows across my lips as I leave the dining room behind and start towards my room to plot out how I will show off my magic.

This should be easy.

CHAPTER EIGHT

Bright light from the clear blue sky outside shines in through the large windows and illuminates the massive room around us. The high-ceilinged hall looks to have been some kind of grand reception room, or maybe a fancy meeting chamber, but it's almost bare now. The only pieces of furniture in the room are two elegant chairs, which have been placed on the slightly raised stone dais along one of the walls. Empress Jessina and Emperor Bane are seated on them.

I study them as they sit there and watch all of us file in through the doors. Because of the way that the chairs are built, neither of them has their wings out. Instead, they are in their human forms. I flick a glance over their bodies. They're wearing different clothes today, but her dress is still silver in color just like yesterday. And so is his fancy shirt. I briefly wonder which dragons had to carry all of their trunks of clothes and other supplies when they flew here. Probably one of their servants.

Shifting my gaze, I glance at the people standing behind them on the pale stone dais. All the other dragon shifters who flew in yesterday appear to be here as well. The leaders of the eight other dragon clans are spread out across the platform, along with other shifters who must be advisors or soldiers or servants or something, but my eyes immediately go to the man who is standing to the right of the two chairs.

Draven Ryat.

As opposed to the Iceheart monarchs, he is wearing the same clothes as yesterday and he also has his wings out. His imposing black armor seems to swallow all the light around him, and that, combined with his massive black wings, makes him look like a dark storm in the middle of the otherwise bright room.

His dark brows are furrowed, and his eyes are sharp as he scans the room as if he's searching for something. Or someone.

I stand close to one of the walls so that I'm not right in the middle of the crowd, but it's becoming increasingly difficult to remain unnoticed because everyone else is giving me a wide berth. All the other contestants who are positioning themselves on the floor below the dais are standing relatively close to one another. But not to me. They leave at least five entire strides between me and them when they come to a halt. It makes me stand out like a lone island in a churning sea. I try not to let it bother me, but there is a dull ache in my chest and a rolling nausea in my gut that I can't entirely block out.

Draven notices that strange formation on my side of the room, and his sharp eyes at last flick in my direction.

Frustration and disapproval flash like lightning in his eyes as he locks them on me. Meeting his furious stare, I just lift my shoulders in an unapologetic shrug. He scowls at me.

A strange burst of laughter threatens to escape my throat. Did he really think that I would just obey him and drop out of the whole Atonement Trials simply because he told me to? Damn, that guy really has an inflated sense of self-importance.

"Silence," Emperor Bane's commanding voice suddenly cuts through the room.

The faint murmur from the crowd of contestants and the gathered shifters stops immediately.

"You have all made it inside the walls, but that does not guarantee you a spot in the first trial," Bane continues, his black eyes sweeping over the gathered fae.

Several people around me shift their weight and some exchange nervous glances.

"Despite your heinous crimes against our people, Jessina and I have generously decided to give you this chance to atone for your sins." A small smile, full of malice and wicked amusement, plays over his lips as he watches us. "So first, you need to prove to us that you actually deserve to be here."

"Indeed," Jessina picks up. "During this first test, you only have one simple objective. To impress us."

She brushes her long white hair behind her shoulder in a highly impatient move and then flicks her wrist at Imar. The tournament administrator quickly breaks away from the group of dragon shifters and instead positions himself on the floor in front of the raised dais. But he is not facing his monarchs. Instead, his blue eyes are turned towards us.

"The rules are simple," Empress Jessina continues. "When your name is called, you will approach Imar alone. Then you will show off your power by making him move."

A ripple goes through the crowd since most people didn't know about this. But thanks to my sneak interrogation during breakfast, I have known for hours and have been able to plan my strategy already.

"Once you have displayed your power, we will decide whether or not you move on to the actual trials," Emperor Bane finishes.

On the floor before us, Imar twists slightly and looks up at the Icehearts. They give him a firm nod.

Turning back to us, he clears his throat and then looks down at the writing board in his hands.

"Alistair Geller," he reads, his voice echoing through the now dead silent room.

On the other side of the crowd, Alistair straightens his spine and starts towards the administrator. Since we're all standing behind, I can't see the expression on his face when he comes to a halt a short distance in front of Imar, but based on his body language, he seems more eager than worried.

Without barely a second's hesitation, he raises a hand and throws a fireball right at Imar's chest.

Imar throws himself sideways a mere second before it can slam into him.

Rage and indignation pulse across Imar's face as he straightens and locks eyes with Alistair again. Atop the dais, lots of other shifters narrow their eyes at the blond fae man as well. Gremar Fireclaw, the leader of the Red Dragon Clan, which Imar belongs to as well, clenches his fist as he glares down at Alistair.

"Approved," Emperor Bane announces.

Alistair bows his head in acknowledgement and then walks towards the other wall that Bane is pointing at. Right before he turns fully to take up position before the wall, I manage to catch sight of the smug grin on his lips.

Imar brushes a hand down the front of his clothes before calling the next contestant. And then the next. And the next.

I study them all closely.

Not only is this test a great way to see what kind of magical powers that I will be up against, it also helps me put a name to the faces I've seen.

When that gorgeous brown-haired woman with the scar and the pink and purple eyes steps up and makes Imar move by growing a tree right underneath him, I learn that her name is Lavendera Dawnwalker. And the muscular guy who I tried to manipulate at the gate, and who called me out at breakfast, apparently possesses some kind of enhanced physical strength, because he simply picks Imar up and then sets him down two strides away.

While the muscular guy, whose name I now know to be

Tommen, walks over to the other wall to take his place next to his friend Alistair, I hear another name that I already know.

"Isera Shaw," Imar calls across the now thinning crowd of contestants.

Isera walks straight up to Imar and, without even breaking stride, summons a block of ice and hurls it at his face. He dodges it, and it slams into the edge of the dais instead. The rectangular block of ice splits in two, one part hitting the floor with a thud and the other sliding along the dais instead. It stops two strides away from where the two monarchs are sitting.

Empress Jessina clenches her jaw and squeezes the armrests of her chair so hard that I'm surprised that I don't hear the wood crack. Next to her, Bane's expression darkens as he looks from the block of ice to the fae woman responsible for it.

Isera simply looks back at them, her face a blank mask.

Another two seconds pass.

Then she flicks her wrist, and the two lumps of ice vanish into nothingness.

Emperor Bane works his jaw and flexes his hand. With his dark eyes locked on Isera, he declares, "Approved."

Isera dips her chin in what can barely be classified as a nod, let alone a bow. But the Icehearts don't call her out on it.

"Maximus Moonsinger," Imar calls once Isera has taken her place by the wall.

One of Alistair's other friends, a guy with blond hair and eyes that are yellow and green, steps forward. I recognize him but I don't know what kind of magic he has, so I pay close attention when he comes to a halt in front of Imar.

A cloud of green smoke appears in the air. Imar tries to dodge it, but Maximus has already thrown a second one. It hits the administrator in the face.

He sucks in a choked gasp.

I start in surprise as his knees suddenly buckle and he crashes down on the floor while reaching for his throat.

Up on the dais, Bane slashes a hand through the air. "Enough."

Maximus makes no other moves, but Imar stops clawing at his throat and instead drags in a deep breath. His blue eyes are dark with anger as he staggers back to his feet. I don't need to feel emotions with my magic to know that Maximus made an enemy here today.

"Approved," Bane says.

Maximus bows. Ignoring Imar's dark looks, he walks straight towards Alistair and his other friends by the wall. I study his back while trying to determine what kind of magic that was. It might be air magic. Or some kind of poison. Or something else.

After dusting himself off, Imar picks up the writing board that he dropped earlier.

"Selena Hale," he calls.

My heart leaps into my throat.

I knew that he was going to call my name soon, but it somehow still manages to surprise me. Drawing in a deep breath, I try to calm my suddenly racing pulse. I've got this. There is no need to be nervous.

With my spine straight and my chin raised, I stride through the thinning crowd and towards Imar. I've already determined which types of emotions he will no doubt be feeling, especially after that stunt Maximus pulled, so this is going to be easy.

Stopping two strides away, I draw in another breath and reach for my magic.

"I'll take this one," a commanding voice suddenly declares.

Losing my grip on my magic, I whip my head up to find Draven stalking across the dais. On the floor, Imar frowns in confusion and looks up at the Icehearts. Jessina just waves a hand.

Behind me, a ripple goes through the gathered fae.

I open my mouth to protest, but Draven has already reached the edge of the dais. With one graceful step, he drops from the raised platform and lands on the floor before me with a thud. Imar takes a step to the side.

My heart jerks and then starts up a nervous pattering as I stare at Draven while trying to reformulate my strategy.

"Well," Draven taunts, a smirk full of challenge lurking on his lips. "Get on with it then."

I suppress the urge to scowl at him and instead simply reach for my magic. It doesn't matter that it's him. I can make this work anyway.

Magic surges through me as I study the ruthless commander in front of me while trying to figure out what he's feeling right now.

Anger.

He's probably angry that I'm still here.

I reach towards him with my magic and push at the pale red spark of anger that should be there.

Nothing.

The realization stuns me so much that I actually blink in surprise.

He's not angry. At all.

While trying to wrap my head around that realization, I reach out again and push at the orange spark of smugness that must surely be there at least.

Once more, my magic meets only an empty void.

I stare at him in disbelief, and then push at the gray spark of boredom.

Nothing.

The Iceheart monarchs shift their weights and raise their eyebrows expectantly, as if wondering whether or not I have already started.

Panic pulses through me.

With desperation surging through my veins, I throw my magic at more emotions. Tiredness, joy, impatience, fear, hunger. Anything I can think of.

And every time, I'm met with nothing but a cold and dark void.

Disbelief crackles through me. How can he feel nothing? Almost everyone feels something at any given time. Only the people with extensive training can block out their emotions entirely like this. Why would he, of all people, prioritize learning such a skill?

The panic inside me grows into full-blown fear as Jessina clicks her tongue and announces, "You have ten seconds to make something happen."

So I do something insane. I do the only thing that I think might be able to shock someone like Draven.

I grab the hem of my shirt and pull it over my head.

A gasp rips through the people around me, but I'm not paying them any attention. All of my focus is firmly on Draven as I yank my shirt off.

It startles him enough that he jerks back a little and blinks in shock.

The moment I see his reaction, I shove my magic straight at him. It slams into the brass-colored spark of shock inside him. Latching on to it, I pour everything I have into it.

Draven gasps and stumbles back several steps as he blurts out, "What the hell are you doing? You can't take off your shirt in the middle of a room full of people!"

I grin at him.

That wicked little smirk reminds him that he wasn't supposed to react and show any emotions. Which in turn triggers a flare of panic. He tries to block it out a fraction of a second later, but I've already latched on to that small yellow spark.

Smug victory pulses through my chest as I pour a torrent of magic at it, blowing his panic far out of proportion.

Draven gasps again and staggers back once more. His eyes are wide and his mouth slightly open.

"Oh fuck," he blurts out. "I shouldn't have done that. Shit. I wasn't supposed to—" He snaps his mouth shut, cutting off his own words, before ending with another, "Fuck."

All around me, the whole room is staring at the usually so powerful and imposing Commander of the Dread Legion who is now panicking like an untrained adolescent.

After quickly putting my shirt back on, I let a wide grin spread across my mouth as I watch Draven.

It took me almost seventy years to learn how to successfully *stack* emotions like this.

Contrary to what most people think, I cannot actually create emotions. Everyone thinks that I can change the way they feel. That I can twist their heart and soul into something unrecognizable.

They're wrong.

I cannot create new emotions from nothing. I cannot make someone angry if they're bursting with joy. I can't make someone hate a person that they love. And I can't make a person love someone that they hate. Or even someone that they've just met. I can only manipulate emotions that are already there. I can increase and decrease what they feel, but I can't make them feel something else. The spark of the emotion needs to be there first.

There are loopholes, or rather *techniques*, that I can use to get around that problem. One such technique is what I did to Tommen at the gate and to Kevlin at breakfast. I say and do something in order to make them feel a specific emotion that I can then increase. It was the same method I used in order to make Draven feel shock now.

Then I used a technique that I call *stacking*. I use one emotion to jumpstart another emotion.

I can't make a person hate someone else out of the blue. But what I can do is to create a situation where the first person feels angry or hurt or betrayed by the second person. Then I can increase those emotions to such an awful degree that it eventually makes the first person hate the second person. Even if just for a second during a moment of weakness or hurt. And then, I can latch on to that brief spark of hatred and flame it into a raging wildfire.

Naturally, it's very difficult to accomplish. It only works under very specific circumstances and only with certain emotions. Love, for example, is entirely impossible to create. I can increase someone's lust to the point where they want to fuck someone even more than they want air in their lungs. But lust cannot create love. Love is too complicated an emotion.

But I can most certainly randomly yank my shirt off in front of the most powerful dragon shifter in the army in order to shock him, which I had calculated would then lead to panic, which I can, in turn, fan into an embarrassingly large flame.

All around me, people are staring at the scene before them. Everyone knows that Draven Ryat would never willingly panic in front of an entire room full of other clan leaders and monarchs and lowly fae alike. It can only happen with the help of strong magic.

I sweep my gaze around the room.

It's displays like this that make people think that I can create emotions from nothing. And I never contradict them. The less they know about my magic, the better.

Up on the dais, a few of the other clan leaders smirk at Draven.

Jessina raises a hand.

I cut off the flow to my magic immediately.

Within seconds, the overwhelming panic that I created in Draven's chest disappears and returns to its original minor spark. He stops stumbling away and instead freezes on the floor. His chest heaves as he stares at me.

If I pushed with my magic right now, I'm pretty sure that I would now find a spark of humiliation in his chest instead.

He stares at me.

The whole room is dead silent. It's so deafening that I can almost feel it hum against my eardrums.

From a few strides away, Draven looks at me like he can't decide whether to torture me into revealing all the secrets of my magic or to simply ram a sword through my heart.

Before he can decide, Emperor Bane shatters the thrumming silence.

"Approved," he declares.

Relief washes over me.

Twisting towards the Icehearts, I give them a respectful bow in acknowledgement.

And then, just because I can't help myself, I turn back to Draven and execute a theatrical bow full of smug victory.

A rush of power pulses through me at being so blatantly disrespectful to someone like him.

With a grin on my mouth, I straighten, spin on my heel, and stride straight towards the other wall.

And I'm lucky that I make it there without Draven's sword through the back of my ribcage.

CHAPTER NINE

To my surprise, I also make it all the way back to my room without getting Draven's sword shoved through my chest. In hindsight, what I did to him back there might have been a mistake. Especially that mocking little bow at the end. But damn, it felt good. And besides, he's the one who decided to interfere and mess with my test first. He deserved everything he got.

The corridor is empty when I arrive at the door to my room. Since I was worried that Draven might try to ambush me, I took the long way back. Everyone else must already be inside their rooms.

I glance towards the room two doors down from me. It belonged to a fae man with incredibly enhanced hearing. Now, it's empty. About ten percent of everyone who walked into that room today was deemed unworthy to continue the trials and were kicked out. He was one of them. I know that I should probably feel bad for them, but I'm really just relieved since it will mean less competition for me.

After sliding out my key, I unlock my door and slip inside.

I only make it two steps into the room before I freeze. Blinking, I stare at the large white box on my bed. That most certainly wasn't there before. And the room was locked. So who put it there? Who else has keys?

Approaching warily, I study the strange package. There is a thick silver ribbon around the rectangular box. Towards the middle is a note, kept in place by the ribbon.

My mind churns. Is it some kind of trap? It can't have been one of the other contestants. The room was locked. And besides, we were all at the test together. It must have been one of the dragon shifters. They probably have a set of extra keys for every room.

Just the thought that they can come and go as they please inside my room makes uneasiness slither through my stomach like a cold snake. But it's not as if I can do anything about it. I need to be here and win these trials, so I must play by their rules.

Carefully reaching forward, I grab the edge of the note and pull it towards me.

Nothing explodes.

Since that's a good sign, I flip the note open as well.

Only a few sentences, written in swirling black script, meet me. I read them quickly. And then I have to read them again. And again.

Congratulations on becoming a full and worthy participant in the Atonement Trials. To celebrate the start of the trials, there will be a ball this evening, and you are cordially invited to attend. Wear the clothes that have been so generously provided for you.

My head spins.

A ball? We're going to have a ball? Why? I thought these Atonement Trials were supposed to be brutal tests of power. But so far, all we've done is to sleep in comfortable beds, eat delicious food, and show off our magic in a safe and comfortable one-on-one display. There has to be more to this. It has to be some kind of trick or something.

After setting down the note on my bed, I gently untie the ribbon. Then I angle my body as far away from the box as I can before I lift the lid, just in case it will explode or there is a venomous snake in there or something.

But when I remove the lid, all that meets me is shimmering silver fabric. Disbelief swirls inside me as I lift it up to find a gorgeous dress. Made of silver silk and white gemstones, it looks like liquid starlight.

I run my hand down the length of it.

A small noise comes from the back of my throat, and I close my eyes briefly, because of how silky smooth and absolutely perfect the dress is.

By Mabona, it's the most breathtaking dress I have ever seen. And someone has given it to *me*. It has to be some kind of elaborate trap.

And if it is, I need to find out.

Reluctantly putting the dress back in the box, I hurry across the room and towards the door. I need to know if anyone else has received a box like this. If it's just me, then I will know that it is indeed a trap.

Yanking the door open, I stride out into the corridor outside.

And slam right into someone's chest.

A huff sounds as the guy stumbles back a step.

I suck in a sharp breath, expecting to find Draven's furious eyes glaring down at me.

But when I raise my gaze, I'm not met by the dragon commander's odd one-colored eyes. Instead, a pair of eyes that are a mix of blue and gold blink at me in surprise. I take a step back, trying to reorient myself.

A fae man with long red hair stares back at me. He has one hand raised, as if he was just about to knock on my door. After another few seconds, he seems to realize that his hand is still raised, because he gives his head a quick shake as if to clear it and then lowers his hand.

"Sorry," he says. A sheepish smile blows across his face. "I was just about to knock on your door but then you flew out of it so fast that I didn't have time to back away."

I clear my throat a bit self-consciously. "Yeah, I'm sorry. I, uhm..." Trailing off, I study his face while running through all the names and magical abilities from the test earlier. At last, a memory clicks into place. "It's Fenriel, right? The guy with the hawk?"

The smile on his face gets even bigger and brighter. "Yes, that's right."

His eyes begin to glow, and a second later, a large white hawk appears on his shoulder. It ruffles its wings and then bumps its beak against the side of Fenriel's head. He strokes the hawk's feathers affectionately and then nudges its chin.

"This is Talon," he explains, and I can hear the pride in his voice as he talks about his hawk. "He has been with me ever since I manifested my magic back when I was a kid." After flashing his hawk another smile, he turns back to me and nods. "And you're Selena, right? The one who had to deal with Draven Ryat instead of Imar."

"Yeah, that's me."

"That was insane. I never thought I'd see him do something like that." He furrows his brows slightly. "Though I still can't figure out how you did it. What kind of magic do you have?"

Dread fills my stomach. I thought that he already knew, and that he was being nice to me anyway. But apparently, he missed what happened at breakfast. I swallow. I really don't want to answer. But hiding it will only make it worse.

So I keep my voice neutral as I reply, "Emotion magic."

Squeezing my hand into a fist, I brace myself for his reaction. For that moment when he understands what that means, and subconsciously takes a step back so that he's not standing too close. For that moment when distrust flickers in his eyes. For that moment when this goes from being a pleasant conversation to a quick goodbye.

Fenriel raises his eyebrows.

I steel myself.

"That's so cool!" he says, a wide smile on his face.

For a few seconds, I just stare at him. Completely dumbfounded. Cool? No one has ever said that my magic is *cool* before.

Since I can't seem to unscramble my brain fast enough, the only thing that makes it out of my mouth is, "Uhm… thanks."

"Anyway, as I was saying, I was just on my way over here to knock on your door," he simply continues, as if my head isn't still spinning. "So here's the thing. When I got back, I found this really strange package on my bed. There was a note inviting me to a ball tonight and also some really fancy clothes that I'm supposed to wear. And I got kind of suspicious that it was a trap or something, so I just wanted to see if someone else had gotten it too."

My mind finally snaps back into the present. Giving my head a quick shake, I clear out the final remnants of shock and then nod vigorously. "Yes, I did too. That's why I was hurrying out of my room. I wanted to see if someone else had gotten it too."

"Oh, okay, good. That's good. Then it's not a trap at least." He cocks his head, a contemplative expression on his face, and absentmindedly pets his hawk again. "I wonder what that's about though. A ball. It seems kind of… odd."

"It's their way of showing us that they own us," a new voice suddenly says.

Both Fenriel and I jump in surprise and then whip around to face the source of the voice. Lavendera, the woman with tree magic, has appeared from the bathing chamber at the end of the hall. I stare at her. I didn't even hear her open the door, let alone walk towards us. Apparently, Fenriel didn't either.

Lavendera just continues moving towards us, seemingly oblivious to our shock.

"They're hosting a ball and giving us beautiful clothes to wear and delicious food to eat in order to show us that they have the ability to make our lives better," she says. She meets our eyes as she comes to a halt in front of us. "They do it so that we will know that they *can* do all that if they want to. That they can abolish the one meal system and can remove the restrictions on clothing and goods. And that they simply *choose* not to."

"How do you know that?" Fenriel asks, his eyebrows raised in surprise.

Her eyes take on a faraway look, and she falls silent. Fenriel and I exchange a quick glance as Lavendera just continues to stare unseeing at the white stone wall behind us for another few seconds. Then she blinks. Repeatedly. And her brain apparently starts working again.

"I've… taken part in the Atonement Trials before," she replies. A brief flash of hopelessness washes over her beautiful features, and she absentmindedly draws her fingers over the scar along her cheek and jaw. Then she abruptly drops her hand and looks us straight in the eye. "My advice? Wear the dress, smile, and do what they want."

Before either of us can reply, she simply strides away.

Fenriel and I stare after her, both of us apparently feeling equally confused.

Then we turn back to each other.

"Well, I guess I'll see you at the ball later then," he says, managing a small smile.

"Yes." I give him a nod. "Good luck."

"Yeah, you too."

"Thanks."

Because by Mabona, I have a feeling that I'm going to need it.

CHAPTER TEN

Apprehension flutters behind my ribs like erratic butterflies. I work as a lookout for the highly illegal and secret fae resistance several times a week, and I've never felt nervous. But now as I walk into a glittering ballroom for a night that is supposed to be pure enjoyment, I feel so anxious that I don't even know what to do with my hands.

It's ridiculous. Deep down, I know that. There is nothing dangerous about attending a ball. And yet, I can't stop my heart from pounding.

I have no idea what I'm supposed to do, because I've never attended a ball before. And I hate not knowing how I'm expected to behave.

Worry rolls through my stomach as I enter the already mostly full ballroom. I waited, fully dressed and ready, until I had heard almost everyone in my corridor leave for the ballroom before I finally made my way down here as well. The thought of standing by myself in a practically empty ballroom, looking nervous and awkward and not knowing what to do, made me feel like I was going to throw up. It's better to arrive when most people are already here. That way, I can slip through the crowd and get a feel for the mood before I engage with anyone.

Candlelight shines from the golden chandeliers in the ceiling and the gilded candelabras across the floor. It makes the pale stone walls shimmer like gold.

However, the Icehearts have done everything they can to cover everything else in silver. The tablecloths and the trays and the containers with food and drink are all made of silver. But the boldest statement of all is that every single fae contestant in this room is dressed in that color as well.

I thought that the dress I received was silver simply because it would match my hair color. But now as I sweep my gaze over the sea of dancing and chatting people, I realize that everyone has received clothes made of silver. Which is *their* color.

My mind drifts back to Lavendera's words from earlier. *It's their way of showing us that they own us.*

She's right. Jessina and Bane Iceheart are leaders of the Silver Dragon Clan. So making us all wear silver clothes is a powerful and not-so-subtle reminder that we belong to them. We do not have free will. We are not our own people. We are their subjects.

Laughter suddenly echoes from my right.

I turn towards it. A group of contestants is standing there by one of the narrow tables that are filled with drinks.

Indecision swirls through me. They look like they might be friendly, but how am I supposed to approach them? I can't just walk up to them and join the conversation.

While suppressing the urge to fidget, I drift awkwardly towards the table as if I'm just going there to grab a drink. The group continues talking and laughing softly. I pick up a glass of what looks like sparkling wine. Then I linger there while I sip some of the surprisingly sweet alcohol.

Once I have gathered my courage, I twist towards the group and edge a little closer.

The two closest people turn towards me and look at me with

a hint of surprise and confusion. But they eventually shift their positions a little to make room for me.

Relief washes through me. Not exactly the smoothest move I have ever made, but it worked, and that's all that matters.

I sip some more wine and listen while they continue talking.

"Have you noticed how many times they've said that the trials are about to start now?" a guy with wavy black hair asks. He lets out a chuckle and shakes his head. "It's always 'welcome to the Atonement Trials' or 'congratulations on making it' or 'it's time to start' but they never actually start the trials."

"I've—" I begin, but a woman with blond hair cuts me off.

"Exactly," she says, and laughs loudly. "They're so dramatic all the time but nothing really happens."

"I don't—" I try again.

"Like come on," the guy says, interrupting me. "We've had two unofficial tests already. When are the real trials going to begin?"

The others hum in agreement and nod. I close my mouth and instead just do the same.

While they continue talking about the upcoming trials, I simply stand there and sip from my glass and nod at the appropriate times.

After a while, the discussion moves on to the topic of clothes. And more specifically, why everyone is dressed in the same color.

"It makes us look ridiculous," the black-haired guy says, and shakes his head.

"Right?" a woman with turquoise and brown eyes fills in. "I feel like a little kid in school or something."

"And why does it even have to be silver anyway?" He turns and runs a hand down his stomach while a mischievous grin lurks on his lips. "It makes me look fat."

The others chuckle and elbow him in exasperation at the obvious joke.

Since I'm pretty sure that they don't want to know the real reason, at least not right now when they're happy and joking, I add softly, "Maybe it's so that they can find us by simply shining a bright light on all of this reflective material."

The blond fae woman looks over at me in surprise, but no one else seems to have heard my joke. She turns back to the group.

"Maybe it's so that they can find us by simply shining a bright light on all of this reflective material," she says, echoing my words but in a louder voice.

Laughter ripples through the air, and the guy opposite her even chokes on his drink.

A kind of empty numbness spreads through my chest as I stare at the blond woman. She doesn't even look at me. Instead, she laughs and winks at the others in response to the appreciative smiles that they bathe her with.

I open my mouth to tell them that it was my joke, but I manage to stop myself before the words can actually leave my mouth. It would only make me sound petty. So instead, I heave a deep sigh and empty my glass.

"Are you always this quiet?"

Starting in surprise, I look up to find the black-haired guy watching me from the other side of the group. This is the first time he has even looked at me since I joined them. My deep sigh must have finally drawn his attention.

"It's just, you came over and joined us a while ago," he continues, his brows furrowed. "But you haven't actually said anything. So, you know, I'm just curious. Are you tired? Or do you just normally not talk all that much?"

Everyone turns towards me. Candlelight glints in their drinks and sparkles in their bejeweled silver garments as they cock their heads and wait for me to answer.

That numb emptiness in my chest swells until I feel like it's going to swallow me whole.

Drawing in a breath, I abruptly set my now empty glass down on the table. "Sorry, I think I just need to get some air."

Before they can reply, I start walking in a direction where I hope there might be a window. Their murmured voices, discussing my behavior, hang in the air behind me. I try my best to block them out.

Music from the group of dragon shifters in the corner fills the large ballroom and mixes with the sound of laughter and chatter and the swishing of clothing. It all presses against me. I feel like I'm drowning. I just need some air. And a few minutes to myself.

Drawing in deep breaths, I escape out into one of the large hallways connected to the ballroom. It's empty, and more importantly, there are two windows at the end of it. I run towards them.

My fingers fumble several times, but I finally manage to get the hatch open.

Cool night air washes over me as I throw the window open.

I drag in a deep breath, filling my lungs. The air tastes like night mist and damp soil and fallen leaves. Closing my eyes, I just remain there for a minute, breathing in the fresh air and clearing my head.

The irony of it all is not lost on me. I can manipulate other people's emotions, but I don't even have control over my own. Everything would be so much easier if I could use my magic on myself. But unfortunately, I can't. So I'm forced to deal with messy feelings and real life just like everyone else.

Once the ache in my heart and the embarrassment in my chest have subsided, I close the window and brush my hands down my dress to smooth it down. While fixing my hair again, I try to boost my confidence. I can do this. I only need to win the trials. It doesn't matter if I fail at making friends at a stupid ball. The only thing that matters is winning the Atonement Trials. And I don't need to do well at this ball for that.

After giving myself a decisive nod, I turn around and start back towards the ballroom.

I only make it halfway down the corridor before a dark shadow falls across the floor.

My heart jerks as Draven walks around the corner and into the empty corridor. He stops when he sees me. I don't. Keeping my chin raised, I continue forwards, intending to walk right past him and back to the ballroom.

But my pulse thrums in my ears. This is the first time I've seen him since I embarrassed him during the power display earlier.

I resist the urge to lick my lips nervously.

His sharp eyes track my every move.

I'm almost there. Almost. Just one more—

Right before I can walk past him, he yanks up his arm in front of me and slams his palm against the wall, blocking my way. I whip my head towards him.

His eyes glint in the firelight as he twists his body, using his size to force me to turn with him until I'm facing him with my back towards the wall. He keeps his hand on the wall, caging me in further.

My pulse patters as I tilt my head back to meet his gaze.

A sly smile blows across Draven's lips as he locks eyes with me. "Going somewhere, little rebel?"

My heart jerks and then beats erratically at the sound of that nickname, even though I know that he doesn't mean it as an actual accusation of treason.

Discreetly, I raise my leg a little and brace my foot against the wall behind me. "Are you following me?"

His eyes gleam again. "Do you need to be followed?"

While keeping my gaze firmly locked on his, I push the silver fabric a little away from my now slightly raised leg. My fingers curl around the hilt of the knife that I have strapped to my thigh underneath the dress.

"No," I reply. "But you do seem to have an unhealthy obsession with tracking me down in empty corridors. Can I suggest a hobby instead? Perhaps knitting since you're so fond of pointy sticks."

A burst of laughter rips from his chest.

He immediately snaps his mouth shut again, cutting off the shocking sound. I stare at him, completely flabbergasted. Did he just... *laugh*?

Draven blinks, looking equally stunned.

Then he gives his head an almost imperceptible shake, as if composing himself, and his usual air of power and command returns. He moves closer. A dangerous expression settles on his lethally handsome features.

"That little stunt you pulled during the power demonstration was very interesting," he says, his voice wrapping around me like dark silk. "I haven't felt panic that strong in centuries."

My fingers tighten around the hilt of my knife, but I keep my voice level as I reply, "You must not have lived a very exciting life then."

"You think I've lived a boring life?"

"You're the one who implied it."

He doesn't take the bait. Instead, he narrows his eyes and studies my face for a few seconds in silence. Since I'm now certain that he hasn't tracked me down to kill me, I carefully release the knife and then let my foot slide the short distance down the wall and back to the floor. After all, if Draven wanted me dead, he would have just rammed his sword through my heart the moment he cornered me.

A hint of curiosity, or maybe confusion, flickers in his eyes.

"You're not afraid of me," he says at last.

It's more of a statement than a question, but I reply anyway. "No."

"Why not?"

"Because fear is a weapon. It gives other people power over you without them even having to do anything." A wicked little smile ghosts across my lips. "I should know. I use it against people all the time."

"Interesting."

A jolt shoots through my body as he suddenly drops his hand

from the wall and instead draws it up my thigh, lifting the silver dress skirt. Lightning skitters across my skin as Draven's fingers brush over my naked thigh. My brain malfunctions and my heart stalls and I can't for the life of me figure out what is going on.

Then his strong hand wraps around the hilt of my hidden knife, and a smirk spreads across his mouth. "Then why were you desperately clutching this blade until just a few seconds ago?"

My heart pounds against my ribs. His hand remains around the hilt of the knife, his knuckles brushing against my skin as he holds it firmly. I can barely think straight when his fingers are that close to the inside of my thigh.

"Because I'm not stupid," I manage to press out in reply. "If you were going to try to kill me, I was going to fight back."

"Hmm," he murmurs. The sound is so low and dark that I can feel it vibrating through the air. He flexes his fingers on the hilt, his intense eyes still locked on mine. "Do you know what the punishment is for attempting to kill the Commander of the Dread Legion in the Iceheart Dynasty?"

I draw in short shallow breaths while several very different and confusing emotions pulse inside me.

The sly smile on his lips grows as he slides my knife out of its holster. The blade glints in the firelight when he expertly spins it in his hand. I suck in a sharp breath as he yanks up the knife and holds it against my throat.

My pulse thrums in my ears.

Moving his hand upwards, he presses the flat of the blade underneath my chin and uses it to tilt my head back.

I just hold his gaze, my chest rising and falling with rapid breaths.

"But..." he begins, that sly smile now back on his lips again. "I could be persuaded to let your threatening actions slide."

"In exchange for what?"

"A dance."

The world goes suddenly silent. I just stare back at Draven, certain that I must have misheard him. But when no other explanation is forthcoming, I blink and shake my head to clear it.

"A dance?" I repeat, stunned shock still lacing my voice as I stare up at him. "You want to dance? With me?"

"Yes."

"Why?"

He pushes my chin higher up with the blade still in his hand. "Take it or leave it."

And because I'm not a complete idiot, I naturally reply, "Alright."

A dark chuckle escapes his chest. "Good choice."

In one fluid motion, he takes the knife from my throat, spins it in his hand, and then offers it to me hilt first. I take it and slide it back into the holster on my thigh while my brain is still trying to figure out what in Mabona's name is going on here.

Draven holds out his arm to me. "Well then, shall we?"

I stare at him. On the surface, the gesture is full of chivalry, but there is something distinctly threatening about the wicked smile on his mouth. I can't help but feel as if I'm about to walk right into a trap. But I can't for the life of me figure out what kind of trap.

So in the end, I just take his arm and let him lead me back into the ballroom.

One dance. It's just one dance.

Surely I can survive that.

CHAPTER ELEVEN

We only make it three steps into the ballroom before I stumble to a halt. Or try to, anyway. Draven simply keeps walking, pulling me with him. But he glances down at me and arches an eyebrow.

"Changed your mind?" he asks.

"I… No. Well, I…" I stammer while that awful realization that hit me a few seconds ago still crackles through my every nerve. It makes panic flicker through me, so in the end, I just blurt out, "I can't dance."

Draven raises both eyebrows in surprise.

"I don't know how to dance," I repeat, futilely trying to pull against Draven's grip while he continues moving us farther out onto the dance floor. "I don't know what to do."

He might be used to attending fancy balls in the Ice Palace with the empress and emperor and all of his powerful friends, but I have never been in a situation where ballroom dancing was even remotely relevant. I've been gutting fish and trying to start a rebellion all my life, for Mabona's sake!

My stomach lurches as Draven at last pulls us to a halt and

spins me around so that I'm facing him. I look up, expecting to see a cruel smirk on his face, and wait for his mocking words.

To my surprise, none of it comes.

"That's alright," he says. And though there is a small and highly amused smile on his mouth, there is nothing mocking about it. "I do. So all you need to do is to follow my lead."

A jolt shoots through me as he suddenly places a hand on my waist and pulls me closer. While my brain is trying to sort through the jumble of thoughts that flashed through it, Draven moves one of my hands to his shoulder and then takes the other in his free one. And then he starts us into the dance. I can't even hear the music we're dancing to because my heart is beating so loudly.

"Consider this practice," Draven says.

His voice cuts through the noise in my brain, and I finally manage to compose myself. The rest of the room comes back into focus. Thousands of candles burn in the glittering chandeliers, the light sparkling against the shimmering walls and the vaulted ceiling. The shifters in the corner are playing their instruments, creating music that is somehow both dramatic and heart-wrenching at the same time. And other dragon shifters, who are wearing clothes in the color of their respective clans, are swirling across the shining floor alongside us.

I meet Draven's eyes. The light from the candles makes it look like the gold in his eyes is coated with smoldering fire. The sight is so intense that I almost forget that he spoke earlier.

With enormous effort, I manage to get my mind back on track.

"Practice for what?" I reply.

A smirk curves his lips. "Obeying my commands without question."

I draw my eyebrows down in a scowl. Shooting him a look full of challenge, I try to pull back and stop moving in the direction he is taking me.

However, the moment I stop following his lead, I stumble in the wrong direction and almost crash into another dancing couple. The two people, who look to be from the Blue Dragon Clan, glare at me.

Draven uses that moment to pull me back to him. Since I wasn't ready for it, I slam right into his firm chest. I swear I can practically feel the sharp ridges of his abs even through our clothes. My cheeks flush a little, and I quickly put some distance between us again.

With that smirk still on his face, Draven tightens his grip on my waist and then moves us into the dance again. And since I really don't know how to dance, I'm forced to admit that I have to follow his lead right now if I don't want to make a fool of myself.

"See?" Draven says, amusement lacing his tone. "Great practice."

"Mabona's tits, you're such an asshole," I mutter.

"Yes, I am." He fixes me with a pointed look. "However, very few people dare to say that to my face."

"At least you're self-aware."

"You expected me not to be?"

Remaining silent for a few seconds, I study him while we continue dancing. He keeps his eyes locked firmly on mine, but still never misses a single step.

"I'm not sure what I expected you to be," I answer at last.

He seems almost surprised by the honesty. Holding my gaze, he looks at me as if he's trying to read answers in my soul. Or maybe to make me read answers in his.

My heart clenches, and everything suddenly feels too intense. Too *intimate*.

I quickly break eye contact and instead busy myself with looking anywhere but his face. My gaze drops down his body. And I blink in surprise, noticing for the first time what he's actually wearing.

Ever since he ambushed me in the corridor earlier, I've been too preoccupied with everything else. His intense eyes. The knife he held to my throat. The very likely possibility that I was going to make a fool of myself on the dance floor. The feeling of his hand on my waist. All of it has taken up so much of my attention that I haven't even noticed what he's wearing. But now that I have, I can't stop staring at it.

For the first time ever, he's not wearing that black dragon scale armor. Instead, he is dressed in some kind of black formal wear.

I stare at his clothes, my mouth slightly open, before shifting my stunned gaze back up to his face. "What the hell are you wearing?"

He jerks back slightly, surprise and disbelief pulsing across his face. Then he draws his eyebrows down in something that looks remarkably like an embarrassed scowl.

"What am *I* wearing?" he counters, and then shoots a pointed look down at my silver dress. "What are *you* wearing?"

"The clothes provided for me." Dropping his hand, I instead grip the flowing black fabric that cascades down his back, and pull at it. "Is that a cape?"

His hand shoots down, grabbing mine and forcing it away from his cape before bringing it back into the correct position for the dance. He tightens his grip on me. Both on my hand and my waist.

"Yes, it's a cape," he huffs.

"Why are you wearing a cape?"

"To make a statement."

"A statement? What kind of statement?" I nod towards the massive black wings behind him. "That you're a moron who doesn't realize that your fancy little cape will get all tangled up in your wings the moment you try to fly?"

He yanks me closer.

Air escapes my lungs as my body slams into his muscular

chest. I try to pull back while refilling my lungs, but Draven snakes his arm around my waist, holding me firmly pressed against him. His face is so close to mine that I can feel his breath caress my lips.

"Azaroth's flame," he curses, but there is a hint of something like amusement in his tone too. His eyes glint as he holds my gaze while speaking almost directly against my lips. "You always act so soft-spoken around everyone else. Who knew that you had such a sharp tongue underneath all that fake submissiveness?"

Heat sears my cheeks, but I'm not sure if it's from embarrassment or indignation or anger or… something else. Taking my hand from his shoulder, I place it against his firm chest and try to push myself back to create a little more space between us. But his arm remains around my back, holding me tightly against him, while he moves us slowly around in a circle as if it's part of the dance.

I swallow and try to come up with some kind of cutting reply. But all that makes it out of my mouth is, "How do you know how I always act?"

"You seriously think I didn't see you with that group over there?" He nods in the direction of the people I tried to make friends with earlier. "How you let them walk all over you."

"I didn't let them walk all over me."

He just arches a pointed brow in response.

I scoff, but I can't argue further because deep down I know that he's right.

"And yet with me, you let that sharp tongue of yours come out to play." He leans impossibly closer and cocks his head. The move makes him slant his mouth over mine, barely a breath away. "Why is that?"

Lightning skitters across my skin as his breath dances over my lips. My heart flutters in my chest and my veins feel like they're on fire.

I know that I should probably make up some kind of excuse

or lie or say anything that will make him less likely to mess with my chances of winning the Atonement Trials. But I don't.

"Because I don't care what you think of me," I reply. "I don't care if you hate me. Truth be told, I kind of hate you too." I stop myself right before I can say, *and that's why I feel so incredibly free when I talk to you.* Instead, I finish with, "And that's why I don't hold back when I talk to you."

A soft laugh escapes his chest. It makes his warm breath hit my lips and slide over my cheeks, sending a ripple down my spine.

"I see," he says.

He relaxes his grip on me, allowing me to draw back slightly again. I try desperately to clear my head as he slides his hands back into the correct position for the dance. My heart thumps in my chest, beating in tune with the swelling music as Draven spins us right into the building climax of the song.

"The cape is a statement," he says, picking up the threads of the conversation that started this head-spinning confrontation. "My entire outfit is a statement." He rustles his wings slightly. "I'm showing off my wings in a half-shift so that people will know that I'm more powerful than them. But I'm also wearing a cape which, as you so astutely pointed out, will get caught in my wings if I try to fly right now. And what does that tell people?"

I consider for a second. Then realization hits me.

"That you're so powerful that you don't even need your wings to win if someone attacks you," I finish for him, finally understanding his reasoning.

"Exactly."

"Huh." I glance down at his outfit before meeting his gaze again and raising my eyebrows. "Clever."

He narrows his eyes. "Was that surprise I heard?"

I just flash him an unapologetic grin.

My stomach lurches as he picks up the pace, spinning us faster and faster as the song approaches its crescendo.

Candlelight flickers around me, and my dress swishes across the smooth floor.

"So, clothes tell a story," Draven says. "I'm wearing this. And you…"

He slides his hand from my waist and up along the side of my ribs. I suck in a shuddering breath that I'm not entirely sure has anything at all to do with the pace of our dance. His fingers skim my back as he keeps his hand high up on the side of my ribs. Lights flicker through my brain as he draws his thumb along the curve right underneath my breast.

"You're wearing a silver dress that you were ordered to wear," he continues. For the first time tonight, a cruel glint creeps into his eyes as he stares me down. "Just like all the other fae in this room, you weren't even allowed to wear your own clothes." He slides his hand back to my waist as he spins us again. "So what does that tell you?"

I open my mouth to respond, but before any words can make it out, the song ends with a dramatic pounding.

Draven spins us one last time and then uses our momentum to dip me towards the floor. My back arches over his hand, and my hair flows down to brush against the floor. Draven leans down over me.

"It says that you're so outmatched against me that you will never be a threat to my power," he whispers against my mouth.

My heart slams against my ribs. Then he abruptly pulls back and yanks me up into a standing position again. I blink, disoriented for a second while Draven releases me and takes a step back.

"Except I was," I blurt out before he can walk away with the last word. "I was a threat to you and your precious image back during that power demonstration."

He scoffs and then flashes me a mocking smile. "Keep telling yourself that if it helps you sleep at night."

His wings shift slightly as he tucks them closer and starts turning to leave.

"Why did you do this?" I ask, almost stumbling over the words in my haste to get them out before he can stride away.

He turns back to me and raises his eyebrows in silent question. I motion vaguely at the dance floor around us, where the other couples are now moving away towards the tables filled with food and drink instead.

"Why did you dance with me?" I ask.

An unreadable expression slides across his handsome features. I have to suppress the urge to back away as he starts advancing on me again. He moves until he's so close that his chest brushes against mine. Then he leans down.

For one insane second, I think he's going to kiss me.

But right before his lips can touch mine, he angles his head and instead continues forward until his mouth is right next to my ear.

A shiver of pleasure rolls down my spine as his breath caresses the shell of my ear. And I swear I can almost feel the bastard smirking.

"Because now," he begins, once more making his breath dance over my sensitive skin, "I have just put a gigantic target on your back."

My heart drops and my stomach flips.

Draven draws back, and when he meets my gaze again, there is a wicked grin on his mouth. He winks. "You're welcome."

Then, before I can so much as curse him, he turns and strides away, leaving me standing in the middle of the dance floor. Alone. My heart patters nervously as I slowly turn to look at the crowd around me.

Dread spreads through my chest like cold poison.

Because Draven is right. Every single contestant is now watching me through narrowed eyes. Some of them flick a glance at Draven before they continue studying me and talking quietly to the people next to them.

"Fucking asshole," I growl under my breath.

Raking my fingers through my hair, I stalk away from the dance floor and towards the first group of contestants that I see. Or rather, the first group that contains a somewhat friendly face. I need to try to mitigate the damage Draven caused before the rumors can spread too much.

Fenriel, the guy with the hawk who stays in the room across from mine, stares at me with surprise and confusion written all over his narrow face. I walk up to his group, snatch up a glass of wine from the table, and down the whole thing before grabbing another one.

"Mabona's fucking tits," I curse.

The other contestants just watch me warily.

But thankfully, Fenriel takes the bait I threw out and asks, "What was that all about?"

I heave a sigh and rake my free hand through my hair again in a gesture of frustration. Then I turn and sweep my gaze over everyone in the group, to make sure that they're listening too.

"A few weeks ago, I kind of spilled a drink on him," I begin, going with the truth. Or mostly the truth, anyway. "And he's still pissed about that, so now he's getting revenge by pretending as if we're friends in order to put a massive target on my back."

I barely dare to breathe as I wait for their reactions.

Relief crashes over me like a tidal wave when most people in the group let out an *ohh* and nod in understanding. Thank Mabona.

After talking a little more to that group, I quickly move to another one. I need to tell as many people as possible the same thing. That way, if people gossip about what happened, the majority will explain to the others what really happened.

Another dance starts back up while I work my way through

the ballroom. The candles burn lower and the laughter grows louder as the evening wears on.

Thankfully, most people seem to accept my explanation of what Draven was really doing. I still move on to yet another group to truly make sure of that.

"What is she doing?" a female contestant with red hair asks right as I drift over to their group.

My heart lurches, and I think they might be talking about me. But then I follow their gazes and realize that they're looking at Lavendera.

The brown-haired woman stands alone by one of the pale stone walls. She's not eating or drinking anything. She's just standing there, staring blankly at an empty spot on the opposite wall.

"I'm telling you, there's something wrong with that one," another woman replies from the group watching her. "She's not right in the head. I've heard that she actually lives out in the thorn forest."

The redhead raises her eyebrows. "Seriously? Is that why we almost never see her in the city?"

"Probably. Or because no one wants to spend too much time with her. I mean, have you heard the weird shit she says sometimes?"

"Yeah." The redhead nods. "I'm willing to bet that it's because she got seriously hurt when she competed in the previous Atonement Trials."

"She has been in the trials before?"

"Yes. That's how she got that scar on her face."

"No, it's not," a third person replies. A guy this time. His eyes are full of sympathy as he casts a glance towards Lavendera. "Haven't you heard the rumors? It's actually Jessina Iceheart who did that to her. She was so jealous of how beautiful Lavendera was that she slashed her across the face with a shard of ice."

The redhead scoffs and rolls her eyes. "Oh come on. That's a myth. Do you seriously believe everything that people gossip about when they're drunk? Why would—"

"Listen up!" Imar's voice suddenly cuts through the chatter and music.

Everyone falls silent.

"Contestants," he continues, sweeping his gaze over all the gathered fae. "You have one more hour left to enjoy this evening of splendor that your emperor and empress have so generously gifted you. Then you will return to your rooms. Because the first trial starts tomorrow."

A ripple sweeps through the room.

Finally. I've had enough of all this fake generosity. It's high time to actually get started with the real trials so that I can win and finally prove to everyone just how invaluable I really am to the resistance.

The dragon shifters, who are just here as spectators to enjoy the show, grin and nod excitedly at Imar's proclamation. Some people on our side do as well, but most shift their weight as apprehension no doubt settles in their stomachs.

"Make the most of it," Imar finishes.

With an ominous smile, he turns and strides back towards where the Iceheart monarchs are seated on two grand chairs. They watch us all with wicked amusement. I flick a quick glance in search of Draven, but I don't see him anywhere.

So instead, I return to my own task. Imar told us to make the most of this hour, and I intend to do just that. After grabbing a new glass of wine, I continue trying to repair the damage Draven did to my reputation.

I use all the tricks I have in order to make people listen to me. Since they saw me dance with the Shadow of Death, most people have at least become curious enough that they don't outright ignore me the way they did in the beginning. It works in my favor, and I manage to speak to most groups.

But as I move towards one of the last groups that I still

haven't spoken to, a strange feeling rolls through my stomach. I trail to a halt, and glance down in surprise. I feel nauseous. Which makes no sense. I'm no longer nervous and worried.

Shaking my head, I start forward again.

Another wave of nausea washes over me and then climbs up my throat.

I slap a hand over my mouth.

Across the ballroom, several other contestants do the same thing.

Panic slices through me as my stomach heaves.

With my hand firmly pressed against my mouth, I run towards the door.

Others do the same.

My insides twist. I sprint through the corridors as fast as I can.

I barely make it to the lavatories before the vomiting starts.

And as I sit there on my knees on the cold stone floor, emptying the contents of my stomach over and over again, I can't get the image out of my head. The image that I caught right before I ran out the door.

The image of Alistair and Maximus. Grinning. Clinking their glasses together.

And then raising their glasses to us in a mocking salute.

CHAPTER TWELVE

I barely feel like a person. I feel more like a husk that someone has scraped all the important bits out of. My stomach is empty, I'm lightheaded, and it feels as if the slightest breeze is going to knock me over.

After I left the ball, I spent most of the night puking my guts up. It finally stopped early this morning. I staggered down to breakfast but only managed to drink some water and eat two bites of bread. Then I went back to bed and thankfully managed to get two hours of sleep. And now, as I stand here in a crowded corridor, waiting for the first trial to be announced, I can't for the life of me figure out how I'm supposed to muster enough energy to win it.

"Food poisoning," Maximus says from across the corridor. There is a mocking grin on his face as he tuts and shakes his head while sweeping a glance over the rest of us. "Such terrible luck."

If we weren't forbidden from killing each other outside of the trials, I'm pretty sure that Maximus would be dead several times over by now.

I wasn't the only one who became ill last night. Several others mysteriously came down with the same sickness too.

And we all know why.

Because Maximus has poison magic, and he somehow used it to spike our drinks.

We just can't prove it.

And the people who contracted this alleged food poisoning were not random. All of them are strong magic users and some of the most difficult competition in these trials. I'm pretty sure that I only ended up on that list because of the little stunt that Draven pulled last night. One more reason to hate the arrogant bastard.

"Careful now, Maximus," Isera warns.

She was one of the people who were poisoned as well. Though she looks in much better shape than I feel.

Maximus flashes her a sharp grin. "Or what, ice lady?"

She just lets out a low chuckle, as if she can't even be bothered to reply to such a ridiculous question.

Before he can bait her again, the large door at the end of the corridor is pulled open. It groans on its hinges, giving evidence that this is not a door that has been opened often. We're somewhere at the back of the castle, and I'm pretty sure that the large door leads outdoors, but I don't know where it leads exactly or what we're doing here.

"Let's go!" someone calls from outside the doors. "Move it."

A ripple goes through our large group, and then footsteps echo between the stone walls as we hurry to follow the shouted command. My head spins with every step, but I try to block it out. It's not as if I have never been exhausted and hungry before. It doesn't matter that I've barely slept and that I spent all night throwing up. I can do this.

I hope.

A loud cheering noise rises as we step out of the corridor and onto the ground outside.

Even though it's an overcast day, the gray light still stabs at my eyes after my ordeal last night, so I raise a hand to shield them while I blink repeatedly. Once my vision has adjusted, I suck in a sharp breath.

We're on the floor of an arena. Packed dirt covers the ground in the shape of a large circle, and then rows of benches rise up and surround the space in several tiers. Dragon shifters fill the seats, and they cheer excitedly as we are herded towards the center of the arena floor.

While stumbling along with the others, I crane my neck and turn slowly to take it all in. My heart rate picks up as I study all the eager faces looking down at us. I don't know what it is that we're supposed to do, but the dragon shifters are eager, and that's never a good sign.

My gaze finds the two Iceheart monarchs. They're seated in two grand chairs in the very middle. That tier is wider, and there are fewer benches on it, so it was probably used by the Seelie Queen when she lived here. Draven stands there as well, along with the other seven clan leaders. From this far away, I can't read the expression on his face. But if he has heard about the poisoning that I suffered because of his meddling, he is probably very pleased with himself.

"Contestants," Imar calls as he strides out to the edge of an otherwise empty section a little to the left of the Icehearts.

Clothes rustle as we all turn towards him. Since we weren't ordered to wear anything specific, I've changed back into my own clothes. Pants and shirt and boots are much easier to move in than a dress. My knife is also securely strapped to my thigh in case I need it for anything.

"Welcome to your first Atonement Trial," Imar says. I can't see his face clearly from this distance, but it sounds like he is grinning. "Today, we will truly cull the unworthy. Only half of you will make it to the next trial."

Several shocked gasps echo from our group. I cast a few quick glances around me. By my best estimate, there are maybe eighty of us. That means forty will make it through to the next round.

All things considered, those are decent odds. Depending on what the trial is, I should be able to make it without too much trouble.

"The objective is this," Imar continues. "Be among the last forty standing inside the circle."

Confusion ripples through our group as we glance around the arena floor. There is no circle anywhere to be seen. However, I'm not stupid enough to draw attention to myself by pointing that out, so I simply turn back to Imar.

Someone else is, though.

"What circle?" Tommen, the guy with enhanced strength, calls while motioning with his arms at the packed dirt around us.

Silence falls over the arena.

Then black smoke explodes across Imar's section, and a red dragon soars out of it.

I jerk back in alarm.

Cries ring out from several others as Imar in his dragon form swoops towards us. Some of the contestants summon magic.

"Attack him and you're dead," Gremar Fireclaw bellows from the section where all the clan leaders are standing.

The magic immediately vanishes, but we all press tighter together in the middle of the arena as Imar circles us. His wings boom in the air, sending blasts of wind towards the ground and kicking up clouds of dust.

Then he opens his jaws.

I tense, gripping the hilt of my knife even though it's useless.

Dragon fire shoots through the air.

More cries rip from our group as we push harder together.

Imar flies in a circle around us, sending a torrent of fire straight at the ground as he flies. The heat from it vibrates through the air. I avert my eyes to protect my vision.

Once he has completed the full circle, he flies back to his empty section. Black smoke yet again explodes across the stone ledge. When it clears, Imar is once more standing there in his human form.

"*That* circle," he announces, and stabs a hand towards the still smoldering ground.

I shift my gaze towards it.

About halfway between our group and the wall with the first tier of spectators is now a trail of scorched dirt. It runs in a perfect circle around us.

Shouts of approval rise from the shifters in the audience.

No one in our group says anything. Not even Tommen.

"The rules are simple," Imar continues, and once again, I swear that I can hear the grin on his face. After pausing for dramatic effect, he finishes with, "There are no rules."

Several shifters laugh from the audience.

"Stay inside the circle," Imar repeats. "That's the only thing you need to do. If you're forced outside the circle, you're eliminated."

"Same if you get knocked unconscious," Emperor Bane suddenly calls.

"Or killed," Empress Jessina adds.

"Yeah, that too," Imar says. He holds up a hand, counting off on his fingers. "If you're outside the circle, unconscious, or dead, you're eliminated."

Dread spikes through me.

Suddenly, I'm starting to regret that I was ever annoyed at their fake generosity and that it took so long to get the real trials started. I'll take dancing at a ball over this any day of the week.

"Once there are only forty people left inside the circle, I'll call an end to the trial." Wicked amusement creeps into his tone. "And you'll definitely be able to hear it, even over all the noise." Once again, he pauses for dramatic effect. "Because I'll be in my dragon form."

No one speaks.

Apparently, Imar had expected a different reaction, because his voice is laced with annoyance as he barks, "Begin."

Then he shifts into his dragon form.

Black smoke billows across the stone ledge, and then a red dragon shoots out of it. He roars, the sound echoing through the arena, and then flies up to the top. Stones crumble and clatter down as he lands on the edge of the highest tier. His tail swishes impatiently through the air as he angles his head towards us.

For a few seconds, no one moves.

Then a thud and a wet gurgle cleave the tense silence.

I whip my head towards the sound.

Shock crackles through me, and I jerk back in stunned surprise as I stare at the scene before me.

Lavendera stands a short distance away. Her arm is outstretched. Two steps away from her, Maximus stares at her with wide eyes. A tree branch is buried so far in his chest that the sharp end sticks out of his back on the other side. He coughs. Blood sprays into the air and dribbles down his chin.

"I hate cheaters," Lavendera announces, and then yanks the branch back out of his heart.

All hell breaks loose.

I throw myself sideways right as a blast of water shoots through the air in the space I was previously occupying. A short distance away, Maximus topples backwards and hits the ground hard. One more gurgle makes it out. Then his chest stills.

Shouts rip through the cool midday air as everyone lurches into motion. Within seconds, the arena floor has descended into chaos.

I roll out of the way as a block of stone flies towards me. Twisting up to my knees, I leap back onto my feet and then sprint away from the worst of the throng. I need space to think. To breathe. To come up with some kind of plan.

Because this is the worst possible trial for someone like me.

I don't have battle magic. I barely have defensive magic. How the hell am I supposed to keep myself inside this circle?

Air explodes from my lungs as a guy with short blond hair slams into me from the side. The force of it sends me crashing down on the ground. I gasp, trying to suck air back into my lungs, as we smack into the packed dirt together. The hit makes my head spin, worsened by the lingering effects of the poison.

Twisting on the ground, I try to get out from underneath him and get to my feet. But the blond man has already shot to his feet and circled around me. I blink furiously, trying to figure out if the poison is still affecting my eyesight.

But then a memory from the power demonstration slams into me.

I don't remember his name, but this blond guy has enhanced speed.

My stomach lurches as Blondie grabs me by the ankle and starts sprinting towards the circle. I cry out in pain as the muscles in my leg pull taut. Pebbles dig into my back as I'm hauled across the ground.

Panic crackles through me.

Throwing my hand out, I search desperately for the hilt of my knife.

The burnt line on the ground draws closer at an alarming rate.

I scream in frustration as I finally yank the blade out. My muscles are still weak from last night, but I throw everything I have into a desperate move as I curl up in a sitting position and slash the knife straight across his wrist.

A howl rips from his throat.

My body skids to a halt as he snatches his hand back. Blood runs down from the cut across the front of his wrist, staining his fingers red. I gasp in a breath and stagger to my feet. Small rocks that were stuck to the back of my shirt clatter down on the ground behind me. My head spins and my stomach rolls, even though there is nothing left in it to expel.

I drag in another shuddering breath as I sprint away.

But Blondie whips his head towards me. Rage burns in his eyes as he clutches his injured wrist. Then he takes off.

He moves so fast that I can barely track his body.

I dash across the ground, but I know that I will never be fast enough to escape him.

The scorched line looms just a few steps to my left. If he catches me, it's over. But I can't outrun him. I need—

I screech to a halt and spin around.

Blondie is moving so fast that he doesn't have time to adjust his course. He barrels straight into me, but I was prepared for it and twist with the motion, spinning him with me.

His increased speed works against him, and he practically flies across the arena floor as I let go of him.

He stumbles across the ground, cutting off his magic, but still crashes down on the packed dirt. Shooting to his feet, he whirls on me.

I grin at him.

Because he's now outside the circle.

He growls curses at me, but I don't have time to listen to them, because three more people are coming my way.

Channeling my magic, I push hard at a spark of calm in their chests.

Only an empty void meets me.

Shit.

Taking off across the ground, I run towards the other side of the circle while I push desperately with my magic at everyone I meet. None of them has so much as a single spark of calm emotion inside them.

Dread washes over me. How the hell am I supposed to keep them from attacking me?

A block of stone shoots through the air.

I leap back, barely managing to get out of the way. The guy who threw it aims another one. But right before he can hurl it at me, Lavendera slams an entire tree trunk into his slide. He flies away and hits the ground close to the circle. But before she can finish the job, Alistair throws a fireball at her.

Backing away, I try to make myself invisible. If I can just stay away from the fight, I'll be fine. It's not—

Pain cracks through my side.

I gasp as a wave of agony rips through my whole soul.

It's so intense that I barely even register that I stagger several steps to the side from the force of the blow.

With black spots swimming in my vision, I stumble and twist towards the source of the blow.

Tommen stands there, his red and brown eyes gleaming with menace, as he grins at me.

My brain fights through the fog of pain and lingering poison.

Tommen. The guy with enhanced strength.

Oh fuck.

He charges towards me.

I swing my arm, swiping my blade at his chest. It forces him to dodge and buys me a few precious seconds to drag air back into my lungs. My ribcage screams in pain at the simple movement.

Fuck. I think he might have fractured some of my ribs.

My brief seconds of grace come to an abrupt end as Tommen launches himself at me again. I try to twist aside, but the pain that spikes through my ribs at the movement makes me falter for a second.

And one second is all he needs.

His boot smacks into the side of my knee.

I scream in pain as my leg bends at an unnatural angle.

But it's cut off as Tommen tackles me.

We hit the ground hard. I gasp in pain. Black spots cover my vision like a wild sea. Yanking my arm out from between us, I stab blindly towards him with my knife. His hand shoots up and wraps around my wrist right before I can sink the blade into his chest.

Pain streaks up my forearm as he grips my wrist so hard that the bones grind together. I cry out and try to yank my arm back.

But he just rips the knife from my hand and then plunges it towards my throat.

I throw my other hand up.

But I know that I will never be able to stop his hand because I'm so hopelessly outmatched against his enhanced strength. So I don't even try to reach his wrist. Instead, I aim for his throat.

The blade slashes along the side of my forearm on its way down.

But my fingers stab right into the front of his throat before he can ram the knife into my chest.

A choked gasp tears from his lungs.

The knife slips from his grip, clattering down on the ground next to me, and he releases my other wrist as both of his hands fly towards his throat. He sucks in strangled breaths, pain pulsing in his eyes.

I try to use that moment of inattention to escape. But he's sitting on my chest. I barely manage to wiggle a little upwards before his eyes snap back to my face. Fury pulses in them.

And that's when I realize that I will never get out from underneath him.

Yanking my arm up, I point up into the sky above us and scream, "DRAGON!"

He whips his head around.

And I push with every smidgen of magic I have.

My magic finds a tiny spark of fear, and I blow it into a fucking explosion.

Tommen screams in sheer terror and scrambles off me. While ducking the dragon that isn't actually there, he sprints away.

For a few seconds, I just lie there in the dirt and gasp air into my lungs.

Pain slices through my chest with every breath, and it pulses through my left leg when I move it. Blood wells up from the cut along the side of my forearm, staining my shirt red and making my fingers slick.

All I want to do is to just close my eyes for a second. But I can't. Because Imar hasn't ended the trial yet. And I still need to win.

So I grit my teeth and struggle to my feet. Picking up my knife, I breathe through the waves of pain rolling through me and survey the battlefield. I try once again to force them to calm down. But it doesn't work. No one feels calm as magic shoots through the air and people fight with fists and magic and everything they have.

Two people spot me just standing there.

I let out a vicious curse as they start towards me.

Anger and frustration rip through my soul. I can't fight these people off. I don't have that kind of magic. And with my injuries, I won't even be able to outrun them anymore. I can't fight. I can't run. I can't calm them down.

So I need to be smarter than them.

A sudden idea hits me like a lightning strike.

Spinning around, I search furiously for Alistair.

I find him close to the middle of the arena, throwing torrents of fire at people and forcing them farther back towards the circle.

The two people running towards me draw closer.

Clenching my jaw, I dart to the left so that Alistair is between me and them.

And then I channel my magic and push at the spark of anger in Alistair's chest.

A gasp rips out of my lungs, and I almost lose the grip on my magic.

The pale red spark of anger inside Alistair's chest is so intense, so massive, that it almost sets me on fire too. It shocks me so much that I can barely breathe. That is not the kind of anger that people feel on a surface level during a battle. The rage inside Alistair is the deep kind. The destructive kind that has been burning in his soul for *years*.

I raise my mental walls higher, protecting myself from his emotions, and then I pour even more fuel into that flaming rage.

He goes berserk.

Fire roars through the air as he attacks everyone in sight. I dart along with his movements, always keeping behind him. Cries of panic echo through the arena as people are forced to flee out of the circle to escape his flames.

I drag in desperate breaths, trying to block out the pain in my leg and ribs and forearm. But even despite all that, there is still a victorious grin on my mouth as I continue to manipulate Alistair's emotions.

Because I don't need to be the strongest or the fastest or have battle magic to win this trial. I just need to make someone else take out all of my competition for me.

Blood runs down my arm and drips from my fingers. I was already lightheaded before this trial even started, but now I feel as if I'm going to pass out any second. There can't be that many people left now. We have to be close to forty. We have to—

A roar cuts through the air.

It's so loud that it almost shatters my eardrums.

I spin around and stare up at the red dragon perched atop the arena. Imar opens his mouth and lets out another deafening roar while his tail swishes pointedly through the air.

The battle staggers to a halt.

Wings boom and clouds of dust rise from the ground as Imar flies back to his empty section on the middle tier. He shifts in a cloud of black smoke and then strides out onto the edge of the platform.

"Congratulations," he calls. "If you are inside the circle and still breathing, you've made it through the first trial."

My knees give out.

Pain pulses through my limbs as I collapse to the ground.

Lying there on my back, I stare up into the gray sky above and drag in deep breaths. My chest heaves. My head spins. A few of my ribs are most likely cracked. Blood coats my entire left forearm. And I think I've torn one of the tendons around my knee.

But I made it.

An insane burst of laughter rips from my lungs.

I made it.

I survived the first trial.

CHAPTER THIRTEEN

Pain pulses through my body with every step as I limp back out of the arena and into the corridor that we came in through. I keep one arm wrapped around my fractured ribs and the other hand sliding along the wall for support. Blood still coats my forearm, dripping faintly on the floor as I move slowly down the hall.

Before we were allowed to leave, Imar told us that we now have three days to rest and heal and to let our magic recover before the next trial. As fae, we thankfully all have increased healing speed. I'm not sure how it works for the dragon shifters, but compared to humans, we heal remarkably fast. And since I'm pretty certain that my ribs are only partially fractured rather than completely broken, three days should be enough time for them to heal. Especially here where I have practically unlimited access to food. Healing consumes a lot of energy, which requires a lot of food. Which is probably another reason why the shifters have never allowed us to have too much of it. But for the first time in my life, I have an abundance of food just waiting for me.

I suck in a sharp hiss between my clenched teeth as a rough hand suddenly grabs me by the shoulder and yanks me around.

Since I don't have enough strength left to stop it, I can do nothing except let myself be spun around. My back hits the wall of the corridor with a thud. Gritting my teeth against the pain, I look up to meet the gaze of my newest attacker.

Alistair Geller looms before me. Rage burns in his orange and green eyes as he buries his fist in my collar, trapping me against the wall.

"You've made an enemy of me now, Soulstealer," he growls in my face.

I furrow my brows in what I hope is believable confusion. "What? Why? We never even faced each other during this trial."

"Don't you fucking dare deny it."

With that mask of bewilderment on my face, I just continue looking up at him.

"Jeb saw what you did." He clenches his jaw and tightens his grip on my collar. "You manipulated my emotions. Made me go on a rampage like a fucking animal."

Aw, crap.

Since there is no point in trying to deny it further, I raise my chin defiantly instead.

"You made an enemy of me first." I shoot him a pointed glare. "When you had your friend poison me."

"If any of you had any proof of that, those fucking asshole shifters would already have killed us."

"It doesn't matter that I can't prove it. It's still true. You know it, and so do I. So I'd say that this makes us even."

"Even?" A vicious laugh rips from his chest. "Oh, we're far from even."

With one hand still buried in the collar of my shirt, he raises his other while his eyes start to glow. Fire flares to life in his palm.

My heart leaps into my throat.

I try to pry his fingers off my collar so that I can escape, but he keeps me in an iron grip.

"You wanted me to use my fire magic for your benefit?" The flames reflect in his eyes as he moves his burning hand closer to my face. "How about I use it *on* you instead? The shifters will never know. They'll just think that you got burned by my flames during the trial."

I struggle hard against his grip, fighting against his hold on me as he brings the flames towards my cheek. But I'm too weak and injured, too drained from the lingering poison and the exhaustion of the trial, to compete with his strength. Heat from the fire washes over my skin. A desperate noise escapes my throat. The flames are almost on my cheek now. A little closer and my skin will start to blister.

Alistair lets out a yelp.

I start in surprise as he is suddenly yanked backwards by a set of twisting branches.

"Are you deaf?" Lavendera demands as she strides up the hall towards us. "They said no fighting outside of the trials."

Relief washes through me.

The other half of our group, the ones who had been standing on the other side of the arena when Imar told us that we could leave, have finally caught up with us. Several of the other contestants cast curious glances between me and Alistair, but they continue past us without stopping. Lavendera stops, though.

Standing with her hands on her hips, she glares at Alistair.

Alistair manages to untangle himself from the branches she used to yank him away from me. Fury still pulses in his eyes as he whirls towards her.

"You," he growls. "Why the fuck do you care?"

"Following the rules is vital," she replies. "And that means no harming each other outside of trials."

"But inside the trials is fine?" His expression darkens and his voice drops lower. "You fucking killed Maximus."

"Yes."

"Why? You weren't even among the people affected by the food poisoning."

"It wasn't food poisoning. It was just poison."

"Still. *You* didn't suffer from it."

"Doesn't matter. He broke the rules." Her voice is flat and emotionless. "So he had to die."

Anger flashes in Alistair's eyes right before they begin to glow again. Fire blooms in his palm, casting flickering light over the pale stone walls. Yanking his hand up, he shoots a stream of fire towards Lavendera's branches that still linger next to him.

But before he can burn them to ash, something flat and pale flashes through the air.

A violent hissing sound echoes between the walls.

I stare at the sheet of ice that showed up to block Alistair's flames.

Footsteps sound from my left. Turning my head, I look towards them.

Isera strides up the corridor. She doesn't look hurt or angry or even remotely bothered by anything. With her chin raised, she simply continues towards us as if she hadn't just thrown a sheet of ice to extinguish Alistair's flames.

From a few strides away, Alistair scoffs and flashes her a mocking grin. "So, the ice lady has emotions after all?"

"Of course I do," Isera replies as she walks. But when she reaches us, she simply continues walking right past without stopping. Right as she passes Alistair, she adds, "I simply do not waste them on insecure little boys like you."

His cheeks flush bright red, in anger or embarrassment or both. He clenches his jaw hard and flexes his hand. Right when it looks as if he's going to summon another ball of flame and throw it at Isera's retreating back, a dark voice cuts through the corridor.

"Is there a problem?"

I whip my head towards the source of the voice and find Draven stalking towards us.

He spreads his wings wider, blocking off the entire corridor, as he advances on us. Lavendera lets her branches vanish into thin air and slips away after Isera while Draven's gaze is temporarily fixed on me. Alistair is about to do the same, but before he can take so much as a step, Draven slides his commanding gaze to him instead.

"I said, is there a problem?" Draven demands. Threats drip from his every word like searing poison.

"No," Alistair quickly replies.

Draven comes to a halt between us. His massive wings flare slightly as he turns and fixes Alistair with a death stare. "No, *what?*"

Alistair clenches his jaw so hard that I can almost hear his teeth crack, and he squeezes his hand into a tight fist. But we all know that no one defies the Shadow of Death. So in the end, Alistair drops his gaze to the floor in submission and forces out, "No, sir."

"That's right." Draven cocks his head. "Now, do you need a reminder of what happens to people who instigate fights outside of the trials?"

"No, sir."

"Good. Then get the hell out of my sight."

Alistair raises his head while Draven turns around to face me instead. And now that Draven can't see his face, he locks eyes with me and flashes me a threatening smile. Then he mouths, "*Watch your back.*"

I narrow my eyes at him as he slinks away. But I don't have time to watch him leave, because Draven is now looming over me instead. Pain and exhaustion still pulse through my body, so I drag in a bracing breath before shifting my gaze to the ruthless commander in front of me.

"And you..." Lightning flickers in Draven's eyes as his gaze drops down to the blood coating my forearm. A muscle flickers in his jaw as he locks hard eyes on me again. "Get that wound stitched up. Right now." He lets out a sharp breath, and then adds, "Before you dirty the whole castle with your blood."

For a brief moment, I consider rolling my eyes at him. But he looks genuinely angry, so I decide not to push my luck. Well, not push it *too much*, anyway. Because I simply can't help myself, I give him a small bow that is just on the edge of being a little mocking.

My voice is laced with a slight trace of teasing as I say, "Yes, sir."

Draven narrows his eyes at me. But he doesn't retaliate. Instead, he simply spins on his heel and stalks back towards the arena.

And if I didn't know better, I could have almost sworn that I saw a hint of amusement on his lips before he turned his back on me.

CHAPTER FOURTEEN

Alistair warned me to watch my back. And I have. In the two days since the first trial, I have carefully checked everything I eat and drink, even though Maximus is already dead, and I have made sure not to end up in a room alone with Alistair or his friends. And because of that, I've been able to heal without getting new injuries.

I did go and get the wound on my arm cleaned and stitched up, which helped it heal quicker. The torn tendon in my leg has also mended itself. And my ribs are almost healed as well.

Physically, I'm doing well.

Mentally, not so much.

I try to ignore the cold weight that presses against my heart as I sneak through the deserted halls of the Golden Palace. As in all other corridors as well, the faelights have been ripped out and replaced by torches. The flickering firelight dances over the pale walls, painting them with ominous shadows. I try to keep my mind on the task at hand, but I can't entirely block out the uncomfortable feelings that have been twisting in my chest like thorny vines these past two days.

When I entered this competition, I thought... I don't know. That I would breeze through the trials? Or something like that.

It sounds ridiculous now. But I just thought that because I wanted to win so badly, it would give me an edge against everyone else. But the more time I spend here, the more I realize that *everyone* desperately wants to win. And I don't know if I'm skilled enough, and ruthless enough, to beat them.

As I turn another corner and sneak down the next corridor, my mind drifts back to the previous trial.

Bitterness crawls up my throat.

That trial was a brutal reminder that I can be eliminated at any time. I was *lucky* that I managed to make it through to the next trial. People like Isera and Alistair have magic that is much more versatile. Mine is so specific. So limited. And that's not even taking into account my own stupidity.

I clench my fist and shake my head at myself as I disappear down another corridor.

During the trial, I didn't even try to win. I just tried not to lose. I didn't even think about ways of making other people go outside the ring. All I thought about was how to keep myself inside by trying to calm people down or create sympathy so that they wouldn't attack me. It was a dangerous and stupid and frankly outright pitiful tactic.

If I wanted to, I could have reached out with my magic and increased everyone's panic and worry. Because I know that most of them felt it. Most of them were worried that they would be pushed outside the ring and were panicking when they were being attacked. I could have latched on to that fear and panic and made them lose their cool entirely. It would have made lots of people blindly sprint away, causing them to end up outside the ring before they even knew what they were doing.

But I didn't.

Because deep inside my stupid heart, I still want people to like me.

I resist the urge to bang my fist against the wall in frustration. This is an important competition, I know that. Important and *rare*. After this, there are one hundred and fifty years until we're given another chance to compete in the Atonement Trials and win the privilege to leave the Seelie Court. I need to win this one. Right now. So that I can make a real difference for our resistance. So why do I still worry about something as trivial as whether or not people like me? It's absurd.

Once more shaking my head at my own stupidity, I slip down the stairs and finally reach a section of the castle that I have never visited before.

The previous trial showed that I can be sent packing at any time, so I need to make the most of this opportunity in every way I can. If I can't win the Atonement Trials, maybe I can at least overhear something important here among the dragon shifters that I can bring back to the leaders of the resistance.

Drawing myself up along the wall, I cast a quick glance around the corner.

Empty.

After slipping around the corner, I sneak down the hall on silent feet. The south wing is quite far from the royal wing, so I doubt that I'll be able to make it all the way to the Icehearts' rooms. But maybe I can manage to spy on some of the clan leaders.

My heart patters against my barely healed ribs as I approach the next corner.

Voices drift out from the corridor beyond.

A jolt shoots through me.

Pressing myself against the wall, I edge forward until I can flick a glance around the corner. I yank my head back, my pulse thrumming in my ears.

Two shifters are standing in the corridor beyond. Thankfully, they were facing each other when I glanced around the corner, so they can't have seen me. I risk another quick look to determine who they are.

My gaze drifts over two sets of black leather uniforms before I pull back again. Black uniforms. That means that they're from the Black Dragon Clan. Draven's clan.

"Lower your voice," one of them hisses.

"I just don't know how much more of this I can take," the other growls back in a voice that is certainly not lowered. "Did you see how he bowed and scraped before them back there?"

An angry breath echoes between the walls. "Yes. And trust me, I despise it as much as you do. Despise *him* as much as you do. But you need to keep your voice down. These walls might have ears."

"I don't care! It has been two hundred years. Two *centuries* of bowing before the Icehearts and watching Draven degrade our entire clan by behaving like their loyal lapdog. How could he sell us out to those fucking vultures?"

My heart lurches. Draven? They're talking about Draven? Shock and disbelief pulse through me. I had heard the rumors, of course. But I hadn't realized just how much his own people despise him.

"I said, lower your voice! You and Draven might have been friends back then, but he's *their* creature now. If he hears you disrespecting him like this, he'll have your fucking head."

"Let him try. Fuck, I can't believe that Azaroth chose him. How could he ever pick someone as corrupt and spineless as Draven fucking Ryat?"

I'm not an expert on dragon shifter culture, but I know that Azaroth is their god. And because only one person in each clan can possess their signature magic at any given time, which also makes that person the clan leader, they believe that Azaroth is the one who chooses which one of them to pass the magic to. Apparently, they're not happy that Draven inherited their storm magic when their last leader died.

"You believed in him once too," the calmer of the two replies. "Remember? You were his best friend."

"Don't remind me. If I had known what he would do, that he would willingly make us all subordinates of the Silver Clan just so that he could get the job as the Commander of the Dread Legion, I would have killed him before he even inherited his magic." He heaves a deep sigh. "I thought… I really thought I knew him." A bitter laugh rips from his throat. "But apparently, Azaroth isn't the only one who was fooled by him."

Resting the back of my head against the cold stone wall, I consider their words. The angry-sounding guy apparently used to be Draven's best friend. And now, he hates him. All of his people hate him.

I wonder if that affects him. Bothers him in some way.

A scoff threatens to escape my throat, and I have to clamp my mouth shut to stop it.

Of course it doesn't affect Draven. Someone who sold out his own people doesn't have those kinds of emotions. If he gave up his whole clan in exchange for the position as the leader of the dragon army, the Dread Legion, then he clearly cares nothing for other people.

"Did you hear that?" the calm one suddenly snaps.

"No."

"Someone is here."

Alarm crackles through me.

Pushing off from the wall, I sprint back down the corridor in the direction that I came from.

And when the two dragon shifters round the corner, I'm already gone.

CHAPTER FIFTEEN

Failure hangs over me like a gloomy cloud, and I find myself scowling as I stomp down the stairs and towards a bathing chamber on a different level. My attempt to spy yesterday yielded no results. And today I've been too preoccupied with trying to predict what the next trial will be that I haven't gotten anything productive done.

My mind churns. It feels as if a swarm of angry bees is trapped inside my skull. And *that* is dangerous. If I'm going to have any chance of making it through the next trial, I need to have a clear head.

The door to the bathing chamber appears at the end of the hall. I glance over my shoulder to make sure that I'm not being followed as I close the final distance to it.

Alistair hasn't dared to attack me again, but I can feel his threatening stare every time he sees me. And I really don't want him to mess with me. Not tonight. This is the final evening before the next trial. I need to make sure that when I go to bed, I'm in the right headspace. So instead of using the bathing chamber in my own corridor, which is where Alistair lives too, I decided to sneak down to one on the other side of the south wing in order to get some space to think and breathe and get my head on straight. Because right now, that is something that I sorely need.

The corridor behind me is empty, so I open the door and slip into the bathing chamber.

Warmth and humid air hits me in the face as I step across the threshold and into a short corridor. I move quietly in case there is someone else here. I'm fairly certain that there won't be, since most of the people who stayed in this corridor have already been eliminated. It was the whole reason why I picked this specific bathing chamber, after all.

Gleaming white faelights cover the pale stone walls as I sneak up to the first doorway on my right and peek inside. Only an empty dressing room meets me there. I pull back and continue towards the actual bath.

The short hallway opens up into a large chamber. The majority of the floorspace is taken up by a massive sunken bath. White stone steps lead down into the water, and then the pool spreads out in a rectangular shape. Water runs down in a soft waterfall on my left, filling the bath, and the excess water then flows out over the bath's right wall, which is lower than the others. That way, the water is always kept fresh.

In here, the soft white faelights have been allowed to remain. Probably because it would be difficult to keep torches alive in a room with so much water and humidity. The gleaming light reflects against the sparkling water, casting glittering reflections on the walls.

I smile at the deserted room before me.

Perfect. This is just what I need.

I hurry back to the dressing room and quickly strip out of the robe I'm wearing. Since I wasn't sure if there would be other people here, I didn't want to bring my own clothes or my knife. So I just put on one of the fluffy white robes that we have been provided for this exact purpose. But it appears as though I might have been overly cautious.

Still, you never know.

After stripping down until I'm completely naked, I pad back to the bath area.

The water glitters invitingly before me.

Walking towards it, I move until I'm standing on the first step down and then dip my foot into the water. A rush of pleasure washes through me. Just like the bath in my corridor, the water is the perfect temperature. Not too cold and not too hot.

With a smile on my face, I walk down the steps until everything except my head is submerged in the warm water. A moan slips from my lips. Leaning backwards, I float on my back while lazily stroking the water with my arms.

Only the sound of softly rushing water fills the room. It drowns out all other sound and leaves me feeling as if I'm floating in a peaceful eternity.

I heave a deep sigh.

This is exactly what I needed. A way to silence all of the doubt inside my head. A way to forget all the mistakes I've made. A way to get myself in the right headspace so that I can focus solely on winning the next trial tomorrow.

While I float there, I try once again to guess what the next trial will be. But it's impossible to know. Even Kevlin, who has done this two times before, says that it's different every time. It might be another battle type trial. Or something that requires more stealth. I sincerely hope that it's stealth, since that's right up my alley.

It's insane that the fae resistance hasn't utilized me more. I would make the perfect spy. I can deescalate conflicts before they happen. And I can create them too, as distractions or as a part of a longer manipulation mission. I could do so much for them. And yet, all these years, they've kept me stuck on lookout duty.

Pain stabs into my chest and squeezes my heart. I've tried so hard to prove myself. To the resistance. To my parents. To the friends I should have had. But no matter what I do, everyone always keeps me at arm's length. As if they think I'm going to... what? Take advantage of them? Force them to like me against their wishes?

It's ridiculous. Just because I *can* manipulate people's emotions doesn't mean that I go around doing it at random. Just like Isera doesn't throw blocks of ice at everyone she meets just because she can. But it's as if there's suddenly this huge difference just because my powers are of the mental kind rather than something physical that people can touch, or at least see.

My heart clenches again, and hopelessness washes over me. How am I ever going to make them accept me? It has been over a hundred years already and—

I sit bolt upright, slamming my feet back down on the floor of the bath and standing up straight.

No. What the hell am I doing? I came here to clear my head. To calm down and reset my mind and get into the right headspace. And what am I doing instead? I'm spiraling into yet another fit of self-pity.

I slap the surface with my hand and scowl at myself. Enough. Enough moping. Enough self-sabotaging. The second trial starts tomorrow. I need to be focused. That's how I'm going to change my life. Change how people see me. Change my future. The future of all fae. I'm going to win.

Water sloshes around me as I stalk back up the steps and out of the bath. Since I apparently can't trust myself when I'm alone with my thoughts, I might as well head back and simply go to bed. Sleep shuts out the destructive thoughts and at least helps give my body more energy.

Drops of water run down my naked body and soak the floor as I stride back to the changing room. I round the doorway with determined steps, heading straight for my robe.

But then slam to a halt.

Dumbfounded, I blink at the empty shelf where I put my folded-up robe. I give my head a firm shake and then turn to look around the room. Did I put it somewhere else?

Only empty shelves and equally empty benches stare back at me. Even the few spare towels that were sitting on some of the shelves are gone.

My mind spins.

Then I spot it. A piece of paper lies on the empty shelf where my robe used to be. I move towards it. Water drips down my legs.

For some reason, I don't dare to touch the paper. So instead, I just lean forward and read it while leaving it there on the stone slab.

Did you really think that I wouldn't see you sneaking away to another bathing chamber? I see everything. And don't even try to rat me out to Draven about this. I haven't broken any rules. I haven't physically harmed you. Only humiliated you. Best of luck, Soulstealer.

For a few seconds, all I can do is to stare at that piece of paper.

The silence in the dressing room is suddenly so loud that I can hear the blood rushing in my ears.

Soulstealer. Only one group of people here calls me that. Alistair and his friends.

Still refusing to believe it, I whip my head from side to side, searching desperately for my robe or a towel or anything that I can use to cover myself with. But there is nothing left.

"Fuck," I curse under my breath.

Dread and panic swirl behind my ribs as I stare at the empty room around me.

Damn. Alistair is smarter than I gave him credit for. He's right. He hasn't broken any rules by stealing my clothes. He hasn't harmed me or attacked me. But he has managed to successfully mess with my head right before the next trial.

Because there is only one thing I can do now.

Walk back through the corridors completely naked and pray to Mabona that no one sees me.

Mortification crashes over me, searing my cheeks. Goddess above, what if someone does see me? How am I ever going to live that down?

I linger in the dressing room, hoping against hope that someone will walk through the door and help me.

But no help arrives.

When my body is completely dry, and no one has miraculously appeared to solve my problem, I'm forced to admit that I'm out of options. I can't stay here. I need to sleep. And I need to get my clothes before the next trial. Which means that I have to walk back to my room like this.

I glance down at the key that I kept tied to my wrist while in the water. At least that bit of paranoia served me well. I still have the key to my room. All I need to do is to make it there unseen.

Walking over to the door, I edge it open and peer out into the corridor.

It's empty.

Slinking out the door, I hurry down the corridor and towards the open doorway to the stairwell. When I reach it, I pause outside and just stick my head through.

The wide stone staircase spirals both upwards and downwards. From my position, I crane my neck in every direction and try to see as far as I can. It's difficult to tell, since the stairs are blocking a lot of the view, but I think it's empty. At least I don't hear any footsteps echo between the walls.

But my heart still pounds in my chest as I sneak onto the first step and start upwards on quick and silent feet.

The stairs wind around and around. I have almost reached the next floor. After that, there are only a few more corridors before I reach my room. Hopefully, Alistair and his friends have better things to do than to stand around in the corridor outside their rooms, waiting for me. But considering that he's an experienced bully, it's not an entirely baseless fear.

Only three more steps left, then I'll be up and out of the stairwell. Just—

A dark figure steps into the stairwell right in front of me.

I stumble to a halt and yank my arms down to protect my private parts. Bracing myself for Alistair's mocking laughter and scathing remarks, I look up to meet his gaze.

Except it's not Alistair.

It's Draven.

The Shadow of Death stands frozen on the first step, his foot hovering halfway to the one below it. His eyes are wide and his mouth slightly open as he stares at me in utter shock. If I wasn't so exposed and vulnerable right now, I would've laughed at the almost comically stunned expression on his usually so composed features.

His gaze darts down my naked body once. Twice. Then, reality at last seems to snap back into him.

"What the *fuck* are you doing?" he demands with such force that I actually flinch.

He at last slams his foot down the final distance onto the step below. The step right above mine.

Instinctively, I back away as he advances on me. But since I wasn't looking where I was going, my foot slips on the edge of the step and I lose my balance. Throwing out my arms, I flail them desperately to try to get my balance back.

However, before I can fall backwards down the stairs, a hand shoots out and grabs my arm.

My stomach lurches as Draven yanks me up and then spins me around before shoving me back first against the smooth wall of the stairwell. A second later, his massive wings flare out and curve around us. They block out everything else and hide both of us from view.

Dragging air into my lungs, I try to catch my breath after the almost fall. But the breath is snatched right out of my lungs again as I tilt my head back to meet Draven's eyes.

Anger and disbelief and confusion pulse across his face as he stares me down.

"What the fuck do you think you're doing?" he demands yet again, sounding just as flustered as he looks. "If this is some misguided attempt to seduce me, you're—"

"Seduce you?" I interrupt, utterly flabbergasted as I stare back at him. "Why the hell would I try to seduce you?"

"To stop me from trying to get you kicked out of the Atonement Trials."

A laugh rips from my lungs, and I shake my head at him in disbelief. Then a sly smile blows across my lips as I hold his gaze. "Oh trust me, Shadow of Death, if I was really trying to seduce you, you would know."

Something almost like heat sears his cheeks for a second, and his gaze drops down my body again for the briefest of moments.

And in that moment, I suddenly remember that I'm still naked. Utterly and completely naked.

I yank my arms back up to cover my breasts and pussy while my cheeks flush a deep shade of red.

Draven snaps his gaze up to my face, and I swear the heat in his cheeks grows worse as well. Then he clears his throat, and that composed mask full of authority slams back down on his face.

"Well then, if it's not for my benefit, then what the fuck are you doing naked in the stairwell?" he demands.

I press my arms tighter against my body as embarrassment washes over me. "It's none of your business."

"Answer the question."

"Are you deaf or just stupid? I just said it's none of your business."

Lightning flashes in his eyes, and he closes the distance between us in one quick stride. His breath dances over my skin as he growls his next words in my face through clenched teeth.

"Answer the fucking question, Selena. Or I swear to God, I will—"

"Fine," I snap, interrupting his annoying threats.

Clenching my jaw, I glare up at him. He just stares me down in silence, daring me to disobey. I force out a frustrated breath.

"I was taking a bath, and someone stole my clothes to mess with me," I admit.

For a fraction of a second, something, some kind of emotion, flashes across his face. But it's there and gone again so quickly that I'm starting to doubt that I even saw it at all.

He flexes his right hand and grinds out, "Who?"

I briefly consider ratting Alistair out, but I decide against it. Because the infuriating fire-wielder is right. Stealing my clothes isn't against the rules, so he won't be punished for it. And if I tell Draven, and he makes a thing out of it, it will only prove to Alistair that he did manage to get under my skin and mess with my head.

So instead, I reply, "I don't know."

Draven forces out a long breath through his nose, as if he is barely managing to restrain himself. He clearly doesn't believe my lie, because he forces out the same word again between clenched teeth. "*Who?*"

"I don't know!" I shoot him a stare full of challenge and incredulity. "If I had seen who took my clothes, I wouldn't have let them just walk out with them, now would I?"

He draws his dark brows down in something between a frown and a scowl. Then he heaves a deep sigh and unclenches his hand. He doesn't admit that my logic makes sense, but he takes a step back.

I remain pressed against the wall, my arms covering as much of my body as I can.

For a few seconds, no one says anything.

Then Draven nods pointedly down at my body. "So your plan was... what? To simply walk back naked for everyone to see?"

He sounds frustrated and annoyed, which just makes me even more angry. He has no right to be annoyed. *I'm* the one who is naked, for Mabona's sake!

"What else was I supposed to do?" I snap back at him. "There was nothing left to cover myself with. And I couldn't just stand there in the bathing chamber all night."

He flexes his hand again and grinds his teeth. I glare up at him. He stares right back at me.

Tension crackles between us like lightning.

I don't even understand why he's so angry. It's not as if my predicament has any sort of effect on him.

At last, he forces out a long sharp breath and takes a step back. His face takes on an unreadable expression. I'm just about to ask what he's doing when he tucks his wings back in tight.

A small cloud of black smoke appears in the stairwell.

I blink in surprise as I stare at Draven.

He has shifted into his fully human form, so his wings are now gone. It's the first time that I have ever seen him without his wings. To my surprise, he looks just as powerful and imposing without them as he does with them.

Then my mind malfunctions as Draven suddenly grabs the hem of his shirt and yanks it over his head.

A small noise escapes from the back of my throat entirely without my permission as I stare at his perfectly sculpted and utterly naked chest. It's an absolute work of art. I get the completely insane urge to run my hands over his firm pectorals and trace my fingers along the sharp ridges of his abs down to that absolutely sinful V that disappears into his pants.

Reality hits me like a shovel to the face.

Jerking my head back up, I blink and then shake my head to clear it.

But the scene before me still doesn't make any sort of sense.

Draven, now only wearing a pair of black pants and a set of black bracers on his forearms, takes a step towards me.

Several different scenarios whirl through my head. Each one more unlikely and insane than the last.

Draven raises his hand and shoves something at my chest.

For a while, I can't make my body do anything. Because I don't understand one single thing about what is happening here right now.

Then my gaze drops down to what he is pressing against my chest.

His shirt. His soft black shirt.

"Put it on."

I snap my gaze back up to his face.

He narrows his eyes at me. "Do not make me repeat myself."

With a light shove, he pushes his shirt harder against my chest.

Utter disbelief swirls inside my skull, and I keep my stunned eyes on his as I reach up and take the offered shirt. He releases it. I just stand there and stare at him. He raises his eyebrows expectantly.

Yanking myself out of my stupor, I hurriedly shake out the large shirt and then pull it over my head. There are slots in the back where his wings are meant to be, but it still covers my nakedness completely.

My heart does a backflip in my chest.

The shirt is still warm. And it smells like him. Like night mist and embers.

Fire flickers through my veins, and my heart pounds against my ribs.

I raise my gaze and meet Draven's eyes again.

That unreadable mask is back on his face.

Grabbing the collar of my shirt, *his* shirt, he pulls me closer as he locks a hard stare on me. "This changes nothing."

Before I can even begin to think of a reply, he releases me with a soft shove, pushing me back against the wall. Then he spins on his heel and stalks down the stairs without another word.

I just stand there against the wall, staring after him.

His intoxicating scent wraps around me and fills my lungs with every breath, and I swear that I can still feel the heat of his body from the shirt that now covers mine.

My heart thumps hard behind my ribs.

My mind spins.

I went down to the bath to clear my head.

But now, my already churning mind is more confused than ever.

CHAPTER SIXTEEN

Brisk morning winds whirl across the palace grounds, bringing with them the scent of damp soil and fallen leaves. It rained last night, and a few puddles still linger in the spots where the grass has been burnt off in patches. Swallowing down a wave of anxiousness, I flick a quick glance at the thirty-nine people who are going to compete in this trial with me.

Isera is standing at the edge of the group, her face an impassive mask as she simply waits for Imar and the other shifters to show up. In the middle of the crowd is Lavendera. Her face is turned up towards the overcast sky, but her eyes are distant and vacant. As if she has retreated far into her mind and is not really here. Fenriel stands a short distance from her, and when he notices my gaze, he gives me a smile and a small wave. I smile back.

Then my gaze snags on three people closer to the front of the group. Alistair and his two remaining friends. Tommen, with his enhanced strength, who now has an even bigger grudge against me after I made him run away in terror like that in the last trial. And Jeb, a slimy guy with brown hair and the ability to create light. All three of them slide their gazes to me.

But before they can say or do anything, Imar strides out onto the grass.

"Line up," he shouts.

Clothes rustle and footsteps thud against the ground as we all quickly position ourselves in one long row, facing Imar.

Right as the last person falls into line, Empress Jessina and Emperor Bane stride across the grass. We all shift slightly, watching them as they close the distance to us.

"Have you forgotten how to greet your superiors?" Imar suddenly demands, his voice now laced with threats.

Annoyance slashes through me, but I still drop down on one knee and bow my head. The rest of the contestants do the same. Since the grass is still damp from the rain, it soaks the fabric of my pants. I grit my teeth as another pulse of irritation shoots through me.

The Icehearts stride across the damp grass, their garments rippling like liquid silver. They come to a halt in front of us, in the very middle, while eight more people approach.

While keeping my chin lowered, I glance towards them.

The eight clan leaders, Draven included, stride across the grass and then take up position on either side of their monarchs.

Silence falls over the palace grounds.

"Back when your Seelie Queen ruled," Empress Jessina begins, her voice laced with disdain, "before we brought justice to your court, you used to lure humans here and play cruel games with them." Raising an arm, she dramatically sweeps her hand out to motion at the massive hedge maze behind her. "You tormented them and made them run through this maze for sport."

My brows furrow. *We did?*

I can imagine the Unseelie Court maybe doing something like that, but did we really do it too? Unfortunately, there is no way to know for certain, because we weren't allowed to keep any of our history. When the shifters conquered us, they burned all of the history books. And since they killed everyone but the children, there was no one left to rewrite those books or even tell us about our history.

"And now," Jessina Iceheart continues. Her pale gray eyes are full of wicked glee as she sweeps her gaze over our kneeling bodies. "Now, *you* will run through this maze to atone for your cruelty."

Clenching my jaw, I squeeze my hand into a fist behind my back. *I* have never forced anyone to run through a hedge maze. I have nothing to atone for.

"In other words," Imar picks up, his tone filled with smug amusement. "Welcome to the second part of the Atonement Trials."

A ripple of anticipation pulses through parts of our group.

"You will be given a box with a glass egg inside," Imar continues. "Your mission is to transport it through the maze without breaking it. Only the people who arrive at the finish line with an unbroken egg will move on to the next trial."

On some unspoken signal, the eight clan leaders suddenly start moving towards the left side of our line. Reaching into pouches at their sides, they each pull out a small and very delicate-looking wooden box.

"These glass eggs are symbols of the precious mercy that we are offering you," Emperor Bane announces. There is an arrogant tilt to his chin as he gazes out at us. "*If* you are worthy enough to win it. So treat them accordingly."

Maybe not symbols of how precious their so-called mercy is, but symbols of how fragile it is, at least.

Once the first eight people have received their boxes, the clan leaders move on to the next section of our row. After reaching into their pouches for another box that they hand over, they move to the next one. Which is my section.

Based on the way the clan leaders are positioned, Draven will be the one to hand me my box. Which I'm sure is no coincidence. He has probably been looking forward to having me kneeling in front of him all morning. Though after what he did for me last night, I'm not entirely certain of where we stand anymore. Maybe we have finally reached some sort of truce.

I raise my head as Draven comes to a halt in front of me.

He is already holding one of those delicate wooden boxes in his hands, but he doesn't offer it to me since some of the other clan leaders aren't in position yet. I search his face for any clues as to what he's thinking.

His words from last night echo in my mind. *This changes nothing.*

Is that true? Has nothing changed?

There are no answers on his face. Only a completely blank mask as he holds my gaze.

The final clan leader moves into position.

As one, they all hold out the boxes towards the kneeling fae in front of them.

I keep my eyes on Draven as I reach up to take the offered box. His fingers brush against mine as he places it in my palms. That small touch sends a bolt of lightning through my veins.

His hands linger a second too long in mine as he holds my gaze. My heart stutters. Something has changed. It must have. Otherwise, why would he be looking at me like this? Is he really going to stop messing with me now? Am I actually going to be allowed to finish the Atonement Trials without his interference?

Right as a burst of hope pulses through my chest, Draven shatters those ridiculous thoughts with one devilish smile.

"Good luck," he whispers so softly that only I can hear it.

The words should have been encouraging, but they are ruined and twisted into a threat by the absolutely villainous smirk on his lips.

My heart jerks at the sight of it, and worry snakes through my spine.

But all I can do is to remain on my knees with the box in my hands while Draven continues to the next section.

Once everyone has received a box, the clan leaders return to their positions on either side of the Icehearts.

Imar steps forward. "Get through the maze with your glass egg intact. Other than that, there are no rules. Understood?"

We nod in acknowledgement.

"Begin," he shouts.

A jolt shoots through me, and I leap up from the ground. From the other end of our row, Isera summons a thick sheet of ice and encases her box in it. Several others who have some kind of elemental magic do the same. Since I have nothing with which to protect my box, I simply sprint towards the entrance to the maze.

The moment I start to move, a faint clinking sound comes from my box. I flick an alarmed glance down at it. But all around me people are dashing towards the opening between the hedges as well, so I can't stop without making someone crash right into me.

So instead, I cut sideways while I run.

Once I'm through the opening, I press my back against the tall hedge that makes up the left wall. And then I open my box.

The world around me disappears as I look down at the thin pillow inside where the egg is supposed to rest.

Shards of glass stare back at me.

My mind spins with disbelief.

He gave me a broken egg. Draven Ryat gave me an egg that is already shattered.

Son of a bitch.

Snapping the box shut again, I look up towards where the shifters are standing on the grass a short distance from the entrance. My gaze locks immediately on Draven. He flashes me a wicked smirk.

If I go back there and try to convince them that the egg was already broken, they probably won't believe me. It will only serve to get me eliminated.

I shoot a vicious glare at Draven, who just grins wider.

Asshole. Fucking asshole.

Shoving the box into my clothes, I whirl around and sprint after the others. Alright, so the egg is already broken. But I have the entire maze to figure out how to solve that.

I catch up to the rest of the group, but I remain at the back as we run between the tall hedges. No one has started attacking others yet. But I keep my distance anyway, just in case someone else figures out that it's possible to limit the number of people who make it through this trial by deliberately shattering their glass eggs.

Booming wings suddenly echo through the cool morning air. I cast a glance over my shoulder to see two massive silver dragons climbing into the sky. My heart lurches as they fly after us.

Cries of alarm rise from the contestants in front of me, and everyone picks up speed.

The Icehearts draw closer at an alarming rate.

Gasps and ragged breathing rip through the air as we all sprint as fast as we can with the two dragons chasing us.

A low rumbling comes from behind.

I cast a panicked glance over my shoulder. Jessina, the slightly smaller of the two dragons, opens her massive jaws. Her sharp teeth glint in the gray light, and a pale shimmering begins at the back of her throat.

My stomach drops.

Oh Goddess above, is she actually going to kill us?

A roaring, rushing, crackling sound echoes through the maze.

I throw myself sideways, crashing into the hedge to my left, right before ice flames explode through the air.

Cries of terror rip from several contestants.

Thuds ring out as everyone throws themselves sideways or flat down on the ground.

Ice streams past above and before us. The crackling ice flames are so cold that they rip the air from my lungs when they pass by me. Pressing myself hard against the hedge wall, I gasp in desperate breaths.

The clinking and crackling sound of hardening ice fills the air.

With my heart pounding in my chest, I stare at the hedge corridor in front of me. The way forward is now blocked by a massive ice wall. It's so tall that it reaches all the way up to the top of the hedges.

On the ground, the other contestants raise their heads to stare at it as well. None of us were hit by Jessina's flames. But we are all trapped on this side of the wall now.

Wings boom from above as the two silver dragons circle above us, eagerly waiting to see how we are going to solve this problem.

I stagger to my feet. The others do the same.

For a few seconds, no one moves.

Then Isera starts sprinting towards the wall. Without breaking stride, she channels her magic and pulls the ice of the wall towards her, creating steps from it. They disappear after she has stepped on them so that no one else can follow.

Above us, Jessina and Bane let out a furious roar. It's so loud, and so full of rage, that I flinch and have to press my palms to my ears.

Isera, however, pays them no mind. She just runs up the wall with confident steps.

Bane swoops down towards her. I hold my breath as he opens his mouth and roars at her again.

She reaches the top of the wall.

He snaps his lethal jaws shut right next to her. She doesn't even flinch. Instead, she summons what looks like a slide on the other side, because she simply leans back and glides out of view.

On the ground, the rest of us stare at the now empty space atop the wall. Bane roars again and then climbs back into the sky to circle it with Jessina. The bursts of wind from his wings are so powerful that some of the closest contestants stumble back a step.

For a few seconds, no one moves.

Then we all lurch into motion.

Lavendera sprints forward next. But to my surprise, she isn't aiming for the ice wall. My mouth drops open as she simply parts the hedge wall before her. With two quick steps, she's through. Then the thick vegetation snaps back into an impenetrable wall.

"Oh, that's so not fair," Fenriel mutters a little to my left. Then he hands his small wooden box to his hawk. "Alright, come on, Talon."

The hawk grabs the box in his talons, lets out a screeching call, and then flies towards the ice wall. Fenriel runs after him.

I give my head a firm shake to clear it and then start towards the wall as well.

Thankfully, the surface isn't smooth. Instead, the ice flames hardened the way they hit, in uneven sections, which has created handholds in the ice.

Even though my egg is already broken, I check to make sure that the box sits securely inside my clothes before I reach for the first handhold. Next to me, on both sides, other contestants are doing the same.

A hiss rips from my throat as I grab hold of the chunk of ice. The coldness sears into my skin. Almost like iron. But at least this ice won't block my powers and sap my energy.

Gritting my teeth against the coldness, I start pulling myself up the wall. I only make it a short distance before the woman next to me slips and falls back down. She hits the ground with a huff, and immediately checks her box. Since the distance wasn't that great, it appears as though the fall didn't cause her or the egg any damage.

However, before she can start back up the wall, a muscular guy with brown hair shoves her aside and takes her place.

Tommen. Alistair's friend and the guy who is determined to get revenge on me.

Shit.

I pick up the pace, trying to climb faster.

My hand slips on the next handhold. Sucking in a gasp, I grip the chunk of ice harder with my other hand and press myself against the wall. While cursing under my breath, I move my other hand back to the handhold, but this time much more carefully.

Unfortunately, being careful means going slowly, which gives Tommen a chance to catch up to me. I try to pretend that I don't see him as he climbs up next to me. Hopefully, he is too focused on his own progress to mess with me.

I cast a quick glance in his direction.

And I'm immediately met by a vicious grin and a pair of glowing red and brown eyes.

While channeling his magic to get enhanced strength, he reaches up to the spot right above my handholds.

And then slams his fist into the wall.

Ice shatters in an explosion of flying shards.

A scream rips from my lungs as my handholds break off from the wall and I tumble down towards the ground. Twisting my body, I barely manage to get into a position where I won't break my legs.

Pain pulses through my side and back as I crash down on the ground. Air explodes from my lungs.

I gasp in shock and pain.

For a few seconds, I just lie there on the damp grass and stare up at Tommen. He looks down at me and grins before starting up the wall again.

Fury crackles through my veins.

Pushing myself into a sitting position, I curl my fingers into the damp grass and channel my magic. Then I shove it towards the excited spark in Tommen's chest.

Just as I predicted, there is a spark there. And it's already massive after his little victory. I pour my magic into it.

Tommen starts climbing faster.

I increase his excitement even more, turning it from enthusiastic anticipation into a wild frenzy.

He climbs faster and faster, desperately eager to reach the top of the wall, until he's moving at breakneck speed.

And then it happens. In his frenzy, he misses the next handhold.

I sit there on the damp grass with a vicious smile on my lips and watch as he plummets to the ground.

He hits it hard. On his side.

Smug victory pulses through my chest like golden sparkles as I'm rewarded with not only the sound of shattering glass, but also breaking wood. His entire box is now ruined beyond repair.

I grin at his shocked expression as he stares down at the splinters and shards on the ground.

Revenge really is sweet.

CHAPTER SEVENTEEN

Air saws through my throat as I suck in deep breaths. The next hedge corridor opens up into some kind of wider space up ahead, and I'm sure that something awful awaits me there.

By my best estimate, I'm about halfway through the maze.

Apart from the ice wall, the other clan leaders have also given us some nasty surprises. Gremar Fireclaw used his magic to create a field of lava a few corridors back, which forced us to climb along the hedge walls to get through it.

I drag in deep breaths and try to calm my pounding heart as I finally reach the end of the corridor.

Just as I expected, a larger space opens up before me.

To my surprise, it's filled with people.

Frowning, I squint at the scene before me. Why are there so many people still here? I'm in the middle of the pack, so all of these people should already be far ahead of me. And why is it so dark?

I glance upwards.

Oh.

The area where the next hedge corridor should be located has been blocked off by a smooth rock wall rising straight up to the top of the hedges. No doubt courtesy of the leader of the Brown Dragon Clan, who has earth magic.

The rock wall then continues up over the entire space, making it impossible to climb over it. The only way forward is a narrow hole in the ground. And since only one person at a time can crawl through what is likely a tunnel that runs the entire length of the next corridor, it has created a bottleneck.

Behind me, leaves rustle.

I glance over my shoulder to find a woman trying to climb up the hedge wall behind me. It's no doubt an effort to make it to the top of that wall, which would then allow her to run across the top of the stone roof instead. But three quarters of the way up, the leader of the Brown Dragon Clan, in his dragon form, suddenly sticks his head over the edge of the roof and snaps his jaws at her. She shrieks and falls back down to the ground.

With a sigh, I turn back to the hole in the ground. He must be guarding the stone roof to prevent anyone from getting past that way. Which means that the only way forward is through that tunnel.

Somewhere higher above the rock wall, other dragons roar impatiently.

I drift closer to the tunnel entrance.

A crowd is already gathered there. Thankfully, Alistair is nowhere to be seen. He has been at the front of the group this whole time, along with Isera, so he must already be through it.

Tension crackles through the air, and irritated voices follow it. It should be a simple case of first come first served, but instead, people are fighting over who gets to crawl through first. I study them for a few minutes, trying to figure out what to do, before deciding to simply wait for my turn.

"Why?" a voice suddenly asks from beside me.

I start in surprise and whirl towards the sound of the voice. To my utter shock, I find Isera standing there. She has been at the very front this whole time. And she is strong enough to force people to let her use the tunnel first, if she wants to. There is absolutely no reason for her to still be here.

Because I'm so stunned to see her, I only manage to blink at her in surprise instead of actually replying.

She doesn't seem bothered by it. As usual, her face is a mask of calm composure. She pushes her long black hair back behind her shoulder as she comes to a halt next to me. But her silver and blue eyes remain firmly on the tunnel entrance ahead of us.

"Why what?" I ask at last, when I've finally managed to gather my wits.

She casts a brief glance at me from the corner of her eye. "Why don't you use your magic against everyone else?"

"Because I'm not Alistair."

"I heard you made Tommen fall from the ice wall."

"That was for revenge. He made me fall first." I motion at the people around us. "These people haven't done anything to me."

"No, but you still need to win." She twists her head, her eyes serious as they lock on mine. "You *could* make them claustrophobic enough that they won't dare to go through the tunnel, couldn't you?"

I hesitate before admitting, "Yes."

She just continues holding my gaze. There is something dangerously intense about her eyes. She usually doesn't say much, or bother to interact with people, but when she does speak, people listen. She has a sort of effortless power about her.

And because of that, I find myself starting to ramble.

"Yes, I could. But I won't." Pain squeezes my heart as I add, "People already distrust me enough as it is. This would only make them hate me and fear me more."

"So?" Isera arches a dark brow at me. "Let them."

I frown in confusion. "What do you mean?"

"If people fear you, use it as a shield. People will always seek to tear you down, because of one thing or another. Be it for how you look or how you behave or who your family is or what magic you have. There will always be people who will use any weakness against you so that they can feel better about their own pitiful lives."

In all our time here, I have never heard Isera speak this many sentences consecutively, to the same person. And not only that, she's being… comforting.

"The trick is to use your own weakness before they can." She holds my gaze. "If you flaunt your insecurities, they can never be used to hurt you."

Her words strike something deep in my heart, and I find myself rocking back slightly on my heels from the impact of it. Use my fears, my insecurities, so that no one else can use them against me. It's a terrifying thought. A *brilliant* thought.

But why in the world would Isera ever share that with me?

Studying her face, I furrow my brows in genuine confusion. "Why are you helping me?"

She breaks eye contact and instead goes back to watching the scene before us. She says nothing.

Now feeling even more confused, I stare at the side of her face. Then I flick a glance at the area before us where people are one by one crawling into the narrow tunnel.

Isera swallows. And for the first time ever, a flicker of dread pulses across her face.

Realization crashes over me. "You're claustrophobic, aren't you?"

She works her jaw and swallows again, but she doesn't answer. With her eyes still fixed on the hole in the ground, she instead says, "I know that you can increase people's fear. Is blocking out someone's fear also within your capabilities?"

"Yes."

Silence falls over us again. Isera's chest rises and falls as she draws in what looks like highly controlled breaths.

"I would owe you a favor," she says at last.

A small smile threatens to spill across my lips. She's too proud to ask the actual question. But I can still hear it clearly in the faint hint of desperation that laces her voice. Asking me this, even without actually asking, has been incredibly difficult for her. But she still did it.

"Alright," I reply.

She snaps her gaze to me, blinking in shock. Apparently, she was certain that I was going to refuse.

After searching my face for a few seconds, she gives me a slow nod. I nod back.

Ice surges up from the ground. I start in surprise as Isera raises a massive block of ice and uses it to push everyone to the side so that the area in front of the hole is clear.

A few curses rise from some of the others.

"Step aside," Isera growls.

Those who had been about to stalk back to the tunnel pause. After one look at Isera's face, they take a step back and motion for her to go first. She, in turn, motions for me to crawl into the tunnel first.

"If I'm behind you, I can make sure that no one tries to mess with you while you crawl through," she explains while we walk closer to the hole.

I raise an eyebrow at her. "And you trust me not to break my promise halfway through the tunnel and simply crawl away without you?"

"Yes."

Her response is so immediate, and so confident, that it stuns me. No one has ever trusted me, with anything, before.

It takes a moment to compose myself after that, but once I'm ready, I drop down to my knees in front of the hole. Isera does the same behind me.

"I'll start blocking it now," I tell her.

She nods.

Channeling my magic, I push towards the bone white spark of

fear in her chest. It's massive, and we're not even in the tunnel yet. I pour my magic into it, decreasing it into the tiniest of drops. Then I start into the tunnel.

The walls of packed dirt are so close that my shoulders almost brush against them when I move. And I have to crawl on my hands and knees, and keep my head lowered, to avoid hitting my head on the ceiling of the tunnel.

A scraping sound comes from behind me as Isera crawls in after me.

The moment she's inside the tunnel, that spark of fear in her chest explodes into a wildfire.

It's so intense, so all-consuming, that I actually gasp from the force of it.

Isera lets out a small noise, almost like a whimper, at the back of her throat.

I throw all the magic I have into smothering that flame of fear. Once it's back to the tiniest of drops, I hear Isera release a deep breath behind me.

We start into the tunnel.

It took me almost a hundred years to learn how to completely separate other people's feelings from my own. If I had tried to do this when I was thirty, I would have drowned underneath the intensity of Isera's fear. I would have felt her claustrophobia as acutely as she herself felt it. But because I've had over one and a half century to practice, I can now fully block out other people's emotions while still feeling them clearly enough that I can manipulate them.

Only the soft scraping sounds of our knees and hands break the silence as Isera and I make our way through the tunnel. But as we crawl, her words keep echoing in my skull.

Let them. If people fear you, use it as a shield.

Maybe she's right. Maybe it's time to start being a little ruthless. What does it matter if the other contestants fear me or despise me or outright hate me? I will be leaving this city as soon as I win the trials anyway.

Glass clinks faintly from the box I still keep inside my clothes.

An idea flashes through my mind. A ruthless and wicked idea.

I know how to win this trial.

The glass egg in the box I received might be broken, but no one ever said that I needed to present the same box as the one I received.

So it doesn't matter that my box is useless.

I'll just steal someone else's.

CHAPTER EIGHTEEN

Panic whirls inside my chest as I dash towards the end of the maze. Stealing someone else's box wasn't nearly as easy as I had expected it to be. I didn't want to steal Isera's since I actually like her, and because we're sort of allies now, so after we got out of the tunnel, I just let her run ahead. And I haven't been able to get close enough to anyone else to swap their box for mine.

My pulse thrums in my ears as I sprint after the small group of contestants ahead of me. Desperation slashes through my soul. This can't be it. I can't get this close to making it through, and then lose just because Draven rigged the game from the beginning! There must be something I can do. It can't end like this.

The group ahead of me reaches the end of the maze.

And then stops short.

Hope explodes inside my chest.

Pushing myself, I sprint the final distance to the end of the hedge corridor. Three people, two women and one man, are standing there, staring at the scene before them. I don't remember the name of the two women, but the guy is Alistair's friend Jeb. The slimy guy with light magic.

"Mabona's fucking tits," the woman with curly black hair curses.

I drag in a deep breath and then raise my gaze to look at what caused her reaction.

In front of us, the palace grounds open up once more, finally allowing us to move unhindered. However, the trial doesn't end once we reach the flat stretch of grass as we had thought. Instead, someone, probably the leader of the Brown Dragon Clan, has raised a narrow bridge made of stone. It starts right before our feet and then curves upwards before finally ending at a window on the third floor of the castle.

"Well, best get this over with," she continues, and takes off up the path.

The other woman starts after her.

A deafening roar splits the air.

The moment that the dark-haired woman steps onto the bridge, a massive black dragon appears in a cloud of smoke from up by the window.

My heart jerks. Draven must have been standing inside the room that the window leads to, just waiting for another contestant to step onto the final obstacle.

Wings boom through the air as Draven in his dragon form climbs higher into the sky. Bursts of air slam down towards the ground, making the grass shudder beneath the strokes of his powerful wings. Then dark storm clouds start to gather.

I stare, transfixed, as Draven channels his clan's signature magic and summons a storm around the narrow bridge. Winds rip through the palace grounds, making the two women on the bridge hunker down. Black clouds spread through the air, casting the whole area in darkness. And then the rain starts.

Jeb sucks in a sharp breath. Reaching to the side of his belt, he unfastens the small wooden box that he had secured there. Very carefully, he opens the lid and checks inside.

My heart pounds and my mind churns as I catch a glimpse of a completely undamaged glass egg inside.

With a start, Jeb suddenly realizes that he's not alone. Snapping the box shut again, he secures it at his waist once more while shooting me a threatening stare.

"Stay at least ten steps behind me," he warns. "Unless you want me to push you off."

A bolt of lightning cleaves the air and cracks into the ground a short distance in front of Jeb. He jumps in surprise. Whipping around, he stares at the huge black dragon, whose attention is now suddenly focused on us.

Before I can reply to Jeb's threat, he hurries forward and steps up onto the narrow bridge. I watch him, my eyes lingering on the small box at his waist while a plan forms in my mind.

It's going to be tricky, and delicate, and very last second. But if I can pull it off, I will make it through this trial.

After shifting my own box into a position that is easier to reach, I draw in a bracing breath and then step up onto the narrow stone bridge as well. It's barely wide enough for one person to stand with both feet side by side. My stomach flips, even though I have barely left the ground yet. I take a step forward.

I half expect the storm to get worse when I step onto the bridge, but to my surprise, it doesn't. Though that's probably just because Draven knows that he doesn't need to make me fall, since he has already broken my glass egg.

Up ahead, the two women have reached the halfway point of the bridge. Both of them are now crawling on their hands and knees to avoid getting blown away by the howling winds. The halfway point marks the place where the drop goes from being painful to being lethal. If we fall during the first half, it will hurt. And it will break any glass egg that a person is carrying. But if we fall during the second half of the bridge, it might kill us.

Anxiousness twists inside me. I need to get this done before we reach the second half.

My instincts are screaming at me to move slowly, but I need to close the distance between me and Jeb, so I walk as quickly as I can. Keeping my eyes fixed on Jeb's back, I avoid looking down while I also spread my arms wide for better balance.

Blood pounds in my ears as I hurry forward and hope that it will be enough.

Lightning strikes up ahead.

One of the girls lets out a shriek.

I flick a quick glance towards them and find that they have almost reached the open window now. My heart slams against my ribs. I can't make my move too close to the ground. But I also can't wait too long in case it doesn't work as quickly as I want it to.

Winds snatch at my clothes and hair as I move closer to Jeb. The cold rain stings my cheeks and makes the stones beneath my feet slippery.

A gasp rips from my lungs as a burst of wind rips across the bridge.

But that was exactly what I had been waiting for.

Ahead of me, Jeb sucks in a sharp breath as well and sways to the side. Flailing his arms, he tries to get his balance back.

I immediately channel my magic and shove at the bone white spark of fear in his chest. Just as I had hoped, I find one already burning there from his almost fall. I feed it with my magic.

Jeb sways again.

Rain whips against my face as the winds keep churning around us. Loose strands that have escaped my hair tie blow into my face and stick to my wet skin, but I don't dare to push them away. I can only focus on two things right now. Not falling off the bridge. And making Jeb fall off the bridge.

I keep feeding his fear. But not too much. Not so much that he will curl into a ball and refuse to move. Just enough to make his moves frantic and clumsy.

Draven swoops down over us and lets out a roar.

It startles Jeb enough that he jerks back.

I push with my magic.

His foot slips.

And he falls off the bridge.

Extinguishing my magic, I throw myself the final distance forward and grab his wrist right before he can plummet to the ground. I drop down so that I'm straddling the narrow bridge, my thighs on either side of it, while I grip the edge with my free hand.

Pain pulses through my shoulder, and I let out a cry, as Jeb's body comes to an abrupt halt with a yank that tears at my arm. The force of his entire body weight pulling downwards is almost too much for me to handle, and I clench my jaw against the strain.

"Grab the side of the bridge," I grind out between gritted teeth.

My hair whips through the air as winds howl around us.

Jeb throws his other hand up, desperately reaching for the edge. My fingers are slick with rain, and my grip on his wrist is starting to slip. The fall won't kill him, but it will break his glass egg. And then my plan will be ruined. I try to heave him a little higher upwards.

"Hurry," I snap.

His hand finally finds the wet stones.

I let out a gasp of relief as half of his body weight is transferred to his other arm. With my hand still around his wrist, I lean sideways and begin pulling the rest of his body up towards the bridge.

He hauls himself up with his other arm too, which decreases the strain on my muscles. Once I no longer need to hold on with my free hand, I press my thighs hard against the sides of the narrow bridge to keep myself in place and instead reach down to grab his belt.

With our combined strength, we manage to get him up and over the edge of the bridge. I release his wrist, and then quickly reach into my pocket.

Jeb gasps air into his lungs as he lies there on his side on the wet stones. My fingers skim over his belt on the way back. Then I slip my hand into my clothes again before bracing my palms on the wet stone bridge and pushing to my feet.

I blink and cast a confused glance around me. The storm has stopped. Frowning, I sweep my gaze over the castle before us. When did the storm stop?

Draven is nowhere to be seen.

But before I can dwell on that any longer, Jeb struggles to his feet in front of me. He immediately reaches towards his side. Relief washes over his face when he finds a small wooden box still attached to his belt. Then he raises his gaze to me and narrows his eyes.

"Why?" he asks.

I hold his suspicious stare with calm eyes. "Because I want a truce."

Understanding blows across his features. After casting a quick glance at the ground that I saved him from plummeting down to, he meets my eyes again and gives me a slow nod. "I'll talk to Alistair."

I nod back.

The scent of wet stones and fallen leaves envelop us as we carefully make our way across the bridge and towards the window. Jeb climbs in first. I follow him.

Inside, most of the contestants are already waiting. Some of them are seated against the walls, looking heartbroken. Open boxes with cracked or shattered glass eggs rest next to them. Others are standing on the opposite side of the room with satisfied expressions on their faces. Isera, Alistair, Fenriel, and Lavendera are among them.

When I enter the room, Tommen looks up from where he is sitting on the floor. His egg, along with the entire box, is broken from when I made him fall from the ice wall, and the splinters and shards lay scattered next to his feet. As soon as he sees me, he clenches his fist in anger.

I ignore him and instead approach the dragon shifters who are also waiting in the room.

Empress Jessina and Emperor Bane are seated on a pair of white wooden chairs in the middle of the room. The other clan leaders are most likely still out somewhere over the hedge maze, creating or maintaining nasty obstacles for the contestants who still remain inside. Imar stands a short distance from the open window. As does Draven. He is leaning his hip against the windowsill, and his golden eyes are fixed on me as I walk up to Imar.

I swear I can feel the smirk lurking on Draven's lips when I take out my small wooden box. Next to me, Jeb does the same.

"You made it through the maze," Imar says. "Congratulations." A sharp glint creeps into his eyes. "Now, let's see if you have treated the symbols of our mercy with the care they deserve."

Snapping his fingers, he points at me and raises an eyebrow expectantly.

My heart thumps in my chest as I lift my box and open it.

"A spotless and entirely unbroken egg," Imar announces as he looks down into my box. "Well done. Congrats on making it through the second trial."

Draven stumbles by the window. Straightening, he tries to quickly compose himself, but his eyes are wide with shock as he stares at me. I suppress the urge to smirk at him.

Imar snaps his fingers at Jeb, who also opens his box.

"A completely shattered egg," Imar declares, and shakes his

head at Jeb. "Careless. Go and join the other ungrateful losers. I want you out of this castle before first light tomorrow."

I'm not even sure if Jeb hears that second part, because he is standing completely frozen, staring down at the shattered remains of his glass egg. *My* glass egg. The one that I swapped right after pulling him up onto the bridge. He really should have been paying more attention. Because the real threat was never the fall from the bridge. It was me.

At last, Jeb seems to realize what must have happened. With his mouth still open in shock, he slowly turns towards me. And when he meets my gaze, his expression darkens like the veil of death.

CHAPTER NINETEEN

My muscles tremble with exhaustion as I stagger through the castle and back towards the south wing. But nothing can dim the sparkling victory in my heart. Not even the dark looks that Tommen and Jeb shot me when I strode out of the room with the rest of the winning contestants.

Because I did it.

Despite Draven's attempt to sabotage me, I made it through the second trial. I'm halfway through the competition now. Only two more trials to go. Two trials that will take our group from twenty-four people to three. And by Mabona, I am going to be one of those three.

Afternoon sunlight streams in through the windows along the corridor, casting pale light over the white stone walls. Despite the brightness, the torches on the wall are burning as well. A reminder of who controls this palace now. As if we would ever forget.

A hand shoots out from the doorway on my right, and strong fingers wrap around my upper arm.

My stomach lurches as I'm yanked through the door.

The door shuts behind me while I stumble to a halt and

straighten on the pale stone floor. There are a few bookcases along the walls, though they're empty, and a round table in the middle of the room. The chairs around it are covered with a thin layer of dust. Evidence that this meeting room has not been used for what is probably centuries.

Other than those pieces of furniture, the room is empty.

Well, apart from the glowering dragon commander who glares at me from only two steps away.

"Mabona's tits," I huff, shooting him an exasperated stare. "You really do need to get yourself a hobby. How many times have you ambushed me in deserted corridors by now?" I shake my head at him. "Don't answer that. I already know. And given that the answer is *a lot*, one might start to think that you're obsessed with me."

Moving closer to the door, I reach for the handle so that I can open it and slip away before he starts doing whatever it is that he plans on doing.

I only manage to get the door open half a foot before Draven slams his palm against it and shoves it shut with a bang. Keeping his hand firmly on the door, he twists and uses his superior size to force me to twist with him until my back is against the door. His eyes sear into mine as he fixes me with a commanding stare.

"How did you manage to present an undamaged egg?" he demands. His voice is laced with frustration, and he curls his fingers against the smooth wood of the door while he clenches his jaw. "You are not able to mend glass. So how did you do it?"

Looking up at him, I let a mask of fake innocence settle on my features. "I just kept it safe through the whole maze." The smile on my lips twists into a sly smirk. "Why? Are you saying that there was a reason why I would need to mend it?"

He squeezes his hand into a fist. A muscle flickers in his jaw as he stares me down in angry silence.

I blow out a frustrated breath and then drop all pretense. It's enough. I've had enough. I'm barely making it through the trials without his interference, and I can't take much more of this. And he's being petty and vindictive for absolutely no reason.

Holding his gaze, I shake my head while true exhaustion washes over me. "Can you stop sabotaging me now? Please. This is starting to get ridiculous. All of this just because of one spilled drink."

"You threw it."

"Fine," I snap, my patience running out. "I threw it." Frustration courses through me like lightning as I glare up at him. "It's still ridiculous. I threw one drink at you because I panicked, and you make it your mission in life to ruin my chances of winning the trials. To ruin my whole damn *life*! It's absurd and petty and ridiculous—"

"It's not just about the drink!"

The words rip out of him with such force that I actually jerk back in surprise. Blinking, I stare at him.

Finally taking his hand off the door, he rakes both hands through his hair and forces out a long breath. Anger and frustration and impatience flash across his face.

"Then what's it about?" I ask, frowning at him.

His gaze snaps back to me, and it's so full of fury that it steals the breath from my lungs. Dropping his hands from his hair, he flexes them at his sides. Anger rolls off his broad shoulders like waves of black smoke. His gaze sears through me, burning my very soul, as he holds my stare.

"If it were up to me, I wouldn't allow these Atonement Trials to even exist in the first place," he growls. "None of you should be allowed to win this competition."

The words are a stab right through my heart. Even though I know that he hates me, and even though I hate him too for being the leader of the enemy army, it still hurts beyond belief to hear that he doesn't think that any of us deserve a chance to win our freedom. That we don't deserve even a chance at a better life.

Anger explodes through me, burning away any scraps of

caution, and I raise my hands and give him a hard shove right in the chest. It surprises him enough that he actually stumbles a step back.

"Get off your fucking high horse," I snap at him. My voice is coming out too high and too strained, but I don't care. "You're no better than us."

He straightens from the shove and narrows his eyes at me.

But now that I've started speaking, I can't seem to stop. Decades of pent-up frustration and anger and resentment pour out of me like a flood.

"You've kept us on our knees at your fucking feet for *millennia*!" I scream at him. "My great grandparents weren't even born when you killed the last of the dragon riders. And the last dragon shifter to be enslaved by fae died centuries ago." Pain tears through my soul as I hold his gaze and stab a hand against my chest. "Why am *I* being punished for a crime that I didn't even commit?"

For one single second, it almost looks as if he understands. Almost looks as if sympathy flashes across his face. But then that arrogant expression of ruthless authority is back on his face again.

"You know nothing of what it's like to be enslaved," he says, his voice low and dark.

"Neither do you! For Mabona's sake, you weren't even born when your ancestors killed their riders."

His eyes flash. "My ancestors had no riders."

A laugh rips from my chest at his fucking ridiculous pride and pettiness. "Oh that's right." I flick a mocking look up and down his body. "Because you're from the elusive Black Dragon Clan that ruled the Western Sea alone while everyone else bickered on the mainland." A vicious smile slides across my lips. "Until you sold out your own people for power."

Dead silence falls over the room.

Draven stares at me, and I swear that I can almost see darkness gathering around him.

He takes a step forward.

And I suddenly come to the horrible realization that I might have gone too far. That I have pushed him too far. Because of those few times when I made him laugh at my snarky comments, and because he showed me kindness when Alistair stole my clothes, I've started to drop my guard around him. I haven't been holding back or choosing my words carefully. But maybe I should have. Because he is still the Shadow of Death. One of the most powerful and dangerous people on this entire continent.

Draven lets out a dark laugh as he moves closer, forcing me to press myself against the door. He braces both palms against the smooth wood, caging me in. I draw in a deep breath as I look up to meet his eyes.

None of the fiery rage remains. Instead, his eyes are now only filled with cold calculation.

"That's right. I sold out my own people, my own friends, for power." A cruel smile spreads across his lips. "So do you really think that being snarky and disrespectful to me is your best move here, little rebel?"

I know that I should probably say 'no, sir' or something equally submissive.

But when it all comes down to it, I just can't bring myself to do it. Draven is the first person that I have been myself around. Most of my life, I have only ever said the things that I know people want to hear. Draven is the first person that I have spoken to exactly the way I wanted to. The one person who I haven't carefully chosen my words around. It has been a breath of freedom in an otherwise suffocating life. And I don't want to give that up.

So instead of saying 'no, sir', which is what he wants to hear, I find myself saying, "You're warning me not to be snarky and disrespectful? *Now*? Today? I regret to inform you, oh Shadow of Death, but I think that ship has already sailed."

He opens his mouth, but no sound makes it out. Blinking, he stares at me in stunned silence while his hands drop away from the door.

"Right," I say, and clear my throat. Raising my hand, I give his cheek a couple of brisk pats. "Good talk."

Draven stares at me, his mouth still slightly open, as if he can't believe what I just did.

Two more seconds pass.

Then he jerks back, and deep shock floods his features as he stares at me wide-eyed.

And while he is busy dealing with the shock that is apparently pulsing through his entire body, I yank open the door and slip away.

CHAPTER TWENTY

I practically skip through the rest of the hallways after that. Goddess above, if I had known that saying what I actually think was this much fun, I would have started doing it years ago. A laugh bubbles in my chest. Mabona's tits, that look on his face was priceless.

But as I make my way back to my room, I still cast glances over my shoulder every once in a while to make sure that he isn't coming to take revenge for my insolence.

Thankfully, I manage to reach my corridor without the Shadow of Death claiming my soul.

The sound of voices fills the pale stone hallway as I round the final corner. I draw up short as I find the corridor before me packed with people. Some of them look to just be chatting with each other before they go back to their rooms. But some look like they're saying goodbye to the others who lost this last trial.

I watch them curiously as I start walking towards my room again.

My heart clenches painfully as I watch some of them hug and pat each other on the shoulder.

When we first got here, there were only a few people who

were already friends. Alistair and his posse, mainly. But, as far as I know, the people hugging each other and saying goodbye now didn't know each other from before.

That tight iron fist around my heart squeezes harder.

Other people have… made friends.

Even here, in a competition that pits us all against one another, other people have managed to make friends. And I can't even make friends during a normal day back in the city.

Am I really that untrustworthy?

"You," a harsh voice suddenly bellows. "You cheated!"

I sigh and admit in my mind that, yes, maybe I really am that untrustworthy.

Jeb elbows his way through a group to my left and stalks up to me. His cheeks are stained red with anger or indignation or both, and his brown hair is a complete mess. As if he has continuously raked his fingers through it in frustration.

Quickening my step, I try to reach my room before he can corner me. I've had enough confrontation for one day, thank you very much.

Unfortunately, I'm still three steps away from my door when Jeb reaches me. He throws out an arm, blocking my path, and forces me to stop walking. I draw in a breath that does absolutely nothing to calm the annoyance and frustration now swirling in my soul. I'm exhausted and sore and so freaking fed up with people. I just want to lie down on my bed and rest for a moment.

Jeb, however, has other plans.

"You," he sneers, and stabs his index finger against my chest. "You cheated."

I narrowly manage to stop myself from replying, *yes, I heard you the first time.* Instead, I draw in another calming breath and ask, "How could I possibly have cheated? I took the same route as everyone else through the maze."

"That's not what I'm talking about. You stole my egg!"

"I saved you from falling."

"Which is when you stole my egg."

"When would I possibly have had time for that? I grabbed you and pulled you up." Raising my eyebrows, I shoot him a pointed look. "And besides, if it hadn't been for me, you would have fallen and shattered your egg anyway."

He scowls and works his mouth a couple of times. His cheeks are now flushed a red so bright that they could most likely have seen it all the way from the Unseelie Court.

"You were probably the one who made me fall in the first place," he accuses with an indignant huff. "And then after you pulled me up, you used your mumbo-jumbo magic on me to make me hand over my egg without me even realizing it."

I suppress a scoff. By Mabona, these ridiculous scenarios that they dream up about what I can do with my magic is getting more and more absurd every day.

"Did you just roll your fucking eyes at me?" Jeb demands, looking both stunned and furious.

I wince inwardly. Aw crap. Did I make that face out loud?

"You've become way too bold ever since you entered this competition," he says, and stabs his finger against my chest again. "You need to remember your place."

"My place is here. In the competition." I hold his gaze with hard eyes. "While you have been ordered to leave the premises by first light. So perhaps you are not the right person to be lecturing someone about learning one's place."

A gasp rips through the corridor. It startles me enough that I nearly jump. I had almost forgotten that there were other people here too.

The realization makes a wave of cold dread crash over me. Oh Goddess, what are they going to think of me now? I have never been this rude, this cruel, to anyone in our city before. And now, all of these people are going to think that I'm a bitch who rubs it in people's faces that I won and they lost.

Panic snakes around my heart, squeezing hard.

Oh crap, I shouldn't have said that.

Before Jeb can even think of a reply, I duck under his arm and hurry the final three steps to my door.

"Hey!" he calls after me. "Don't you fucking dare—"

I slam the door shut, cutting off his threat.

Groaning, I bury my face in my hands. Goddess above, I shouldn't have said that. My interaction with Draven made me feel bold and indestructible. But I can't go around acting like that with everyone else too. They will only hate me even more.

With a sigh, I slide my hands up and rake them through my hair.

Exhaustion slams into me like a tidal wave.

"Fuck," I mumble under my breath.

Dropping my arms back down by my sides, I walk over to the closet and the mirror instead. With muscles that still tremble from an entire day of getting through a massive hedge maze, I slowly start stripping out of my clothes so that I can check myself for injuries.

There is a large bruise covering my hip and side from where I hit the ground when I fell from the ice wall. My forearms are covered with tiny cuts from when I had to climb along the hedge to evade the lava. And the muscles in my shoulder ache from when I caught Jeb as he fell.

The more garments I take off, the more cuts and bruises I discover.

It's not as bad as my injuries after the first trial, but I still can't deny that the competition is becoming more and more intense.

Uncertainty swirls inside my soul as I study myself in the mirror.

Deep down, I know that I don't have the right kind of magic to win these trials. Elemental magic, or at least some kind of physical magic, will always be better suited for things like this. And there are so many strong people competing against me.

Staggering backwards, I slide down to the floor by the bed,

resting my back against the wooden bedframe. It's cool against my flushed skin, and sooths some of the bruises. I draw my knees up and brace my forearms on them as I stare at myself in the mirror. My exhausted face stares back at me.

Maybe Isera was right about more than one thing back in that maze today. I could have used my magic to make everyone else too claustrophobic to get through the tunnel. In fact, I can do lots of things like that. Maybe it's time to take her advice and start playing more offense. To start actually trying to make other people lose, so that I will have a better shot at winning.

Nausea twists my stomach at the thought.

I can't do something like that. I can't be that cruel. That selfish. We all just want to be able to leave this shitty life behind and start fresh somewhere else. And who am I to take that away from them?

Besides, what would people say about me if I win like that? They would gossip about how I only won because I crippled everyone else. That I didn't deserve it. That they were always right about me. That I can't be trusted.

A small voice inside me whispers a sentence that I barely dare to hear.

Does it matter?

Does it matter if people gossip and talk and curse my name? Does it matter that they hate me? I will have won the Atonement Trials and will be given permission to leave the Seelie Court. I can travel anywhere. I can make a real difference for the fae resistance. So what does it matter if people I barely know despise me?

Cursing under my breath, I drop my head and rest my forehead on my arms while I heave a deep sigh.

Why must I care so much about what other people think of me?

I want to win. Desperately. But I also want people to like me. And that has held me back in these trials.

The magic I've used on people up until now hasn't even scratched the surface of what I can really do. But if I use my powers in full, I know that people will hate me for it. And that makes me want to throw up.

I want to be accepted. It's half of the reason why I signed up for this bloody competition in the first place. But I also want to win.

It's a circular problem that I can't solve without sacrificing something.

I want to win so that I will be accepted. But to win, I need to do things that will make people hate me. So if I win, people will accept me. But they will also hate me.

Another groan escapes my chest and I thump my head against my forearms.

I don't know what to do.

All I know is that I need to make a decision.

Fast.

CHAPTER TWENTY-ONE

I jerk awake as a loud bang echoes through my room. Sitting bolt upright, I throw myself out of bed and twist the faelights to turn them on right as another crash sounds.

Light floods my room.

For one single second, I can't understand what it is that I'm looking at.

There is a giant hole in the middle of my wooden door. As if someone has punched through it. Or kicked through it.

Then a boot crashes through the door, and reality slams back into me.

Wooden splinters fly through the air as the entire middle part of the door shatters.

Throwing myself across the room, I dive towards the knife on my dresser right as two men burst through the hole in the door.

Tommen flashes me a vicious smile as he and Jeb straighten inside my room. "Payback time, bitch."

I don't even have time to scream for help before they launch themselves at me.

Panic crackles through my veins.

Leaping back, I slash my knife in front of me. It forces them to stop their attack long enough for me to land. My back hits the dresser with a thud, making the wood rattle. I cast a panicked glance around the room, trying to figure out how to escape. But I barely manage to scan half of the room before Tommen lunges at me again.

His fist speeds towards my face. I duck it and slash at his chest. A cry of pain rips from his throat as my knife grazes part of his chest, drawing a thin line of blood.

Fury burns in his eyes.

I jump back as he aims another punch at my head. But my back slams into something else.

Arms reach around me from behind, trying to trap me. Jeb's harsh breath hits the back of my neck. With panic blaring inside my skull, I stomp my heel down towards his foot. He's wearing boots, and I'm barefoot, but it manages to cause enough pain for him to lose his grip on me. I dive away right before Tommen can slam his fist into my stomach.

Rolling across the floor, I twist around and swipe at their hamstrings.

Jeb curses as my knife nicks the side of his thigh.

I yank my blade back, aiming another strike.

Pain shoots up my arm as Tommen's boot connects with my wrist.

The knife flies from my grip. It hits the wall to my left and bounces down on the floor in a clattering of metal. I gasp as I jerk back, narrowly avoiding a strike to my ribs.

Across the room, Jeb snatches up my knife while Tommen throws himself at me. I leap sideways, rolling over my bed. The rumpled sheets tangle around my ankles, and I have to kick them away when I hit the floor.

Metal glints.

On instinct, I yank up an arm to block it.

Pain explodes through my forearm as the knife cuts a deep slash right across it.

I cry out in shock and pain, but I don't even have time to block out those emotions, because Tommen aims a kick at me from the other side. Throwing myself flat on the ground, I roll underneath the bed in an attempt to find temporary shelter. But hands wrap around my ankles.

A gasp rips from my lungs as I'm yanked out from underneath the bed.

I'm only wearing that delicate silk nightgown and the sheer white robe that goes with it, so more pain pulses through me as my bare skin scrapes against the floor.

The moment one of the hands disappear from my ankle, I blindly kick my leg upwards. A grunt of pain echoes into the pale room as I hit something soft.

But my victory is short-lived as a boot slams into the side of my ribs.

I hear the crack before I feel it.

Agony slashes through my whole chest as several of my ribs shatter from the magic-enhanced kick. Rolling over on my side, I try to crawl away. Another boot takes me in the side of the head.

Lights flash before my eyes as my head snaps to the side.

I think I cry out in pain, but it's difficult to hear over the ringing in my ears.

Black spots dance before my vision, and the room sways around me. I kick out with my leg again.

Another burst of pain sears through me, so intense that it blinds me for a few seconds, as Jeb rams the knife into my thigh. I gasp into the ceiling, but I'm not sure if any sound makes it out. Blood pounds in my ears.

Jeb yanks the knife back out with a wet sliding sound.

For a moment, everything is still.

I try to move. To fight. To run. To do something. Anything.

But all I can do is to lie there on the ground. Blood wells up from the cut across my forearm and the wound in my thigh. Agony pulses through my chest as every labored breath disturbs my shattered ribs. My head throbs and the room spins. My vision is starting to go black at the edges.

Above me, Jeb and Tommen flash me a cruel smile.

Then Jeb raises the knife.

Desperation and hopelessness crash over me. So intense, so cold and all-consuming, that I want to bawl my eyes out.

This is how it ends. After a lifetime of sitting on the sidelines. A lifetime of accomplishing nothing. A lifetime of being treated like crap. This is how it all ends.

Jeb rams the dagger straight towards my eye.

A violent wind crashes through the room.

Broken wood from the already shattered door shoots through the air and smacks into the white stone walls with a loud *crack*. The knife is ripped from Jeb's hand by the wind and clatters against the wall behind me as Tommen and Jeb are thrown backwards several steps.

Cries of alarm tear from their throats and echo between the stone walls.

They whirl towards the door, crouching into attack positions, right as a shadow of death stalks into the room.

No, not *a* shadow of death.

The Shadow of Death.

Draven Ryat stalks into my room, looking like vengeance and fury itself. He is only wearing a pair of black pants, leaving the rest of his lethal body on full display. His imposing black wings loom behind his broad shoulders, and black storm clouds billow around him.

Pure rage burns in his golden eyes as he comes to a halt on the floor.

Then his gaze flicks down to me, and that rage darkens into something not of this world. Something so terrifying that ice skitters across my skin at the mere sight of it.

Draven slides his gaze back to my two attackers.

All color drains from their features.

Jeb opens his mouth. But he doesn't have time to so much as beg before Draven summons a literal storm. Black clouds whirl inside my room as another violent wind crashes through it and hits my attackers. From almost point-blank range this time.

I hear the loud cracks of thunder as lightning flashes through the churning clouds. It zaps into Tommen and Jeb. Thuds sound as they slam into the wall behind them, but I don't see it, because the darkness at the edge of my vision has spread almost completely over my eyes now.

Agony pulses through my whole body. I just want to close my eyes and sleep.

The last thing I feel before oblivion drags me under is a pair of strong arms lifting me up.

CHAPTER TWENTY-TWO

Soft sheets caress my skin. Blinking, I rub a hand over my face and heave a deep sigh. I haven't slept this peacefully and this deep in ages. I feel completely rested, and my body is filled with renewed energy.

I jerk upright in the bed.

Rested. Filled with energy. My body.

Memories of last night crash over me. The shock as Tommen and Jeb broke my door down. The fear as they attacked me. The pain as they hit me and stabbed me. The hopelessness as they were about to kill me.

And then…

Draven storming into my room like the Shadow of Death.

My breath catches.

Which oddly enough doesn't hurt. I glance down at my body in stunned surprise.

I know that several of my ribs were completely shattered last night. And I might have increased healing speed, but it's not *this* fast.

My gaze drifts to my arm and then my leg. The wounds there are gone. Not even a scar is left.

Which can only mean one thing.

The powerful healing magic from the leader of the Orange Dragon Clan.

For an entire minute, all I can do is to stare down at my body. My now completely healed and well-rested body. I haven't felt this good in decades. Not only did that powerful healing magic fix my most recent injuries, it also got rid of the exhaustion and weakness and sheer utter tiredness that has clung to my bones for years due to the prolonged lack of food and the long hours of work. I didn't even realize how much it has weighed on my soul until now when it's gone.

Drawing in a deep breath, I marvel at the feeling of my lungs expanding fully. Without pain or pressure crushing them.

I rub a hand over the spot on my thigh where Jeb stabbed me. There is a tiny speck of blood on the hem of my short white nightgown, which means that I'm still wearing the same one that I wore last night. But someone has swapped the thin lace robe for a different one. No doubt since my original one had a slash through the arm. Not to mention that the fabric covering that arm was completely soaked in blood from the cut across my forearm.

The realization that someone has healed me and changed my robe brings forth another question.

Where in Mabona's name am I?

Still sitting in the middle of the bed, I stare at the room around me. It's certainly not my room. Instead of walls and floor made of the same pale stone as the rest of the palace, this room has the added luxury of floorboards and wall panels made of rich dark wood.

There are bookshelves along one wall, and a grand desk by the other. They're all made of the same elegant wood. As is the double bed that I'm occupying. I glance down at the dark sheets that cover the soft mattress before I begin searching for the most important features of the room.

The doors.

There is one door on the wall to my right and another opposite me across the room. The wall on my left holds a series of windows. Sunlight which, from the angle of it, looks to be from a bright midday sun streams in through the windows and illuminates the luxurious room. I study it for another second.

I'm still somewhere in the Golden Palace, of that I'm certain. But it's not the south wing.

"On your knees," a harsh voice bellows from somewhere outside the windows.

My heart stutters as I recognize the voice.

Scrambling out of bed, I hurry over to the windows and look out at the scene before me. Or rather below me.

The windows overlook a courtyard on what appears to be the east side of the palace, close to the front doors. This room is up on the fourth floor, but I can still see clearly what happens on the ground below. And when I do, my mouth drops open.

All of the contestants who made it through the second trial are standing in a half circle with their backs towards my window. In front of them are three people. Draven, Tommen, and Jeb.

My two attackers from last night are on their knees while Draven stands behind them, looming over them like an executioner. He is holding his massive sword in his right hand, and his face radiates ruthless power and cold fury.

"You were given one very clear rule," Draven says, his voice cutting through the air like the strike of a whip. "No fighting outside of trials. And yet, these two spineless cowards decided to attack another contestant in the middle of the night." His eyes burn with threats as he sweeps a hard look over the half circle before him. "What is the punishment for that?"

Someone apparently answers, but because they aren't shouting the way that Draven is, I can't actually hear what they say through the closed window.

"Exactly," Draven replies. He flexes his hand on the hilt of his sword. "Execution."

On the ground, Tommen and Jeb tremble and cower down.

My gaze drops down to the two of them. Shock and confusion pulse through me as I take in their appearances.

Yes, the punishment for attacking another contestant is death. But these two haven't simply been shackled and brought out to be executed. They have been *tortured* too.

Both of Tommen's arms are bent at unnatural angles, and when he opens his mouth slightly, I notice that all of his teeth are missing. Blood and bruises cover both his face and Jeb's. Jeb also has vicious-looking stab wounds and cuts all across his body.

My heart patters against my ribs as I stare at them. Based on the extent of their injuries, the torture must have gone on for most of the night.

Draven stalks around them until he is standing in the empty space on Tommen's left. Tommen sways slightly on his knees but tries to keep his back straight as Draven comes to a halt.

"Beg forgiveness, and I will grant you a clean death," Draven commands, his voice pulsing through the air.

Tommen's mouth moves, but from up here, I can't hear what he says. But apparently, Draven is satisfied with whatever it is that he says, because he raises his massive sword.

And then cuts Tommen's head clean off his shoulders.

I gasp.

Down on the ground, several of the contestants jerk back as well.

Tommen's head hits the ground and then rolls halfway around before coming to a halt. His body topples forwards and slams into the stones with a thud that I can hear even through the closed window. Blood spreads across the pale stones.

Jeb pees his pants.

The dark stain spreads across the entire front of Jeb's pants as Draven flicks blood off his sword and then stalks around so that he is standing on Jeb's right. Before Draven can even say anything, Jeb throws himself down on the ground, pressing his forehead against the stones before Draven's feet. His hands reach desperately for Draven's boots. The Shadow of Death kicks his hands away while a disgusted look twists his features.

"Please, I don't want to die," Jeb cries. And *his* words I can actually hear, because he too is screaming. "Please. Please. I'm begging you."

Draven only stares down at him with merciless eyes. "You really should have thought about that before you dared to attack Selena."

"Please—"

"You have five seconds to raise your head and face your death like a man. Or I will kill you right there in the dirt like the spineless worm you are."

A ripple of fear courses through Jeb's already broken body, and he presses his forehead harder against the ground while frantically begging for mercy.

Draven spins the sword in his hand so that the point is facing downwards. Then he simply rams the blade through Jeb's back.

A scream of pain rips from Jeb's throat. Draven yanks the blade back out. More screams echo through the midday air as Jeb rolls over on his side. His body convulses and he coughs blood onto the pale stones before him.

Draven doesn't even bother to watch him as he dies slowly and in pain instead of the quick death Tommen got. Instead, he raises his bloodstained blade and points it at the other contestants. Several of them flinch.

"Let this serve as a reminder." He points to where Jeb is still writhing and coughing blood on the ground. "This is what will happen if you try to kill Selena, or any of your fellow contestants, outside of the trials. Understood?"

Everyone quickly nods.

"Good." Draven yanks his sword down and effortlessly slits Jeb's throat, at last ending his torment. "Dismissed."

Everyone scatters immediately.

I pull back from the window while confusion swirls inside my skull. There was something odd about what just happened. It didn't look like a simple execution of a random contestant who broke the rules. Instead, it felt almost... personal.

Shaking my head, I push those strange musings aside. I have more important things to deal with right now. Like getting out of here.

Moving away from the window, I hurry over to the closed door on the wall opposite the bed. I pause for a second, pressing my ear against the wood, and try to see if I can hear anything.

No sound makes it through the door.

After casting a glance over my shoulder, I carefully edge the handle down. Thankfully, it's not locked. I open the door a tiny crack and glance through it.

Disappointment flits through me when it turns out to just be a spacious private bathroom. After checking to make sure that there is no one in there, and no way out either, I close the door again and instead hurry over to the other door.

I repeat the same process. First, I just listen against the wood to see if I can pick up any sounds. Then I push the handle down.

To my great annoyance, this door turns out to be locked. I glare at it and rattle the handle a few times too for good measure. The stubborn door remains uncooperative.

With a sigh, I move back from the door and instead sweep my gaze over the rest of the bedroom. There might be a key somewhere in here.

I get to work.

When I'm halfway through one of the bookcases, a metallic clicking sound suddenly comes from the door. I whirl around and grab the closest hard object I can reach. Which turns out to be a book. I have just managed to raise it in a position ready to swing when the door is pulled open.

My heart jerks as Draven walks through.

Without even looking towards me, he pulls the door shut behind him and locks it again. Then he at last turns towards the bed. He stops. Blinks. Apparently surprised to not find me in the bed, he casts a stunned look around the room.

His gaze lands on me.

For a moment, no one says anything.

Then he flicks a quick glance at the book I have raised to swing with both hands. And for a second, I swear that a hint of amusement blows across his lips.

Then that arrogant expression is back on his features, and he nods towards the book. "Planning to hit me with that, are you?"

The sound of his voice yanks me out of my stupor. With a huff, I set the book down and then cross my arms over my chest instead. I wait for Draven to say something else.

He doesn't. He only continues watching me with an expression I can't read.

That flustered feeling in my chest falters, and the memories from last night once more flash before my eyes. I let my arms drop back down by my sides, suddenly feeling awkward and uncertain.

"You saved me," I say, my voice coming out sounding as confused and uncertain as I feel.

The unreadable mask stays on his face as he simply replies, "Yes."

"How?"

"I'm pretty sure you were still conscious for that part."

"No, I mean, how did you know that I needed help?"

"It was a very loud fight."

"No one else in our corridor heard it."

"I have better hearing than they do."

"But—"

"Most people just say *thank you* when someone saves their life."

I snap my mouth shut as my cheeks flush. Because Goddess

above, he's right, isn't he? Regardless of everything else that he has done to me, he did save my life last night.

So I swallow and then clear my throat before saying, "Thank you."

A small smirk plays over his lips. "See? That wasn't so hard, was it?"

I shoot him a scowl, already regretting that I ever thanked the bastard. Then my gaze flits down to the smooth skin on my forearm, where the deep cut used to be. Raising my gaze, I meet his eyes again.

"You made the leader of the Orange Dragon Clan heal me," I say. It comes out like something halfway between a statement and a question.

Draven shrugs and then starts towards one of the closets. "Yes. I couldn't very well have you bleeding all over my room, now could I?"

Shock hits me like a brick to the face. My mouth drops open as I just stare at him.

"This is your room?" I manage to blurt out eventually.

"Yes."

I blink at him in stunned disbelief. "Why did you bring me here?"

He stops halfway to his closet and instead turns to look at me again. After flicking a dismissive look up and down my body, he arches an eyebrow at me. "I didn't do it because I care about you, if that's what you're wondering. I just saw a chance and took it."

Heat flushes my cheeks, because for a moment there, I did wonder if he might actually have done it because he cares about me. About my safety, if nothing else. But apparently not.

Trying to block out that flash of embarrassment, I instead ask, "A chance for what?"

A truly villainous smile spreads across his lips as he holds my gaze. "A chance to keep you locked up in here so that you will miss the next trial."

CHAPTER TWENTY-THREE

My frustration builds as the sun slips entirely beneath the horizon and darkness blankets the world while I still haven't managed to find a way out of Draven's room. No matter how much I search for miracles, there are only two ways out of the room.

The windows, which don't even open. And even if they did, we're four stories up. If I tried to jump out, I would die.

That only leaves the door. Which is fully and completely locked.

I scowl at the rows of black shirts in Draven's closet after searching through it for what has to be the seventh time. The shirts just look back at me impassively, utterly disinterested in my infuriating problem. I slam the closet door shut.

Turning back towards the rest of the room, I scan it once more while I try to come up with some sort of plan.

Apart from the two times he came back to give me some food to eat, Draven has been elsewhere the entire day. At first, I was grateful for that because it gave me a chance to thoroughly search through his entire room. But once I realized that there is no key in here, his absence just became another point of frustration. He obviously has the only key to the door, which means that he needs to actually be here for me to have a shot at stealing it.

The lock clicks from across the room.

Whirling around, I sprint towards the door.

Draven is faster.

He has managed to open the door, slip inside, and then close and lock the door behind him before I can reach him.

I stumble to a halt on the smooth wooden floorboards, spinning my arms in an effort to keep my balance and stop myself from slamming right into his chest.

He arches a dark eyebrow at me. "Going somewhere, little rebel?"

Scowling, I cross my arms and shoot him an annoyed look. "Yes, I was, actually. Since you have failed to provide me with what I need."

"Oh really? You have water. And I've brought you food not once but *twice* today. And tomorrow, you might actually get three meals, since I'm assuming that you will be conscious during breakfast this time."

I give him a flat look while uncrossing my arms. Then I motion pointedly down at my body. "Clothes. I need clothes."

His gaze slips down to my body.

I'm still only wearing that white silk nightgown that ends halfway down my thighs and the sheer lace robe over it. Neither piece of clothing offers much protection. The robe is practically see-through, and the nightgown is short, sleeveless with only thin straps over the shoulders, and has a plunging neckline.

Compared to the imposing black armor that he is wearing, I feel almost naked. It's a very clear visual of how massive the power imbalance between us is right now.

"You have clothes," he states when he slides his gaze back up to my face.

Annoyance flickers through me, and I motion down at my body again. "You call this clothes?"

"You're the one who put them on in the first place. I didn't make you wear them."

"To sleep. Not to prance around in all day."

Amusement tugs at his lips for a second. Closing the distance between us, he lifts his hand and slides it along my jaw. A small shiver of pleasure rolls down my spine at his featherlight touch.

"Oh trust me," he says as a smirk spreads across his face. "You don't need to worry about prancing around in your nightgown. Since you won't be leaving this room."

And then he gives my cheek a couple of brisk pats. Exactly the same as I did to him in that deserted room yesterday.

It stuns me enough that I just blink at him in surprise. Then my brain catches up, and I shove his hand away while shooting him another scowl. He lets out a low chuckle. I huff.

Then I let a sly smile curl my lips as I flick a knowing look up and down his body. "Admit it. The real reason why you won't allow me to get my clothes is because you like the sight of my body in this tiny little nightgown."

He draws his eyebrows down and lets out a dismissive snort. "Why would the sight of your body elicit any sort of reaction from me?"

"Because I'm hot."

He rolls his eyes. "And humble, apparently."

"You're one to talk."

"I'm going to take a bath."

His sudden change of topic catches me off guard, and he uses that moment of stunned confusion to walk right past me and towards the bathroom door. Snapping out of my stupor, I turn and look at him as he disappears into the bathroom and closes the door behind him.

I heave a deep sigh.

Earlier in the day, I briefly entertained the idea that I could steal his sword while he's sleeping tonight and then use it to threaten him into opening the door and releasing me. However, I was quickly forced to discard that idea. For the same reason that Draven walked into his bathroom still wearing his entire set of dragon scale armor.

Since dragon shifters switch between dragon and human form, they quickly had to figure out a solution to the clothes problem. The shift leaves them naked, which naturally became an annoying obstacle in most situations. So they designed something that would help them get around it.

I don't know how it works, or if normal civilians wear the same thing, but all shifters who are in the army wear bracers that can store their clothes and equipment. So when they shift into dragons, the armor and sword they were carrying get magically preserved in those bracers. And then when they shift back to human form, their dragon scale armor, and the equipment that was attached to it when they shifted, returns to their bodies.

Where those bracers go while they are in dragon form is beyond me. But I've always assumed that they become part of their dragon scales, since the bracers look to be made from the same material.

Unfortunately for me, though, this means that Draven can store his sword inside his bracers while he's sleeping. Which means that I can't steal the bloody thing.

While Draven takes a bath, I occupy myself with searching through his room one last time. Just in case I missed anything.

I didn't. There is nothing in his room that can help me escape. Unless I decide to hurl books at him or try to strangle him with one of the plain black shirts in his closet. Neither option seems to have a high probability of success, though.

The door to the bathroom is opened.

I spin around, getting ready to make one more attempt to trick him into letting me leave.

But the words get stuck in my throat, and my entire brain stops working, as Draven strides through the door and back into the bedroom in only his bracers and a pair of black underwear.

His wings are gone, leaving him in fully human form. And those bracers and that pair of underwear, which is practically nothing more than a pair of tight shorts that end halfway down his thighs, do very little to conceal his lethal body. I can count every ridge of his defined abs and follow every curve of his biceps. Drops of water cling to his messy black hair, and one of them slides down the side of his neck.

He reaches up and rakes a hand through his hair. The move makes the muscles in his arm and chest flex slightly. My gaze drops down to the bulge visible against the front of his underwear.

Heat pools at my core.

Mabona's fucking tits, did he have to be both hot and well-equipped?

"Now who's staring?"

A jolt shoots through me. I hadn't even realized that my mouth was open, so I snap it shut and flick my gaze back up to Draven's face again.

There is a wide smirk on his lips as he raises his eyebrows expectantly, waiting for me to answer.

My cheeks flush.

He lets out a low chuckle. "So maybe you should consider what dirty thoughts are present in your own head before you accuse me of wanting to stare at your body in that *tiny little nightgown*." He mimics those final three words in my voice.

I glare at him.

With another dark laugh, he strolls over to the bed and throws back the cover, revealing the smooth dark sheets beneath.

The sight of it sends another jolt through me, and a question that I hadn't even considered flashes through my mind.

My intention was to ask that question, but instead, what makes it out of my mouth is, "You're going to bed."

Draven pauses with his hand on the cover, which he has now

moved aside, and casts a glance at me over his shoulder. "How very observant of you."

I'm already flustered, and his flippant response just makes it worse. So instead of asking the question in a way that doesn't sound so pathetic, I end up just blurting out, "Where am I going to sleep?"

Apart from the bed, there is nothing in this room that can remotely be used as a bed. No couch. Not even a soft rug. Just a desk and some closets and dressers.

A devilish glint appears in his eyes as he meets my gaze.

"On the floor, of course," he says.

I gape at him. "You can't be serious."

"Where else would you sleep?"

"In the bed."

A sly smile curls his lips, and he raises his eyebrows at me. "You want to share my bed?"

Heat sears my cheeks. I try to let out an annoyed huff, but unfortunately it comes out sounding more embarrassed than irritated.

"You know what I mean." I flick my wrist in the direction of the bed. "There is more than enough room for both of us. You on one side and me on the other. No *sharing*," I shoot him a pointed look, "required."

For a few seconds, he just watches me in silence. There is an expression on his handsome features that I can't read. It might be amusement. Or annoyance. Or approval. Or something else entirely.

At last, he just turns back to the bed and climbs onto it without another word. The wood creaks slightly underneath the weight of his muscular body as he adjusts his position.

Standing there on the floor, I watch him while trying to figure out what this means.

Draven is lying on his stomach, with his arms up and his hands tucked underneath his pillow. He has positioned himself slightly more towards the middle of the bed rather than staying firmly on one side.

Squinting at the bed, I try to measure the space that remains on the mattress. It looks like I could fit quite comfortably there. My gaze darts over to Draven's muscular back. Does this mean that he has agreed to let me sleep in the bed?

Since he hasn't said anything, I decide to assume so. After giving my head a short shake to clear it, I stride over to the other side of the bed and reach for the edge of the cover.

Right before my fingers can brush against the soft bed, a small cloud of black smoke pulses through the air.

Draven's massive wings explode into view.

I start in surprise, jerking back a little.

When I have gathered my wits again, I'm met with the most infuriating sight yet. Draven's huge black wings are spread out to his sides, blocking the entire rest of the bed.

I curl my fingers into a fist and force out an angry breath.

"Asshole," I growl.

"What was that?" he demands without even lifting his head.

"You heard me."

"Yes, I did." At last, he raises his head and locks eyes with me from over his broad shoulder and his massive wing. "Watch your mouth, little rebel. Or I might find another use for it."

A pulse shoots through me. All the way down to my core. I suck in a breath as fire licks my veins.

Blinking, I shove the unexpected feeling aside and instead shoot another glare at Draven. And then, because with his damn wings taking up the whole bed, I can't do anything else, I curl up on the floor next to the bed and try to fall asleep.

To my surprise, my body doesn't ache with stiffness when I wake up. Rather the opposite. My body is surrounded by soft covers and a fluffy mattress and smooth sheets.

Startled, I sit bolt upright and glance around me.

Shock ripples through my soul.

I'm in Draven's bed.

And so is he.

He is lying on his stomach on his side of the bed, while I'm occupying the other.

My gaze lands on him right as he jerks awake too. His eyes meet mine. And then alarm pulses across his face.

Sheets flutter through the air as we scramble out of bed at the same time. I pull my sheer robe tighter around me while Draven stalks around the bed. That look of alarm is gone from his face. Now, only a dark scowl remains as he advances on me.

"I thought I told you to sleep on the floor," he says.

"I did sleep on the floor," I retort.

"Clearly not." He comes to a halt barely a breath away. So close that I can feel the heat that radiates from his bare chest. "Since you obviously crawled into bed with me anyway."

Swallowing down a sudden burst of embarrassment, I raise my chin and put as much conviction into my voice as possible. "No, I didn't."

"Then how did you get into my bed?"

My mind desperately tries to sort through any possible memories from last night, but I come up blank. I'm sure that I slept through the night. And I don't sleepwalk. So there is no way that I climbed into bed with him.

"I don't know," I huff. "And how could I have even gotten into it? Your wings were blocking the whole bed." I jerk back in surprise as I realize something else. Flicking my gaze over Draven's body, I blurt out, "Where are your wings?"

He starts slightly, and then flicks a quick glance over his shoulder, as if expecting his wings to be there. They're not. There is a distinctly flustered expression on his face as he turns back to me and replies, "I must have shifted at some point during the night. Which is when you saw your chance and crawled into bed."

"You randomly shift form in the middle of the night without even knowing it?"

That flustered look on his face deepens, and he lets out a huff. "I might have. I don't know."

"You don't know? Do you really expect me to believe that?"

"You ask too many questions."

Before I can retort again, he grabs my chin and tilts my head back so that he can lock hard eyes on me.

"I told you to stay on the floor," he begins, his voice now dripping with threats. "And you climbed into my bed anyway. Try that again, and I swear to God, I will handcuff you to it instead."

My stomach flips. And because that unnecessarily attractive bastard is standing there half-naked and with bed-mussed hair, looking hotter than sin, my mind shoots straight into forbidden places while a throbbing sensation pulses between my legs.

With my pulse suddenly thrumming, I find myself saying, "You like handcuffs in bed, huh?"

He yanks his hand away from my chin as another flash of alarm shoots across his features. It's there and gone again within a fraction of a second, so I can't tell if it was because he's repulsed by the idea or if it was because I'm on to something.

Flexing his hand, he levels a very impressive scowl on me. "I meant handcuff you to the leg of the bed. So that you will be forced to stay on the floor."

A very untimely grin dances over my lips. "Sure you did."

He narrows his eyes at me. "Keep talking, and I'll get those handcuffs right now."

I open my mouth to bait him again, but then stop myself before I can say anything else. I know that I should stop talking now. In fact, I should probably have stopped talking a while ago.

Because if he decides to actually follow through on his threat and handcuff me to the floor, it will make it more or less impossible for me to find the key and steal it from him.

But I can't quite find it in myself to act all submissive and apologize. So instead, I simply give him a knowing smile.

He stares me down for another few seconds, as if trying to convince both me and himself that he won that round. Then he blows out a forceful breath and spins on his heel.

"Troublesome, infuriating," he mutters under his breath as he stalks into the bathroom, "insubordinate little—"

The rest of his words are cut off as he shuts the door behind him.

But as I stand there and watch the now closed door, one question still remains.

If I didn't climb into the bed on my own, how in Mabona's name did I end up there?

CHAPTER TWENTY-FOUR

I'm lying in a luxurious sunken bath, submerged in warm water and enveloped by the pleasant smell of scented soap. I should feel relaxed. Calm. At ease. But instead, all I can feel is an overwhelming sense of stress. It's so intense that I can practically feel my soul vibrating with it.

Every second that passes is another second that brings me closer to my doom. Yet another day has passed without me being able to escape. I only have tomorrow left now. The day after that, the third trial is supposed to start.

I have tried everything I can think of, but I can't find the key. Or another way to get out. I even used my magic to try to manipulate Draven's sympathy so that he would release me. But he noticed the moment that I tried to channel my magic and threatened to handcuff me again. So my best bet is still the key. Which I still haven't found. But tonight, I'm going to make another attempt.

Draven must be keeping the key somewhere on his person while he sleeps, so all I need to do is to wait for him to fall asleep, and then I can search him for it. Which is why I have spent almost two hours in his bathroom.

I glance towards the closed door. He must have fallen asleep by now. I went into the bathroom right when he announced that he was going to bed. And it can't possibly take him longer than two hours to fall asleep.

Water sloshes down my body as I stand up and make my way out of the sunken bath. There are several fluffy white towels waiting in neat piles in one of the cabinets. So I pull one out and wrap it around myself. I kept my hair up in a bun, so I only need to dry off my body.

My mind churns with different strategies as I drift towards the door. I just need to check if he's sleeping. If he is, I can quickly put my clothes on and get to work. But if he isn't, I need to take my time getting dressed.

Still only wearing the towel, I push the door open a tiny bit and peer out. Only one faelight has been left on, leaving the room mostly in darkness. I open the door a little wider and squint towards the bed.

Surprise flits through my chest when I find it empty.

Standing there with my hand still on the handle, I stare at the empty bed. Did he leave?

I open the door wider and sneak out while glancing around the room.

The bathroom door is shoved shut behind me with a thud.

It startles me enough that I nearly jump out of my skin. Whirling around, I come face to face with Draven. He is standing by the wall, in a spot where he was hidden behind the door when I opened it. Just like last night, he's only wearing a pair of black underwear and his black bracers. The rest of his perfect body is on full display as he stands there, leaning one shoulder against the wall with his arms crossed and one ankle crossed over the other.

A knowing smirk plays over his lips as he watches me. "Did I startle you, little rebel?"

"What? No. It's just..." I ramble, my mind scrambling to compose itself again. "I imagined you in bed."

That sly amusement on his face grows deeper. "Oh?"

"I mean I thought about you in bed."

He raises his eyebrows, his eyes practically gleaming with satisfaction now.

I shake my head frantically. "No, I mean I thought you *were* in bed. Sleeping. That's it. Not... I didn't think about you in bed. I wasn't even in a bed. I was in the bath and..."

Goddess above, I really need to stop talking.

Draven pushes off from the wall. My heart stutters as he starts towards me. His eyes glint in the faint light as he backs me towards the wall. I draw in an unsteady breath, trying desperately to find my wits again. Goddess damn it, I'm supposed to be smart. And yet the things that have come out of my mouth this past minute could have made the village idiot envious.

My back hits the wall with a soft thud. I grab the top of my towel, trying to keep it in place, while Draven closes the final distance between us. My heart slams against my ribs.

Draven braces one hand on the wall next to me, and then cocks his head. "Tell me, Selena, were you really thinking about me while you were sitting there naked in the bath?"

"Yes." I shake my head hard. "No. I mean, yes, but not like that."

"Oh really? Then what were you doing in there for *two hours*?"

"Planning your demise."

A laugh escapes his chest before he manages to smother it. But the amusement lingers in his eyes like golden sparkles as he holds my gaze. "Is that so?"

"Yes."

At that, a villainous expression, dripping with challenge, descends on his handsome features. Moving his free hand, he brushes his fingertips over my thigh, right above the knee. A jolt zaps down my spine at the touch.

"So if I were to slide my hand up your thigh and brush my knuckles against your cunt right now, I wouldn't find it soaking wet?"

My breath catches in my lungs. I know that I should try to deny it, but all I can do is to stare at him while my heart pounds in my chest.

Draven slides his hand higher up my thigh.

A shiver of pleasure courses through me.

He stops, waiting for me to protest. To shove him away. To tell him to stop.

I don't.

His fingers make lightning dance over my skin as he traces them up along the inside of my thigh. My breathing grows heavier. I drag in shuddering breaths as his hand reaches my pussy.

He keeps his eyes locked on me. Studying me. Searching my face. Waiting for any indication that this is not what I want.

I try to convince myself that I don't want this. Try to convince myself that I'm repulsed by the thought of Draven's hands on my body. But I can't. Because when he's standing there, looking like that, looking at *me* like that, I want nothing more than to feel his hands worship my body. It doesn't matter that we're enemies. Because right now, he's looking at me as if he sees me, the real me, in a way no one ever does.

His knuckles brush against my throbbing clit.

A moan rips from deep within my chest.

Snapping my mouth shut, I throw my head back and rest it against the smooth wooden wall behind me.

Draven keeps his eyes on mine as he twists his hand and instead draws his fingers over my pussy. Another bolt of pleasure shoots through my spine. Curling my hand into a fist, I draw in a deep breath through my nose and try to suppress another moan.

He traces teasing circles around my clit until a whimper slips from my lips. Then he begins rubbing my throbbing clit with his thumb.

Pleasure spikes through me, and light flickers before my eyes.

I drag in shuddering breaths as he expertly plays with my clit.

Tension builds inside me.

Pressing the back of my head harder against the smooth wood, I squirm against the wall as Draven drives me closer and closer to an orgasm.

My heart pounds against my ribcage.

My clit throbs and my pussy aches with need.

I feel like my very nerves are on fire.

Short shallow breaths escape my heaving chest.

He increases the pressure of his fingers and picks up the pace slightly.

Something between a moan and a whimper rips from my lungs. My legs tremble, and I writhe against the wall as the pleasure reaches unbearable levels.

Draven watches me, completely enraptured. He's staring at me as if he has never seen anything like it before. As if every moan that escapes my mouth is the most fascinating thing he has ever experienced. As if *I'm* the most astonishing thing he has ever known.

The sight of him looking at me like that makes me feel lightheaded.

He rolls my clit with his thumb while he slides his index and middle finger down my pussy.

I gasp as his fingers brush against my entrance while his thumb continues moving in a way that sends bursts of pleasure streaking up my spine.

My whole soul thrums as I tumble headfirst towards an orgasm.

Draven's intense gaze sears into me.

Just one more second. One more stroke. One more—

Shock and alarm suddenly pulse across Draven's face. He

shoots a wide-eyed stare down at his hand, as if he can't believe what he's doing.

And then he yanks his hand back.

My knees give out.

I crash down on the floor. Throwing my hands out, I brace myself on the smooth wooden floorboards and bow forward over my knees as I drag in desperate breaths.

My entire body is vibrating with pent-up tension. My whole fucking soul is twisting in on itself, waiting for the release that was just one damn breath away. The release that never came.

A strong hand grips my jaw, forcing me to crane my neck and look up from the floor. And when I do, my eyes meet Draven's golden ones.

That enraptured look of absolute fascination has now been wiped completely off his features. Instead, only a smug look full of mocking victory is visible on his stupidly attractive face.

"Just as I thought," he says with a wicked smirk on his mouth. "Soaking wet."

I want to scream.

I think I do scream. In frustration and sheer utter desperation. My body still vibrates with need and pent-up release that never came.

Glaring up at him, I clench my jaw.

I'm going to get him back for this.

Fucking bastard.

I'm going to get him back for this if it's the last thing I do.

CHAPTER TWENTY-FIVE

My time is about to officially run out. I try to draw in calming breaths as I stand pressed against the wooden wall, watching the door next to me like a hawk. But with every passing second, the panic that has been clawing at my chest all day only grows worse.

After Draven left me there on my knees last night, unsatisfied and about to combust from the pent-up release, I went back into the bathroom to take matters into my own hands. Once my body was no longer vibrating with tension and my head was clear again, I finally figured out where he keeps the key while he sleeps. Magically sealed inside his bracers along with his armor. So naturally, I tried to steal his bracers that night. And again this morning. Then I also tried to steal the key from him when he came back with my lunch.

That… did not work out well for me.

When he left, he told me that it was time to get the handcuffs.

That was hours ago, and I have been existing in a state of panic and stress ever since. The third trial starts tomorrow morning, and if Draven actually shackles me to something in his room, it's game over for me. So I only have one chance left now. One single desperate chance.

I need to attack him right when he opens the door. Before he can lock it behind him. Before he can handcuff me to his bed. Before he can even close the door behind him.

One chance.

And I have to make it work.

The sun is slipping lower on the horizon, painting the sky with streaks of purple and red. It casts splashes of deep color on the wooden walls. I stare at them as I remain right inside the door. Draven has to return soon.

Dread cuts through my chest as a sudden thought hits me.

What if he doesn't return? What if he decides to simply sleep somewhere else tonight and leave me here all alone? Then I won't even have the chance to try again.

The lock clicks.

My heart lurches.

Both relief and panic crackle through my veins.

He's here. It's time.

I grip the large book harder in my hands. There weren't all that many possible weapons to choose from, so a thick leather tome was the best I could find. It will have to do. I raise the book higher in a two-handed grip.

My pulse thrums in my ears.

This has to work. Please, Mabona, this has to work.

The door is pulled open.

A black boot appears across the threshold.

I slam the book straight at Draven's face right as he steps through.

He yanks his arm up.

And right before the book can crash into his face, his forearm appears in front of it and takes the hit instead. I growl in frustration. His other hand shoots up, yanking the book out of my grip. I snatch my hands back right before he can catch my wrist as well.

He tosses the heavy tome to the floor and whirls towards me. The book hits the floorboards with a loud thud, but my eyes are fixed on the door. The still open door.

I feint a kick between Draven's legs.

By instinct, he flinches.

Twisting around, I dash forward.

My foot makes it one step across the threshold.

Then my stomach lurches as strong arms wrap around my waist, lifting me off the floor and hauling me back into the room.

"No!" I yell in frustration.

Fighting with everything I have, I try to break his grip on me and get my feet back down on the floor. Draven grunts with exertion as I yank and shove at his arms while kicking my heels towards his shins. One arm disappears from around my waist. I wiggle, managing to slip through his grip and land on the floor again.

The door bangs shut as Draven throws it closed behind us. But before he can lock it, I make another attempt to sprint towards it.

"Azaroth's fucking flame," he curses under his breath as his hands snatch at me while I try to twist out of his grip. "Did you oil up your entire body for this or what?"

I'm almost free, slipping between his hands, when he switches tactics. A gasp rips from my lungs as he hooks his foot behind my ankle and yanks my leg forwards. The move makes me stumble, and he uses that moment to bring us both down on the floor.

My back hits the smooth wooden floorboards with a thud. I let out a huff as my breath escapes my lungs. Before I can get my wits back, Draven's knees hit the floor on either side of me. I try to roll away, but my hips are now trapped between his thighs as he straddles me.

Panic pulses through me, and I aim a punch at his face.

His left hand shoots up and grabs my wrist before the strike can hit. I suck in a sharp breath. Pulling furiously, I try to yank my wrist out of his grip, but I might as well have been fighting an iron manacle. Raising my other hand, I grab at his fingers, trying to bend them off my wrist. He simply reaches out with his other hand and wraps that around my free wrist as well.

A frustrated noise tears from my throat as Draven pushes both of my hands back towards the floor. I try to fight him, try to stop my arms from moving, but I'm so ridiculously outmatched against his strength.

My forearms meet the smooth floorboards as Draven pins my hands to the ground above my head. I yank and struggle, but I'm thoroughly trapped underneath him now.

Grinding my teeth, I glare up at him.

Amusement dances in his eyes as he leans down over me until his face is right above mine. "Did you really think that would work?"

"It might have," I growl while yanking at his grip.

He nonchalantly flexes his fingers around my wrists in response. A casual reminder that he doesn't even need to use his full strength to keep me pinned.

I wiggle furiously underneath him.

And because of the way he's leaning forward over me now, the move makes me grind myself against him.

A jolt shoots through me.

Since I'm still only wearing that short and thin nightgown, I can feel every ridge of his body as if I were naked. Lightning flickers through my veins as my pussy rubs against the harsh material of his armor. And the hard bulge between his legs.

My mind goes blank for a second as I try to remember if there is some kind of special protection on his armor in that spot. Some kind of material that is extra hard. I can't remember.

But it doesn't matter anyway. All that matters is getting out from underneath him.

Yanking against his grip, I squirm furiously again.

He draws in a sharp breath. Tightening his grip on my wrists, he levels a commanding stare on me. "You really need to stop moving."

"You really need to get off me," I retort while continuing to struggle.

His eyes shutter as my hips grind against his again.

The sight of it stuns me so much that I stop moving for a second. My mind spins. Apparently, I'm not the only one affected by this.

With my stunned eyes locked on his, I deliberately roll my hips against him once more. Emotions flash across his face, and his wings flare.

They spread out above me like a black ceiling, cutting us off from the rest of the world. I stare, completely transfixed at them. They're imposing and beautiful and lethal all at the same time. My gaze shifts to his face, which is so close to mine that I can feel his every breath against my lips. Heat pools inside me and my pulse thrums.

I squirm again, deliberately grinding my pussy against him once more.

A violent ripple courses through his body.

"Fuck," he presses out, his voice coming out strained and hoarse. "That's it, I'm getting the handcuffs."

My heart jerks. Because for a second there, as he holds my gaze with those intense eyes of his, I don't know if he meant that as a threat or an offer.

But then he abruptly releases my wrists and climbs to his feet. I blink, trying to clear my head, while he strides across the room and towards his desk. Sitting up, I watch him pull a pair of handcuffs from one of the pouches on his belt.

Metal clanks as he straightens the short chain between the manacles and then bends down. I scramble to my feet right as he snaps one side of the handcuffs shut around the leg of his desk.

Based on the color, the shackles look to be made of steel rather than iron. But I still don't want them anywhere near me.

Draven straightens from the desk and turns to face me again. No traces of flustered pleasure remain on his features. Only ruthless authority.

"Since I apparently can't trust you anywhere near my bed, I'm locking you to the desk instead," he declares.

A pulse of embarrassment shoots through me when I think that he means that he can't trust me near his bed because of what just happened on the floor. Because I rolled my hips against him like a horny teenager. But then I realize that he probably means because I tried to steal his bracers last night while he slept. The embarrassed heat in my cheeks fades a little but doubt still crawls into my chest. Did I imagine those hints of pleasure on his face? Maybe I misinterpreted the signs. Maybe he felt nothing after all.

With that expression of cold command still on his face, he raises the hand that isn't currently holding the manacles, and twitches two fingers at me in a clear order to approach.

I take a step back instead.

He narrows his eyes at me. "Do not make me come over there and get you."

My heart slams against my ribs. I can't let him handcuff me to that desk. I need to get out. I need to win the next trial. Win this whole competition. I need to help the fae resistance. I need to make people accept me.

Draven forces out a long breath and places the other manacle on top of the desk. Then he starts towards me. I cast a desperate glance around the room, trying to calculate if I can somehow make it past him and get to the door. As if he can read my mind, he spreads his wings wider, blocking the way.

I start to back away, but then change my mind and instead stand my ground. Draven keeps advancing on me. He doesn't stop until he is standing so close that his chest almost brushes against mine. Holding my gaze with commanding eyes, he raises an eyebrow expectantly.

"What do you want?" I blurt out. The words rip out of my chest, full of frustration and desperation. Holding his merciless stare, I shake my head slowly. "What do you want me to do? Do you want me to beg? Is that it?"

Before he can answer, I drop to my knees before him.

"Do you want me to lick your boots and suck your cock?" I demand.

Emotions flash across his features again, shattering that blank mask on his face.

And because I was standing so close to him, my face is now right in front of his cock, which is why I can clearly see the bulge in his pants grow larger. My eyes widen as realization pulses through me. I flick my gaze back up to his face, and find him clenching his jaw and flexing his hand.

"You're turned on by this," I state, completely stunned.

His hand shoots down and wraps around my throat. With golden eyes that are burning with fire, he growls, "Do not use your magic on me."

Forbidden desire pulses through me at the feeling of his hand around my throat like that. He's not choking me. Only showing me that he holds the power here. But he's wrong. Because his hard cock is straining against his pants right in front of my face.

A devilish smile spreads across my lips. He is not the one with the real power here. I am.

"Are my eyes glowing?" I ask.

His gaze flits between my lips and my eyes before he finally grinds out, "No."

I flash him a knowing grin. "Then whatever you're feeling is all you, Shadow of Death."

Another bolt of emotion pulses across his features. For a second, it almost looks like desperation.

With his hand still around my throat, he takes a step forward and to the side. It pushes me backwards and off my knees so that I'm instead sitting on my ass on the floor. Draven, who is now standing next to me instead of in front of me, leans down over me.

His other hand slides through my hair at the back of my neck.

Dark desire pulses through my core as he threads his fingers through my hair and takes it in a firm grip. Tilting my head back, he brings his face closer to mine. My clit throbs as he slants his mouth over mine.

"Is this what you want?" he demands.

His breath hits my lips with every word, making a shiver of pleasure roll down my spine.

"You want me to bend you over a table and fuck you like I own you?" he pushes, his voice dark and hoarse. "You want me to handcuff you to my bed and make you come so hard that you're screaming my name? Is that what you're hoping to accomplish with this?"

I grin against his mouth. "I think you're projecting, darling. You're the one who got all hot and bothered when I got down on my knees and offered to suck your cock."

A low growl rumbles from deep within his chest.

In one fluid motion, he releases his grip on my hair and instead pulls me to my feet. But he keeps his hand around my throat as he warns, "You're playing with fire, *darling*."

Holding his gaze, I raise my forearm and push his hand away from my throat. He lets me. I take a step closer to him. He draws in an unsteady breath.

I flash him a sly smile. "Good thing I have experience with that then."

Then I snake my hand around the back of his neck and yank his mouth down to mine.

A groan rips from his chest.

The sound of it makes my heart flip.

Sliding both hands into my hair, he pulls me closer and kisses me back so fiercely that I gasp into his mouth. He bites my bottom lip, sending a jolt through my spine. My mind spins as his tongue tangles with mine. Oh fuck, he tastes like wind and rain and lightning. Like fire and sin. And my undoing.

I slide my hand up to the back of his head, raking my fingers through his hair and pressing his lips harder against mine while he dominates my mouth. Whatever air manages to make it into my lungs is snatched right out again with every commanding stroke of his tongue.

It takes me longer than I want to admit to remember that *I* was supposed to be in control of this. I was supposed to be the one holding the power here.

He kisses me like he's fighting a war. Like he's trying to make me surrender my whole soul to him. And Goddess above, when he grips my hair and dominates my mouth like this, I'm almost tempted to do it.

While still kissing him furiously, I reach up and press my other hand against his chest. A low noise comes from the back of his throat when I touch him. Taking a step forward, I start moving us away from the wall of windows.

He lets me back him across the room while still kissing me senseless.

It takes everything I have to keep my mind from malfunctioning every time his lips press against mine. No one has ever touched me like this before. Kissed me like this before. As if he can't breathe without me.

Wood and metal clank as we hit the desk and the back of Draven's thighs sends it sliding back and banging against the wall. I draw my hand down his chest and then reach up and grip his wrist. With my mouth still on his, I move one of his hands from my hair and down to my hip. Another low moan escapes him as I roll my hips against him before pulling my hand back. His fingers skim over my hipbone, making my short nightgown slide upwards. Pleasure skitters down my spine.

I reach forward, past his hip.

And then snap the manacle shut around his wrist.

He sucks in a sharp breath as I wrench myself away from him and leap backwards out of his reach.

Utter incredulity shines on his whole face as he stares at me.

His chest heaves and his hair is slightly mussed from when I raked my hand through it.

He looks completely and thoroughly kissed.

And confused.

Eyes wide with stunned disbelief, he glances down at the handcuffs that now trap him to the desk.

I flash him a wicked grin as I back towards the door. "That's what you get for leaving me unsatisfied last night."

Then I wink and, at long last, escape right out the still unlocked door.

CHAPTER TWENTY-SIX

To say that Draven is looking murderous would be the understatement of the decade. The flames in his eyes could have set a medium-sized ice palace on fire. He flexes his hand, and a muscle flickers in his jaw, as he glares at me from across the large gathering hall.

I blow him a kiss.

Lightning flashes across his face. And if it weren't for the fact that his precious Iceheart monarchs were seated not three strides away from him, I'm pretty sure that he would have stormed across the room and killed me on the spot.

"Uhm..." Fenriel begins from next to me. His blue and gold eyes flick between me and Draven. "What's that all about?"

"Oh he's just angry that I managed to recover in time for the trial," I reply with a light shrug.

It's a lie. But a fairly innocent one. The other contestants don't know that Draven has kept me locked up in his room these past three days. Or that he had the leader of the Orange Dragon Clan heal me after the attack. They all think that I've spent the past three days in an infirmary or something, slowly healing from my wounds. And I haven't corrected them because… well, because it's too complicated to try to explain everything that has been happening between me and Draven. So after I escaped, I just returned to my own room as if nothing had happened.

"Huh," Fenriel replies. "And he tried to put a target on your back during the commencement ball too." A contemplative look blows across his narrow face as he pushes a few long red strands of hair back behind his pointed ear. "What even is the deal with you two?"

Before I can try to figure out how to reply to that, Imar strides through the door and into the large gathering hall. A ripple goes through the remaining contestants who crowd the floor around me.

"Welcome to the third trial," Imar says as he comes to a halt in front of us and clasps his hands behind his back. "Today, we will weed out the last dregs of unworthy ingrates before the fourth and final trial."

Anger flickers through me, and I can barely stop myself from scowling at the trial administrator. Unworthy ingrates? We have nothing to be grateful for. And we are already worthy. I clench my fist. By Mabona, as soon as I win these trials, I'm going to make sure that people like him never set foot in our court again.

"Today," Imar continues, "you will face twenty-four opponents."

We all glance around at each other, assuming that he's talking about us. But to my surprise, Imar sweeps his arm out and points towards the door.

Another shifter from the Red Dragon Clan pushes the two double doors open.

Surprise ripples through our group when people from our city stumble in through the doors. An anxious murmur starts up. Both from them and from several of us. I study the fae men and women who shuffle nervously across the floor and spread out across the room.

Imar motions towards them. "These are the people from your city who have volunteered to help out in today's trial."

I barely manage to suppress a scoff. Volunteered? More like volun*told*.

"There are twenty-four of them," Imar continues. "Just like you." Then he pauses for dramatic effect as he sweeps his gaze over us. "Ten of them are carrying a small wooden coin somewhere on their person. They will not hand them over willingly, so your mission is to acquire one." A wicked smile tugs at his lips. "By any means necessary."

Several of the volunteers swallow and anxiously shift their weight while casting worried glances between us and Imar.

"There are only ten coins," Imar announces. "And without a coin, you won't move on to the final trial. Other than that, there are no rules." He flicks his wrist. "Begin."

My heart leaps into my throat at the sudden start.

All around me, people lurch into motion and scramble to catch up as well.

I remain frozen on the floor as indecision tears through my soul.

Isera's words from the last trial echo through my mind. *Why don't you use your magic against everyone else?*

I *could*. I could use my powers to mess with everyone's emotions. This is the perfect kind of trial for that. Everyone is in the same room, and I can stand on the sidelines without being attacked. This is the perfect opportunity for me to sabotage all the other contestants. The perfect opportunity to make them too frustrated or too worried or too uncertain to finish the task. The perfect opportunity to make everyone else fail.

Nausea rolls through my stomach. Am I really that kind of person? Am I really someone who would sabotage people who have done nothing to me?

My gaze drifts to Fenriel, who has summoned his hawk and is apparently waiting for the bird to scout the room from above.

Even though we're in a stressful trial, there is a smile on his face as he watches his hawk soar through the air.

I drag in a breath while pain squeezes my heart. Could I really sabotage someone like Fenriel? Or Isera, who I consider something of an ally now? Or Lavendera, who protected me against Alistair back in that corridor after the first trial?

Indecision whirls through me like a violent storm.

A scream of fear cuts through the room.

I whip my gaze towards it.

Halfway across the room, Alistair has just shot a torrent of fire at one of the volunteers. The guy threw himself on the ground to evade the flames and is now pushing up to his knees. I watch as he holds out a trembling hand to Alistair. A wooden coin wobbles in his palm. Alistair picks it up.

And then starts towards the next volunteer.

Panic washes through the room as everyone realizes something Imar alluded to. There are only ten coins, and without one, you can't move on to the final trial. But he never said that each person could only collect one coin. So if Alistair gets three of them, there will only be eight people in the final trial. And if he gets five, there would only be six people.

The room explodes into frantic movement as everyone else hurries towards the other volunteers to see if one of them has a coin while also fighting each other for it.

For a moment, I just study Alistair.

Then my mind settles.

I am not like him.

I want to win. Desperately. But I don't have to sabotage other people to do it. I don't have to play the game the way Alistair plays it. I can't. Because I still care too much about what other people think. Still care whether they like me or not.

But that doesn't mean that I can't win. I don't need to be cruel to win. I just need to be smart.

Lurching into motion, I channel my magic and throw it across every volunteer in the room.

Almost all of them have a purple spark of worry in their souls. Since I can't just sense emotions without manipulating them, I decrease those sparks of worry ever so slightly while I scan through them all until I find the ten people who have the biggest sparks.

The ones who are carrying one of those coins know that they need to resist if we try to take one. If they don't, the dragon shifters will no doubt punish them. But if they resist too much, we might hurt them. Which means that the people with the coins will feel the most worry.

A fae woman with curly red hair a little to my left has a spark of worry the size of her entire chest. I cut off my magic and start towards her. One of the other contestants is already there. It's Trevor, the guy with stone powers. He raises a block of stone that he looks to be threatening her with. She takes a step back while shaking her head, no doubt trying to convince him that she doesn't have a coin.

I call up my magic again and shove it straight at Trevor.

Just as I had hoped, I find a cerise spark of impatience in his chest. While continuing to walk towards them, I pour a flood of magic into that spark.

Trevor curses and slams his block of stone down into the floor. Then he spins on his heel and hurries over to another volunteer.

I reach the woman two seconds later.

Dread washes over her features when she sees me. But I think it has more to do with the fact that I'm another contestant rather than any fear of me specifically.

"I don't have a coin," she presses out right as I come to a halt in front of her.

My eyes begin to glow as I summon my magic again while I

reply, "I can read people's emotions, so I know that you do in fact have one of the coins."

Alarm flits across her face, and she swallows but doesn't say anything.

"And I know that you don't want to be standing here holding one," I push while I continue to work my magic on her. "It makes you a target. But as soon as people see you hand over a coin to someone else, they will leave you alone."

My magic pours into the spark in her chest. Into that cream-colored spark of logic.

"I'm asking nicely." I give her a pointed look. "The next person won't."

She bites her lip, her gaze flicking around the room. She knows that I'm right. About all of it. She doesn't want to be standing here. She just wants this to be over. And very few other contestants will simply ask nicely.

I manipulate her emotions until those very logical thoughts become so impossible to ignore that she sucks in a sharp breath and then nods vigorously.

All around us, the room has descended into a frenzy. Magic flash and people scream and yell in anger and fear and frustration as twenty-three contestants scramble around the room and try to convince twenty-three volunteers to hand over coins that they may or may not have.

And at the edge of it all, I stand calmly and smile as I hold my hand out to the redhead before me.

She smiles back at me, her face full of the strong relief and certainty that only clear logic can bring, as she drops a wooden coin into my open palm.

I curl my fingers around it while victory glitters inside me.

I don't need to ruin everyone else's chances to win. I don't need to be cruel or violent or threatening.

I just need to outsmart them.

CHAPTER TWENTY-SEVEN

The dining room is now so empty that the clinking of our utensils echoes between the pale stone walls. I glance around the room while I eat my dinner in silence. There are only ten of us left, and everyone is sitting at their own table. The tension in the air is so thick that I could have cut it with my knife.

"Wow," Fenriel suddenly exclaims as he sits down after getting his food. "You'd think that we're all waiting for our execution tomorrow. Not the start of the final trial."

Several people jerk their heads up and twist around to glance at him. I do too. His plate and utensils produce a soft thud as he sets them down on the pale wooden table in front of him. Light from the torches along the walls casts dancing shadows over his red hair and makes his eyes glitter as he raises his eyebrows and looks around at all of us.

"Come on, people." He flashes us all what appears to be an entirely genuine smile. "We made it to the final round. We're the best of the best. We should be celebrating."

His excitement is infectious, and smiles tug at several people's lips. Despite myself, I smile too.

Ever since I passed the third trial two days ago, I've just been waiting for the other shoe to drop. For Alistair to attack me or for Draven to try to lock me up or for the Icehearts to just randomly decide that I don't qualify for the final trial after all. Everyone else put on great displays of magic in order to get their wooden coins. Some even had to fight Alistair for them. But because my magic isn't as flashy or noticeable, it looked to everyone else as if I just walked up and asked the volunteer and then was given it without any real effort.

Back then, I could feel Jessina and Bane watching me through narrowed eyes, full of cold calculation. And I was so sure that they were simply going to declare me unworthy and take away my win. But thankfully, that hasn't happened. Not yet, at least.

But the final trial starts tomorrow morning, and I'm still here, so I allow myself a small breath of relief and smile at Fenriel's excitement.

He leans back in his chair and stretches his legs out underneath the table. My heart aches with jealousy at how carefree he looks. I don't think I've ever felt that at ease in my entire life.

"What would you do?" Fenriel asks, and looks around at all of us. "With your freedom, I mean. If you win the Atonement Trials tomorrow, what are you planning to do with your freedom?"

A few people exchange startled looks. We've never shared personal details with each other before. After all, in here, we're all rivals.

I glance around at the people in the room with me. Isera is sitting at a table by the wall, eating her food as if she's the only person in the room. As usual, her face is an impassive mask, and she hasn't looked up even once since Fenriel started talking.

Alistair is sitting at his table in the middle, which is now empty except for him since all of his friends have already been eliminated. He has paused with his glass halfway to his lips and is watching Fenriel with orange and green eyes that are full of suspicion.

A short distance from him, Lavendera is sitting at her own table. The plate of food before her is completely untouched, and she's absentmindedly tracing patterns on the pale wooden tabletop with her finger. Her eyes are fixed on the white stone wall across the room as she stares at something that only she can see.

"I would open up a bakery."

We all start in surprise and turn towards the source of the voice.

Trevor, the blond guy with stone magic, blushes a little when he notices our surprised looks. But then he clears his throat and shrugs before elaborating. "I'd find a nice human town, without any dragon shifters, and open up a bakery. I would bake all of those incredible pastries that I've only read about in books." A broad grin spreads across his face. "And then I'd eat them all."

Soft laughter ripples through the room.

"I mean, I'd sell them too," he adds with a smile. "Eventually. But first, I'd just eat them."

Fenriel excitedly slaps the tabletop with his palm and then points towards Trevor. "See? That, right there, is a true life goal!"

Another round of chuckles spreads through the room.

The tension that used to vibrate in the air evaporates almost immediately, and it's suddenly much easier to breathe.

I eat some more of my food while someone calls from across the room, "What about you then, Fenriel? What would you do?"

Fenriel lets out a satisfied sigh and leans back in his chair again. "I would set out on an adventure." Another grin spreads across his mouth as he crosses his ankles and reaches up to rest his hands behind his head, the very image of relaxed comfort. His face takes on a dreamy expression as he gazes up at the ceiling. "I want to travel the world. Wander through the great forests. Climb the Peaks of Prosperity. Explore the land all the way to the Western

Sea." He shifts his gaze back down to us and flashes us another smile. "With Talon, of course. He would love to soar freely too."

Unexpected warmth spreads through my chest, and I find myself smiling too. That does sound like a wonderful dream.

Sitting up straight, he turns towards Isera, who is still eating her food without bothering to look up.

"What about you, Isera?" he asks, trying to bring her into the conversation too. "What would you do?"

At long last, she looks up from her food.

Silence descends over the dining room as she meets Fenriel's gaze. Her eyes betray nothing. No hint of emotion. As usual, her entire expression is just a blank mask.

I get the overwhelming urge to reach out with my magic and push at different emotions, just to figure out what she's really feeling. But I don't do it. I never use my powers on people without their permission if I can help it. And Isera trusts me for some reason, or at least she did back in that tunnel, so I don't want to do anything to ruin that.

Everyone holds their breath as they wait for her to reply.

She just looks back at us.

And then goes back to eating.

A sigh of disappointment escapes several throats.

"You would try to find your mother, wouldn't you?"

Isera jerks her head up. Shock and alarm flash across her face like bolts of lightning. It's the strongest emotions I have ever seen on her face, and the sight of it stuns me so much that I sit back in my chair.

"What did you just say?" she demands. Her grip tightens around her knife, and for a moment, I think she might be getting ready to summon her magic too.

Kevlin, the person who made that shocking statement, just looks back at her with a steady gaze. "I said that you would most likely try to find your mother. Wouldn't you? Your father was killed by a shifter patrol when you were only two years old, so your mother is all you have. But she was one of the three winners of the last Atonement Trials," he motions vaguely at the world around us, "so she's out *there* somewhere."

My mouth drops open in surprise.

Clothes rustle as we all turn to stare at Isera.

She is gripping her knife and fork so hard that I'm surprised the metal hasn't started to bend. A muscle flickers in her jaw as she grinds her teeth before forcing out, "How did you know that?"

"I competed in the last Atonement Trials too, remember? I knew your mother. We were friendly. Or at least until she beat me in the final trial and took the last spot as the third winner."

Isera's chest rises and falls with uncontrolled breaths, but she says nothing. Without reading her emotions, I can't tell if she's angry or hurt or maybe panicked. Eventually, she forces out a long breath and relaxes her grip on the utensils.

"Yes," she says at last. "If I win, I would try to find my mother." Pain flickers in her silver and blue eyes for a second. "She said that she was going to come back for me and take me with her. She never did." She works her jaw. "I was ten." Bitterness crawls into her tone as she adds, "I don't need her. I raised myself. But yes, if I win, I would track her down and confront her lying ass about why she broke her promise."

My heart aches as I watch her.

Silence hangs over the dining room. It's so loud that I almost hear it ringing in my ears. I know that we've all had a shitty life in different ways. After all, there is not much happiness to be found in a conquered court. But Goddess above, has Isera really been on her own since she was ten?

"Satisfied?" Isera demands, her voice suddenly as sharp as her ice magic, when she realizes that we're all staring at her. "You wanted an answer. Now you have it."

Then she snatches up her knife and fork and promptly goes back to eating while ignoring the rest of the room.

Fenriel clears his throat. Loudly. And a tad awkwardly. He casts his gaze around the room, seemingly looking for some inspiration on how to smoothly change the topic. Apparently, he doesn't find it, because he just ends up blurting out, "What about you, Lavendera? What would your life look like if you won?"

For a few seconds, Lavendera just continues staring at the wall. Then she blinks, gives her head a short shake, and shifts her gaze to Fenriel. He watches her with hopeful eyes.

"It would probably be filled with lots of pain," she announces.

And then she goes back to staring at the wall.

Fenriel lets out a groan from the back of his throat and rubs his forehead while the rest of us stare at the incredibly beautiful but very strange fae woman. Lavendera just continues watching the pale stones for things we can't see.

"I would settle down in a nice cottage in the woods," someone calls from my left.

"There!" Fenriel exclaims, and sits forward excitedly while pointing towards the guy who said it. "That's another great life goal, right there."

Laughter sweeps through the room, and the tension that had begun to settle again evaporates once more.

I continue eating and drinking while several other contestants share their dreams for what they would do if they won. When Fenriel asks me, I just make up a generic dream since I can't very well announce publicly that I'm planning to kickstart the fae resistance.

Torchlight glitters in Fenriel's eyes as he lifts his glass.

"Well then," he begins. "Cheers to great life goals!"

"Cheers!" most of us reply.

Only Isera, Alistair, and Lavendera don't join in.

The rest of us empty our glasses.

While setting down his now empty glass, Fenriel turns

towards Alistair and gives him a mischievous grin. "You didn't poison this one, did you?"

Alistair blinks in surprise, looking genuinely stunned.

Fenriel just grins wider while amusement sparkles in his eyes. "Too soon?"

For the briefest of moments, the ghost of a smile steals across Alistair's lips. I stare at him in shock. I don't think I've ever seen him smile at a joke before. At least not a joke that wasn't somehow cruel. But he looks genuinely amused by Fenriel's playful jab.

"Hey, you never told us what you would do if you won," Trevor calls.

That fraction of a smile vanishes from Alistair's face in a flash. A ruthless expression slams back down over his features as he cuts a scathing glare at Trevor. "Why would I ever tell you lot anything? All you need to know about me is that I'm going to win tomorrow. And if any of you dare to stand in my way, I *will* fucking kill you."

Shoving to his feet, he kicks his chair out of the way and then stalks out of the dining room without another word.

I watch his retreating back while a sense of loss spreads through my chest.

All throughout the dining room, that tense atmosphere returns with a vengeance. Everyone glances around, their eyes now full of suspicion again, as we're all reminded of the merciless fact that there can only be three winners. We're not a team. We're not friends. We're contestants fighting for the same chance to make our own dreams come true. At the expense of everyone else's.

We might all hate the dragon shifters together, but we are still in this tournament alone.

I heave a sigh.

Enemies by necessity.

CHAPTER TWENTY-EIGHT

Tilting my head back, I stare at the wall of trees that rise up before me. A sense of foreboding spreads through my chest like cold poison. I swallow. Don't tell me that we're actually going in there?

"Welcome to the fourth and final trial," Imar calls across the grass.

Winds rush across the fields, snatching at my hair and clothes. I swallow and tear my gaze from the forest ahead before sliding it towards the cause for the sudden strong winds.

Ten dragons circle us from above. The air from their beating wings makes my hair whip across my face. Reaching up, I push it back so that I can see properly. Sunlight reflects against silver scales as the Icehearts cut downwards.

Gasps rip from two of the other contestants as the massive silver dragons fly so close to us that the tips of their wings almost slash across our faces. I flinch. As do most of the others. Only Lavendera remains completely motionless at the end of our straight row.

Glancing towards her, I briefly wonder if the Icehearts did

something similar during the last trial and if that is how she ended up with that scar across her cheek and jaw.

The back of my neck prickles.

I don't even need to turn around to know that it's Draven who has flown up behind our backs. His imposing black dragon form looms behind, blocking out the sun and casting the grass around us in ominous darkness. My breath catches in my throat, and for one second, I'm convinced that he's going to open his jaws and burn us all to ash. A shiver rolls down my spine. I suddenly understand exactly how he earned the nickname *the Shadow of Death*.

We stagger forward a little from the forceful winds as he beats his wings right behind our backs. Then he sweeps around us towards where the Icehearts are. The other seven clan leaders follow.

Booming sounds echo across the landscape as the ten dragons slam down on the grass. Black smoke explodes through the air. Then the shifters stride towards us. The seven clan leaders are in their human form, while both the Iceheart monarchs and Draven performed a half-shift. Sunlight glints against two pairs of silver wings and is swallowed by a pair of black wings.

I discreetly study Draven's face, trying to read his mood.

Only his customary expression of ruthless power meets me.

My heart patters against my ribs. He still hasn't retaliated from when I handcuffed him to his desk, and I can't help but wonder if that is because he's gearing up for something massive during the final trial today.

A ripple of apprehension mixed with nervous excitement courses through our now small row of contestants as Jessina and Bane come to a halt on the grass right in front of us. As usual, Draven takes up position on their right, two steps behind, while the rest of the clan leaders form a row behind them.

"During the Age of Strife," Empress Jessina says, using the name that the shifters have for the historical period when fae were dragon riders, "you proved that you are a wicked and untrustworthy race. After we liberated ourselves from the bonds of servitude, we knew that we had to protect the rest of the world from people like you."

I clench my jaw and squeeze my hand into a fist.

"So we raised this grand forest." She sweeps a hand out to motion at the twisting forest of trees and thorns behind her. "And it has protected the world from your cruelty ever since."

From the corner of my eye, I can see Alistair squeeze his hand into a fist as well.

"Now," Emperor Bane picks up. "To atone for that past cruelty and to prove that you are worthy of redemption, it is only fitting that you must face the forest in your final trial."

Another ripple of apprehension courses through me. Very few people who go into the forest ever return.

I flick a glance towards the twisting trees. Then my gaze darts over to Draven for a second.

I expect him to glare at me or shoot me threatening stares or something. But he doesn't look at me at all. In fact, he hasn't looked at me even once since he landed on the grass. As if we're suddenly complete strangers again who have never interacted before. As if he didn't lock me up in his room a few days ago. As if we didn't share the same bed. As if he didn't pin me to his wall and drove me to the brink of an orgasm with just his fingers. As if that furious kiss never happened. As if I never handcuffed him to his desk.

For a moment, I feel an absolutely pathetic sense of disappointment.

Now that I'm faced with this sudden indifference, I realize with a start that I actually quite enjoyed our banter and bickering and even our fights. It has been a breath of fresh air. A moment of freedom for me. A rare opportunity to just be myself without having to worry about pleasing anyone. Riling him up has been surprisingly fun. So in spite of his infuriating interference during these trials, I've begun to look forward to our interactions.

But I suppose that's over now. If I win today, I will be officially recognized as a winner of the Atonement Trials by the Iceheart Dynasty, and there is nothing Draven can do to take that away from me. And if I lose, I will be stuck here for another one hundred and fifty years, just like he wants, and there is nothing I can do about it. So regardless of the outcome, we are now officially done with each other.

"Somewhere inside this forest is a stone altar," Imar announces, yanking me out of my thoughts. "And on that stone altar are three rings. Your mission is to find and retrieve one of the rings." His blue eyes gleam in the sunlight as he flashes us a foreboding smile. "And to make it out again alive."

Dread washes over me as I cast another glance towards the forest. We're supposed to find a ring? Inside *that* gigantic mess of trees and vines and thorns? My heart starts pounding faster in my chest. How the hell am I supposed to win this trial? I know nothing about how to navigate in the woods. And my magic is useless for this kind of thing too. There's no way that I will be able to find the rings on my own.

"The three people who first kneel before your emperor and empress and present one of the rings will be crowned the winners of this century's Atonement Trials," Imar continues. "You can only present *one* ring. Other than that, there are no rules."

"This is going to take days," Trevor blurts out from a little farther down to my left.

We all start in surprise and cast stunned glances at him, shocked that he even dared to speak up. The Icehearts narrow their eyes at him, as if they're displeased with his sudden outburst. Draven only continues staring straight in front of him, his face devoid of everything except that usual menacing air.

"Most likely, yes," Imar replies.

"But how are we supposed to survive in the forest?" Trevor continues, his eyes wide with disbelief. "Without water or food or equipment."

Imar lifts his shoulders in a nonchalant shrug. "That is up to you to figure out."

I suppress a sigh as I gaze out at the unwelcoming forest before me. Great. Just great.

"Do whatever is necessary to obtain one of the rings." Imar gives us a knowing look laced with both mockery and threats. "Because only three of you will be granted the privilege of leaving this city. And there will be one hundred and fifty years until the next Atonement Trials."

Tension crackles like bolts of lightning through the air as we all exchange dark glances. Eyebrows are drawn down, jaws are clenched, and eyes are filled with determination. We all have different reasons for wanting to win. But we all want it *desperately*.

As I scan the faces of my fellow contestants, I know without a doubt that there will be no alliances now. No holding back. No mercy. We are all in this to win.

I drag in a deep breath as I shift my gaze back to Imar.

He flashes us a wicked smile. "Begin."

I sprint towards the tree line.

CHAPTER TWENTY-NINE

My heart slams against my ribs and air cuts through my throat as I sprint right into the forest. All around me, the other nine contestants do the same. Dry twigs crunch underneath my boots as I run. But with every step, an overwhelming sense of panic and desperation clangs louder inside me.

I have no fucking clue what I'm doing.

I don't know where I'm going or how to even begin to locate the stone altar with the three rings. I don't even know why I'm running.

Trees and twisting branches flash past as I hurtle blindly into the woods. The other contestants quickly disappear from view as we all spread out. Out here, this close to the city, there is more space between the trees. But I know that the tangle of trees will only get thicker the farther in we get. How am I supposed to find anything in here?

Think.

Blades of grass rip from the ground as I suddenly dig my heels in and skid to a halt. Throwing out my hand, I catch myself on a brown tree trunk as I come to a complete stop. My heart pounds in my chest. I draw in a deep breath.

Think. Goddess damn it, I need to think.

I haven't won a single trial by sheer force of power. I have gotten through them all because I've played it smart. I need to do the same thing now.

I panicked when Imar just abruptly called the start like that, and I started running because that felt like the right thing to do. It's a race against the clock after all. Ten contestants and only three rings. But just dashing blindly through the forest is not a strategy. It's a dumb reaction caused by stress.

My chest heaves, and my brain is still flickering with that lingering sense of alarm and panic and stress that flooded my entire system when Imar called the start. Pressing my palm against the rough bark of the tree, I close my eyes and just focus on breathing in and out.

I need to use my head. That's how I'm going to win. Not by outrunning everyone else in a mad dash through the woods. By outsmarting them.

Once my heart has stopped slamming against my ribs and my brain has stopped spinning, I open my eyes again and take stock of my situation.

I'm never going to find that stone altar on my own. I don't have the necessary skill set, knowledge, or magical ability for it. So who does?

My mind drifts back to that night during the commencement ball when I overheard a group of contestants gossip about Lavendera. One woman's words echo in my mind.

I've heard that she actually lives out in the thorn forest.

Narrowing my eyes, I drum my fingers on the tree trunk while I consider that bit of gossip. If it's true, then Lavendera will know these woods better than anyone. She also has tree magic. If anyone can find the stone altar with the rings, it's her.

Hope surges through me.

Straightening, I whip my head from side to side, trying to catch sight of the brown-haired woman.

Only twisting trees stare back at me. Dark green vines and snaking branches filled with thorns curl around the trees and hang down from the boughs like vipers waiting to strike. And not a single contestant is in sight.

I blow out a sigh and then straighten my spine.

It's fine. I can still figure this out.

Channeling my magic, I cast it out around me in all directions.

This is a trick that took me a lot of time to master. But it's a very convenient use of my magic. By sending it flowing out around me like this, I can scan an area for people even though I can't see them.

Well, technically, I can't just scan for people since I can't sense emotions as such. I can only manipulate them. So what I do is to push out with my magic with the intention of increasing or decreasing an emotion. And once my magic latches on to that spark of emotion inside someone's chest, it creates a sort of tether which allows me to feel which direction they're in. As long as I keep increasing or decreasing whatever emotion I latched on to, I will be able to feel where that person is at all times.

The only problem is of course that, if I can't see them, I don't know *who* I'm latching on to.

Since I figured that worry should be a rather normal emotion right now, I aimed for that when I threw out my magic.

Several purple sparks of worry flare up as my magic hits them. I turn in a circle, gazing out at the trees in all the directions where I can feel those purple sparks. It's impossible to tell exactly how far away they are. And more importantly, I have no idea if one of those worried sparks belongs to Lavendera.

Scrunching up my eyebrows, I release them and instead try another emotion.

Stress.

Seven sparks appear.

I blow out a sigh and cut off the flow of my magic again.

This won't work. I need something more specific. Some kind of emotion that I know belongs to Lavendera.

Leaves rustle above my head as a strong wind sweeps through the forest. I stare at the mass of trees before me as a suddenly overwhelming sense of hopelessness washes over me.

Because I have no fucking clue what goes on inside Lavendera's head.

Half of the time, she is just staring at spots in the distance with a vacant expression in her eyes. The other half, she says the strangest things.

I have no idea if she is feeling angry or sad or confused or excited or indifferent. Or if she simply feels nothing at all.

"Shit," I curse under my breath.

Flexing my hand, I try to dispel the flash of worry and stress that pulses through me. After shaking out my hand, I roll my shoulders back and then give my body a good shake too.

"Alright, come on," I tell myself. "You can figure this out."

Who else has abilities that are suited for finding something in the woods and also has a very clear and distinct emotion that I know will belong to them?

The memory of Alistair's shockingly strong rage drifts through my mind. If I scanned for anger, I would no doubt be able to find Alistair. But he has fire magic. His chances of locating the rings are about as bad as mine.

Realization strikes like a lightning bolt.

Fenriel.

He has a hawk, for Mabona's sake! That hawk can scout ahead for miles and see everything from above. If anyone is going to find the rings, it's him.

A wide smile spreads across my lips.

Because Fenriel is also unique in another way. He is the only one among us who is always cheerful and excited.

Reaching for my magic, I throw it out in search of a glittering silver spark.

There.

Up ahead and a little to my left, one single spark of excitement burns inside the forest. And I know deep within my bones that it can only ever be Fenriel.

With hope now pulsing through me once more, I push off from the tree and sprint in that direction while I keep the steady stream of magic connected to Fenriel's spark. I increase it only enough to retain the magic connection. Not enough to change his mood too much.

Once I feel the spark getting close, I slow down. A hint of long red hair becomes briefly visible through the foliage.

Relief washes through me. It is Fenriel.

He appears to be jogging, and I can't overtake him, so I slow down to a jog as well.

And then, I simply follow him.

Hours pass by as I stalk Fenriel through the woods, always staying out of sight while still keeping my magic connected to him and boosting his excitement ever so slightly. It truly is a brilliant plan.

Apart from one thing.

Fenriel has the stamina of a fucking horse.

He keeps jogging at the same steady pace hour after hour. He has only stopped once, to drink from a brook we passed. I nearly inhaled the whole brook as I gulped down water while trying to refill my lungs at the same time. Then Fenriel took off again, so I had to cut my rest short and scramble after him.

We've passed some bushes with berries on them, and I don't know if Fenriel picked some on the way to eat. But I didn't dare to touch them. I have no idea if they're poisonous or not.

So instead, I just follow Fenriel. Hour after hour as he jogs through the woods.

And Mabona's fucking tits, my body is going to give out any second now.

I'm slim, just like everyone else in our city, since we're only allowed such small amounts of food. However, I have no clue what Fenriel does for a living, but I spend most of my days sitting on a stool and gutting fish.

Being slim and being fit are not the same thing.

I'm so not used to jogging for hours on end. Just getting through that maze last week took everything I had. This... This is going to kill me.

My throat and lungs burn as I drag in desperate breaths, and my legs tremble with every step as I try to keep pace with Fenriel. He's not even moving that fast. But it's the continuous running without barely a moment of rest that is killing me. If he doesn't stop for a break soon, I'm going to collapse.

Fenriel's excitement spikes.

It's so sudden, and so unexpected, that I actually gasp. That glittering silver spark in his chest flares up into a massive thrumming beacon.

And it was not my doing.

I stop moving. He does too.

There is only one reason why he would feel excitement that strong.

He has found the stone altar.

My chest heaves and my limbs tremble with exhaustion as I stand there on the grass, staring at the thick mass of trees ahead. Fenriel's spark of excitement remains in place. I drag lungfuls of air into my body.

Then Fenriel takes off at a sprint.

My heart leaps into my throat.

Every muscle in my body is screaming at me to stop. To just sit down. To lie down and rest.

But I can't. Because Fenriel has found the rings. And I need to get one of them.

Blocking out the pain and exhaustion that courses through my body like fire, I take off between the trees and sprint after Fenriel.

My heart slams so hard against my ribs that I think it's going to shatter them and collapse my lungs. But I keep running. Branches whip past my face and a stray thorn slices into my cheek as I sprint past. Yanking up a hand, I impatiently wipe off the thin line of blood that appeared.

Anticipation courses through me.

There looks to be an opening up ahead.

Pushing my legs to go as fast as they can, I dash towards it, shoving branches and vines and thorns aside with my arms.

I crash through the trees and into a clearing.

Fenriel is standing next to a stone altar in the middle of the small clearing. His hawk Talon is perched on his shoulder, and there is a triumphant smile on his lips as he holds up one of the rings.

My gaze snaps down to the altar. Two gold rings remain there.

Hope surges through me.

I take a step forward right as someone else steps into the clearing.

Lavendera blinks when she sees me and Fenriel, and comes to a halt only two steps in. She cocks her head. I open my mouth to say something right as the sound of snapping branches comes from Lavendera's side of the glen.

She doesn't even turn around. But both Fenriel and I snap our gazes towards the noise.

My heart drops as Alistair, Isera, and Trevor sprint into the clearing.

CHAPTER THIRTY

For one single second, we all just stare at each other. Then everyone's eyes turn towards the stone altar and the two gold rings that remain. Fenriel, who was holding up the third one, snaps his fingers closed around it and yanks his hand down.

The clearing explodes into chaos.

I throw myself sideways as a block of stone shoots towards me. Across the grass, Fenriel whirls around and tries to sprint away.

Fire roars through the air, creating a wall of flames in front of Fenriel, at the same time as Alistair, Isera, and Trevor dash towards the altar.

Rolling to my feet again, I leap up from the grass and sprint towards it as well. But I'm on the wrong side of the clearing. They arrived in a spot that was much closer to the altar than mine. So before I've even made it halfway across the clearing, they have already reached the stone altar.

Desperation slashes through my soul as I watch Trevor and Alistair snatch up the remaining two rings.

Isera arrives one second later, her fingers almost managing to brush the ring that Alistair grabs. A block of ice explodes into existence, wrapping around Alistair's entire hand. He cries out in shock and then slams his burning palm over the ice encasing his hand.

Fenriel makes another attempt to sprint away with the ring he already has, but this time it's Isera who throws up a massive wall of ice. I gasp as it shoots up from the ground, encircling the entire clearing and locking above us like a dome. Her message is clear. No one fucking leaves until she has one of the rings.

I silently thank her for that because I also need to get one of the rings before the others can disappear with them.

Sprinting across the grass, I aim straight for Trevor while bombarding him with pulses of magic in order to find something that sticks. Stress. Panic. Fear. Exhaustion.

Exhaustion.

My magic finally finds a spark in his chest to latch on to. I pour my magic into it.

To get here at the same time as us, Trevor must also have been running constantly all day. He, and Isera and Alistair too, probably had the same idea as me. Follow Lavendera as she searches for the stone altar.

My concentration slips for a second as I'm struck by a sudden thought. Flicking my gaze from side to side, I scan the clearing for Lavendera. Shock pulses through me when I realize that she's nowhere to be found.

Stone shoots towards me.

I leap to the side barely a second before a block of stone flies past in the space where my head was supposed to be. Snapping my gaze back to Trevor, I growl a curse and then increase the strength of my magic.

Tiredness washes over his features, and he staggers to the side as I blow his exhaustion from a spark to a wildfire. He shakes his head violently, trying to block out the emotion. Raising a trembling hand, he shoots a hail of pebbles at me.

I jerk back, but it's no use. There are too many of them to

avoid, so I just yank up my forearm to protect my face and twist sideways. Pain pulses through my body as the pebbles hit me in the back and side.

Fire roars across the grass to my left.

It explodes into hissing steam as it slams into Isera's ice wall.

I gasp in a breath and spin back towards Trevor to see him raise a block of stone. Panic pulses through me, and I push at his exhaustion with everything I have. His knees buckle, and he loses the grip on his magic. I'm just about to sprint towards him and snatch the ring from his hand when a block of ice cracks into the back of his head.

His eyes go wide with shock before his brain catches up with the hit. Then he blacks out and slams face first into the grass.

I let out a yell of frustration as Isera snatches the ring out of his hand while shooting three consecutive blocks of ice at me, Alistair, and Fenriel. I throw myself sideways, rolling to my feet, while the blocks of ice shoot past on the grass. Alistair burns them off with his flames.

More blocks of ice speed through the air as Isera shoots them at us, barely aiming, while she backs towards the edge of the clearing. I zigzag across the grass, trying to get to Alistair and steal his ring while he's busy battling Isera.

Magic flashes through the air. Hissing and crackling noises echo between the ice walls. I suck in desperate breaths, trying to keep my legs moving. My lungs burn, my muscles ache, and everything inside me is screaming with exhaustion from the constant running and the lack of food and water. But I have to get one of the rings. I have to.

Alistair ducks and Fenriel dives away as Isera shoots more blocks of ice at us to keep everyone back. I'm forced to throw myself forwards to avoid one of them, landing right in the line of fire between Isera and Alistair. Panic crackles up my spine as I jump to my feet and try to dash away.

But before I can move more than a stride, Alistair shoots

another torrent of fire towards Isera at the same time as she makes the ice ceiling crack above our heads.

Talon, Fenriel's hawk, who had been trying to claw through the ice and create a hole at the top of the dome, lets out a screech of victory and swoops towards Fenriel.

I see the disaster that is about to happen as time seems to slow to a crawl.

Dread crackles through me like lightning, and I scream a warning, but I already know that it will be too late.

The hawk swoops down, oblivious to the torrent of fire that is about to shoot through the air. And Fenriel, who is busy leaping back up to his feet and spinning back around, doesn't see it. I know, without a doubt, that when he turns around and sees what's about to happen, it will be too late. Too late for him to make the hawk change direction. Too late for him to even release his magic and make the hawk vanish.

Talon is going to get incinerated.

Without thinking, I do the only thing I can.

I throw out my arm, grab the hawk mid-air, and yank it to the side.

Pain sears through me and I scream in agony as the flames roar past a fraction of a second later and singe my arm. The hawk lets out a high-pitched call of alarm. I release it, and it immediately flies straight towards Fenriel.

For a few seconds, everyone goes dead silent and still inside the clearing.

Fenriel is staring at me with wide eyes. His face is pale as death and full of lingering terror. A few strides away from me, Alistair casts a shocked look between me and Fenriel and Talon. Isera reaches the ice wall. Hesitation flickers in her eyes as she casts a glance at me.

Then she demolishes the wall, drops a strangely shaped chunk of ice right next to my feet, and then sprints away with her ring.

The sound of shattering ice makes Alistair lurch into motion.

Closing his fist around his own ring, he whirls around and hurtles into the trees in the other direction.

I'm left standing there in the middle of the clearing, staring at their disappearing backs while my arm throbs in pain. I flick a glance down at the ground. The chunk of ice that Isera dropped by my feet is still there. Confusion swirls through me as I stare down at it. It's round, but shaped like a tunnel rather than a cylinder, and it's about the length of my forearm.

Realization slashes into me. Bending down, I snatch up the chunk of ice and slide it onto my forearm. It fits perfectly, and Isera must have somehow adjusted the temperature of it too, because it's only pleasantly cool instead of being so freezing cold that it would've risked causing frostbite.

A sigh of relief comes from the back of my throat as the strange magical ice soothes the burns that Alistair's flames caused.

"You saved him."

Whirling around, I blink in shock as I find Fenriel still standing there. Some of the color has returned to his face, but he is still staring at me with wide eyes.

"You saved Talon," he repeats.

Since I don't know what to say, all that makes it out of my mouth is, "Yes."

That word seems to make everything come crashing down around him. He staggers a step to the side and chokes back a sob. Talon lands on his shoulder and nudges Fenriel's cheek with his beak.

I just watch them in silence. I didn't even know if the hawk could die, since he's a product of magic, but based on Fenriel's reaction, it appears as though he can.

Fenriel swallows down another choked breath and reaches up to stroke the hawk's feathers. Then he starts towards me. I remain rooted in place with the chunk of ice wrapped around my forearm. The burns weren't too bad. They're painful, but they will heal. Probably by tomorrow. Especially now since I could treat them with the strange ice straight away.

While striding towards me, Fenriel raises his hand. Then he tosses something towards me. I yank up my uninjured arm and catch it on reflex.

Stunned shock pulses through me as I stare down at the object now in my hand. One of the gold rings. With eyes wide, I raise my gaze to Fenriel.

"Take it," he says.

And because my brain is slow with both pain and exhaustion, all I can manage to reply is, "You're giving it to me?"

"Without Talon, nothing matters. My life is meaningless if he is not by my side." His gold and blue eyes are dead serious as he holds my gaze. "You saved him. I owe you more than a simple ring."

My mouth drops open, and I just stare at him.

All the usual cheerfulness and excitement is gone from his expression now. Instead, cold ruthlessness, the likes of which I have never seen on his face before, spreads across his features.

"Take the ring," he says. It sounds almost like an order. A muscle feathers in his jaw as he clenches it while he squeezes his hand into a fist. His eyes are locked on the woods to my right as he grinds out, "I'm going after Alistair."

I stare after him in shock as he stalks right past me and continues towards the tree line. The hawk flaps his wings on his shoulder and then flies into the air. Fenriel takes off at a sprint.

With my mouth still open, I stare at him until his long red hair disappears completely behind the foliage.

I look down at my hand.

The golden ring in my palm glints faintly in the late afternoon sunlight. I close my fingers around it while stunned disbelief washes over me. I have one of the rings. I can win the trial.

Trevor groans on the ground.

Panic shoots up my spine as I remember that he is still here.

And Lavendera is here somewhere too. I need to get away before either of them decides that, between me, Isera, and Alistair, I'm the easiest target.

After sliding the ring onto my finger, I whirl around and sprint back in the direction that I came from. I keep running until my legs can't take it anymore. Sinking down on the ground, I brace my back against a tree trunk and gasp in deep breaths.

Exhaustion rolls through my entire body.

But I'm far enough away from the clearing that the others shouldn't be able to track me. So now, all I need to do is to run back out of the forest.

A sudden realization slams into me like a shovel to the face. The thought is so jarring that I swear my ears are ringing.

After looking down at the ring on my finger, I drag my gaze up and stare out at the forest before me while that terrible realization sweeps through my whole soul.

I managed to get all the way in here by following Fenriel.

But without him, how the hell am I supposed to find my way back out again?

CHAPTER THIRTY-ONE

My head spins. Staggering across the uneven ground, I desperately try to block out all the exhaustion and pain and hunger. The hunger should be nothing new. But after these weeks in the Golden Palace, my body has started to get used to the luxury of three meals a day. And now it twists, empty after almost an entire day without food. An entire day of running. And fighting.

I glance down at my forearm. The ice has long since melted, taking its soothing coldness with it, and my arm now throbs with pain as my body tries hard to heal the wounds. But because of the lack of food, the healing is excruciatingly slow.

Another wave of desperation washes over me. I really need to find something to eat. But most importantly, I need to figure out where I am.

By my best estimate, it has been two hours since I left the clearing with the stone altar. And I've walked in the direction that I think is south, but I'm somehow still no closer to finding my way out of this infernal forest. I glance at the trees around me.

The sun is slipping lower on the horizon, painting the

treetops with splashes of deep red. I draw in a strained breath as I come to a halt. The setting sun is a problem, because it will bring a blanket of darkness over the woods soon. I need to try to reconfirm which direction is which.

Because the canopy is so thick, I can't even see the Peaks of Prosperity from in here. And without them as a landmark to navigate by, it's difficult to know if I have been walking in the right direction all this time. I need to either find another clearing. Or climb a tree.

My forearm pulses in pain at just the thought of it. But I can't just wander around aimlessly and hope to come across another clearing, so I grit my teeth and grab the nearest branch. It creaks slightly as I begin pulling myself up.

Vines sway around me like snakes as I haul myself up towards the next branch. I shove them aside with my free hand while bracing my weight on the branch underneath me. Thorns slash at my skin.

I suck in a sharp breath between my teeth. Narrowing my eyes, I glare at the vines and the thorns that twist around them. As if trying to climb a tree wasn't already difficult, now the damn thing is fighting back too.

With much more careful movements, I push aside a tangle of vines and then jump to reach the next branch above me. The vines immediately swing back into place. Thorns scrape against my skin as I climb. I grit my teeth and try to ignore their pricking.

My muscles tremble with exhaustion as I throw my arm up towards the final branch. I can barely manage to pull myself upwards. A cry of desperation rips from my lungs. Using every smidgen of strength I have left, I shove off from the branch below and haul myself upwards.

Fresh air washes over me as I break through the thick canopy. I drag in a deep breath. While holding on to the tree trunk, I close my eyes for a second and just breathe in the cool air. Out here, it tastes like pine trees and fallen leaves and crisp mountain air.

Just feeling the open air flood my lungs, washing away the suffocating sensation from the hours underneath the twisting vines and thick canopy, makes strength return to my body.

Once my head feels a little clearer again, I open my eyes and gaze out at the landscape around me. The thorn forest spreads out on all sides. Dread washes over me when I realize that I'm much farther from the city than I thought. Twisting my head, I glance between the mountain range visible far to the north and then towards the open area south from here where our city is located. Even if I walk in a straight line, it's going to take almost an entire day to reach it. And without being able to see the Peaks of Prosperity, I won't even know if I *am* walking in a straight line.

A miserable sigh escapes my chest. Mabona's tits, I fucking hate this stupid forest.

Shaking my head, I get ready to climb back down again. I still have another pressing problem to solve. The sun is about to set, and I need to find somewhere safe to sleep.

My limbs tremble with exhaustion as I climb back down again.

But I only make it halfway before my gaze snags on something that I missed on the way up.

A cluster of what looks like... fruit.

Squinting, I study the strange pieces of fruit. It's not something that we grow in our orchards out on the fields around our city. In fact, I have never seen a piece of fruit like this before. It's green and kind of oval in shape.

I reach towards the closest one.

Hesitation flickers through me. What if it's poisonous?

Pain pulses through my forearm again. I glance down at the burn wounds that are struggling to heal.

Goddess damn it. I need food for the healing to work the way it's supposed to. I shift my gaze back to the strange fruit. I'll have to risk it.

Reaching out, I pick the closest one and then bring it to my lips. While sending a prayer to Mabona that this won't kill me, I take a bite right in the middle.

A soft and juicy texture meets my tongue.

I let out a moan from deep inside.

Goddess, it's delicious.

My body is urging me to just gobble it all up straight away, but I force myself to wait. After that first bite, I remain standing on the branch and just holding on to that piece of fruit for at least five minutes. If it's poisonous, or hallucinogenic, I need to know before I inhale the entire cluster of fruit.

When five minutes have passed and I haven't died, I bring the green fruit back to my mouth and then scarf it down within a matter of seconds. Then I reach for another piece of fruit. And another. And another. Until I've eaten them all.

Energy floods my veins once more, and a tingling sensation starts in my forearm. I heave a deep sigh of relief. Now, my body can finally begin to heal the burns properly.

Feeling much more clear-headed, I climb the rest of the way back to the ground.

The sun has slipped even lower towards the horizon, and a murky haze has now crept into the forest around me. I swallow down a sense of dread as I scan the gloomy trees around me. I have no idea what this forest is like at night, and I would prefer not to find out. After all, there is a reason why the people who go into this forest rarely come back out again.

After checking the knife I still keep strapped to my thigh, I turn in the direction I now know to be south and start forward at a brisk pace. I need to find somewhere safe to sleep before all light is gone from the world.

Branches and thorny vines snatch at my clothes and hair as I hurry across the uneven ground. I shove them away while whipping my head from side to side, desperately searching for something that will provide me with a bit of protection.

My gaze snags on something to my left.

Trailing to a halt, I turn towards it fully and squint as I study it.

Gnarly branches have grown from the tree trunks and down towards the ground, creating an almost cave-like structure with an opening at the front. Hope sparkles inside me. This is perfect. If I sleep in there, I can stay hidden both from other contestants and whatever else lives in these woods.

Rolling my shoulders back, I start towards the large opening in the curving branches. A *crack* sounds as one of the roots that cover the ground snaps in half underneath my weight.

Right as I'm about to glare down at the root, another sound drifts through the forest. A low and rumbling groan.

The blood freezes to ice in my veins.

Stopping dead in my tracks, I stare at the dark opening ahead. My heart slams against my ribs.

The deep rumbling comes again.

"Oh fuck," is all I manage to say.

Then a monster charges out from the tree cave.

CHAPTER THIRTY-TWO

All blood drains from my face as a wolfbear charges straight at me. It's exactly what it sounds like. A mix between a wolf and a bear. Except it's three times the size of a normal bear.

I scream as it lunges for me. Diving sideways, I barely manage to escape the swipe of its knife-sharp claws. It crashes into the tree next to where I was standing only a second before. I roll across the roots and leap to my feet.

The wolfbear swivels its massive head towards me.

I bolt.

A furious roar comes from behind me.

Fear slashes through my chest as the wolfbear gives chase.

My heart hammers against my ribs as I dash through the forest. Heavy thuds and loud crashing sounds echo behind me, getting closer with every second. A whooshing comes from behind.

On instinct, I duck and throw myself sideways.

A massive paw swipes through the air where my head used to be one single second afterwards. I crash into a thick tree trunk. Pain spikes up my shoulder as I slam into the rough bark.

The wolfbear roars in frustration and skids to a halt.

Shoving off from the tree, I barely manage to swing myself around the trunk before the beast charges into it. Leaves rustle and branches rattle as its heavy weight smacks into the tree trunk with enough force to make the tree bend.

Panic grips my heart.

I jerk back, trying to sprint away again, but the animal lunges towards me. Gasping, I yank myself back behind the trunk. With my heart slamming against my ribs, I circle the thick tree trunk, keeping it between me and the monster. The wolfbear growls at me as it fails to reach me once more.

Heavy panting comes from its mouth, and saliva drips from its sharp teeth as it opens its maw and makes another attempt. Its jaws snap shut mere breaths away from my face as I jerk backwards.

The panic inside my skull builds into a blaring crescendo as I dart from side to side, desperately trying to keep the tree between me and the death waiting for me.

Another roar of anger echoes from the beast's throat. And instead of trying to run around the trunk to get to me, it charges right into it.

Wood cracks as the wolfbear slams its shoulder into the trunk. Leaves rain down around me. A cry of fear rips from deep inside me.

Yanking out my knife, I grip the hilt hard as the monster pulls back from the trunk again. My breathing comes in fits and starts as I stare at the massive beast before me. It bares its teeth at me, saliva dripping from the sharp canines. I drag in unsteady breaths.

The wolfbear charges.

Every instinct inside me is screaming at me to run. But I force myself to remain where I am. Right as the beast crashes into the trunk again, I leap to the side and swing my knife.

Wood cracks, sending chips flying. Branches rattle and roots groan as the tree tips backwards from the force of the hit.

I aim for the monster's throat as I slam my blade down at it from the side.

The beast twists right at the last second, and my knife buries itself in the animal's shoulder instead.

The wolfbear roars in pain.

Gasping in shock and fear, I stumble backwards, yanking the knife out again.

Another roar tears from its throat. It swings its head from side to side, swiping madly with its paw. I use that brief moment of pain and disorientation to escape.

Whipping around, I sprint away between the trees.

My pulse thrums so fast in my ears that I can barely hear anything over the loud pounding of my own heart and my own ragged breaths. Ramming the knife back into its sheath, I throw out both hands in front of me and shove at the vines and thorns that are trying to block my way. The thorns slice at my arms, but I don't dare to stop.

A tiny sprout of hope manages to flicker in my chest for one second when the forest behind me remains silent.

Then it's promptly crushed and drowned in a cold black lake of fear and desperation as the wolfbear roars and charges after me again.

I yank vines out of my way while a whimper of terror rips from deep within me. Heavy thuds close in on me from behind. I sprint with everything I have while desperation rips through my whole soul. My feet pound against the ground. But the wolfbear keeps gaining on me. Fast.

The thick tangle of trees abruptly gives way to a clearing. I sprint into it while whipping my head from side to side, trying to find something that will protect me. On the other side of the clearing, a twisting nest of thin trees and vines rise up like a wall.

Hope surges through me again.

If I can just get there, I'll be able to weave through the narrow spaces. But the wolfbear is too big. It will get stuck in the clearing.

My lungs burn as I race towards the safety of the tree wall.

Wood snaps behind me.

I cast a glance over my shoulder right as the wolfbear crashes into the clearing after me.

With my heart slamming against my ribcage, I sprint with everything I have.

But it's not enough.

The beast leaps.

Diving forward, I throw myself flat against the root-covered ground right as the wolfbear flies past above me. My hair whips in the wind that its massive form creates.

It slams into the ground in front of me. I leap to my feet right as it spins around to face me.

Dread and terrible hopelessness wash over me as I stare into its yellow eyes. We're right in the middle of the clearing, and the massive beast now stands between me and the safety of the thick foliage wall on the other side.

Channeling my magic, I try to force it to feel tired or bored or anything at all. But it's useless.

Heavy snorting sounds come from its muzzle as it pants. My chest heaves as well. And I know, without a doubt, that this is it. When it attacks this time, I won't be able to evade it.

The wolfbear growls and bares its teeth.

Then it raises its massive paw and lunges at me.

A roar that could have shattered the heavens explodes through the air.

Then something huge slams down behind me with enough force to make the ground shake.

I gasp in shock as a massive dragon head swings around from behind me.

Another blood-curdling roar splits the darkening sky as the dragon opens his gigantic jaws and bellows at the wolfbear.

Stunned shock pulses through my body as I slowly turn my head and look over my shoulder.

A massive black dragon crouches behind me.

My heart flips.

Draven.

He has lowered his head and curved his neck around me, keeping his massive body behind my back, his neck protecting my right side, and his head slightly in front of me as he roars at the wolfbear again.

I whip my gaze forwards again to see the wolfbear jerk back. Then fury seems to pulse across the animal's face, and it rears up on its hindlegs. I flinch and turn my head to protect my face as it swipes its claws towards me.

Fire sears through the air.

Another gasp rips from my lungs as a torrent of flames streams through the air. From this close, the heat is so intense that I can feel it vibrating against my skin.

The wolfbear only has time to shriek for one second.

Then the fire incinerates it completely.

My heart slams against my ribs as I straighten and turn fully towards the wolfbear again. Only embers and ashes remain. They float in the air, pulled up towards the darkening sky by a cold evening wind.

For a few seconds, all I can do is to stare at them.

Then I turn towards Draven.

He pulls his head back from around me and straightens.

Awe pulses through me as I stare up at his massive form. His huge black wings are spread wide to the sides, and red light from the dying sun reflect against his night black scales. My heart clenches. Goddess above, he really is breathtaking.

Black smoke explodes across the clearing, and the massive dragon disappears into it.

A moment later, Draven in his fully human form stalks out of the smoke. As usual, he is wearing his black dragon scale armor, complete with his massive sword.

I open my mouth to thank him for saving my life. But I don't even manage to get the first word out.

Because Draven is looking at me as if he's about to murder *me* next.

CHAPTER THIRTY-THREE

Black storm clouds gather around Draven as he advances on me. Thunder rumbles from them, in tune with the anger that seems to roll off his muscular body. He flexes his right hand as he locks a commanding stare on me.

"Azaroth's flame," he curses, his voice coming out more like a growl. "What the hell are you doing?"

I jerk back, stunned by his anger. Recovering, I give my head a quick shake and then draw my eyebrows down in a scowl. "What am *I* doing?"

"I let you out of my sight for half a day, and I come back to find you fighting a *wolfbear*! Are you out of your mind?"

"I wasn't fighting it. I was trying to *survive*."

"Then you should have run from it. Not faced it down like some kind of lunatic."

"I *was* running from it. But in case you didn't know, the average person cannot actually outrun a wolfbear." I blink as the rest of his words finally catch up with me. Narrowing my eyes, I watch him as he comes to a halt right in front of me. "Wait… What do you mean *let you out of my sight*? Were you watching me?"

He draws up short, seeming startled by the question for a second. Then he crosses his arms over his chest and scowls down at me as if I'm stupid. "Of course I was. I'm one of the people in charge of making sure that the trial runs smoothly." Suspicion creeps into his eyes. "Which begs the question, what the hell are you doing all the way out here?"

"I was trying to find my way back."

"Why would you be..." He trails off as his gaze darts down to my hand. Shock crackles across his features, and when he snaps his gaze back up to my face, his eyes are wide with disbelief. "You. *You* have one of the rings?"

Crossing my arms over my chest defensively, I drag my eyebrows down deeper and glower at him. "No need to sound so surprised."

"Of course I am. I saw Alistair, Isera, and Trevor follow Lavendera to the stone altar. How the hell did *you* manage to find it?"

I stew in annoyed silence before admitting, "Fenriel's hawk found it. And I followed Fenriel."

"How? You're not skilled enough to track someone through the woods."

"Wow. Your faith in my skills really is touching."

"Just answer the question."

"Fenriel is the only contestant who ever feels excited. So I tracked him by that emotion."

Surprise pulses across Draven's unnecessarily handsome features. And for a moment, he almost looks... *impressed*. Then ruthless authority slams back down over his features, and he snaps his fingers at me before holding out his palm. "Alright, hand it over."

My eyebrows shoot up.

He narrows his eyes, and his voice drops lower and darker as threats lace his tone. "Give me the ring, Selena."

I scoff. "Is that an order?"

"Did it sound like a suggestion?"

Uncrossing my arms, I hold up my right hand with the back of my hand towards Draven and my fingers straight. A faint hint of red light from the setting sun glints in the smooth gold ring. Draven raises his eyebrows expectantly and shoots a pointed look down at his open palm.

I flash him a smile dripping with challenge. "You want it?" I flip him off. "Come and get it."

He jerks back, looking stunned. But I don't stop to watch it. Instead, I whirl around and sprint towards the dense wall of vines and trees across the clearing.

I figured that the same tactic I had planned for the wolfbear will work on Draven too. The space between the trees is so narrow that I will be able to squeeze through it. But Draven, even without his wings, is much broader and bulkier than me. He will never be able to follow me through it.

An insane burst of excitement rushes through me as I dash towards the tree line. Behind me, Draven lets out a curse. Then the black storm clouds that hung around him start expanding.

My heart jerks as the clouds spread rapidly across the clearing, further darkening the already gloomy area. Winds whirl across the grass, snatching at my clothes and hair. I hurtle across the ground.

Right as I reach the dense wall of trees, a gust of wind slams into them, making them rattle. I twist sideways to slip through the narrow gap, and while doing so, I also cast a quick glance behind me.

Draven isn't running after me.

Instead, he is simply striding across the ground as if he has all the time in the world. His steps are confident. Powerful. And there is a slight smirk on his lips. As if there isn't a single shred of doubt in his mind that he will catch me.

We'll see about that.

Squeezing through the gap between the first row of trees, I

twist my body and slide sideways towards the next one. There is no way that Draven will be able to follow me. Twisting and slipping, I make it about four full strides into the mass of vines and thin tree trunks.

Then a bolt of lightning cracks into the trees.

I suck in a sharp breath and whip my head towards the entrance to the tree wall. The thin trunks at the front groan. Then crack. Then topple outwards.

My pulse thrums in my ears as I watch the outmost row fall aside right in the spot where I slipped in earlier. A moment later, Draven strides in. Storm clouds swirl around him like black smoke. Through the tangle of vines, his eyes find mine. A wicked grin spreads across his face.

"Shit," I breathe.

With alarm blaring in my skull, I lurch into motion again. Squeezing between the next set of trunks, I move as fast as I can. But the ground in here isn't made of grass or soil or even firm roots. Instead, it's made up entirely of those thin vine-like trunks. They're hard, and slippery, and they produce strange clanging noises when I step on them. Like a hollow wooden tube when you strike it. But most importantly, they're *round*. So every time I step on one, my foot slides sideways towards where that thin tree meets the one next to it.

I twist my ankle several times as I scramble across the slippery ground.

Lightning cracks into the trees right behind. I suck in rapid breaths as wooden groaning and crashes follow it. My heart thumps in my chest. I spin around while weaving through the next gap.

A hand locks around my wrist.

My stomach lurches as I'm yanked backwards.

Air explodes from my lungs in a huff as I slam right into a rock-hard chest.

Tilting my head back, I'm met by Draven's smirking face.

"Did you really think that would work?" he taunts.

Reality snaps back into me, and I try to yank my wrist out of his grip. His fingers remain firmly locked around it while he reaches up with his other hand. Panic shoots through me as he reaches for the gold ring on my finger.

In a burst of desperation, I yank out the knife from my thigh holster and swing it towards him.

He jerks back in shock, loosening his grip on my wrist, as the blade slashes through the air right in front of his face. Using that moment to my advantage, I rip my wrist out of his grip and lurch forward, aiming to slip past him and dart back out into the clearing.

I've barely managed to make it two strides past him when something heavy slams into my back.

A yelp slips from my lips as Draven and I crash to the ground. The round wooden trunks that make up the ground dig into my hipbone as I land on my side next to Draven. Scrambling furiously, I try to get my limbs free and crawl away.

Hands appear on my hips before I can get my own hands and knees underneath me. Another startled noise rips from my lungs as Draven yanks me back and flips me around. My back hits the ground with a thud, followed a second later by Draven's knees landing on either side of my hips as he straddles me. The force of our bodies hitting those strange trunks makes that hollow clanging noise echo around us again.

I try to swing the knife at Draven's face again, but this time, he's ready for it. Grabbing my wrist mid-air, he holds my hand steady as he yanks the blade out of my grip. In one fluid motion, he spins the knife in his hand and then presses it against my throat.

Drawing in a sharp breath, I stop struggling underneath him.

"Azaroth's flame," he curses, and shoots me an exasperated scowl. "You nearly took my eye out. Who knew you were so violent?"

I huff. "You're one to talk."

Amusement flickers in his eyes for the briefest of moments. Then that expression of complete and utter authority descends on his features again. While holding my gaze with commanding eyes, he nods towards my hand. "Alright, you know how this goes."

I curl my hand into a fist, feeling the cold metal ring dig into my skin. Desperation rips through my chest.

"Why are you even doing this?" I ask. It comes out almost like a shout. And it's far more high-pitched and breathless than I had planned for it to be. "I made it through all of the other trials. I got the ring. Why can't you just let me win?"

He holds my gaze with serious eyes, and I can tell that he means every word when he says, "Because you don't deserve it."

I slam my fist into the ground in frustration. "Look, I'm sorry about throwing the drink at you. If I had—"

"I don't care," he cuts me off, his voice as merciless as his eyes. "You could beg and plead and bargain with me all night, but it still wouldn't make a difference." Cold steel kisses my skin as he slides the knife up higher, pressing the flat of the blade underneath my chin. "Hand it over. Now."

My heart slams against my ribs as I stare up into his unyielding eyes. And in that moment, I know that I have no other choice.

So I heave a deep sigh and then take off the ring. While holding his hard stare, I drop it in his waiting palm. He slips the ring into one of the pouches along his belt.

"Good." A small smirk tugs at his lips. "You're finally learning to obey my orders."

I narrow my eyes and level a glare full of challenge on him. "This isn't over."

I might have been forced to hand it over right now because he has me pinned to the ground underneath him with a blade at my throat. But as soon as he turns his back on me so that he can't see my eyes, I'm going to manipulate his emotions and make him give it back to me.

"Yes, it is," he replies, and slides my knife into one of his own holsters. "Because now, I'm going to fly away from here and drop the ring somewhere else. And you're going to go back to the city and accept that you have lost."

"I will never accept that I have lost. I swear by your god and mine, I'm going to fight with everything—"

A white bolt of lightning slams into the ground right next to me. It's so forceful that the ground shakes.

I gasp, the sound cutting my threat short. The air around me taste of ozone.

"Listen to me," Draven presses out between clenched teeth before I can recover. "You—"

Wooden groaning noises suddenly come from right underneath me.

Both Draven and I whip our heads towards it.

But before either of us can so much as open our mouth, a loud crack cuts through the dark evening air.

My stomach lurches as the hollow wooden trunks beneath us give way.

And we plummet into a dark abyss.

CHAPTER THIRTY-FOUR

Pain shoots through my body as I slam back first into another set of hollow trunks. And then another. And another. Each one gives way as soon as we hit it, making us plummet too fast for us to even have a chance at grabbing on to something. I grunt in pain at each rapid hit.

Draven wraps his arms around me and throws his weight sideways. It makes us spin in the air so that he's below and I'm above instead.

Hollow wood shatters and splinters fly around us as we tumble downwards in the gloomy darkness.

Suddenly, the layers of trunks end and we're falling through the open air for a few seconds. But before Draven can even shift and summon his wings, we slam into the ground.

Air explodes from Draven's lungs as he crashes back first into the ground with me on top of him. My back still aches from the first couple of layers that I smacked into when we fell, but because Draven flipped us around and took the brunt of the fall, I'm mostly unharmed.

He grunts and drags in a strained breath.

I suddenly realize that I'm still lying on top of him, my entire body pressed against his. It probably isn't helping him get air back into his lungs. I try to scramble off him, but his arms are still wrapped tightly around me. So instead, I brace my palms on his firm chest and just raise my head to meet his gaze.

"Are you okay?" I ask.

He drags in another breath and then presses out, "Yeah." His eyes find mine. "You?"

"You're the one who took most of the hits," I point out.

His gaze flits down to his arms, which are still wrapped around me. He blinks, looking startled, and then quickly releases me. I climb off him immediately and get to my feet. My heart suddenly pounds in my chest for some reason.

Another groan comes from Draven's throat as he sits up. Raising his hands, he rakes them through his now messy hair and heaves a deep sigh. Then he pushes to his feet as well.

For a little while, we just stand there side by side, staring up at the spot where we fell through.

It's hard to make out all the details in the murky darkness, but we appear to be inside an underground forest. The ground beneath my feet is made up entirely of thick and lush grass, which is now flattened by our landing. Trees spread out around us, but it's not the same kind of trees that can be found in the thorn forest above. These have a slightly surreal and almost magical look to them. But most importantly, there is no sky above our heads.

Instead of a setting sun and a sky painted in dark red and purple, there is a solid ceiling made of those strange thin trunks above us. It spans the whole area around us as far as I can see. And right above us is a narrow hole. Through it, we can see layer upon layer of those thin tree trunks, creating a thick barrier between the world above and whatever place we have ended up in.

"Well… fuck," Draven mutters.

Cocking my head, I study the broken edges of the trunks.

"You must have weakened the structural integrity of the wood with your lightning strikes."

I can feel Draven slowly turning his head and looking down to stare at me. Tearing my gaze from the narrow hole above, I meet his gaze. His expression is full of disbelief.

"Weakened the structural integrity of the wood?" he echoes.

"It means you broke it."

A scowl pulls at his brows as he huffs, "I know what it means."

"Uh-huh."

He mutters something under his breath.

Tilting my head back, I glance up at the hole again. But right before I can ask if he can fly us back up, a sudden burst of uncertainty pulses through me. I flick a quick look at Draven instead. Because the real question is: if he *can* fly up, would he take me with him?

My gaze drifts down to the pouch where he put the ring that he forced me to hand over, and his previous words echo through my mind again. *Now, I'm going to fly away from here and drop the ring somewhere else. And you're going to go back to the city and accept that you have lost.*

He was planning to leave me up there. And he desperately wants to make sure that I lose this trial. So what's to stop him from just flying out of here on his own and leaving me to search for another way out? It would solve both of his problems.

However, before I can decide whether or not to ask him and to put the idea in his head that he can fly away and leave me, he volunteers the answer himself.

"I can't fly us back up through that hole," he says.

My heart flips, and a ridiculous burst of giddiness sweeps through me. *Us*. Fly *us* back up. That's what he said. I have to suppress a very untimely grin, since the news in itself, that he can't fly through the hole, isn't very good.

"It's too narrow," he explains, scowling up at the hole. "I won't even be able to extend my wings halfway."

And because of the realization that he never planned to leave me trapped down here alone, I'm suddenly filled with energy. So I flash him a teasing grin and reply, "Really? You're bragging about your wingspan?"

He starts in surprise and snaps his gaze back down to me. There is an absolutely adorable flustered look on his face for a few seconds before he manages to compose himself again. Narrowing his eyes, he takes a step closer and fixes me with a pointed stare.

"You really are making up for lost time, aren't you?"

I blink. "What do you mean?"

"All of those snarky remarks that you've been swallowing down over the years, you're taking them all out on me now." Raising his hand, he draws his fingers along my jaw and then brushes his thumb over my bottom lip. "Such a sharp little tongue hidden behind a polite smile all this time."

My breath hitches. A shiver courses through my spine as he slides his thumb back over my bottom lip again. I can barely concentrate on anything except the soft brush of his fingers.

Then he lets out a low chuckle and drops his hand while taking a step back. "And to answer your question, I was simply stating a fact. That the hole is too narrow for me to extend my wings." A sly smile blows across his mouth as he gives me a look. "But yes, I do also have a very impressive wingspan."

The memory of when I was on my knees right in front of his crotch, and the huge bulge I saw in his pants, flashes through my mind. And before I even know what I'm saying, I find myself replying, "I can imagine."

"Imagine?" He arches an eyebrow at me. "You've seen my wings several times now." A devilish glint shines in his eyes. "Unless you were referring to something else?"

"Like what? Your ego?"

"You already knew that that's massive too."

"At least you're self-aware."

"And once again, you sound surprised by that."

"Can we just focus on the problem at hand?" I huff, suddenly feeling embarrassed about that flicker of pleasure I felt when he caressed my bottom lip. Holding his gaze, I wave a frustrated hand at the world in general. "We fell through the ground into another forest below the real forest. We don't know where we are. We have no food and no water. And we don't know how to get back up again." I shoot him an expectant look. "Did I miss anything?"

He shrugs. "We're also losing the light."

I heave a sigh. "Yeah. That too." Looking up at the ceiling again, I wave a hand at the thick layers of tree trunks. "Can't you just shift into a dragon and break through it?"

"God, why didn't I think of that?" he replies in an overly dramatic voice before leveling a flat stare at me. "Maybe because I'm a huge fucking dragon, and if I shift in here, this whole bloody ceiling is going to shatter and crash down right on top of us."

Drawing my eyebrows down, I shoot him a scowl. "Could've done without the sass."

"*You* are trying to lecture *me* on sass?"

"Alright. Fine. I get it. No shifting into a dragon."

Silence falls over our gloomy underground forest. Then Draven blows out a breath and nods.

"Alright then," he says. "We'll make camp here tonight and wait for the light to return in the morning. Then we can start looking for another way out."

"Agreed."

Reaching into one of the pouches on his belt, he pulls out something that clinks metallically. "Here, take this."

And like an absolute idiot, I trust the bastard and reach out my hand.

He snaps one side of a pair of handcuffs shut around my wrist. I jerk back, but it's already too late. Another click sounds as Draven locks the other manacle around his own wrist, handcuffing us together.

Drawing my eyebrows down, I hold up my now shackled wrist and glower up at him. "Seriously?"

He smirks. "In case you get any ideas about trying to steal back the ring and run off in the middle of the night."

I roll my eyes at him. But I *had* actually considered doing exactly that, so I suppose I can't be too outraged about it.

Without warning, he turns around and strides towards the closest tree. And since we're now stuck together, I stumble after him. Because he's both bigger and stronger than me, I can't do anything except follow him. And mutter under my breath.

"What was that?" he asks over his shoulder.

"Nothing."

"That's right."

I scoff, but it's interrupted when he abruptly sits down on the ground. He drags me with him, and I practically fall on top of him. Heat sears through me as I end up straddling his lap.

He flashes me a smile full of wicked mischief. "Trying to mount me again, are you?"

My cheeks flush, and I push against his shoulders, trying to scramble off his lap. "Mount you?" I huff. "When have I ever tried to mount you? You're the one who flipped us around in the air." Drawing my eyebrows down, I scowl at him. "And how did you even find me in the first place?"

"I've said it before and I'll say it again. Most people just say *thank you* when someone saves their life."

Suspicion curls around my spine as I study his face, which now bears a nonchalant expression. "How did you know that I was in danger? You said that you weren't watching me."

"I've already told you that as well. You're very loud." He raises his eyebrows and gives me a pointed look. "I mean, seriously. Have you ever heard yourself scream?"

Embarrassment sears my cheeks.

Giving him one final shove, I untangle my limbs from his and instead sit down on the ground next to him. I would have preferred to move farther away, but I can't because of the handcuffs. So I just try to ignore him and lie down on my back.

Thick grass envelops my body, feeling almost like a soft mattress.

Draven lies down as well.

Silence once more falls over us. No winds rustle the trees down here, but we're still halfway through fall, and without the sun's warmth, the nights are cold.

Rolling over on my side, I pull my legs up closer to my chest, trying to conserve my body heat. But I have to keep my right arm draped behind me since it's locked to Draven's left wrist.

I'm not sure if it's a dragon shifter thing, but I swear that I can almost feel the heat radiating from his body. It barely reaches my back, which just makes the rest of my body feel even colder.

A shiver courses through me.

"You're cold," Draven says.

It's a statement and not a question, so I don't bother replying.

He heaves a deep sigh behind my back.

I suck in a surprised breath as he rolls over on his side and lifts my upper body from the ground. Moving his hand over my head, he positions my arm so that its draped down over my stomach instead while he slides his own arm, the one shackled to mine, underneath my body. Then he pulls me towards him.

My heart stutters as my back connects with his chest.

Before I can even ask what he's doing, he wraps his free arm around my body as well and then summons his wings. Black smoke drifts into the cold evening air. Then a massive black wing spreads out over us like a tent.

Lightning flickers through my veins and my heart slams against my ribs.

Draven lets out a sigh and adjusts his position. Every tiny movement makes his body shift against mine. Once he's satisfied, he stops moving. And at that point, I'm flush against his chest. I swear I can even feel his heartbeat thump against my back.

My pulse thrums in my ears.

But Draven says nothing. As if this is the most natural thing in the world.

I lie there in his arms, feeling his comforting warmth envelop me, and stare at the black wing around us until I'm sure that he has drifted off to sleep. Then, I finally breathe the words that I was too proud to say earlier.

"Thank you," I whisper softly into the silent night. "And thank you for saving me from the wolfbear."

His chest rises and falls against my back as he continues sleeping.

But then, right when I'm about to close my eyes as well, he *replies*. And his voice is the gentlest I've ever heard.

"You're welcome, little rebel."

CHAPTER THIRTY-FIVE

Morning light hits my face. Raising my left hand, I rub sleep from my face and then blink my eyes open. At first, my brain can't process what I'm seeing.

There is a black barrier between me and the rest of the world. Pale light streams in through the gap between it and the thick grass I'm lying on. Then my mind at last catches up.

Oh. Right. The fight. The fall. The underground forest. Draven's wing. And his body pressed against my back.

My heart jerks.

It takes all of my willpower to stop my body from doing the same.

Lying completely motionless, I draw in breaths that have suddenly become unsteady.

I'm curled up on my side with Draven behind me. He is pressed so tightly against me that I can feel his chest expand against my back every time he breathes. His left arm is still underneath me, locked to my right one, and his other is draped over my side. His right hand rests possessively on my chest, right over my heart. Which is now beating erratically. I wonder if he can feel it.

Twisting my head, I glance over my shoulder. Draven's eyes are still closed, and his chest rises and falls with the deep rhythmic breathing of sleep. My gaze flicks down towards his belt and the pouch that contains the ring.

I scowl in annoyance when I notice that that particular pouch is pressed against the ground by his left hip. And since my right hand is trapped to his wrist on the other side, there is no way that I will be able to even reach the pouch. Let alone steal the ring from inside.

So I turn my head back and instead try to scan the area around us. But all I can see through the gap between his wing and the grass is the bottom of a few trees. I heave a sigh.

My gaze drifts over his wing instead.

It blocks out a lot of the light, but from in here, when the light shines from the other side, it's a little more translucent. It makes the veins that run through the membrane more visible. Intrigued, I follow them with my eyes as I study the wing intently.

I don't think I have ever been this close to a dragon shifter's wings before. From a distance, they look hard and severe. But this close, the inside at least looks like it might actually be soft to the touch.

Completely fascinated by my discovery, I raise my free hand and gently draw my fingers over the wing. I suck in a small breath when I find it soft and smooth. Almost like velvet.

A moan rips from Draven's throat.

And his cock, which I only now realize is pressed against my ass, hardens immediately.

It sends a jolt through my spine.

Stunned, and more than a little curious, I trace my fingers over his wing again.

A strangled noise comes from the back of his throat, and he snaps his eyes open.

"Selena," he says. It sounds like it's supposed to be a warning, but his voice is choked and rough. "What are you doing?"

My heart begins pounding in my chest, but I keep my eyes fixed on the wing before me as I reply, "I was just curious about what your wings felt like."

Before he can respond, I brush my fingers over the soft membrane again.

This time he actually gasps. His cock hardens even more, and he squirms on the ground.

The reaction shocks me so much that I can't help but to slide my fingers a little farther down the wing.

Draven's hand shoots up from where it was resting over my heart to instead circle my throat.

"Careful," he warns, his voice still rough.

With his hand around my throat, I can't turn my head to meet his gaze, but I try to catch sight of his face from the corner of my eye. "Are they sensitive?"

"Let's just say that there are only two reasons to touch a dragon shifter's wings. To inflict pain. Or pleasure."

My pulse thrums underneath his hand as he flexes his fingers around my throat. He angles his head slightly, and now his breath caresses the shell of my ear as he speaks.

"So unless you plan to torture me or fuck me, can I suggest that you stop tracing your fingers over my wings like that."

Pulling my hand back, I clear my throat while heat sears my cheeks. "Sorry."

He lets out a low humming sound in acknowledgement. It makes his breath caress the shell of my ear again, and a shudder of pleasure rolls down my spine. I swear I can feel him smirking behind me.

Apparently satisfied with that little revenge, he finally releases my throat and pulls away.

The sudden loss of his warm body against mine is almost jarring.

I drag in a deep breath to center myself again while Draven folds his wings back in. Then they disappear with a small cloud of smoke as he shifts into his fully human form. That surprises me, since I have almost only ever seen him in his half-shift form before, but lingering heat still sears my cheeks from when I touched his wings, so I decide not to be even more intrusive and ask about that too.

A faint metallic click sounds as Draven unlocks our handcuffs. I raise my eyebrow at him in silent question.

"If you try to steal the ring and escape now that we're awake, I *will* catch you," he explains. "So there's no need to keep you shackled to me."

I scoff in annoyance but don't argue since I'm pretty sure that he's right.

"Alright, let's go," he says as he pushes to his feet. "We need to scout the area and figure out if there is another way out of here."

After raking my fingers through my hair and retying the string that holds some of my hair back from my face, I stand up as well and give my body a good stretch to ease some of the stiffness after sleeping on the ground.

Then Draven and I set out to explore this strange underground forest that we ended up in.

Just as I surmised last night, the area around us is mostly filled with trees of a kind that I have never seen before. There are no fir trees or pine trees. Instead, all of them are covered in leaves of different shapes. Some are round and some are long and thin while others are jagged. The actual trunks vary as well. They're either straight or twisting, thin or thick, tall or short, covered in vines or mushrooms or nothing at all. There is no real unity. Even the ones that look to be of the same species have some features that differentiate it from the others.

The longer we walk, the more I get the feeling that not a single tree is exactly like another in this forest.

But the strangest part of all is the colors.

There are normal green leaves, of course. But a lot of the trees also sport foliage in colors that simply shouldn't be possible. One twisted and gnarly tree that we pass has leaves in a bright pink color. Another, a tall and proud tree with a straight trunk, has leaves the color of a roaring fire. Yet another displays leaves that glitter silver in the daylight.

I gaze around me, wide-eyed, as Draven and I travel deeper into the forest.

How these trees can even grow down here is beyond me. Daylight filters down through the layers of thin trunks that make up the ceiling above the entire forest. It illuminates the landscape and paints it in a warm glow. But there are no direct rays of sunlight that reach down here.

"Do you hear that?" Draven suddenly demands.

Stopping dead in my tracks, I whip my head from side to side. Then I hear it too.

"Water," I say, relief washing over me. "Running water."

We hurry towards the sound and find an entire river cutting straight through the forest. I drop to my knees at the bank and gulp down water. Draven does the same.

Once we've slaked our thirst, we push to our feet again. A considering look blows across Draven's features as he looks up and down the river.

"This is the River Andunir," he says, staring out at the water.

The River Andunir is the river that runs through the thorn forest and into Lake Andun outside our city before it continues into the woods on the other side.

I squint at the water too. "How do you know?"

"It runs all the way from the Peaks of Prosperity to your city, and it cuts underground in several places." His eyebrows are furrowed as he looks up at the strange forest around us. "I had no idea that there was something like this down here, though."

"Huh." I glance in the direction that the water is flowing, which must then naturally be south since the river runs that way. "So if we just follow the river, we will eventually reach the part where it flows back up again."

"Exactly."

Excitement ripples through me. Alright, we finally have a way out. Now, I just need to figure out how to steal the ring before we get there.

After drinking some more water, we set out along the river.

Neither of us speaks. I can almost feel the tension vibrating through the air between us. But I also don't know what to say. After what happened this morning, I suddenly feel uncharacteristically uncertain around him in a way that I never have before.

Draven's gaze flicks to me.

I glance towards him, but by the time my gaze finds his face, he is already looking at the grass and trees ahead. But I know that he was glancing at me. I could feel it.

Only the sound of softly running water fills the air as we continue walking.

Draven glances at me from the corner of his eye again.

"What?" I huff, turning my head to stare at him while we continue walking.

He starts in surprise and then twists his head towards me as he echoes, "What?"

"You were staring at me."

"No, I wasn't."

"Seriously? Now you sound like a child."

"Why does everyone else's dreams matter more than your own?"

I jerk back, stunned by the drastic change of topic. Frowning in genuine bewilderment, I hold his gaze and shake my head in confusion. "What do you mean?"

He blows out a forceful breath and rakes his fingers through his hair. Then he slides his gaze back to me, his golden eyes now full of something like exasperation. Or maybe frustration.

"I've seen how powerful you are," he says. "Back during that first trial, when Tommen almost killed you, you blasted him with your full power, right? Manipulated his fear?"

I nod in confirmation.

Draven holds my gaze with dead serious eyes. "Did you know that he pissed his pants?"

Shock pulses through me, and I draw back a little.

"Yeah," he confirms. "You made him so afraid that he pissed his pants."

"Oh." I blink at the colorful forest before me as that thought swirls inside my skull. "No wonder he had such a grudge against me."

Silence descends over us for a few seconds.

Then Draven heaves another sigh. "You can do things like that, and yet you always hold back."

"I don't always hold back," I retort, my voice coming out sounding petty and defensive.

"Almost always. Instead of fighting at full power, you make yourself less. Why?"

His words echo what Isera asked me earlier as well. Why don't I use my powers to make other people lose so that I will have a better chance at winning?

"I don't know." I squirm a little as uncomfortable feelings snake through my chest. "It's just... We're all trying to get out of this town and I just..."

"You always put everyone else's needs and wants ahead of your own. You always take care of everyone else. But who takes care of you?"

"I do."

The words are out of my mouth before I can stop them. And as soon as I've spoken them out loud, my heart clenches in pain as if an iron fist has squeezed it. I drag in a strained breath, and rub a hand over my heart, as if that can help ease the tightness inside my chest.

It's the painful truth. I always try to make sure that everyone else feels comfortable and at ease. But no one ever does the same for me. No one has ever put my needs and wants first.

Clearing my throat, I try to sound normal as I repeat, "I do."

But the words come out like a frail whisper. And I hate it. So I shove the ache in my heart aside and instead reach for something else. Some other kind of emotion. Anger. Why did he need to ask something like that? Here? Now?

"Why do you even care?" I snap before he can respond. Anger laces my voice, making it a little less brittle. "Why do you care if I fight to win or not? *You* are the one who is trying to make sure that I lose. So what gives you the right to ask me something like that?"

He opens his mouth to retort, but then he just draws his eyebrows down in a scowl and snaps his mouth shut.

We continue walking in incredibly tense silence after that.

The hours drag on.

Once we're past what must at least be midday, my legs wobble with every step. I've had precious little to eat in the past two days, and my body consumed most of the energy from the fruit yesterday when it healed the burn wounds on my arm. I stumble a little as I take another step.

Draven's hand shoots out and grabs me before I can fall.

"What's wrong?" he demands.

I don't want to admit to any weaknesses, especially since he doesn't even look tired at all, but I know that hiding it out of stubbornness and pride would just be plain stupid.

"I haven't eaten a lot," I admit. "And I had some burn wounds that needed healing, which consumed most of the energy from the food I found yesterday."

His eyes flash like lightning. "Burn wounds?"

"I was in a fight for the rings."

Anger flickers across his features. Then he abruptly grabs me by the arm and starts pulling me deeper into the forest instead of continuing along the river.

"What are you—" I begin, but he cuts me off.

"We're finding you some food." He shoots me a look. "I can't have you passing out because I'm not going to carry you."

A question that I have been pondering all day is right there on my tongue. Why haven't you already left? Why haven't you just shifted into your half-shift and flown away along the river without me? But I don't dare to ask that question out loud. Not yet, anyway. So I simply follow him deeper into the woods.

Eventually, we find some fruits and berries that look vaguely edible. Draven tries them first, claiming that he will better be able to withstand poison or other unwanted side effects. When he deems them safe, he hands them all to me. I practically inhale them all.

Once I reach the end of my little feast, I slow down and instead study Draven's face while I chew.

Noticing my staring, he frowns and meets my gaze. "What?"

"I was just thinking that I'm kind of glad that you managed to evade the knife that I slashed at your face before."

The confusion in his eyes deepens, and he shakes his head at me in silent question.

I flash him a grin. "It would have been a shame to damage such a pretty face."

A surprised laugh rips from his chest.

He snaps his mouth shut almost immediately, cutting it off, and shoots a stunned look down at his own chest. As if he can't believe that that sound came out of his own body.

There is still a hint of amusement playing at the corner of his lips as he looks up and meets my gaze again. "You have an uncanny ability to—"

An arrow shoots right past his face.

CHAPTER THIRTY-SIX

I throw myself backwards as a cloud of arrows zips through the air. Hitting the ground behind the fallen tree I was sitting on, I roll across the grass while arrows crack into tree trunks around us with sharp thuds. Leaping to my feet again, I take cover behind a thick tree.

Across the grass, Draven is backing away as the arrows force him away from me. Black clouds and winds materialize around him as he summons his magic. But that only makes the stream of arrows grow more frantic.

I cry out in alarm as an arrow buries itself in the tree right next to my cheek. Jumping backwards, I try to scramble out of the storm of arrows that pelts us both.

"We need to split up," I call as I duck and twist. "We're too big of a target together. We need to split their attention."

"Don't you dare—" Draven begins, but I cut him off.

I know that I'm right. As long as they can surround us and shoot at us both at the same time, we'll be trapped.

"We'll meet up at the river," I yell.

Anger flashes across his face as he shoots winds and lightning at the trees where the arrows are coming from. I yelp and leap back farther as an arrow almost takes me in the chest. It's time to go. Now.

"The river is miles long," Draven snaps back at me. "Which *part* of the river?"

"The wet part!"

Frustrated growls and crackling lightning strikes answer me, but I don't stop to listen. Instead, I whirl around and sprint right into the woods in the other direction.

If half of our ambushers follow me, Draven should be able to take out his half as soon as he is no longer surrounded. So all I need to do is to lead my half away, give them the slip, and then circle back around.

Thankfully, my energy has now returned since I manage to eat most of the food before we were attacked.

With my heart pounding in my chest, I dash between the colorful trees. Arrows zip past me. But there is no sound of footsteps behind me. That just makes even more dread crash over me. How can an entire group of people be following me without making any sound?

Grabbing a tree trunk, I swing myself around it and dart to the left.

An entire rain of arrows speeds past right in front of my face.

Crying out in shock, I screech to a halt and backpedal furiously. Sharp thuds echo as the arrows strike tree trunks to my right. I whip around and sprint in the other direction instead.

The same thing happens several more times. When I try to take one turn, so that I can loop back towards the river, an entire cloud of arrows streaks right past my face.

It isn't until it happens a fourth time that I finally understand what's going on.

A chill snakes down my spine as realization floods my mind.

I'm being herded.

But by then, it's already too late.

I jerk to a halt, almost stumbling and falling over, as an entire wall of drawn bows materializes in front of me. Flailing my arms, I fight to recover my balance. And when I finally straighten, bows with nocked arrows are pointed at me from every direction.

My pulse thrums in my ears. I drag in deep breaths, trying to calm my racing heart, while desperately trying to make out who the bows belong to.

Then at last, a figure from straight ahead steps out of the foliage around her.

Except that the foliage follows her out too.

My jaw drops.

Shock clangs inside my skull like giant bells as I stare in open-mouthed disbelief at the person in front of me.

A dryad.

Mabona's fucking tits, it's a *dryad*. I've heard stories about them, but I didn't think they lived here. All the legends say that they live in the deep forests to the north. I stare at the female dryad before me.

She's shaped like a woman wearing a flowing dress. Except her dress is made of branches and vines and leaves. And so is her long hair, which ripples around her as if on a phantom wind. Red flowers grow around her head like a crown. The splashes of red are a stark contrast against her pale green skin. Millenia's worth of wisdom seem to swirl in her brown eyes. As if she has lived through all the ages of this world. Seen it all. Lived it all. And knows it all.

My mouth dries out as she locks those intense eyes on me.

"What is a fae from the Seelie Court doing in our woods with a dragon shifter?" she asks. Her voice is low and smooth, but she spits out those last two words as if they taste foul.

I swallow. "Trying to find my way back out of here."

She cocks her head, the vines in her hair rippling with the motion. "How did you get here?"

"We fell through a hole in the tree trunk ceiling thing," I stammer.

"Where?"

"I'm not exactly sure. About four hours walk, I think." Raising my arm, I point in the direction we came from. "That way."

"What were you doing in the woods in the first place?"

"I'm a contestant in the Atonement Trials."

Silence falls over the woods. A few bowstrings creak faintly as the dryads holding them pull back a little farther. I draw in a breath and try to keep my focus on the only dryad here who is not currently pointing an arrow in my face.

She narrows her eyes at me. "What is the Atonement Trials?"

I'm momentarily stunned that she doesn't know, since it's such an integral part of our lives. But I suppose that if they live down here, there is no reason for them to have heard about it.

"It's a competition," I explain. "The Iceheart monarchs host it once every one hundred and fifty years. They make us fight each other until there are only three left, to prove that we're worthy. And the ones who win are given permission to leave the city."

A sharp hissing sound rips from all the dryads around me. I flinch, thinking that they're going to shoot me.

"The Icehearts," the dryad leader snarls in a voice full of poison. Then she narrows her eyes at me as a contemplative look passes over her face. "I knew that they trapped you in your court. After all, you rarely venture into the forest. But I did not know that they make you fight each other for sport."

Clenching my jaw, I squeeze my hand into a fist. "It's our only shot at a better life."

She cocks her head again, and that considering look blows over her beautiful features once more. The silence around us is so loud that I can hear the air rushing in my ears.

"You hate them," she says at last. It's half statement, half question. "You really, truly, hate the Iceheart Dynasty, don't you?"

Since I'm fairly certain that she isn't going to run and tattle to Empress Jessina, I answer honestly. "Yes."

"Hmm."

I just hold her gaze, not sure what else to say.

"You're following the river to get out," she says, and once more, it's somewhere halfway between a statement and a question.

"Yes," I answer. "I want to get out of here as fast as possible."

She watches me in silence for an uncomfortably long time, as if she's trying to read the sincerity on my face. Then she finally nods.

And without another word, she turns around and begins walking away while all the bows are lowered.

"Wait," I blurt out. "You're just... letting me go?"

As soon as the words are out of my mouth, I know that it's a really dumb thing to say. I was just ambushed by a horde of dryads after I trespassed on their territory, and they're letting me just walk out of here. I should have just taken my miracle and run. But meeting them, meeting a dryad, threw me so far off my game that my brain is still scrambling to catch up.

The leader turns back to me.

A spike of fear shoots through my spine as she smiles. It's not a comforting smile. It's the sharp smile of a predator who's about to rip someone's throat out. Age-old fury burns in her eyes as that smile slashes across her lips.

"You hate the dragon shifters," she says. Malice, potent enough to sear through the very ground beneath us like acid, seeps into her voice. "We hate them more."

Just looking at the vicious rage on her face steals the breath from my lungs. And before I can recover it, she has already disappeared into the magical forest with the rest of her companions.

For an entire minute, I just stand there, staring after her while my heart pounds in my chest.

Then a sudden realization crackles through me like lightning.

Whipping around, I stare in the direction I came from. The direction where I left *my* dragon shifter.

My heart pounds as the dryad's words echo in my skull. *You hate the dragon shifters. We hate them more.*

Dread and fear wash over me.

Draven.

CHAPTER THIRTY-SEVEN

Fear twists in my stomach as I race back towards the river. What if the dryads managed to overpower him? What if they're torturing him? What if he's already dead?

My heart clenches at the mere thought.

I stumble and almost crash into a twisting tree as a sudden question flashes through my mind.

Why do I even care?

Why should I care if Draven gets hurt or killed? He has done nothing but sabotage me ever since he first saw me on the Dragon Field. I should be hoping that he's hurt or dead, because that would make it so much easier to steal the ring back and win the trial. So why is dread and panic currently twisting between my ribs and strangling my lungs?

Deep down, I know the answer to that question. And the truth is as shocking as it is disturbing.

I have started to care about Draven.

Yes, he's ruthless and domineering and an absolute bloody menace. But he's also unexpectedly kind and thoughtful and funny. He has protected me from attackers and a wolfbear, and he gave me his own shirt so that I wouldn't have to walk through the halls naked for everyone to see. He sees me. Sees all the parts of me, even the ones I try to hide from the rest of the world. And he makes me laugh.

With him, I feel free. Free in a way that I have never felt before. I don't have to hold myself back or make myself less for him. I don't have to choose my words carefully. For some reason, he makes me feel like the real me is enough. Like *I'm* enough. With him, I never feel as if I have to adapt my personality to fit the people around me. I can just be me.

Panic crackles through me as I sprint through the forest. But panic for a different reason this time.

Because Goddess above, I actually like Draven Ryat.

What the hell is wrong with me? He's the Commander of the Dread Legion. The leader of the enemy army. I should feel nothing but rage and hatred towards him. And yet, I can't forget the feeling of his warm body holding me last night. The feeling of his hands as he brought me to the brink of an orgasm in his room. The taste of his mouth as he kissed me like he was starving for it.

Confusing and highly conflicting thoughts whirl inside my soul as I leap over fallen trees and dash towards the river.

But when I at last skid to a halt in front of the flowing water, the grass around me is empty. My pulse thrums in my ears as I whip my head from side to side. But Draven is nowhere to be found.

My heart clenches.

Channeling my magic, I use the same technique that I used on Fenriel earlier. I try to find and latch on to one of his emotions so that I can follow that bond towards his location.

I throw out my magic, searching for a spark of anger.

Nothing.

I try annoyance.

Nothing.

Impatience. Frustration. And several other emotions that he surely must be feeling.

But every time, I'm met with nothing.

A growl of frustration escapes my own throat. What could he possibly be feeling?

On a whim, I throw out my magic towards a spark of worry.

I gasp.

The purple spark of worry in Draven's chest is so massive, so all-consuming, that I have to scramble to pull my shields up so that I won't be affected by the emotion as well.

Stunned, I just stare in the direction that the emotion is coming from. Draven is *worried*. And not just a little worried. Based on the intensity of the flame, he's so worried that he must not even be able to breathe properly.

Giving my head a few quick shakes, I snap out of my stupor and instead start running towards him. Since I need to manipulate the emotion to keep my connection to it, I decrease it ever so slightly while I dash across root and stone. But the worry is so overpowering that it barely makes a difference.

My heart jerks as Draven at last comes into view a little farther down the river.

He is pacing the grass like a caged wolf, clenching and unclenching his hand while whipping his head from side to side.

When his gaze finds mine, he stops dead in his tracks. For the briefest of moments, I swear I can see relief flicker in his eyes. But that unyielding expression that he so often wears remains firmly on his face and betrays no emotion as he looks at me. As if he couldn't care less whether I showed up or not.

But because my magic is still connected to him, I can feel that raging flame of worry in his chest go out with a *whoosh*.

I cut off my magic. Still stunned by his reaction, I walk the final distance to him. He just watches me with unreadable eyes.

"Took you long enough," he mutters when I come to a halt before him.

I was planning to say something snarky in reply, but instead, I find myself saying, "You were worried about me."

Alarm flashes across his face for a second. Then he draws his eyebrows down in a scowl and crosses his arms. "No, I wasn't."

"Are you forgetting that I have emotion magic? I could literally *feel* your worry. It's what I used in order to find you. I followed your intense worry to get here."

His angry scowl falters a little, and he clears his throat. "Yes, well..." He huffs. "If you died, your parents would probably riot. And I have better things to do than burn cities to the ground."

Before I can even open my mouth to respond, he grabs me by the arm and starts pulling me with him as he spins around and stalks forward.

"Now, let's go," he declares. "Before we're attacked again."

"Yes, about that..." I shoot him a pointed glare as I stumble along beside him. "Do you know what would have been good to have when I was trying to survive that attack? My knife."

A flicker of guilt blows across his face. Then he slams that mask of ruthless authority back down on his features. But he does in fact slide out the knife that he took from me earlier and then hands it back to me.

"If you try to stab me with this, I'll bring out the handcuffs again," he warns.

With a scoff, I take the blade and ram it back into my thigh holster. Then I open my mouth to speak again.

I'm just about to ask him how he managed to get away from his half of the dryad ambushers when hesitation pulses through me.

I don't even know if *he* knows that they were dryads. And given what they said to me about hating the dragon shifters, I doubt the Iceheart monarchs would be thrilled to learn that there are dryads living underneath these woods. If Draven doesn't already know and I tell him about it, he's going to tell his emperor and empress about it too. After all, he is their loyal lapdog. I don't know what the history is between the dryads and the dragon shifters, but since I don't want any dead dryads on my conscience, I decide to take this secret with me to the grave.

So instead, I just yank my arm out of his grip and shoot him an annoyed look at being manhandled like this. A look that he promptly ignores. Rolling my shoulder back, I straighten my shirt again and let out a huff. The silence between us is suddenly thick and tense.

There are several things I want to say, things I want to ask about, but I can't. I need to keep my mouth shut so that he won't ask questions that I don't want to answer. But I also can't stand the crackling silence.

So just to fill it, I say, "My parents wouldn't have rioted, by the way. So you wouldn't have had to burn our city to the ground."

He glances down at me, his eyebrows raised. As if he's surprised that I volunteered any information about myself. To be fair, I'm a little surprised too.

"They wouldn't have rioted if their only child was killed?" he asks.

"No. We have a… complicated relationship." Pain spikes through my heart, and I suddenly regret bringing this up, because I really don't want to talk about this. So I hurriedly switch the focus to him and force teasing mischief into my voice as I ask, "What about you? Does the Shadow of Death even have parents or were you just birthed by an angry storm cloud?"

He laughs.

Goddess above, it's such a pleasant sound. And with it, the tension around us disappears as if swept away by a strong morning wind.

"No, I have parents," he replies. Then he tilts his head to the side and shrugs. "*Had* parents. They died when I was about sixty. Natural causes. Nothing dramatic. And I was already Clan Leader by then, so I had a lot of other people to worry about too."

I whip my head towards him. "Wait, what? You became the leader of your clan when you were that young?"

"I was actually thirty-seven, if we're being specific."

My eyebrows shoot up. "Are you serious?"

He shrugs, as if it's no big deal.

I squint at him, studying his face. But just like all fae and shifters, he looks to still be between twenty-five and thirty years old. Since there is no other way of knowing, I decide to just ask. "How old are you now?"

"Two hundred and eighty-six."

I stop dead in my tracks.

Light shines down on the magical forest around us, illuminating the trees and making the colorful leaves shine like jewels. To my right, the river flows steadily to the south. And for a few seconds, that soft rushing sound is the only thing that breaks the silence.

Then I turn towards Draven and lock stunned eyes on him. "Two hundred and eighty-six. You're only two hundred and eighty-six?"

He frowns, looking genuinely confused by my disbelief. "Yes."

"But… but…" I stammer. "How is that even possible? You're the Commander of the Dread Legion, for Mabona's sake! How can you be so ridiculously powerful when you're this young?"

For a few seconds, he just stares at me. It looks like he can't figure out if he's supposed to be flattered or insulted. Then he shoots me a pointed look, seriousness descending on his features again.

"Why should I tell you something like that?" He arches a dark eyebrow at me. "We're enemies, aren't we?"

I heave a deep sigh and rake my fingers through my hair. He has a point. But I'm suddenly tired. Tired of… everything.

So while I start walking again, I reply, "Because we almost died. And I just want to…" I sigh again. "Just tell me something true. Something real."

He walks in silence next to me for a while. Just when I think he's not going to answer, he finally speaks up.

"So you know how the shifter who inherits the clan magic becomes the leader?" he asks.

I nod. "Yes."

"Our previous leader died when I was thirty-seven, and Azaroth chose me for some reason. So I inherited the magic when I was quite young, which meant that I could start developing it from an unusually young age."

"So that's the secret? A lot of time to practice?"

"No." A soft chuckle rumbles from his chest. "The secret is a grumpy as hell old dragon."

Blinking, I look up at him in surprise.

There is a wistful smile on his lips as he gazes out at the forest before us while we continue walking.

"One day," he begins, "when I was out on one of our islands, practicing with my storm powers, this huge gray dragon showed up."

"Gray?" I stare at him in shock. "There are *gray* dragons too?"

He shakes his head. "Not on this continent. But she wasn't from here. She said that she was on vacation, of all things." Another one of those soft and absolutely incredible laughs ripples from his chest. "Anyway, she saw me trying to practice. And she *laughed* at me." With that smile still on his lips, he shakes his head. "I was so offended. Because, back then, I was arrogant and cocky—"

"As opposed to now?"

He rolls his eyes and gives me a soft shove in the shoulder.

But because I wasn't prepared for it, I stumble sideways and almost crash into a strange tree with a very thin vine-like trunk. The top of it is shaped like an upside-down bell, and it sways when I hit the soft vine that holds it up. Thick pale green liquid sloshes over the edges of the bell and splatters the ground. I leap out of the way before the sticky substance can hit my boots.

Narrowing my eyes, I glower at Draven.

He just grins, looking entirely unapologetic.

Blowing out a long breath, I shake my head and then move back to his side as we start up along the river again.

"Anyway, I was offended and cocky, so I challenged her," Draven picks up. He lets out a low chuckle and shakes his head. "She mopped the fucking floor with me."

I raise my eyebrows at him, surprised that he would admit something like that.

He just shrugs, as if he isn't even embarrassed about it. "She was incredible. The best storm wielder I have ever seen. And by some stroke of insane luck, she decided to spend her vacation on our islands. So she trained me. She taught me things about storm powers that none of our previous leaders even knew." He sighs. "I still don't know exactly who or what she was, but I got the feeling that she was old. Really old."

"Was?" I ask softly. "She died?"

"No." He chuckles again and shakes his head. "Like I said, she was just on vacation. So after a few years, she went back to her home. Wherever that is. She said that she had to go back and make sure that the troublesome underworlders hadn't burned everything down."

"What's an underworlder?"

"No idea. But I assume that it's some kind of vicious demon or something."

"Huh."

"But, yeah, that's the secret behind my power." His golden eyes glint as he glances down at me and shoots me a mischievous smile. "No grand birthright. No divine fate. Just an old, grumpy as hell, steel gray dragon on vacation."

"Wow." I watch him, my eyebrows raised. "That was so not the answer I was expecting."

"I'm not surprised. Most people just—"

A sudden idea hits me like a lightning bolt, drowning out the rest of his sentence as my head instead clangs with both excitement and apprehension.

Next to me, Draven keeps talking. But I can barely even focus on his words enough to nod at the appropriate times anymore.

Because I have just figured out how to steal the ring from him.

CHAPTER THIRTY-EIGHT

Nervous apprehension buzzes inside my chest. It feels as if I have a swarm of agitated bees trapped inside my ribcage. I draw in what I hope are normal-sounding breaths as I try to make my heart stop beating so hard.

My genius plan involves three things that need to happen in a very specific order. But the longer we walk, the more worried I get that the first thing is never going to happen. Or that it's going to happen too late and there will be no chance to even execute the second step. Or that Draven is going to figure out what I'm doing and handcuff me again. Or that he will hear the very incriminating thumping of my heart.

With that anxiousness vibrating inside my soul, I keep throwing out my magic in search of a group of people who should be feeling either excited or impatient. But just like the past three hours, I don't find anything.

I'm very well aware of the limits of my magic, and how close I need to be to feel someone else's emotions. So once I can feel a group of people who are either impatiently or excitedly awaiting the return of the victors in this trial, I will know that we are close to reaching the end of the river. And as soon as I know that, I can set the second stage of my plan in motion.

But if that doesn't happen soon, it will all be too late.

My heart slams against my ribs as Draven and I walk along the river. We must be far into the afternoon at this point, which means that we should be reaching the city soon.

Come on, come on, I plead desperately in my mind.

Worry clangs inside my skull.

My magic connects.

It takes all of my willpower not to gasp when I finally latch on to several cerise sparks of impatience. And they're all located in the direction of the city.

Excitement explodes through me.

Finally.

It's close enough that I should be able to make it there without Draven catching me. *If* I time it correctly.

My pulse thrums in my ears as I flick my gaze around the area, searching for the one thing that I need to enact the second part of my plan.

Dread strangles my throat when I don't find any. Only trees with green and orange and pink leaves, and a softly flowing river, stare back at me.

I fight to keep my breathing even. Shit. I need to do this now. Before Draven also figures out that we're almost out of the underground woods.

We continue walking.

Every nerve inside my body feels like it's charged with lightning.

I force even breaths into my lungs.

Please, I beg silently.

My heart lurches.

There.

The tree I was desperately searching for finally appears up ahead.

My heart is beating so fast that I can barely keep my hand steady as I discreetly slide my knife out of its holster. Draven's eyes remain on the path ahead. I draw in short breaths. The tree gets closer.

If I screw this up, it's over.

I need to time it perfectly.

Apprehension crackles through my veins like bolts of lightning.

Two steps left.

And... now!

I slash the knife through the thin vine-like trunk with one precise slit.

Then I ram it back in my holster and continue walking.

A faint rustling sound comes from behind us.

My heart pounds in my chest.

Please, please, tell me that I timed it correctly.

The rustling turns into a whooshing sound.

Draven spins towards it right as the giant bell-shaped top tips over and dumps all of its slimy green content right over us.

I yelp as I whirl around as well, hoping that it sounds like genuine shock. My gaze immediately darts to the cut I made in the vine that held up the bell. Because of its weight, the bell tipped forward once I cut through the vine. Then it snapped completely, leaving no evidence that I had anything to do with it. And besides, half of my body is also covered in that slimy green substance, since it tipped over me too.

However, Draven is far worse.

He stands there on the ground, his arms raised halfway up, and just stares in disbelief at the broken plant. There is an absolutely flabbergasted expression on his features. His hair, his face, and his entire body is completely covered in slime. That thick green liquid runs down his cheekbones and drips from his jaw and from his raised arms.

I burst out laughing.

Slime flies through the air as he whirls towards me. "I swear to God, if you had anything to do with this, I'll…"

Then he trails off when he notices that my entire shirt and face and hair are soaked with it too. The only parts of me that escaped relatively clean are my pants, though there is some splatter on my left thigh.

A growl rips from his chest as he instead shoots a death glare at the broken plant. Then he yanks his arms down, flicking slime down at the ground.

"Azaroth's fucking flame," he grumbles under his breath as he stalks towards the river.

His boots make wet squelching sounds with every step.

My stomach lurches.

This is it. This is my one chance to steal back the ring.

While wiping slime out of my face, I follow him towards the river. My heart pounds in my chest. If he decides to just walk right into the river with his armor on, my entire plan will be for nothing. I need to make him take his clothes off before he gets into the water.

So before he can even think about stepping into the river fully clothed, I grab the hem of my shirt and yank it over my head.

Draven stumbles a step as he snaps his gaze to me.

I just lift my shoulders in a shrug. "It's nothing you haven't seen before. You saw me naked in that stairwell, remember?" Choosing my words carefully, I add, "And besides, I can't wash the slime off properly with my clothes on."

Draven opens his mouth, but then closes it again. There is a slightly flustered look on his face as he glances between me and his own body. Then he grunts in what sounds like resignation.

After trying to wipe some more slime off his hands, he reaches for his belt and starts unbuckling it.

My heart patters in my chest as I steal a discreet glance at the pouch where the ring is hidden. But I keep my face a neutral mask as I unbutton my own pants.

A thud sound as Draven drops his belt on the grass. Then he starts on his armor. I take my time shimmying out of my pants. Then I pretend to just remember that I'm still wearing my boots. With a calculated shake of my head at my own silliness, I sit down on the grass with my pants down at my ankles and start unlacing my boots.

More thuds sound as Draven drops the top half of his armor on the grass.

My pulse pounds in my ears as I pull off my boots while waiting until Draven finally grabs the hem of his black undershirt. Then he pulls it upwards.

The moment that the fabric blocks his vision, I strike like a fucking viper.

Leaning sideways, I shove my hand into the correct pouch and yank out the ring.

His eyes are only covered for a few mere seconds, but by the time he pulls the shirt fully off and glances down at me again, the ring is already hidden in one of my boots. And my pants are also fully off, to account for what I was doing while his eyes were covered.

Heat flushes Draven's cheeks when his gaze instead lands on my now almost entirely naked body. And just to distract him even more, I choose that moment to slip my hands inside my panties and push them downwards. He snaps his gaze away while the flush on his cheeks deepens.

I almost laugh. Both at his embarrassment and at my genius. It worked. I have the ring. And he doesn't know.

Now, all I need to do is to quickly wash off and then come up with an excuse to leave for a few minutes. Maybe to go and pee in the woods or something. And then I'll run like hell to the finish line and win this goddess damned trial.

Giddy with excitement, I strip out of my remaining clothes and then grab my slime-covered shirt in one hand as I walk down to the edge of the river. The water flows softly around my ankles as I step into it. It's surprisingly warm, given that we're halfway through fall. But maybe this strange underground forest somehow affects the temperature in this section.

Water laps around my calves as I bend over and dunk my shirt in the water.

A strangled noise comes from behind me.

Still bent over and rinsing off my shirt, I glance behind me, surprised at the odd noise.

I find Draven standing frozen on the grass a few steps behind me. His hands hover halfway to his underwear, not moving, as he stares at me.

Heat washes through my body when I realize that I'm standing completely naked and bent over right in front of him.

"Fucking hell, Selena," he presses out, his voice rough.

I snap my gaze back to the water and hurriedly finish washing off my shirt. Then I straighten and move back to place my shirt on the grass so that it can dry. But I can barely concentrate on my mission anymore because Draven's gaze is burning into my skin everywhere I go.

Fire flickers through my veins at the desperate look in his eyes. But I try to ignore it as I move back to the river. I have a mission. A plan. I just need to wash off my hair and body, and then I'm escaping with the ring.

Water sloshes around me as I wade into the river and dive in. The world around me disappears, to be replaced by the sound of rushing water in my ears, as I run my fingers through my hair to get the slime out. Then I push off from the riverbed and break the surface again.

A splashing sound comes from behind me. My heart flutters. Draven is now in the water too.

I make sure to keep my back to him as I wash off all the slime. My gaze darts towards my boots several times. I have a plan. All I need to do is to follow it. No distractions.

Steeling myself, I turn around and start back up towards the grass.

Right as I turn around, Draven breaks the surface after being submerged.

The air is snatched right out of my lungs as my gaze lands on him.

All of that weird green slime is now gone. Instead, water clings to his black hair and runs down his skin. My clit throbs as he reaches up and drags his fingers through his hair, pushing it out of his face. His muscles shift with the motion.

Fuck, did he have to be so damn hot?

He freezes mid-motion as he notices my stare. With his hands still halfway through his hair, he just stands there, watching me as if stunned. My gaze slips down his firm chest. The water level is right above his hips, and I swallow as I watch the water gently lap against his stomach.

"Selena," he says, his voice dark and full of warning.

I snap my gaze away from his body and quickly start towards the grass again.

Goddess damn it, I have a plan. Dry off a little. Put my clothes back on. Make an excuse. And then run like hell.

No distractions. Absolutely no distractions.

The sound of sloshing water comes from behind me when I reach the grass. And because I am an absolute idiot, I turn towards it.

My heart skips a beat as I find Draven walking out of the water as well. His wet hair has now been swept back from his face, and drops of water run down his body. His utterly naked body.

Fire licks through my veins as I stare at the masterpiece that is his body. Every curve of his muscles and every sharp ridge of his abs are just begging to be touched. He stops, still ankle deep in the river, when he once again notices my gaze.

But this time, I can't look away.

I follow a drop of water that slides along his abs and down that sinful V, and I'm struck by an overwhelming impulse to grab him by the hips and lick that water drop off his skin.

Then the drop of water slips lower.

I suck in a short breath.

Fucking hell, he wasn't lying about his wingspan. I stare at his massive cock, which hardens more with every second, while forbidden images flash through my mind. Images of him pushing me up against the small rock wall a short distance to my left. Images of him putting a hand around my throat and fucking me hard. Images of him bending me over and trapping my arms behind my back and fucking me like—

"Selena."

My name rips from his lungs like a warning, a threat, and a plea.

Raising my gaze, I meet his eyes again. What little air I had managed to get back into my lungs disappears in a small gasp as I find him staring at me with desire burning like wildfire in his eyes. Swallowing, I lick my lips.

He clenches his jaw and flexes his hand.

"You really need to stop looking at me like that," he warns, his voice low and rough.

The mere sound of that dark and strained voice makes my skin prickle with pleasure.

Drawing in an unsteady breath, I hold his searing gaze. "Or what?"

He starts forward again. Water sloshes around his ankles as he walks the final couple of steps out of the river and then continues across the grass. My heart pounds in my chest as he advances on me. I can barely think straight when he moves until he is standing so close to me that I can count every drop of water that slides down his muscular chest.

His eyes are dark with desire as he locks them on me. "Or I'm going to push you up against that rock wall and fuck you like you're mine."

Heat sears through my veins.

He takes a step forward, using his body to make me take a step back.

"I'm not fucking kidding, Selena." He keeps advancing while I keep retreating. "You have ten seconds to drop your gaze, or I swear to God, I'm going to fuck you until your legs give out and the only moans coming out of your mouth are my name. And then I'm going to keep fucking you until you will never be able to even think about touching another man because all you can think about is my hands on your body and all you can feel is my cock inside you."

My heart stutters. Sucking in shuddering breaths, I stare up into his golden eyes while heat pools inside me and my clit throbs harder. A thud sounds as my naked back hits the stone wall. Draven keeps moving until he's right in front of me, trapping me against it.

"Ten seconds," he warns.

My pulse thrums in my ears. "We're still enemies."

"Yes." He keeps holding my gaze. "Eight seconds."

"And after we leave this underground forest, everything will continue as it always has."

"Correct. Six seconds."

"So nothing we do right now will make a difference."

"Agreed."

"Because it won't change anything anyway."

"Exactly." He shakes his head slowly and warns, "One second, little rebel."

There is an almost pleading note in his voice, as if he knows that if we cross this line, it's going to ruin us both.

But I don't look away.

My chest heaves and fire flickers through my veins as I stand there naked against the rough stone wall and hold his gaze with determined eyes.

"Fuck," he breathes, and it sounds like that word was ripped from the very depths of his soul.

Then he slides both hands into my hair and crushes his mouth against mine.

Lightning crackles through my veins, and I gasp into his mouth. Raising one leg, I wrap it around his hip and pull him tighter against me as I press my hands against his firm chest. A moan rips from his lungs as I draw my fingers down towards his stomach. His cock hardens against me.

He slides one hand down to rest on the side of my neck and reaches down with the other to grip my thigh. His fingers dig into my skin as he holds my leg up while dominating my mouth. I gasp as he bites my bottom lip and then claims my mouth again.

I rake my fingers down his hard abs, drawing a shudder from his body.

"Your wings," I press out between furious kisses. "Please. I want to feel your wings."

While continuing to kiss me senseless, he performs a half-shift. I suck in a breath as he flares his imposing black wings. He devours that sound as he steals the breath from my lungs with another desperate kiss.

I trace my fingers along that enticing V and down towards his cock while I reach up with my other hand. My right hand closes around his thick cock at the same time as I brush my left hand over the soft membrane of his wings.

He chokes on his breath. I show him no mercy. Sliding my hand up and down his throbbing cock, I trace my fingers along his wings again.

A gasp rips from his lungs. Breaking the kiss, he bows forward and presses his forehead against my shoulder while his body trembles. The most incredible moans spill from his lips like dark honey.

My mind can barely process it. Draven Ryat, the Shadow of Death and Commander of the Dread Legion, one of the most powerful and dangerous dragon shifters in the world, is completely undone by my simple touch.

I keep sliding my hand up and down his cock and trailing my fingers over his wings, utterly transfixed by the way his body reacts. Shudders rack his powerful frame and dark groans rip from his lungs. His cock is so hard underneath my hand that I can practically feel it pulsing against my palm.

Heat sears through me and my clit throbs at the sight of him like this.

Continuing my precise movements, I push him closer to the edge. Goddess above, I can't wait to see what he looks like when he comes. I slide my hand up and down again. His body practically vibrates with tension.

Then, right before he can come, he suddenly snaps his head up. His eyes are wild and hazy with lust as he blinks furiously. A jolt shoots through me as he abruptly releases my neck and thigh and instead grabs my wrists. I suck in a sharp breath as he yanks my hands away from his body.

Rough stone scrapes against the back of my hands as Draven pins them to the rock wall above my head. Adjusting his grip, he pushes my hands together and then wraps one hand over both of my now crossed wrists. My chest heaves as I tilt my head back and stare up at him.

"Fucking hell," he growls under his breath, his voice rough and strained.

I pull against his grip on my wrists, but they are now firmly trapped against the wall above my head.

A wicked glint appears in Draven's eyes as he slowly shakes his head at me. "I'm going to make you fucking squirm and beg for that."

"You—"

My words get cut off by a gasp as Draven draws his free hand over my pussy. A shudder of pleasure rolls through my body. With that sly glint still in his eyes, he cocks his head.

"I told you that I was going to ruin *you,* little rebel. Not the other way around." A devilish smirk curls his lips. "So you are mine to play with, mine to torment, mine to edge until you're begging me to fuck you."

Before I can even begin to form a response, he rolls my clit between his fingers.

Lightning zaps through my spine. Arching my back, I throw my head back and gasp.

"That's it." He traces his thumb over my clit. "Moan for me."

Pleasure spikes through me.

He adjusts the position of his hand and continues to rub my clit with his thumb while he slides his index and middle finger down to my entrance. I pull against his grip on my wrists and bite back a moan. He tightens his fingers around my wrists.

"I said, *moan,*" he commands, his voice pulsing through my very soul.

While continuing to tease my clit with expert precision, he pushes one finger inside me.

A moan tears from my lungs.

Leaning down closer, he smirks in triumph. "Good. Now beg."

Pleasure streaks through my body as he begins pumping his finger while his thumb keeps rubbing my clit. I squirm against the rough stone wall as a shudder courses through my body.

Draven adds a second finger.

A whimper spills from my lips, and I throw my head from side to side as he slides both fingers in and out while he intensifies the sweet torture that he is inflicting on my clit.

My entire body thrums with need.

He slants his lips over mine. "Beg."

Another shiver of pleasure rolls down my spine when his breath caresses my lips. I pull against his grip on my wrists again and writhe against the wall in an effort to relieve the tension now building inside me.

Lightning shoots up my spine as Draven spreads his fingers wide inside me and then quickly moves them back and forth before he pumps them up and down again. Desperate moans spill from my lips. Draven brushes his mouth along my jaw while his thumb keeps working.

The tension inside me builds into a crackling storm. I gasp in breaths, my chest heaving, and squirm as the edge of an orgasm draws closer.

But Draven never lets me fall over it.

As soon as I'm close to it, he slows his movements before starting back up again.

Pitiful whimpers escape my lips. My whole body trembles with pent-up need. I squirm and gasp and throw my head from side to side. But there is no relief. No mercy.

And so, I break.

"Please," I gasp out. "Draven, please."

He chuckles. It's low and dark and it dances over my skin. Leaning impossibly closer, he smirks against my mouth.

"Good girl."

Something between a whimper and a moan rips from my soul.

Draven pulls his fingers out and removes his hand. My heart slams against my ribs as he instead takes a firm grip on my thigh and lifts my leg up. Then he positions his cock against my entrance. Resting my head against the stone wall, I try desperately to keep hold of that frail thread of sanity that is all that remains while a storm of pent-up tension and need whirls inside me.

"Eyes on me," Draven orders.

Dragging in a breath, I tilt my head back down to meet his gaze.

His eyes burn with possessive need. It's so intense that it takes my breath away.

He thrusts inside me.

My eyes widen, and I gasp as his thick cock slides into my soaking wet pussy. Faint flickers of pain ripple through me as my pussy stretches to accommodate his massive size. But Draven doesn't rush me. He's not rough or impatient. Instead, he keeps pushing at a slow but steady pace.

I drag in an unsteady breath as he sheaths himself completely. Then he stays like that for a while, giving me time to adjust. My heart thunders in my chest. Fuck, the feeling of him filling me completely is like nothing I have ever experienced.

With his eyes locked on mine, he slowly slides out a little. And then thrusts in again.

A groan rolls from my throat as pleasure shoots through me. He slides out halfway and then slams back in again. A little harder this time. My back thuds against the rock wall. He does the same thing again.

I stare into those beautiful eyes of his as he starts up a steady pace.

He flexes his fingers around my trapped wrists. Then he shifts his grip on my thigh, lifting my leg a little higher.

A gasp tears from my throat as he thrusts in again.

The new angle creates the most incredible friction.

A satisfied smirk blows across Draven's lips. Keeping my leg in that position, he picks up the pace. Pleasure shoots through my spine with every thrust, and I have to blink repeatedly to stop my eyes from rolling back in my head.

His thrusts become firmer. More possessive.

I drag in shuddering breaths as the tension inside me builds.

My body trembles with pleasure and desperate need as Draven fucks me exactly the way he said he would. Like I'm his.

His fingers dig into my thigh and his hand pins my wrists

above my head as he fucks me like he owns me. And the feeling of it makes my heart skip several beats and my head spin.

My back thuds against the rock wall as he slams into me with dominant thrusts.

The tension inside me reaches unbearable levels. Desperate moans drip from my lips as I tumble towards the edge of an orgasm.

Draven's eyes sear through my very soul as he commands, "Come for me, little rebel."

Release explodes through my veins. Throwing my head back, I gasp as pleasure floods my every nerve.

My pussy tightens around his cock as he keeps fucking me through the orgasm. Incoherent pleas spill from my lips as the feeling of his cock grinding against my throbbing clit with every thrust sends lightning shooting through my spine. White lights flicker before my eyes.

My moaning is drowned out by a deep groan.

I snap my gaze down to Draven's face right in time to see pleasure flood his features. It's one of the most extraordinary things I have ever seen.

His cock pulses inside me as he comes.

I just stare at the astonished look on his face and that incredible pleasure that fills his eyes and makes them glitter like the brightest of gold. I feel lightheaded.

When the last ripples of pleasure fade out, I can barely form a coherent thought. I just lean against the wall while my chest heaves. Draven looks equally stunned.

For a little while, our heaving breaths and the soft rushing of the river are the only sounds that break the stillness.

Then Draven releases my wrists and thigh and pulls out.

The sudden loss of him inside me is so jarring that I almost stumble. Throwing a hand out, I brace my palm on the rough stones behind me.

"Well, would you look at that?" There is a sly glint in Draven's eyes as he cocks his head. "You can still stand."

Blinking, I stare at him in confusion.

He closes the distance between us again and slides his hand up my throat. With a firm grip right underneath my jaw, he tilts my head back and locks eyes that are gleaming with wicked delight on me.

"I told you that I was going to fuck you until your legs give out." He smirks. "Which means that you and I are just getting started, little rebel."

Using his grip on my throat, he pulls me away from the wall and instead spins me around so that I'm facing it. Then he releases my throat and gives my ass a firm slap.

"Now, put your hands on the wall and bend over."

CHAPTER THIRTY-NINE

My chest heaves. Lying on the grass, I stare up at that strange ceiling of thin round tree trunks above us while I try my best to drag air into my lungs and piece my mind back together. Next to me, Draven does the same. And his chest heaves as badly as mine.

"Fuck," he presses out between deep breaths.

"Yeah," I reply.

For a while, we just remain there, lying side by side on the thick grass. The river continues gently flowing past a few strides away.

"That…" Draven begins eventually.

Was absolutely fucking mind-blowing, I finish in my mind. It was, by far, the best sex I've ever had. Draven wasn't kidding when he said that he was going to ruin me. I don't know how I'm ever supposed to fuck someone else after this. How I'm supposed to just forget what his hands felt like on my body. How his cock felt inside me. How he managed to wring every drop of pleasure from my soul.

But I can't say any of that out loud.

So instead, I finish his sentence with, "Never happened."

Tilting his head to the side, he looks over at me. For a fraction of a second, I swear I can almost see pain flicker in his eyes. But it's gone so fast that I'm starting to doubt that I ever saw it. And when he speaks, his voice is calm and composed.

"Agreed," he says.

Sitting up, I plaster a smile on my face and force a joking tone into my voice. "After all, what happens in the magical forest, stays in the magical forest."

He lets out a short laugh, but it sounds as forced as mine. "Exactly."

Suddenly feeling incredibly awkward, I clear my throat and then push to my feet. Then my gaze darts towards my clothes, and my heart leaps into my throat.

Shit. My plan. I need to leave. Now. Before he figures out that I have stolen the ring.

Draven lets out a soft groan as he climbs to his feet as well. I hurry over to my clothes and start putting them on as fast as I can without it looking too suspicious. Hoping that he chalks my jerky movements up to awkwardness after the abrupt end to our intimacy, I yank my shirt over my head and pull my pants up before I sit down to put on my boots.

The ring presses into the sole of my left foot as I put the boot on. I need to remove it before I start running, but first, I need to get out of sight.

"I need to pee," I announce.

Draven heaves a deep sigh. "And I need to clean off my armor."

My gaze flits towards where he dropped his armor earlier. Satisfaction shoots up my spine. This is perfect.

I managed to wash off my shirt before we got distracted, so it's already clean. And it's even almost dry. But he went straight into the water, so his armor is still covered in green slime.

"That's why you should have done it before you decided to

fuck my brains out," I say, making sure to keep that neutral teasing tone in my voice. As if everything is normal.

He shoots me a pointed look from over his shoulder. "Yeah, well, it was very difficult to concentrate on anything when you were looking at me as if *you* wanted to fuck *my* brains out."

Heat sears my cheeks.

Using that to my advantage, I clear my throat and pretend to be even more flustered than I am. "Yes, well... Anyway, I'm going to go pee."

Before he can reply, I turn around and hurry straight into the woods.

As soon as I'm out of sight, I crouch down and unlace my boot. Pulling out the ring, I slip it onto my finger and then lace my boot back up again. Splashing sounds come from down by the river. I cast one last look towards it, even though I can't see anything through the trees.

And then I sprint away like the little thief I am.

My legs are still wobbly from the intense orgasms that Draven wrung from my body, so I almost stumble over a root as I dash across the grass. Channeling my magic, I throw it out towards that cluster of impatient sparks that I felt earlier. They're still there.

While drawing in deep breaths to steady my pounding heart, I run with everything I have towards it.

Eventually, the ground starts sloping upwards.

A jolt of anticipation shoots through me.

My muscles shake with exhaustion as I dart uphill.

An opening appears up ahead. The river, which has picked up speed from a downhill angle, rushes fast now as it's forced over the small hill and up through that hole. Keeping close to the side of it, I duck my head and run through as well.

The twisting thorn forest appears around me.

I whip my head from side to side. Based on the position of the sun, it's already late afternoon. Just as I estimated, it took almost an entire day to reach the city from the position deep in the forest where all of this started.

To my left, the river crests the tiny hill and rushes downwards on the other side.

Hope sparkles through my chest as I spot the city wall through the trees. But the cluster of impatient sparks is coming from the fields between the city and the Golden Palace, so I take off through the woods and towards that spot instead.

My heart thumps excitedly in my chest.

But somewhere deep inside, there is a sharp jabbing pain that refuses to go away. Because I can't help but feel guilty. Guilty for tricking Draven. Guilty for fucking him and then just leaving. Guilty for pretending that it meant nothing to me, when in reality, it flipped my entire world upside down.

That guilt and pain twist inside my chest like thorny vines. I shouldn't have slept with him. I shouldn't have crossed that line. We're enemies. We will always be enemies. He has been actively trying to ruin my life and get me kicked out of the trials from the day he saw me on that field.

And even if we could put that behind us after I win the Atonement Trials, it won't change what he is and what I am. The commander of the dragon shifter army and the fae rebel who is trying to destroy everything he is protecting. It would never work. *We* would never work.

We're on opposing sides in a conflict that has spanned millennia. Whatever we could have been was doomed from the start. So I should never have crossed that line. It would have been better to not know what it feels like to have him. Because now, I don't know how I'm supposed to forget.

My feet pound against the ground as I sprint towards the edge of the woods.

A jolt shoots through me as hints of people become visible through the trees. Afternoon sunlight glints against two pairs of silver wings. Excitement pulses through me.

This is it. Just a little farther, and then I'm going to win the Atonement Trials. I'm going to be given winner status and permission to leave the Seelie Court and be given funds to set up a new life in the world outside. I'm going to be able to start building a network of rebels in the human cities and coordinate a real resistance. I'm going to make a difference. I'm finally going to matter and I—

A body slams into me from the side.

Air explodes from my lungs as I crash down on the ground with a heavy body on top of me.

CHAPTER FORTY

Gasping air back into my lungs, I throw my elbow out as I try to roll away. A grunt of pain echoes as my elbow connects with something soft. The weight crushing my side eases for a second. I use that second to throw my body sideways and finally roll over on my back. Dragging in another breath, I blink furiously to clear my head and expect to see Draven above me.

Dread washes over me when I instead find Kevlin straddling my chest.

He must have been hiding here by the finish line, waiting for people to return with the rings. Goddess damn it, that's a clever strategy. Why spend days searching for the rings when you can let everyone else do it and then just ambush them and steal a ring when they return?

I yank my hand away as he lunges for the ring on my finger. Squeezing my hand into a fist, I try to keep the ring safe while I jerk up my leg and slam my knee right into his ass.

A yelp rips from his throat. Because he was leaning forwards over me, trying to get the ring, the hit from behind sends him tumbling over my head and rolling off me. I scramble around and push to my knees right as he whirls around as well. Pain shoots through my face as he slams his fist into my jaw.

The force of it is hard enough to snap my head to the side. Black spots dance before my eyes as I shoot to my feet while reaching for the knife at my thigh. But before I can draw it, Kevlin aims a kick at the side of my knee. Abandoning my attempt to reach my knife, I'm forced to leap back to avoid getting my kneecap shattered.

"Just give me the fucking ring," Kevlin growls at me, his eyes wild as he advances on me. "I have waited over three hundred years for this! I'm not going to lose a third time."

I yank out my knife right as blinding light explodes across the forest.

A gasp rips from my lungs, and I throw my hand up to protect my eyes. But it's too late. Kevlin, just like Alistair's friend Jeb, has light magic. And when he summons it in a gloomy forest, the sudden difference is so intense that it leaves me temporarily blinded.

Blinking furiously, I try to get my vision back while I slash blindly around me with the knife. A hiss informs me that I almost managed to hit Kevlin with it, but he just keeps coming.

Winds rush through the trees, making the leaves rustle. It masks the sound of Kevlin's feet as he moves.

Panic clangs inside my skull as I spin in frantic circles while swiping my knife in every direction. I have no idea where he is. All I can see is a harsh white light. I blink furiously, but the effect of his blast isn't diminishing.

That's when it hits me.

He hasn't turned off his magic. It's still blasting around us.

Terror crashes through me.

He's going to keep me blinded like this until he can get the ring.

Squeezing my fingers into an even tighter fist, I hold on to the ring as hard as I can while I slash with my knife and reach for my own magic. Shoving it around me, I try to increase Kevlin's fear. But he is not afraid. I try exhaustion. Boredom. Pity. Compassion. Anything I can think of that will help me. But he feels none of those emotions.

Still blinded by the light, I swipe through the air where I hope he is standing.

Pain spikes through my elbow as a punch lands. The strike to my elbow hits it right in the wrong spot, making my muscles spasm and my fingers fly open. The knife flies from my hand. But I don't even have time to hear where it lands, because a weight slams into me from straight ahead.

My head snaps back from the force of the sudden hit, and I topple backwards with Kevlin on top of me. My back hits the ground with a thud, knocking the breath out of me again. Before I can recover it, a hand closes around my throat.

"Give it to me," Kevlin snarls as he squeezes my neck. "Or I swear to Mabona, I will strangle you and then take it from your corpse."

Panic blares through my skull as he cuts off my air. Still blinded by his light, I move my hand up far above my head so that he won't be able to reach the ring, and then I yank my leg up and try to slam my knee into his ass again. But this time, he is sitting on my hips rather than my chest, so the move accomplishes nothing. I throw my other hand out, desperately searching for the knife that must be somewhere around us.

Kevlin hisses as I squirm and struggle underneath him, but his hand stays around my throat. My lungs burn.

Fuck, I need to think. Think!

My fingers only find grass and soil and roots. No knife.

A scream of frustration and panic and sheer utter desperation builds in my throat. But with him choking me like this, I can't even let it out.

Bucking my hips, I try to throw him off me. It only serves to make him lift his weight for a few seconds. But I use those seconds well as I yank my free hand back and punch him straight in the balls.

He screams in pain.

I push with my magic, throwing everything I have into that violet spark of pain inside him.

Another bloodcurdling scream rips from his chest as he releases my throat. I gasp in a deep breath while the blinding white light disappears in a flash.

I blink furiously as silhouettes of the forest start returning to my vision. I still can't see properly, but the weight of Kevlin's body disappears from above me as he scrambles away while screaming in pain. Keeping my magic pouring into him, I gasp air into my lungs and try to force my vision to return faster. My heart pounds against my ribs. I need to find the knife. And get off the ground. Twisting around, I start struggling up while still dragging air back into my lungs. I need to—

Blinding agony shoots through my leg as Kevlin stomps his boot down on the side of my ankle.

I scream, losing the grip on my magic.

Bones crack as Kevlin shatters my ankle.

The light is gone but I can barely see anything because of the black spots that are now dancing before my eyes. Pain sears through me, shooting like lightning up and down my leg, as I try to crawl backwards.

Kevlin, still bent over in pain from my strike to his balls, gasps in breaths through clenched teeth as he throws out an arm and grabs me by the collar. I slam my elbow into the crook of his, breaking his grip. But before I can get away, he slams his other fist into my cheek.

My head snaps to the side while more stars dance before my eyes. I suck in a sharp breath as Kevlin buries his fist in my collar again while I'm still trying to recover. With a yank, he pulls me back towards him and up onto my knees. I blink furiously, trying to clear my head, while I pound my fist against his hand.

He releases my collar. But before I can even feel relief over that, he grabs my left wrist and yanks my hand towards him. I keep my fingers tightly squeezed into a fist, protecting the ring. But he doesn't even try to pry my fingers up. Instead, he bends over and shoves my hand down on the ground.

Then he raises his foot.

Alarm screams through my head. I try to yank my wrist out of his grip, but it's too late.

He stomps his heel down on my hand.

I scream as the bones in my hand crunch underneath his boot.

Desperately, I try to summon my magic and manipulate his pain again. But the agony pulsing from my own ankle and hand is so blinding that I can't concentrate enough to channel magic.

My gaze darts around the ground, frantically searching for the knife instead.

Hope pulses through me.

But it's drowned out by another wave of blinding agony as Kevlin stomps on my left hand again. I almost pass out as the already shattered bones grind further together.

"Stop," I gasp out. "Please, I'll give it to you. Just stop. Please."

Kevlin stops with his foot hovering over my hand. He is still crouched down and slightly bent forward so that he can hold my wrist pinned to the ground while also being able to bring his boot down on it.

My vision swims and my head spins as I slide my right hand along the ground towards his feet.

"Please," I beg again.

His eyes are hard and merciless as he stares me down. But he returns his foot to the ground. His hand remains around my left wrist, though.

"Alright," he says. "Unclench your hand."

"I can't." A whimper of pain spills from my lips. "You've shattered everything in it."

A frustrated sigh rips from his lungs.

Then he finally lifts my hand off the ground, allowing me to raise the rest of my body too.

The moment he moves, my right hand wraps around the knife that was lying on the ground behind his feet. I straighten as he pulls my left hand towards him and bends my finger up so that he can take the ring himself.

Another cry of pain rips from me, and I lose the ability to move for a second as agony spikes through me.

Panic blares inside my skull.

Kevlin pulls the ring off my finger right as I slash the knife across the back of his thighs, severing his hamstrings.

He screams in pain and his legs buckle.

The ring flies through the air as he crashes down on the ground. Blood runs down the back of his now useless legs. I yank my wrist out of his grip and scramble across the ground before he can grab me again.

A ray of afternoon sunlight shines down between the trees and hits the ring where it rests on the ground a few strides away. The gold glints in the warm light. I crawl towards it.

Kevlin's screams echo from behind me as I drag myself towards the ring that will make this all worth it. The ring that will save me. That will give me a new life.

When I'm still two strides away from the ring, a pair of boots become visible right behind it.

Dread and panic and a terrible sense of hopelessness washes over me as I snap my gaze up to find another contestant standing there.

Lavendera looks down at me in silence before shifting her gaze to where Kevlin is writhing on the ground. Then her gaze drops down to the gold ring before her feet.

I want to scream my lungs out. My hand is broken and my ankle is shattered while Lavendera looks entirely unharmed. There is nothing I can do to stop her if she decides to take the ring. I won't even be able to chase her to the finish line.

Her pink and purple eyes stay locked on the ring for a few seconds. Then she looks up at me.

I don't even know if I'm breathing anymore.

Lavendera heaves a deep sigh.

And then walks away.

Lurching into motion, I scramble the final distance to the ring and snatch it up. The gold is cool and smooth against my palm as I clutch it in my uninjured hand.

My gaze shoots to Lavendera's retreating back. Confusion and disbelief and overwhelming gratitude swirl inside me.

And because I need to know, I call after her, "Why?"

She stops and turns around to face me again. There is a strange and faraway expression on her face as she sighs again. "Because it can't be me."

Then she walks away.

Struggling to my feet, I just stare after her until another voice shatters the silence.

"You can't do this!" Kevlin screams at me from the ground. "I've worked so hard for this. Fought so hard for this."

While keeping all of my weight on my uninjured ankle, I twist around to face Kevlin. Desperation pulses across his whole face.

"Please," he begs. "This has been my dream for over three hundred years. And I can't wait another hundred and fifty years for the next chance."

Draven's words from earlier suddenly echo inside my skull. *Why does everyone else's dreams matter more than your own?*

A harsh laugh rips from my lungs. Because he's right. They don't matter more than my own.

Holding Kevlin's gaze, I shake my head while something steady settles inside me.

"I don't care," I reply.

And then I turn my back on him.

The edge of the forest is right in front of me. Pain spikes through my leg as I begin hobbling towards it.

All I need to do is to make it out onto the grasslands outside where Jessina and Bane Iceheart are waiting. After everything I've been through to get to this point, everything I've done and everything I've endured, there is now only a short stretch of forest and an even shorter stretch of grass standing between me and victory.

I stumble towards it on my one good leg.

But I only make it a few steps before a heart-stopping sound booms through the forest behind me.

The sound of beating wings.

CHAPTER FORTY-ONE

Everything inside me screams in pain and exhaustion and sheer fucking desperation as I try to run with a broken ankle while the beating of wings grows louder behind me. Lightning shoots up my leg with every step, and the agony is so blinding that I can barely see the forest before me. I cry out in pain as I stumble through the trees.

I have to make it. Please, Mabona, I have to make it.

Begging to any deity that will listen, I shove my way through tangles of vines. Thorns slice into my skin.

The beating wings draw closer.

With a scream, I shove myself out between two twisted tree trunks right as a dark shadow sweeps through the air above me.

My legs give out and I crash down on the grass right at the edge of the massive field between our city and the Golden Palace.

A second later, Draven slams down on the ground a few strides away.

Lightning flashes in his eyes as his gaze locks on me where I'm crawling forward across the grass. My heart jerks violently at the expression on his face. He looks like he's about to slaughter every person in this court and then burn the whole forest to the ground.

Clenching his fist, he takes a threatening step towards me and opens his mouth to say something. But right before the first word can make it out, another voice breaks the silence.

"Draven," Empress Jessina says. "You're back. Were you monitoring the trial all night?"

Draven freezes in place. There looks to be a war going on behind his eyes as he stares at me.

"Yes," he at last replies.

"Any issues?"

His golden eyes sear into me, burning through my very soul. Behind his thigh, where only I can see it, he flexes his hand again. It looks like he's about to pick me up and simply throw me back into the forest. But I'm gambling on the fact that he can't interfere while Empress Jessina and Emperor Bane are watching. However, based on the way Draven is clenching his jaw, it looks like he might ignore their orders and do it anyway.

I barely dare to breathe as I hold his gaze.

Then he forces out a breath, and that usual mask of calm authority slams back down on his features.

"No," he replies, his voice respectful and composed. Then he turns around to face the empress and lowers his chin in deference. "No issues."

Without another look back, he strides over to the Iceheart monarchs and takes up his customary position a little behind them to the right.

I can't even feel the relief that should be washing through me, because the pain and exhaustion that course through my every vein are so all-consuming that I can barely breathe. Agony sears through me and black spots float in my vision as I crawl across the grass with a broken hand and a shattered ankle. Whimpers of pain spill from my lips.

Both Iceheart monarchs, all eight clan leaders, and four of the other contestants are standing there on the grass, watching me. But I can't even muster enough energy to be embarrassed. I don't care if I'm crawling on the ground. I don't care about the pitiful noises that escape my throat. All I care about is that I'm about to win.

Empress Jessina watches me with cool gray eyes, somehow managing to look both amused and bored at the same time. Emperor Bane studies me as well, but there is a vicious smirk on his mouth as he watches me crawl up to their feet.

Pushing myself up to my knees, I drag in a deep breath to steady my spinning head. Then I hold up my right hand and unclench it.

Gold glints in the afternoon sunlight as I present the ring to them.

Bane's smirk widens.

"Finally," Jessina says, and flicks her wrist impatiently. "We have the third winner."

I snap my gaze towards the four other contestants on the grass, realizing that two of them have already brought the other rings.

Isera, Fenriel, Alistair, and Trevor stand there a short distance away. Isera looks cool and composed, and completely unharmed. Alistair, on the other hand, has bloody claw marks all over his face and arms. Most of the blood appears to have dried at this point, but a few of the slashes on his face must open every time he blinks and moves his mouth, because drops of blood slide down his skin.

I stare at him before shifting my gaze to Fenriel. He and Alistair must have gotten into quite the fight. Or rather Alistair and Talon the hawk. But pain swirls in Fenriel's eyes too, and I can see that he is sporting burn wounds both on one of his arms and his left thigh. Next to him, Trevor is swaying slightly where he stands. Dried blood covers the back of his head, and his eyes are sliding in and out of focus.

Empress Jessina snaps her fingers and points to the ground in front of her feet. "Come on then. Let's get this over with."

My heart pounds in my chest, and I hold my breath, hoping that it's Isera and Fenriel who will step forward.

A faint groan slips from my lips when Isera and Alistair are the ones to approach.

Both of them keep a blank mask on their features as they walk up to the Icehearts and then drop down on one knee next to me.

"I hereby declare the final trial finished," Empress Jessina calls. "And the victors are Isera Shaw, Alistair Geller, and Selena Hale."

Triumph sweeps through my soul like a glittering wave.

Behind Jessina's shoulder, Draven is glaring at me with burning fury in his eyes. But even he can't dim my joy now. Because I did it. I won the Atonement Trials.

"Tomorrow morning, three of our soldiers will come here to collect you," Emperor Bane picks up. "They will fly you to the Ice Palace where the formal winner's ceremony will take place in front of our entire court."

Empress Jessina levels a commanding stare on all three of us. "Our soldiers will arrive at sunrise. If you are not already waiting on the Dragon Field when they arrive, you will forfeit your place as winner of the Atonement Trials." Her eyes sharpen. "Don't be late. We wait for no one."

All three of us bow our head in acknowledgement.

"Excellent," she says.

Then she snaps her fingers again. But when I look up, I realize that it's not meant for us this time.

"Rin," the empress calls. "Heal the winners."

Rin Tanaka, leader of the Orange Dragon Clan, steps forward without a word. Her long black hair ripples over the shoulders of her orange dragon scale armor as she walks up to us. She stops next to Alistair, who is kneeling closest to where she was standing previously, but her gaze darts over to where Fenriel and Trevor are standing.

"And the others?" she asks.

"No." Jessina scowls at her as if that should have been obvious. "They lost."

For one second, I swear I can almost see a flicker of anger in Rin's black eyes. But when she speaks, there is no change in her tone. Her voice is as smooth and calm as before.

"Of course," she replies.

Alistair lets out a strangled noise of relief as she begins healing the vicious claw marks across his skin. My ankle and hand throb in pain, and I glance longingly towards Rin as I wait for my turn.

"What about the other contestants?" Fenriel suddenly asks from across the grass. He casts a worried look towards the woods. "Trevor and I only came back here because we had to drop out because of our injuries. But what about the ones who are still in the forest. How will they know that the trial is already over?"

Emperor Bane shrugs, making his silver wings rustle behind his broad shoulders. "They'll figure it out eventually."

"What if they don't?"

"Who cares?" He shoots Fenriel a sharp look. "If they don't return, it means they weren't worthy of living anyway."

All five of us contestants, even Alistair, jerk back a little at his cruel words. Fenriel opens his mouth, and it looks like he's about to argue, but then Bane flares his wings slightly.

The subtle threat is loud and clear.

Dropping his gaze, Fenriel bows his head and takes a half step back.

"I'm bored, Bane," Jessina announces. "And I'm tired of breathing the same air as these uncivilized people. It's high time we leave this filthy court and return to the Ice Palace."

There is a malicious smile on Bane's lips as he sweeps his gaze over us. I squeeze my uninjured hand into a fist and clench my jaw, but I remain on my knees with my chin lowered.

"Agreed," Bane says. "Let's go."

Spinning on their heels, they start striding farther out onto the field. Sunlight gleams in their silver clothes and wings.

Jessina casts a glance over her shoulder. "Draven, come."

For a few moments, Draven's gaze lingers on me. There is an unreadable expression on his face now. And for some reason, that is almost worse than his previous anger.

Then, without a word, he tears his gaze from me and strides after his monarchs.

Black smoke explodes across the grass as all three of them shift into dragons.

The grass trembles as strong winds whoosh down over it when the three dragons beat their wings and take flight. Still on my knees, I sit there on the grass and wait for my turn to be healed.

Jessina and Bane let out loud roars that make the woods shake in fear. Then the two of them soar upwards and towards their Ice Palace somewhere far up north.

Draven, in his massive black dragon form, hovers over the field for a few seconds.

His eyes sweep over me one last time.

Then he too flies away.

CHAPTER FORTY-TWO

After Rin Tanaka healed my broken and exhausted body, I headed straight back to the city. There was nothing for me to pick up from my room at the Golden Palace. I'm already wearing everything that I brought with me. Everything that's mine. So while the seven clan leaders shifted into dragons and flew off, I walked straight to the Golden Gate. Isera and Alistair did the same.

And now, as I walk through the city, everything suddenly feels different. It has only been a few weeks since the Atonement Trials started, but it feels as if years have passed. Everything that I've been through, everything that I've done, has somehow changed me. But I'm not sure exactly how.

The streets I walk through now feel smaller. And the buildings somehow look more impersonal. But worst of all, the city and the people in it suddenly feel distant. I feel as if I'm a stranger walking through town, and not someone who has lived here her whole life.

The feeling is so jarring that I almost miss the tavern I was heading for. Stumbling to a halt, I take a step back and reach for the door.

Inside, miserable-looking people are drinking their sorrows away while there is far too little food on far too few tables. A soft murmur hangs in the air and a fire burns in the hearth to my right.

In here, life simply... goes on. As if the Atonement Trials never happened. As if my life hasn't been utterly changed.

I give my head a few short shakes, trying to push aside the strange feeling. Then I approach the bar.

"The mask is white," I say as I catch the tavern keeper's eye.

He starts in surprise at hearing the code phrase that we use to secretly identify ourselves as members of the resistance. Then he clears his throat. "And very hard to take off."

I nod at the correct answer, which signals that he is a member of the resistance as well and that it's safe to talk.

"I need this delivered," I say, and slide an envelope across the scratched wooden counter.

Reaching out, he casually takes the envelope and slips it into his apron pocket before giving me a nod. "Consider it done."

After nodding back in thanks, I turn around and walk back out again.

Since I don't know who the leaders of the resistance are, I couldn't just walk up to one of them and tell them that I have won the Atonement Trials. So I wrote that in the letter that will now be delivered to them instead. In it, I also suggested that they recruit Fenriel to our cause. Not only is he a genuinely kind person, he also has his hawk that can potentially fly out of the Seelie Court. And that could be the perfect way for me to relay information to the resistance leaders, and for them to tell me what they need me to do.

Brisk evening winds whirl between the crooked wooden buildings as I stride through town and towards a house closer to the northern wall.

Once I reach it, I stop in front of the door and draw in a few bracing breaths.

Nausea twists in my stomach.

Not once during the entire course of the trials have I been as nervous as I am right now. It's ridiculous. But facing the two people in this house will always be worse than anything the dragon shifters can subject me to.

After dragging in one more breath, I raise my hand to knock. But then I stop. A short laugh escapes my chest. And instead, I simply push down the handle and walk right across the threshold.

"Hello," I call as I walk into the house. "Dad? Mom?"

My parents scramble out of the kitchen. They stop, looking completely stunned, when they find me standing in the living room.

"Why didn't you knock?" my mom blurts out.

I open my mouth but then just close it again. That's her first question? The last time I saw them, I told them that I was entering the Atonement Trials. Now, they see me for the first time in weeks. And her first question is why I didn't knock?

Blowing out a breath, I give my head a quick shake to clear it and then compose myself.

"I just came to tell you that I won the Atonement Trials," I announce.

Shock pulses across their faces. I keep my chin raised and my spine straight as I bear their scrutiny.

"So that means that you're leaving?" Mom eventually says.

Not even a *congratulations*. Or *well done*. Or anything.

Blocking out the painful twist in my chest, I just nod. "Yes."

"Good."

My heart drops and a frustrated kind of disbelief crashes over me. "Don't you mean good *luck*?"

"Right." She clears her throat. "Good luck."

Pain bleeds from my heart as I stare at them. Then it all just boils over.

"Look," I begin, my voice coming out all hurt and angry. "I

know that I'm not the daughter you hoped for, but would it really kill you to just be proud of me for once in your lives?"

"Be proud of you?" Dad interjects. "What in Mabona's name is there to be proud of?"

"All my adult life, I've done everything I can to please you. And yet, all you do is resent me. Why—"

"Of course we resent you!" Mom snaps. The words seem to rip out from the very depths of her soul. Her eyes are full of anger and hurt as she stares me down. "You ruined our marriage."

Pain slashes through my chest. "I was a *child*."

"I don't care!" she screams the words at me with all the force of a physical hit. With that anger still in her eyes, she motions between herself and Dad. "We *loved* each other. And you broke us. You took our emotions and twisted them up so badly that we could never be sure if we were truly angry with each other or if we were happy or calm or stressed or if we had any feelings at all. Or if it was all just your vicious meddling." Tears well up in her eyes. "You *ruined* us. You ruined everything."

I rock back on my heels as if she had hit me across the face.

In my chest, I swear that I can hear my heart crack.

The silence in the living room is so loud that it pulses against my eardrums.

Swallowing back the lump in my throat, I open my mouth to say something. To defend myself. To try to explain, yet again, that I couldn't control my powers back then. That I didn't mean to manipulate their emotions. That I worked myself into exhaustion trying to master my powers faster than anyone ever had before.

But then I just close my mouth instead.

Nothing I say is ever going to change how my parents feel about me.

They don't care anymore.

And now, neither do I.

So I just turn on my heel and walk away without another word.

None of this matters anyway. All that matters is that I have won the Atonement Trials. And tomorrow, my new life, my wonderful life away from all of this, is finally going to begin. I just need to make sure that I'm standing on the Dragon Field before sunrise.

No one, *no one,* is going to stop me from claiming my place as a victor in front of the entire Iceheart Dynasty tomorrow.

Hesitation blows through me.

No one *can* stop me, right? Like Draven. He can't just use his power and influence as the leader of the dragon shifter army to somehow stop me from claiming my status as winner of the Atonement Trials.

Can he?

CHAPTER FORTY-THREE

I'm striding across the grass and out onto the Dragon Field an entire hour before the sun will rise. To my surprise, Alistair is already there. And Isera arrives ten minutes after me as well. Apparently, none of us wants to risk missing our one shot at getting out of here.

Cool morning winds sweep across the grasslands and rustle the leaves in the thick forest around us. I stare at those twisted trees and snaking vines and sharp thorns, and I can't help but wonder if the rest of the contestants are still in there. Hopefully, they heard the Icehearts roar like that before they flew away, and took that as a sign to return.

I glance at Isera and Alistair from the corner of my eye.

Both of them just stand there next to me, their spines straight and their eyes fixed on the Peaks of Prosperity that the dragons should be flying over on their way here.

I shift my weight as the silence continues stretching.

"So…" I find myself saying after a while, because the tense silence is grating on my frayed nerves and is making me more worried that Draven is somehow going to show up and ruin this for me. "Still not going to tell us what you're going to do with your freedom?"

Alistair starts in what looks like surprise, and then turns his head to stare at me. As if he can't believe that I'm talking to him. When he realizes that I am in fact addressing him, he draws his pale brows down in a scowl.

"No," he declares.

"Seriously?" I shoot him a pointed look. "After the winner's ceremony today, we're going to split up anyway and probably never see each other. So what does it matter?"

He glares at me in silence for a few seconds. Then he blows out a forceful breath and rakes a hand through his curly blond hair. "I'm going to get the hell out of here and never return."

The venom in his words shocks me.

I raise my eyebrows. "You hate this place that much?"

"Not this place." He flexes his hand. "The people."

"*You* hate the people here? But you're the one bullying everyone."

His orange and green eyes flash with fury. "You know nothing about me. Now shut the fuck up before I snap your skinny little neck."

Shaking my head, I scoff and then turn back to stare at the forest before us. "I'm glad Fenriel's hawk got revenge on you."

"Me too."

Both Isera and I whip around to stare at Alistair.

"What?" I ask.

He shrugs, suddenly looking a little self-conscious, and then repeats, "Me too." He casts me a glance from the corner of his eye. "I'm glad you pulled him out of the way. I don't like hurting animals."

"Then maybe you shouldn't have shot a torrent of fire at him."

"I didn't shoot it at the hawk." He scowls and flicks an annoyed look at Isera. "I was aiming for *her*."

Isera just flashes him a sharp smile in reply.

"Wow," I say. "That was not what—"

"Incoming," Isera suddenly snaps.

My heart leaps into my throat. Whirling back around, I gaze towards the Peaks of Prosperity.

Hope and excitement swell in my chest as I spot three silver dragons approaching. This is it. This is the moment I leave the Seelie Court and start my new life.

Turning my head, I look back at the city in the distance. It wasn't all bad. But I'm still glad to be out of here. Glad to start over somewhere else where people don't immediately distrust me as soon as they hear my name.

"Uhm, guys?" Alistair begins, suddenly sounding worried. "The empress said they were going to fly us to their court. How do you think they're going to do that?"

"I doubt it's on their backs," Isera answers. "Since they've been punishing us for thousands of years for doing just that."

The three silver dragons draw closer.

Nervous anticipation pulses through me. Swallowing, I check my meager possessions. Which only consist of the clothes I'm wearing and the knife in my thigh holster.

"They're not slowing down," Alistair notes.

Wings boom through the air as the three dragons sweep down over the grasslands and speed right towards us.

I suck in a sharp breath.

They stretch out their legs and open their claws.

Alarm spikes through me. "Don't tell me that they're—"

My stomach lurches as one of the dragons grabs me with its claws and lifts me off the ground as it flies past.

I would have screamed if I had any air in my lungs, but I can't even seem to remember how to breathe as the dragon makes a sharp turn in the air and then starts back towards the Peaks of Prosperity. My muscles are tense. I'm afraid that the smallest movement is going to make me slip through the dragon's claws and plummet to my death below.

But the claws are steady around me as the dragon speeds across the thorn forest. And when we get closer to the Peaks of Prosperity, my mind has started to come to terms with my current situation and has accepted that I probably won't fall to my death. My muscles relax and that incredible sense of excitement returns.

I gaze down in astonishment as we sweep over the grand mountain range and leave the thorn forest behind as we continue across the continent.

Winds whip in my hair and clothes. The air up here is cool and brisk and tastes of freedom. An absolutely ridiculous grin spreads across my mouth. I gasp as I spot cities and villages on the horizon. We're too far away to see them, but they must be human cities. Or maybe dragon shifter cities. Or do humans and shifters live together in shared cities?

Since I've spent my life trapped inside a forest of thorns, I have no idea what the rest of the world is like.

But now, I'm finally about to find out.

I grin at the open horizon as we soar through the air. I'm going to see it all, learn it all, do it all. Goddess above, I'm going to finally start living.

To my surprise, my excitement doesn't dim in the slightest even after hours of flying. Because there is always something new to see. A new city or a new mountain range or a new lake. Sights I have never seen before. And the view from up here is unparalleled.

Eventually, the three dragons who are carrying us pull together in a tighter formation.

That's when I see it.

A great ice castle on the slopes of a mountain, and a sprawling city beneath it.

Air escapes my lungs in a whoosh as I stare at the sheer size of that city. My gaze drifts to the magnificent castle.

The Ice Palace. Home of Empress Jessina and Emperor Bane and the center of power in the Iceheart Dynasty.

I have heard about the splendor of it, but nothing could have prepared me for the real magnificence of it. An imposing wall made of white ice circles it. And beyond, a massive palace with gleaming domes and twisting spires reaches for the heavens. All of it glitters like diamonds in the afternoon sunlight.

My stomach lurches again as the dragons soar over the defensive walls and swoop down towards a wide courtyard at the front of the palace. I stumble as I'm dropped the final few feet to the ground. After so long in the air, it takes my legs a moment to adjust.

Drawing in a deep breath, I push my windswept hair out of my face and then straighten. Next to me, Isera and Alistair do the same. The three dragons who carried us here climb back into the sky again.

I blink at the scene before me.

Two massive doors made of ice tower over us. They're open, and through them, I can see a grand entrance hall. But in front of it all stands a tall man in white formal wear with silver decorations.

"Follow me," he says by way of greeting.

Without even waiting to see if we comply, he spins on his heel and starts towards the open front doors. I scramble to follow him on legs that still feel a little unsteady. Isera and Alistair stumble the first few steps too as we all hurry to catch up with the man.

"You are to wash up and change into the clothes provided for you," he announces while still continuing to walk ahead of us.

"Okay," Alistair replies.

A new wave of worry sweeps through me as I step across the threshold and into the grand entry hall beyond. Because somewhere in here is Draven. And there is still time for him to take revenge. My heart patters against my ribs as I swallow and glance around the glittering hallway, half expecting to find the Shadow of Death lurking there.

"When does the winner's ceremony begin?" I ask as the man leads us down the hall and towards another door.

He finally turns his head and looks back at us. And I swear I can see a small smile ghost across his lips as he answers with three words that make my heart flutter.

"In one hour."

CHAPTER FORTY-FOUR

Light fills the entire throne room. It glitters against the ice walls like starlight and casts sparkling reflections on the people in the room. To my utter shock, I realize that the light is coming from faelights. They might despise our people, but apparently, they see no problem with using our inventions for their own benefit.

Craning my neck, I gaze up at the dome above. Faelights have been set into the entire ceiling, making them shine like permanent stars. The irony isn't lost on me that their palace is filled with our faelights while our palace is filled with their torches.

"Stop five paces from the dais," our guide instructs in a soft voice as he leads us through the throne room. "The man bows and the ladies curtsy."

A jolt shoots through me. Curtsy? I don't know how to curtsy. I've only ever knelt or bowed in front of the dragon shifters before.

I flick a glance at my companions. Isera has her customary blank expression on her face, so it's impossible to tell if she's nervous. But it wouldn't surprise me if she actually knows how to curtsy properly. Alistair, on the other hand, looks like he just wants to get this over with.

My gaze drifts down to our clothes. All three of us are wearing formal clothes in different shades of silver. It's a very effective reminder that the Icehearts own us until they say otherwise.

The clothes were laid out in a dressing room that I was escorted into. I had planned to use the hour before the start of the ceremony to sneak around in the palace. After all, it's the perfect opportunity to gather some intelligence for our resistance. But as soon as I stepped into the room, it was flooded with attendants who were there to help me bathe and dress and to do my hair. Getting all of it ready took the entire hour. But after this ceremony is finally done, I will have all the time in the world to do whatever I want.

My flowing silver dress rustles faintly against the floor as I continue following our guide through the throne room. The dress is elegant but more lowcut than I was expecting. The wide straps of the dress rest more on the side of my shoulders than on top of them, leaving my collarbones bare. Isera's dress is in a similar style, and several of the male dragon shifters in the room let their gazes linger on our cleavage as we pass.

I resist the urge to reach up and undo my elaborate hairdo. All of my hair has been pinned up and twisted into swirls and braids that are fastened with glittering silver pins, so there is nothing obscuring the view of my neck and collarbones and cleavage. Isera's long black hair has been pulled up in a similar style too, and I can't help but feel as if this was the reason for that. The Icehearts want us to feel exposed so that they can enjoy one final power play.

The rest of the people in the massive throne room are dressed in formal wear too, but as opposed to us, theirs are not exclusively made of silver fabric. Instead, all kinds of colors are represented among the crowd. It makes me feel as if I'm walking through a colorful sea as I continue down the main aisle with rows of courtiers spreading out on both sides.

But as we draw closer to the raised dais on the other side of the room, all of my focus narrows down to three people.

Two massive thrones, made from the same sparkling material as the rest of the castle, are positioned in the middle of the platform. Empress Jessina and Emperor Bane are seated on them. As usual, they are wearing elegant clothes in their signature silver color. Jessina's white hair has been pinned back from her face before it flows down her back while Bane keeps his black hair falling like a straight waterfall behind him. Their silver wings are spread wide, extending far past their icy thrones.

And to their right stands a figure dressed in all black.

My heart does a backflip in my chest as my gaze lands on Draven.

Among all the fancy formal clothes, he alone wears his black dragon scale armor. His black hair has been swept back from his face as if he has just nonchalantly dragged a hand through it, and his imposing black wings loom behind his shoulders.

I study his face as we close the final distance to the dais. I expect to see anger or annoyance or a threatening glare. Or any kind of emotion. But there is nothing. His handsome face is a blank mask, and he watches me with completely expressionless eyes. As if I'm nothing more than a random person who happened to wander into the castle. As if these past few weeks never happened. As if we never happened.

Pain twists my heart.

Annoyance immediately follows it, and I shove the pain aside. Why should I care if he is looking at me as if he doesn't even know me? He's at the top of my list of enemies, at the top of our rebellion's list of enemies, so none of this matters anyway.

Our guide, the man in the white suit from earlier, stops five steps in front of the dais and executes a sweeping bow. "Your

Imperial Majesties, may I present the winners of this century's Atonement Trials."

Still bent over, he shoots the three of us a pointed stare. I snap out of my tangled thoughts and quickly drop down in a curtsy.

Someone snickers from the crowd, which causes others to do the same.

Heat creeps into my cheeks. Clenching my jaw, I try to block out their judgmental laughter and instead focus solely on the Iceheart monarchs in front of me while our guide retreats into the crowd. I straighten from my apparently terrible curtsy.

"Alistair Geller, Isera Shaw, and Selena Hale," Emperor Bane says. His powerful voice carries across the sea of people and echoes against the glittering ice walls. "Congratulations on winning the Atonement Trials."

We all bow our heads in acknowledgement.

"Today, your entire life will change," he continues. "You will leave your old life behind and embark on something new."

My heart flutters with excitement, and it takes all of my willpower to stop a wicked grin from spreading across my mouth. *Oh I will be embarking on something new, alright. My mission to bring you down.*

"To formally recognize you as winners, you will be presented with a gift that symbolizes your change in status," Jessina picks up, and snaps her fingers.

Three people approach from the edge of the dais while Jessina and Bane stand up from their thrones. They start towards us with regal steps. My heart leaps and then patters against my ribs when Draven starts towards us as well.

The three people who are approaching from the sides are each carrying a small decorative cushion in a pale blue color. Something rests on top of each pillow, but I can't see what from down here.

Only the soft swishing of Jessina's dress breaks the silence as she, Bane, Draven, and the three people with the cushions descend the steps from the dais. They spread out before us. Emperor Bane takes up position in front of Isera and Empress Jessina comes to a halt in front of Alistair.

My heart does another ridiculous flip when Draven stops in front of me.

The three people with the cushions take up position to the right of each of them, holding out the pillow to them so that they can reach the object on top of it. I know that I should probably look at the object, but my eyes are locked on Draven's.

Standing there in front of me, he simply watches me with that same neutral expression. I try to read any sort of emotion in his eyes, but there is nothing.

A strange sense of calm resignation washes through me. This is how our time together ends. Not with a furious fight but with cold indifference.

"You will each be given an iron collar," Empress Jessina says. "As a symbolic representation of your servitude to us and how your years of imprisonment in the Seelie Court are now at an end."

Her words yank me out of my thoughts, and I snap my gaze down to the object on the pillow.

Just like she said, an iron collar rests there on top of the pale blue cushion. I suppress the urge to roll my eyes at the yet again very obvious power play.

Draven's golden eyes sear into mine as he stands there before me.

I stare back at him.

"With the transfer of these collars," Emperor Bane begins in a voice dripping with authority, "we hereby declare you winners of this century's Atonement Trials."

Relief and excitement and sheer triumph pulse through my soul.

As one, the three of them reach for the cushions.

I jerk back in confusion as they lift up the collars from the pillows.

But before I can so much as step back, Draven spins back towards me.

And snaps the iron collar shut around my throat.

I gasp as the iron presses against my skin. It cuts off my connection to my magic immediately. And while the size of the collar isn't great enough to cause me to collapse, it still weakens me and burns cold against my skin, as if I have a band of ice around my throat.

The shock of it makes me stumble back. Next to me, the same thing has happened to Isera and Alistair too.

But before I can retreat more than half a step, Draven's hand shoots out and wraps around my throat. With a firm grip, he pulls me back towards him and leans down.

To my left, Jessina and Bane are doing the exact same to Alistair and Isera.

Draven slants his lips over mine, just a breath away from touching.

And this close, where only I can see, that blank mask finally cracks. Pain and sorrow swirl in his eyes as he holds my gaze.

Then he whispers, so softly that even I can barely hear it even though his lips are right in front of mine.

"I wasn't trying to sabotage you, little rebel. I was trying to save you. From *this*."

Then he breathes in, sharply.

And sucks my magic out of my body.

I gasp.

Because of the iron collar, I can't reach my magic. But I can feel it as it drains out of my body with Draven's sharp inhale. And because our magic is so connected to our energy, it weakens me so much that my knees buckle.

Draven releases my throat, and I crash down on the ground since my legs can no longer support me. My knees hit the ground with a thud, and I just barely manage to yank up my arms and brace my palms on the smooth floor before I can topple forward and smack my forehead into it.

Next to me, more thuds sound as Isera and Alistair hit the floor as well.

I gasp in unsteady breaths. My body is so devoid of energy that my muscles tremble. I can barely manage to remain on my knees. But worst of all is my mind.

Shock clangs inside my skull like giant bells.

Draven *inhaled* my magic.

It will return, of course. Our magic is connected to our energy, so with enough rest, our magic builds back up to its previous level even if we drain it completely.

But I had no idea that *someone else* could drain our magic too. That the dragon shifters could drain it from us.

Tilting my head back, I stare up at Draven with wide eyes.

"Why?" I press out.

Something flickers in his eyes for a second, but then that unreadable mask is back on his face.

"Aww," Jessina says, and leans down to draw her hand along Alistair's jaw where he sways on his knees in front of her. "I love this moment. The moment when they realize that it was all a lie."

Isera, who was bent over with her palms pressed against the floor, drags in a shuddering breath and looks up at the three dragon shifters before us. And for the first time ever, I see fear in her eyes.

"What?" she gasps out between heavy breaths.

"The Atonement Trials is a lie." Empress Jessina flashes us a cruel smile. "It was never a way for you to earn your freedom. It is, and always has been, a competition to find the people who have the strongest magic among you. Because that is what we want. Your magic."

"Yes," Bane joins in. Reaching down, he gives Isera's cheek a few patronizing pats that look almost forceful enough to be slaps.

Malice shines in his black eyes as he stares her down. "Welcome to your new existence. As our life slaves."

Alistair tries to pull away as Jessina reaches for him, but it only makes him topple sideways. While trying to push himself back up, he presses out, "What are you talking about?"

Jessina flashes him a smile that is all teeth. "We can feed on your magic, your energy, to live forever."

My eyes widen as shock crackles through my veins.

"During the war, when we rose up and slaughtered all the dragon riders, we realized that we could collar you with iron and then feed on your magic to boost our own energy. Eventually, we realize that it also kept us from aging."

"You…" I begin, my tongue stumbling over the word. "You were alive back then? When fae were dragon riders?"

"You mean when we were your slaves?" she snaps, her voice turning vicious. "Yes, we were. Bane and I are the only dragons still alive from those days. But we remember. We remember your cruelty and your entitlement. And now, it's your turn to suffer."

"But the previous winners," Isera blurts out. Panic and fear now pulse unhindered in her eyes. "Where are—"

"They're dead."

Isera jerks back as if Jessina had slapped her.

"It's one of the unfortunate side effects," Bane explains with a shrug. "Since we continuously drain your magic and energy at the same rate all the time, you eventually die. It takes roughly one hundred and fifty years. Which is when we hold a new competition."

All color has drained from Isera's face as she stares up at him. "Dead. She's… dead?"

Bane frowns. "She?" Then realization pulses across his face. "Oh. Isera *Shaw*. Elena Shaw was your mother, wasn't she?" He chuckles, and then a malicious grin spreads across his mouth. "Elena was *my* life slave. How fitting that I will now be your master too."

Pain and heartbreak swirl in Isera's eyes as she stares up at the emperor who now owns her. Next to them, Jessina strokes her hand along Alistair's jaw again in a highly possessive manner.

Which means that I will be a life slave to...

Turning my head, I stare up at Draven Ryat. The Shadow of Death. Commander of the Dread Legion. One of the three most powerful and dangerous dragon shifters in the world. And now, my master.

My entire soul recoils at the mere thought.

Draven holds my gaze, his eyes once more unreadable as he watches me kneel there before his feet.

I curl my fingers into fists.

It doesn't matter that he tried to stop me from winning. It doesn't matter that he tried to prevent this. Or why.

Because at the end of the day, he still went through with it. He still put that iron collar around my neck and drained my magic.

Clenching my jaw, I glare up at him as rage burns through me.

I am not his slave. I will not let him drain my energy while he keeps me collared and kneeling at his feet. I would rather kill myself than spend the rest of my life as his slave.

Or better yet... I would rather kill *him*.

BONUS SCENE

Do you want to know what Draven was thinking during that final chapter? Scan the QR code to download the exclusive bonus scene and read the final part from Draven's perspective.

Made in United States
Troutdale, OR
03/06/2025